# THE SEIZURE

# THE SEIZURE

David Fraser

COLLINS
8 Grafton Street, London W1
1988

William Collins Sons & Co. Ltd
London . Glasgow · Sydney · Auckland
Toronto · Johannesburg

BRITISH LIBRARY CATALOGUING IN PUBLICATION DATA

Fraser, *Sir* David, *1920-*
The seizure.—(Treason in arms).
I. Title II. Series
823′.914[F]   PR6056.R2864

ISBN 0-00-223163-8

First published 1988
© Fraser Publications Ltd 1988

Photoset in Linotron Times by
Rowland Phototypesetting Ltd
Bury St Edmunds, Suffolk
Made and printed in Great Britain
by Robert Hartnoll (1985) Ltd., Bodmin, Cornwall

# CHAPTER 1

'I'm not sure,' said Harry Wrench, 'that I fully understand you.' He looked across the lunch table at his host, a man perhaps ten years older than he. Harry was thirty-two, the man facing him looked at least forty. His name was Bruce Clandon, he was manager of a City of London branch – one of many – of a major clearing bank; and Harry Wrench, a young but rising star in a merchant bank, still had no clear idea why he had been invited to lunch with Clandon. Alone.

Clandon said, 'I'll do my best. Unfortunately I have to talk a bit obliquely about some of it.'

He poured some more excellent claret into Harry's glass. They were lunching in the small, panelled dining room at the bank, next to Clandon's office. The board of the bank – of this branch of it, originally small and independent before swallowed by one of the huge conglomerates of the banking world – met here, lunched here, discussed here policy, prospects and results. Now there were only Bruce Clandon and Harry Wrench eating at a small table set to one side of the room. Outside a large window the sheer brick wall of another of Holborn's mid-Victorian buildings shut out most of the day's light. A bank messenger came in with dishes from time to time; apart from that infrequent interruption Clandon and Wrench were alone. The sound of traffic was muffled, the window seldom opened although it was early June. The room was quiet.

Clandon said, 'This client of ours – a man we know very well, an entirely sound man – needs the money rather urgently. He intends to sell a piece of land – of which he's got a certain amount – to raise it. No problem – but that will take a bit of time.' He dissected the food on his plate rather fussily.

'Well?' Harry Wrench felt at ease, his excellently cut dark

suit sitting well on his broad shoulders, his waist still slender, his rather swarthy face alert and good-humoured. 'Well?'

'Any loan to him is utterly safe. Furthermore he'll pay a high rate of interest – of course. Say, for six months.'

'You've not explained to me,' said Harry Wrench, 'why you don't lend him the money yourself. Normal service, surely? You know we don't do this sort of thing for individuals, it's not our line.'

'Of course it isn't. But I would propose a loan to a small property company which our client owns. That would enable the company to repay him some loan stock, give him some cash. Which is what he needs. We're bankers to the company, there's no problem.'

'Then why not lend him half a million yourselves?'

Clandon looked at Harry, narrowed his eyes and began talking even more softly than usual, although always a particularly soft-spoken man. Harry had to concentrate his attention to hear every word.

'The difficulty,' Clandon murmured, 'comes from the purpose for which our client needs the money. I cannot avoid knowing this.'

'And you can't,' said Harry robustly, 'avoid telling me about it. If you want us to lend the man money.'

'Of course. You can be sure there's nothing – er –'

'Crooked. Near the wind.'

'Precisely. Our client's integrity is beyond question. So are his motives. But the object he has in mind – well, our board, I mean the main board of the bank, have issued very strict instructions that we are not, I repeat not, to advance money in these particular circumstances. To anybody.'

'What circumstances?'

Clandon said, almost inaudibly,

'Our client's name is James Harting. He farms in a middling way in Essex. Well off – on paper. He's not a rich man in terms of easily disposable assets. He happens to be a personal friend of mine. He's a widower.

'In March this year, James's daughter, Joanna, was on a skiing holiday in Austria with friends. For some reason the

6

party didn't travel back together. Joanna, it seems, decided to return by train and ferry, by herself. She didn't turn up. Disappeared.'

'How old?'

'Nineteen. Only child, he adores her. Ten days later, ten agonising days, he received the first note. The first demand.'

Clandon had mumbled the names and it was only at this point that Harry made the connection:

'Harting! Of course! The girl was kidnapped!'

'Exactly. And is still held. As far as the press is concerned, there's been no communication. On this occasion those brutes have kept it all perfectly quiet and James hasn't wanted publicity. Nor have the police.'

'What are the police doing?'

'There's a well-established drill. Interpol, similarity to other cases and so forth. The police – here and in Europe – are adamant that it would be wrong to pay up.'

'How much do they want?'

'It comes to half a million, sterling. They want dollars. Presumably they know how to handle dollars securely. Naturally everybody has wanted James to keep communications open, without handing over. Now he's had an ultimatum.' Clandon's voice was still very low, but Harry knew from it that it was the friend rather than the banker talking.

'They've given James three weeks. After that they've described – disgustingly – what they intend to do to Joanna. He believes them. The police say it's bluff, it's nonsense, that they're working on some leads. They reckon she's probably somewhere in Germany. They're absolutely opposed to paying up, of course.'

'And Harting wants to?'

'Wouldn't you?'

Harry said nothing. There had been a photograph of the Harting girl in the newspapers, a charming photograph. Cursed with a vivid imagination, he could almost hear James Harting's voice as he argued with police, civil servants; as he talked, no doubt near desperation, to his banker friend. After a minute Bruce Clandon said,

7

'We – the bank – have recently put out very firm guidance in such cases. No connivance whatsoever in paying ransom demands, blackmail.'

'If you persuade us to lend Harting the money, in a disguised sort of way, you'll be conniving all right, won't you?'

'Yes,' said Clandon. 'Yes, I will.'

'You won't say anything to your board, I take it.'

'No need. James will have persuaded Brandon Sellars to make a short-term loan to his private company.'

Harry Wrench had now worked for Brandon Sellars Securities, a medium-sized merchant bank, for five years. The proposition wasn't impossible and Clandon knew it. Clandon remarked, almost in a whisper,

'I will simply have made the contact, and can, of course, ensure that all is presented – sensibly – from a banking and accountancy point of view. James will have got his price for his land and repaid the loan before the end of this year, before the end of 1972.'

Harry looked at him and sipped his glass of claret. He knew that Clandon had picked his man with care. Clandon was the slightest of acquaintances but he certainly realised that Brandon Sellars trusted the judgement of young Harry Wrench, but that Harry was still sufficiently junior to keep the transaction from turning automatically into an issue of principle, of policy. The sum involved was peanuts, the interest rate better than one would get on a deposit elsewhere at the moment. Brandon Sellars wouldn't lose. Security? He had Clandon's word about Harting's position, Harting's intentions. Undesirable publicity if things went wrong? Condonation of blackmail payment? Avoidable, surely –

Harry said, conversationally, 'This property company your friend owns –'

'In excellent order and expanding,' said Clandon, getting the other's drift immediately, 'small commercial properties, regular rent reviews, minimal management expenses, first-class advice. We've helped build it up, of course. Now the books are pretty well clear. Good cash flow.' Clandon looked at his fingernails and said quietly,

8

'A perfectly good place to deposit money at fifteen per cent.'

They had finished lunch and Harry said,

'One question. Perhaps two.'

'Of course.'

'Is this anything to do with the Irish business? I know you've talked about Germany, but –'

'But these people are said to help each other, help other causes with money and so forth. I know. Well, I can tell you, quoting James, that the group who say they're holding Joanna are not thought by the police to have any IRA connection.'

'Who are they? Have they a name?'

'They call themselves the European Liberation Movement. Why kidnap a very ordinary English girl, you might ask – Joanna's not a millionaire heiress or anything like that.'

Harry remarked, 'The papers seemed to think, if I've got it right, that they may have confused her with that American girl, Fenner, the oil man's daughter.'

'That's so. The Fenner girl was staying in the same hotel. The two girls are rather alike. Presumably these devils were planning a big, well-publicised operation. Then, in error, they find themselves with Joanna. And have done enough homework to reckon they can tap her father for half a million and get it. Petty cash.'

He was looking down at the table. Harry stood up and held out his hand.

'Thanks for lunch. I'll let you know by ten o'clock to-morrow. I'll have to think. And talk a little.'

'A very little, I hope.'

'That can be managed. I'll ring.'

Clandon nodded, and said, still softly, without much ex-pression, 'She's my goddaughter. I'm very fond of her.'

Then he saw Harry to the main door of the bank.


'Franzi Langenbach's asked me to stay in this house in Italy he's built for himself.'

'Ah!' Miranda Wrench's tone was non-committal. Her

brother Harry was giving her dinner at Rules, and Harry knew her very well – too well to offer much hope of allowing her heart's feelings to be guarded for long. But, anyway, what were they? Franzi had written an extraordinary letter after his last visit two months ago and she supposed her reply had been pretty extraordinary, too, considering that they'd never –

Considering that, two mature people in 1972, they'd met only socially since faraway childhood skiing friendship. Met as often as not with Harry. Considering that they'd talked intimately only once – lunch together during Franzi's last visit to England, but a lunch and a talk of which Miranda could remember everything: Franzi's urgent need to confide about himself, his background (or some of it), his ambitions, his anxieties; and her own reserve, her inability to speak much about her own life despite a strong desire to do so to such a gentle, enchanting listener. When they'd left that lunch table Miranda knew she desperately hoped she'd see Franzi Langenbach again. And again. Soon.

Almost immediately had come his departure to New York. He seemed to spend a lot of life airborne, never in one place for long. And then the letter.

Now Miranda said again, 'Ah!' smiled at her brother and raised her eyebrows.

'When did he ask you? Are you going?'

'He gave me an open invitation when he was here last. Told me to suggest myself in July. Think I will – probably for two or three days, then move on – Rome, Naples. I don't know Italy. I can get away for a fortnight probably.'

'Good idea. Where exactly is Franzi's house?'

'In Umbria. Near the Adriatic coast. Sounds lovely. Franzi's coming over here soon and I'll see if he still means it.' Harry was, Miranda knew, looking at her hard, and without surprise she heard him say,

'Why not come too?'

'I might not be able to get away from the gallery in July. It's next month. I'd have to make some changes.' Miranda ran a small but successful picture gallery in Fulham.

'I'm sure you could if you tried. You like him, don't you?'

'He's charming.'

Miranda looked round the upper room at Rules where they were dining. The dark walls, the Victorian and Edwardian prints and cartoons were always oddly restful, the atmosphere redolent of ancient high jinks, 'Nineties dandies, aspiring actresses, little suppers'. It was someone else's world, but nostalgic and agreeable. Miranda's voice was very cool and her reflective, detached smile was so well done that even Harry was uncertain. They didn't exchange confidences these days, in their thirties. But foolhardy, risking it, determined not to appear running from the subject, she said,

'He's had a strange upbringing, German on both sides of course. Last time he was here he told me something about it. His mother died in a Nazi concentration camp. She'd helped some British officer escape.'

'She had indeed,' said Harry, who had gossiped about Franzi from time to time. 'She'd helped a chap called Marvell escape. We've met the Marvell sister, remember? That nice woman Marcia Rudberg, who's married an Austrian, lives in Sussex at a place called Bargate her father left her, and had anyway spent the war in Germany herself – another odd story I should imagine. Does Franzi remember his mother?'

'Yes. He – it was painful to him even to speak of her. He obviously adored her. Of course he was only a small child when they – when they took her.'

So they'd talked heart to heart, Harry thought. And what of my sister's heart? He nodded.

'What about Franzi's father?'

'He was a German air force officer. Franzi didn't talk about him. I gathered there were considerable properties in Germany which have ended up with Franzi.'

'Yet he lives in America –'

'Not all the time. He goes to Germany quite often. He's got an old aunt or something there. Arzfeld, I think the name is. His mother was von Arzfeld. Not to mention frequent visits to England, as we know. He sees the Rudbergs in Sussex you mentioned, I know that. And he's built this house in Italy.'

'Jet set surgeon! There was an article in an Italian illustrated magazine all about him, *Oggi* or one of those. Did you see it?'

'I think perhaps I did,' Miranda said, wondering if the indifference was overdone. There had been coloured illustrations of Franzi Langenbach superimposed against the Manhattan skyline. Franzi standing beside a sleek-looking Mercedes in an Italian landscape. Franzi on skis. Miranda's Italian had been just sufficient to make out the gist of the article, half mocking, half reverent. Brilliant young surgeon. Youthful phenomenon. Playboy with a serious side. Franzi with various exciting and excited-looking girls in restaurants and nightclubs. The captions had indicated gilded origins, too. There was a photograph of the ancient Schloss Langenbach.

It was time for a change of subject without the change being so marked as to appear an evasion.

'Take care in Italy, Harry! They seem to set off bombs all the time – there was that ghastly one at the Rome railway station in April.'

'Things always look worse from abroad. Think of Northern Ireland and how it looks to us in England, let alone the Italians.'

'Still – we really seem to be living in the age of terrorism, don't we? In Italy that extraordinary business of Feltrinelli's death. And in France, that Renault man kidnapped –'

'My dear, it's instead of war. We're not suffering an actual war. We're exposed instead to these fanatics. They've just rounded up this young woman who's the last of that gang in Germany. The girl's flat was a complete armoury, according to the papers. Sub-machine guns, grenades –' Harry's mind went to the morning's conversation with Clandon.

'It's an epidemic,' said Miranda forcefully. 'What do they want?' Harry fancied his perception in the matter.

'Terrorists of the kind we're talking about will identify with as many issues as possible. They'll feel involved with any resentment powerful enough to produce violence. Palestinians – you name it. After all it was Japanese suicide squads who shot down twenty people at Tel Aviv airport two weeks ago.

They want to destroy for the hell of it, so that a new, beautiful, clean, uncorrupted world can be built on the ruins.'

'No compromise. No reform.'

'Exactly.' Harry smiled in a sad, knowledgeable way. He felt master of the subject, felt that he had studied the jargon of revolution sufficiently to express it in terms used by its devotees. 'Exactly, the present set-up is hopelessly tainted, everywhere. It's unjust beyond hope of redemption. It's got to be destroyed. This is the terrorist phase of the Revolution. First you organise, then you terrorise –'

'Who are you quoting?'

'Mao Tse-tung. First you organise, then you terrorise, so that people are afraid to resist, afraid to support the authorities, lose all confidence in society's ability to protect them –'

'Then?'

'Then things are ready for guerilla warfare.'

'Well,' said Miranda, 'I don't believe these creatures would have their successes, or as much success anyway, without TV. They thrive on publicity.'

'Of course! The Revolution needs to be communicated. So does terror. We feel more nervous the more we see. So we imagine more. Perfectly proper communication – and I'm not saying we shouldn't have it – does the terrorists' job for them.' Harry summoned a waiter and produced his credit card.

Miranda could not avoid seeing Franzi Langenbach's face whenever her concentration slipped, nor stifle her awareness of Franzi's letter, that letter, in her handbag where it had been since its arrival. 'Do you know,' the letter had asked, 'that when you walked into the room, to lunch with me, the whole world changed, all other sounds faded except the sound and expectation of your voice, all other people melted into the background so that they could hardly be distinguished by my eyes, they were shadowy, not clearly defined. Meanwhile you stood there, and smiled, and said, "Sorry I'm late," and it was as if a very, very strong light was on you, isolating you from everything and every colour and shape around you, picking you out. It was alarming and unnerving and my heart raced and I talked nothing but egotistic nonsense and all the time I wanted to take you a thousand miles away –' and so on.

Miranda thanked her brother for dinner, her generous merchant banking brother. He said,

'Think hard about Italy. I'm sure Franzi could put us both up.' She said that she would and accepted a taxi lift home to Chelsea.

It was, as it happened, exactly one week later, on Sunday 25th June, that Reno Vanetti took Carla and Vittorio for a drive.

He'd never talked about his car and Vittorio had wondered about it and now noted with approval the lines of a Fiat – 1971, not bad. It was, he thought, the one in which Reno had originally driven him from Arezzo at their first encounter, of which he recalled little clearly. Dark blue and remarkably clean considering the squalor of their lifestyle – and it really did seem to be Reno's own. As if letting Vittorio a little further into a charmed inner circle, Reno murmured,

'Bruno looks after it.'

'Bruno,' explained Carla, 'has a garage. The other side of Perugia, the Assisi road. A friend. A comrade.' Carla was Carla Rosio. Vittorio, as far as anybody bothered, was Vittorio Parano.

They climbed steeply from the valley lying along the eastern side of the hill city of Perugia, climbed a narrow, winding road with periodic exquisite glimpses of the Umbrian countryside. They reached a high point in the road: to their east and ahead of them began the rolling forested hills that stretched as far as the Adriatic, parallel rivers intersecting the green slopes. Everywhere there was an atmosphere of gentle luxuriance. The mountains were gracious rather than forbidding, the valleys lush, the fields speckled with wild flowers. The roofs of villages and farmhouses were of varying tints of red and orange, harmonious with earth, with tree bark, with ochre-coloured walls. It was June, with the sun shining on Umbria.

Carla said conventionally, 'A beautiful day!'

'Vittorio doesn't think much of the beauties of nature!'

Reno's voice was sardonic and it stung Vittorio, who had so far been enjoying the air, the sky, the sense of revived strength after weeks cooped up in a dingy attic. He said,

'Vittorio appreciates beauty, Reno. Why not? Does a man have to be born rich to love beauty, is that it?'

He knew he'd scored. Patronising bastard! And they thought they had the right to lecture him all the time about the duty to change the world in honour of the poor! Now, because he was a slum kid from an institute, a small criminal on the run, they thought he didn't have a heart to beat faster beneath the Umbrian sky – patronising, superior bastards! Vittorio's irritation was the stronger because he knew Reno's comment was not unjust in a general way. There weren't many among the roughs, the villains, the outcasts who'd peopled Vittorio's world so far who cared a fig for any sort of beauty except a woman's flesh, nor many who ever used the word. Beauty! But he, Vittorio, *did* care, *did* recognise, *did* respond, he told himself angrily, and it hurt him to be dismissed as an insensitive oaf by Reno – a deprived insensitive oaf, no doubt, a victim of the system, but all the same somebody you couldn't share a lot with. Sitting in the back of the car, emboldened by his annoyance (because he still feared Reno), he leant forward and said,

'Eh, Reno? Can't the poor appreciate beauty too?'

Reno said, indifferently, 'Of course. But bourgeois enthusiasm for picturesque nature generally masks total insensitivity to the miseries of others, peasants, poor people who are enslaved by that nature, and who don't have time to say "How beautiful!" They're too over-worked and over-tired!'

'I daresay,' said Vittorio, 'but I'm not an over-worked, over-tired peasant!' Reno was making it worse all the time, he thought. 'Peasant' indeed!

Reno turned and smiled at him, simultaneously steering the car round a dangerous bend on the unfenced road. Reno's smile was rare and charming. Vittorio felt mollified despite himself and Reno drove on, on and on, up and up, humming a little tune. After a few more miles Reno said,

15

'You read *Oggi*, Carla?'

'Of course.'

'An idea?'

'An idea. Maybe a good idea.'

'He finds peace here, it said. The warmth, the colours, a painter's landscape – it appeals to his northern desire for a softer world than the north provides. You read all that?'

'That and more!'

'I was on the telephone this morning, Carla. We have quite a generous allocation for a particular task, if we propose one. That business with the English girl has worked, our friends told me. We're all right – very much all right.'

Reno pulled into a passing place and got out of the driving seat. They had now travelled many miles from Perugia and were high among the wooded hills with occasional breathtaking views to a valley far below, a valley from which small tributary glens reached back into the mountains. Vittorio saw that Reno had taken from his pocket a neat pair of binoculars, very expensive-looking, and was examining something intently. Then Reno spoke gently to both of them, keeping his eyes to the front, binoculars up.

'Come and look. The one to the right of the single row of cypresses – next to the right of the last cypress.' He added softly, 'From now on you're both on duty.'


'Harry Wrench?'

'Speaking.'

'Bruce Clandon. Thank you. It will be in the papers tomorrow. They've agreed to let her go.'

'I'm glad,' said Harry, meaning it profoundly. It wasn't every day, he thought, that it was possible in the line of business to do such straightforward good; to bring unalloyed happiness. He repeated, 'I'm glad,' and Clandon said, 'Thanks again,' with a lot in his voice, and rang off.

# CHAPTER 2

From the first they had made Vittorio tell them again and again about the earliest murder he had committed. Neither Reno nor Carla approved of these episodes from Vittorio's uncommitted, politically uneducated past, when deeds, as he carefully explained, had always been inspired by anger, greed or lust. Vittorio was a natural if exaggerated actor. He enjoyed anecdote and the more shocking the crime or indefensible the circumstance the greater his enthusiasm in recounting his part.

'*Rabbia*,' he would say, rolling the eyes. '*Brama*,' he would murmur, nodding with a resigned and self-satisfied half-smile, 'that was all it was, *brama*, desire. It drove me mad, I was savage at that time, I can tell you!'

They were far from persuaded that Vittorio's stories were true in their entirety – or even, perhaps, true at all. This scepticism was to some extent comforting since Reno, while flattering himself on his freedom from the trammels of bourgeois morality, was puritanical, and disliked the gloating note with which Vittorio explained the animal nature of his motives. Carla, even more dubious of the truth of the tale, grew quickly impatient with Vittorio's immature bragging on these occasions. But despite this they encouraged him. They were absorbed by the detail, the method, the sense that, liar though he might be, they were listening to an expert, to one who knew about killing, robbery and most associated arts. And they liked – or professed to like – his total absence of remorse.

'Just a minute, Vittorio. Did you put on gloves before forcing the garage door?'

Vittorio would smile.

'Sharp! That was the only place I needed a glove. A lot of people would have overlooked it!'

And later –

'Wasn't there some noise when the fellow went down? How were you sure there wouldn't be a row? There were people in the next room – he might have knocked over a chair, grabbed something as he fell –'

'I knew *how* he'd fall, if he was hit like that, you see?' – Vittorio did some miming – 'I timed it and I spaced him. He went down absolutely clear of chairs and tables and suchlike. I arranged it, you see?' He laughed. 'It's experience!'

In matters of detail he was remarkably convincing.

They had found Vittorio by chance two months earlier, at the end of April. He had been, as for a large part of his life, lying low and avoiding the police. He had also been in rather a bad way. The newspapers had recently been full of the robbery of an antique dealer's shop in Florence: the antique dealer, left for dead after savage bludgeoning of the skull, had lain unconscious in hospital for days, finally recovering but with memory and sense damaged for ever. Reno had been driving back from Florence to Perugia shortly afterwards and had gone into a small bar he knew on the outskirts of Arezzo. The owner was as near as such a man could get to being a sympathiser, and it was a place which all sorts frequented with no questions asked. The police took a percentage and in return there was generally warning before a visit.

It was mid-afternoon, and hot for April. Reno ordered a Coca-Cola; he drank alcohol seldom. Looking round the bar he noticed a young man sitting by himself in a corner, in the shadows. Strikingly good-looking, the young fellow wore a gold bracelet, jeans and a black anorak. Reno nodded to him.

The owner of the bar said in a low voice, 'Trouble, that one!'

'Trouble?'

'Won't go. Wants me to keep him here. I can see why! We get on all right with the authorities, not too many problems, you know – but –'

'But?' Reno spat out the interrogative, '*Ma?*'

'But I can't play the fool. I can see it won't be long –'

'What are you talking about?'

'He's been here two hours,' said the man, still near inaudible, 'and I doubt if he can stand.'

Reno glanced casually towards the young man, who was slumped over the table, his eyes unfocussed. The proprietor said,

'One grappa! He's dead sober!'

Reno nodded.

'Bullet?'

'Shsh!' said the other. They were alone, the three of them, in the little bar, brilliant sun outside, all shadow within. A cat moved round the room, miaowing at regular intervals. Reno said, without expression,

'I'll persuade him, if you like.'

'Better not get involved. He may shift when people start coming in.'

But Reno had been thinking, and shrugged his shoulders. After another minute and the ordering of a second Coke he walked over to the young man's table and sat down. They exchanged nods and Reno observed pain and fatigue, enormous fatigue, in the very beautiful brown eyes. He sipped his Coke and said,

'A grappa?'

The other shook his head.

'Thanks. I – I'd better –'

Reno leant forward and spoke very softly.

'You might like somewhere quiet for a bit. You look as if you've had a rough time. I've got a decent place, outskirts of Perugia, nobody will bother you. Nobody. I've a car outside.'

He saw the mix of longing and caution in the other's eyes. Saw, too, as he had sensed when first entering the place, something else – more than a touch of savagery, an elemental quality behind the silkiness and the looks. But just for the moment the fellow was vulnerable, was on the run, had been hit and hit hard. Something might be made of him, Reno thought; and there was a need.

He said, 'Got a name?'

He snapped the query, softly but with calculated roughness, asserting superiority. He reckoned that this young man was a creature quick to resent, dangerous-tempered, one normally to humour a little. It was important to take and retain the upper hand while this one was wounded, frightened and suppliant. It wouldn't last and it was essential to begin as Reno intended to go on.

'I'm Vittorio,' the young man shrugged, as if to say that was quite enough.

'Well, Vittorio, are you interested? Ask this fellow behind the bar, he'll tell you I'm not a pervert, not getting you along so I can kill you, or thrash you, or even make love to you!' Reno smiled thinly.

The other murmured, 'So why?'

'I think,' said Reno, 'that I might have interesting employment for you. That's why. When you feel more like it. And if you wish.'


And so Vittorio came to live with them. He collapsed on the journey to Perugia and at first needed rest and little else. A bullet from the gun of a security guard – surprisingly employed by the Florentine antique dealer – had caught him across the stomach, ploughing up flesh, superficial but painful. He'd lost a good deal of blood and the wound had turned septic. His companion in robbery had been arrested the day after the event.

'Pulled in on suspicion,' Vittorio said confidently, much later on when they all three knew each other better, 'they won't nail it on him. And he'd never talk.'

They knew that he was nervous. He had done one short prison sentence in Milan when eighteen and had much disliked it. He told them that now he knew his way around he'd quickly become a top man in any prison, but they realised that this was bravado. Vittorio feared conviction and sentence. Prison had been dominated by the old hands, the organised ones, the members of societies beyond Vittorio's experience. He had found himself victim rather than predator, a little fish whose violent skills aroused there no terror, whose every trick could be trumped. He had, they guessed, loathed the homosexual approaches inevitably forced upon him, although Vittorio did not refer directly to these well-known features of Italian prison life. He did not regard prison lightly, and they found this helpful. Meanwhile he grew stronger, ate voraciously, asked few questions to start with and slept the night and day through.

On the fourth day Carla brought him a half litre of red wine. They had put him on a mattress in a little room behind the apartment door, almost a cupboard, with a skylight window in a sloping roof. Apart from this the apartment – bare of furniture except for two ancient tables, beds for Reno and Carla, a few cushions and some packing cases – consisted of two rooms, floors piled high with books and newspapers. There was a tiny kitchen and a shower room. Reno spent a good deal of every day reading, but went out a certain amount on unspecified business. Vittorio knew that he was out now.

Carla put the wine on the floor beside Vittorio, who was awake and looking more animated, she thought. Carla had some rudimentary, mainly self-taught knowledge of medical aid; Reno had once brought back two books he had ordered her to study. She had dressed Vittorio's wound on the first evening. It looked messy, but she knew enough to realise it would be all right if it could be cleaned up and the infection killed. Now she said,

'I'd better change the dressings. I got some new lint this morning and some stuff the man in the shop said would be really good at clearing up the muck.'

'It feels all right. Leave it till tomorrow.'

'No, I want to do it now.'

'So do I,' said Vittorio, and ran his right hand up under Carla's skirt to the thigh, fingers strong and caressing. Carla was bare-legged, the weather hotter daily. Her skin felt delicious to the touch, firm and silk-like, yielding but not in the least flabby.

'So do I, Carla. I want to do it now!'

She straightened, looked at him smiling up at her, his eyes tender.

'Carla –'

Carla bent down and with her right palm hit him extremely hard on his left ear. Vittorio's mouth changed shape. His lips had been half-parted, gentle, lascivious. Now they bared his teeth like a dog snarling at a stranger.

'Ah-h-h – you –!'

She stepped sharply back. He was not yet robust enough to be agile and his right arm, stabbing out with the savagery of a tiger's paw to grab her, missed and collapsed by his side on the mattress. Vittorio was breathing deeply, eyes full of anger and lust fixed on Carla. She moved swiftly through the open door of the tiny room. Three minutes later he heard Reno re-enter the apartment. Vittorio lay back and listened to rapid speech from next door, low and indistinguishable. Little bitch! What did she think he was? And she wasn't at all bad, either, with that reddish hair, green eyes, a good body, slim legs, very smooth skin from what he'd seen of it. He considered the next move.

Then Reno came in and sat down on the floor beside the mattress. Reno looked at him and then picked up the jug of wine and drank a little from it. Vittorio put on a proud look. He supposed Carla was Reno's, although they were, he thought, odd together; it was hard to tell exactly what Reno felt. Now Vittorio imagined Reno would take advantage of his, Vittorio's, weakness. He would deal with him for making a mild pass at the girl, threaten him, turn him out, beat him perhaps. He decided that if so he would simply make it clear that, one day, Reno would die for it. He was pretty sure Reno was not one to kill from jealousy. Vittorio smelt such characteristics, he could tell. Nevertheless, he doubted if Reno would be impressed by any menaces Vittorio could utter. He was rather afraid of Reno. He looked at him with a defiant half-smile and wished he didn't feel so damnably feeble.

Reno said nothing, put the jug down and lit a cigarette.

'Cigarette?'

'Thanks,' said Vittorio. It couldn't be peace. It was going to be a cat-and-mouse affair. He kept his eyes on Reno, seeing a slender young man with a pale, narrow face and dark, receding hair. It was, Vittorio thought uneasily, a clever face.

Reno never moved fast, had none of Vittorio's cat-like agility when fit, appeared deliberate, methodical, even rather clumsy. Vittorio doubted if he was particularly strong and was sure he, Vittorio, could spread Reno all over the apartment floor and ceiling if it ever came to it. But he doubted, too, if it ever would come to it, and there was something about Reno which was dominant and unnerving. He asked himself, as he had frequently but without great interest since arrival, what the hell was their game? They knew, or suspected, a good deal about Vittorio. He knew nothing at all about them.

They smoked and watched each other. Reno said nothing. After a bit Vittorio felt a compulsion to break the silence.

'Carla's going to dress my belly!'

Reno still said nothing. He tapped ash fastidiously on to the floor, for all the world, thought Vittorio, as if he were sitting in a smart restaurant with a silver ashtray beside him. Several more minutes went by. Reno finished his cigarette and threw the stub expertly through the open skylight. His voice, as always, was quiet, without emphasis.

'Why do you suppose we've helped you?'

Vittorio, naturally, had wondered this. He supposed they were some sort of vagabonds, rebels, layabouts, do-nothings, runaways, God knew what. Crooks, he supposed sceptically, but amateur crooks, they didn't fit into his experience, filled as it already was with a gallery of characters from most parts of the Italian criminal fraternity – small-timers all, he had inevitably to acknowledge, although he would not have dreamt of saying so aloud. Now he smiled with what he hoped would look like cynicism rather than the puzzlement he felt. He put a shrug into the smile, as if to say,

'What business of mine?'

and actually said,

'You saw I was in a bad way – you've been good to me –'

'Yes. Why?'

'Well, I gathered from Ramini –' Ramini was the proprietor of the Arezzo bar.

'What did you gather from Ramini?'

'He nodded to me – when you suggested –'

23

'Well?'

'He wouldn't have nodded – Ramini has a lot of friends, that's well known. He doesn't know me but obviously knows you. I was hardly conscious but I reckoned that nod meant – well, meant that I could, that I'd be all right, to go with you.' Feeling for words Vittorio managed, 'That I could trust you.'

'Trust?' said Reno forcibly. 'What do you mean, trust?'

This was becoming difficult and Vittorio reached for the jug and had a swig of wine. Reno didn't seem to expect an answer and after a little, brow wrinkled in thought, said very softly,

'Vittorio, have you ever killed a man?'

This was easier.

'Yes, if you want to know.'

'So have I. How did you do it?'

'First time,' said Vittorio, thinking fast, 'a knife. I learned to use a knife early. You see –'

He talked away, feeling a sort of relief. After a while, during which Reno had said nothing beyond the injection of a periodic, brief question to clarify some point of narrative, Vittorio uneasily realised he was unsure – to put it no more strongly – whether Reno believed a word he was saying. At the same time he felt perfectly certain that when Reno had said 'So have I' it was the exact truth. Furthermore, Vittorio had sensed this from the first hours of consciousness in that place. Reno had said something, one or two things, commented on the newspapers he was interminably reading, spoken not boastfully but with quiet effectiveness, in a way which only made sense if the man speaking knew what it was to take life deliberately. Vittorio could never have analysed this in a thousand years, but there is a freemasonry of murder and Vittorio had no doubt that Reno belonged to it, although he found it difficult to imagine circumstances or cause. Yes, Reno had killed.

Vittorio talked until exhausted. Some sense of prudence kept him from discussing in any detail the exploit in Florence from which he had received the security man's bullet in the flesh. The time would probably come for that, and Reno could not fail to suspect it; but not today. The affair had received a

24

lot of publicity, he'd known that, half conscious that he was, when on the run. He'd listened to the radio in a succession of bars, before slipping out, fearing suspicion, the closing of a trap. Then Reno had found him, Reno who now sat listening, tapping ash on the bare, dusty boards of the floor beside Vittorio's mattress, frowning, perhaps about himself, about Carla, about what they did, his protectors, his hosts, his saviours, his gaolers – whatever they were, saying nothing about themselves, nothing at all.

Vittorio felt very tired. Then, after a long silence, Reno stubbed out his fourth cigarette, looked thoughtfully at Vittorio and said,

'I am now going to tell you one or two things.'

In the process of telling him 'one or two things' Reno elicited yet more from Vittorio. He preferred to impart information and simultaneously extract it, create a dialogue, say, 'Well, I'll tell you how it was – but I expect something like it has happened to you, too, hasn't it? Hasn't it?' From Vittorio, tired but responding to Reno, compelled by Reno, Reno learned of a childhood passed in the slums of Turin. Vittorio remembered no father, no mother. He had recollections of some sort of institution; it sounded a religious house, an asylum for destitute infants.

'They used to thrash us – for anything! We had to be silent at meals – filthy meals! We were always hungry –'

He'd been luckier than many, he said. There was no way of testing the veracity of these reminiscences. Nor was it possible to discover how old Vittorio was, because nobody had ever told him. He became confused when Reno tried to clarify the age at which he (allegedly) escaped from the institution.

'How can I say? Eight years, maybe? Seven?'

Since then he had survived by thieving, armed robbery on a few occasions when somewhat older, intelligent evasion of the law. Despite his fatigue Vittorio was enjoying so much talk about himself, and almost forgot that Reno was about to tell him 'one or two things'; almost forgot, too, to be afraid of Reno's clever, concentrated stare. He began to boast.

'Before going to Florence – just before we met –'
'I understand.'
'I spent six months in Milan. That's what I like – big city. I was getting on pretty well there – I had a partner –'

Reno showed no particular interest and Vittorio checked himself. There should be no talk about partners. Even to Reno. Especially to Reno.

'And I had a girl there – or two, to be exact. One was a blonde, a real blonde, Austrian as a matter of fact. Fantastic! I've lost her photograph –'

Reno said conversationally,
'When did you last see her?'
'Six weeks.'
'And no woman since?'
'What do you take me for? Of course I've had women since! I was well fixed up in Florence before – well, before things happened.'
'And you'll soon be around again, Vittorio, eh?'

Vittorio reflected that the subject was a delicate one, which Reno must always have been intending to approach.

'That's right,' he said with an uneasy grin, 'soon be fit now.'

'Vittorio, we hope you'll stay with us quite a while. Maybe join us in certain important things we're doing. First, I want to tell you a little about Carla. You are not to try to make Carla, not to try anything on with her at all.'

'Of course!' said Vittorio to himself, 'because she's yours!' He kept his mouth shut, his eyes watchful.

'Carla will be angry if you forget this. I assure you that is true.'

'So you think!' formed itself in Vittorio's mind, but he said non-committally, 'OK' in an Italo-American voice, or so he fancied.

'Carla,' said Reno, 'is a sensitive woman. She had a bad start to life. Her mother – she was fond of her mother – was raped by an American soldier when a young girl. Nine months later Carla was born.'

'Rape, eh?' said Vittorio, nodding wisely, concealing a smile.

'So Carla believes, or pretends to believe. I suspect,' said Reno, 'that it was as likely to have been an exchange for a tin of American sausage meat. Who can tell? It doesn't matter. Carla has no idea about her father except that he was an unknown and unwanted American. She knows no more about her father than you do, Vittorio.'

He lit another cigarette for each of them.

'As I say, she loved her mother, who died when she was nine years old. She was – well, her beginnings have given her a, shall I say a distaste for – for casual encounters. Unless unavoidable.'

Vittorio looked ruminative. Apart from the message, he couldn't get over Reno's precise, careful way of putting things, using words one didn't hear every day! Now Reno was staring at him as if unsure whether he'd understood.

'I mean, she hates being pulled about, pawed, attacked as if she was just a piece of flesh. She's a person – an intelligent, important, talented person. So, very naturally, she only likes a man who – who treats her with full understanding of that fact.'

They smoked in silence, almost a friendly silence. Reno said, still without emphasis,

'Remember that! I may say Carla's a pretty good shot. Don't assume she's soft because she's a girl.'

Vittorio nodded, suppressing a grin about Carla's skill with a gun which he thought a silly remark. As expected, he was being warned off and by now he was reconciled to the fact that if he was to stay on terms with these people – and he suspected it was going to be necessary for some time – Carla had better be left alone. He was unsure how much he accepted of Reno's high-flown sentiments about the loftiness of her personality. She was a woman, wasn't she? And this was Italy, for God's sake! But he felt the force of Reno's conviction, of Reno's character and – no doubt – Reno's possessive love for Carla. He was being warned off and he'd take the warning.

Reno broadened the conversation.

'Carla, you can imagine, doesn't care much for America and all that. Nor do I.'

Vittorio said nothing to this. Personally he had a strong desire to cross the Atlantic. Now Reno was talking in a curiously gentle voice.

'Vittorio, like Carla, you had a harsh start to life. Like hundreds of thousands of others, in Italy and everywhere else.'

'You bet I did!'

'Is that right, do you think? Is it inevitable that children should be born, grow up without education, proper food, prospects – kicked around, at the bottom of the heap? Should that go on for ever?'

'It's not going to happen to *my* son,' said Vittorio, pushing his chin out, 'I'm on the way up!'

'Perhaps. But it will happen to others. Must that be so? Do you never dream of changing it – changing it utterly?'

'*Come*?' said Vittorio, with sincere surprise. 'How, change it utterly?'

Reno said, after a pause,

'Can you remember any occasion when you completely changed your own way of doing things?'

As a matter of fact Vittorio could. He had once decided that a little small-scale pimping would be comparatively easy money, and had acquired first one, then two girls, each of whom had fallen for him. He'd been firm with them but not excessively brutal and it had looked both promising and pleasant. Then –

'Then I dropped it. Got out.'

'Why?'

Vittorio, although vain, knew that only the truth would work with Reno, at least on this occasion.

'There were big boys around, you see. I'd not realised. It was their patch. It was a case of getting out or ending up down the main drain of the city, in very small pieces!' He laughed. Since he couldn't tell the story as a triumph, it had to be related as of one who had at least walked with great danger and survived.

'So you got out – you changed your way of life. Can you find one word to express exactly why?'

28

It was obvious, and Vittorio didn't like enunciating it but Reno had still got those unblinking eyes on him. Hypnotic, almost.

'Fear, of course!'

'Exactly! It is only fear which makes people abandon – or adjust – a way of life which suits *them*, however intolerable it may be for others. Others like young Vittorio. Like young Carla. Only fear leads to the desertion of a system so that the system itself crumbles.'

Vittorio, almost timidly, murmured,

'And young Reno?'

Reno ignored this. With the sure perceptions of the survivor he had always been, Vittorio suspected that Reno knew of the sufferings of the poor, the hungry, the exploited, the beaten, from the experiences of others, not his own. Reno's confidence was a plant with secure roots. Reno stubbed out yet another cigarette on the floor, looked earnestly at Vittorio and said,

'Our business, you see, is to change the world. And the first step is to induce fear in those who run it in their own interest. And in their own way.'

Vittorio, uneasy, tried near-facetiousness:

'Change the world! You and Carla? How soon?'

'There are others. We are far from alone. We have comrades here in Italy – some here in Perugia. And we have comrades, dedicated to the same idea, as sick of the system as we, in other countries – Germany, England. You must have read.'

'I suppose so,' nodded Vittorio. He felt confused. Reno smiled at him and said,

'Vittorio, soon you'll be better. You'll want to go out, have a drink, maybe pick up a girl, have a look at town. You'll need money. You only had this on you.' He held up Vittorio's wallet. Vittorio felt no resentment. It was natural in a man who'd driven him here and taken him in. He had no recollection of arriving – they told him he'd passed out in the car. He remembered that, for various disagreeable reasons, there had only been seven thousand lire in the wallet. He took it from Reno who said,

'Seven thousand lire.' Vittorio nodded. He completely trusted Reno by now – at least in things like this.

'I hope you'll stay with us. We have certain problems. Just at present this isn't one of them.' Before Vittorio's eyes he took thirty thousand lire, six five-thousand-lire notes, from his pocket, gently took back the wallet and slid the notes into it. Vittorio took it from his outstretched hand with astonished suspicion. Reno got smartly to his feet.

'Now I have to go out. We'll talk again tomorrow. And Vittorio – we can help you. And you can help us.'

'Reno –'

'Yes?'

'You know you said, just now, "So have I".'

'Well?'

'Are you going to tell me about that?'

Vittorio told himself that it was absurd as well as demeaning to his self-respect that his mouth was dry. But it was. Reno was always considering him so carefully, like something in a zoo. How old was Reno? he wondered. Twenty-five or twenty-six maybe? Smooth hands. High, pale forehead. Vittorio tried to summon up reserves of contempt – this fellow had lived soft! He knew nothing! He tried to look knowing, even sceptical as he lay on the mattress squinting up at Reno. He, Vittorio, had told plenty and learned little. Maybe Reno was a phoney, a pompous fake for all his super-ciliousness, his handouts, his questioning! And as for the girl!

But Vittorio knew it was not so. Reno said quietly,

'There were eleven bodies. Seven died instantly. It was in the papers – all the papers, everywhere. Three weeks back.'

'How? Where? Why?'

'Bomb. Rome. To change the world.'


So they were those sort of nuts! Vittorio had been thinking it over. He had, he supposed, guessed something of the kind from their mixture of evident ruthlessness – he felt no incli-nation to doubt Reno's exploit – a ruthlessness combined with a sort of fastidiousness, an intellectualism (although Vittorio had few words in which to express these thoughts to himself). But in the following weeks – and as he got stronger they became companionable, the three of them – he found that when Reno and Carla were talking to each other, as often as not he couldn't understand a word they were saying. He watched them carefully, suppressing a natural envy; Carla's movements, the sheen of her skin, the sound of her washing herself in the poky little shower room – all this was hard to bear. Vittorio thought he must go off for a bit soon. His wound was healing nicely. Perugia wasn't a town he knew, but he would enjoy exploring it, no problem. For the moment, however, Reno simply said,

'Best to stay in for a little longer,' and Vittorio obeyed. He was stronger but still damnably weak.

He saw that they were dependent on each other, those two. Reno was the boss – not simply as a man (very much not, Vittorio thought, simply as a man) but as a clever one, a deep one, a driving force. But Carla was intensely practical. Vittorio reckoned that she was probably as dedicated to their cranky revolutionary ideas as her lover, and she spoke of 'them' – the authorities, the powers-that-be, the managers of the existing system of society – with a hatred which was even more explicit and virulent than Reno's; this may, as Reno had indicated, have derived from bitterness about her origins, about her mother's story, but it was articulate, well worked out. The long sentences, thought Vittorio, the words, the jargon she used – you'd never suppose all this was because her mother had been screwed by a GI! Vittorio knew better than to appear cynical but he had difficulty in understanding. He nodded, sighed and played along.

In their turn they showed insatiable curiosity about his own deeds, his methods, the lore of his profession: petty crook, occasional killer (truth to tell, very occasional, but he knew how to make his stories grip), pretty-boy womaniser. Vittorio Parano. He'd adopted the second name somewhere along the line and knew of no other.

Much of the time, lounging on cushions on the floor, they read newspapers and illustrated magazines, and talked about news items. Reno had originally wondered whether Vittorio was at home with the printed word, but in fact Vittorio read fast. Carla, serious, green-eyed, long eyelashes, sallow but smooth skin of which he was hotly aware, constituted herself his tutor while Reno went on his mysterious expeditions. She threw a *Sera* across at him one day at the beginning of June.

'That you, Vit?'

There was a report about the Florentine antique dealer. The article was strongly written – victim of outrage, still incapable of helping the police, unlikely ever to do more than exist without mind or senses for the rest of his life, if it could be called life, an unremembering, unloving, unfeeling thing once called man. It was an indignant article calling for stronger measures against violent criminals. Vittorio's companion in the robbery was awaiting trial and the article pointed out that two men had been involved.

> Giacomo Benetti, security guard on the premises, who behaved with conspicuous bravery, certainly wounded the second man, perhaps fatally. The police are, however, convinced that he is not in the region of Florence. Wherever he is, if he is alive, he can reflect on the fact that a decent, honest, cultivated man is now rotting like a vegetable because of his actions.

Vittorio grunted. He'd never talked about it but he was perfectly aware Carla and Reno guessed about him. His grunt, his absence of denial, confirmed. Carla said,

'Your friend won't come up until October, they seem to think. How much will they get out of him? Or have they got out of him, do you suppose?'

'Pietro's tough, a good fellow. He'll not talk –'

But he knew it was bombast. Pietro would soon talk if there were some strong inducement, like a lenient sentence.

'You were wearing a mask,' said Carla, reflecting on the reports from the press, taking his complicity for granted. 'The security man, Benetti, has no description. Can't recognise. Right?'

He muttered 'Right,' with a faint smile. He wished Pietro

hadn't hit the old fellow so bloody hard, and gone on hitting him. It had been completely unnecessary. One little tap and he'd have known nothing. As it was, people were agitating, people were indignant, the press wouldn't drop it. If you're going all out, thought Vittorio, do it properly. He had nothing like the experience he described to Reno and Carla but if he killed it would be because he meant to. Pietro had been loutish and put them both in deep. The job had been thoroughly botched and detracted from his own reputation for expertise. It must lower him in Reno and Carla's eyes. He scowled at the newspaper and turned to the football pages.

Carla still seemed to have plenty on her mind.

'There should be no need for you to do these things, Vittorio. You realise that you've been forced into them by society?'

'Of course!' He tried to look melancholy.

'Because society itself is organised as a crime – a gigantic crime of one section cheating and depriving another, and framing laws only to protect the cheats and keep the deprived that way. What the bourgeois world calls morality, the rules it devises, is simply a way of persuading the deprived to accept their deprivation. You understand me?'

'Of course, Carla.'

She was looking especially delectable this morning. He wondered how long Reno would be out, but his resolution held. He was still astounded that one of these female revolutionary nuts could be so good to look at – he'd have pictured them as plain and resentful if he'd ever thought about it.

'What bourgeois society calls criminal –' said Carla, 'robbery, killing those who make the system work – isn't criminal in any true sense. On the contrary it's a duty, and to avoid that duty is to condone the system. That's the point.' She said it very prettily, and Vittorio reflected that he had probably avoided duty a good deal less than Reno and Carla. Still, there were those eleven bodies in Rome! Lazily, he said,

'And when you – you and Reno, he told me, and I suppose

33

you were both in it – when you blew up a lot of people in a Rome station, they were all people making the system work, were they?'

For at heart Vittorio was less easy about this brave rejection of all conventional morality than his companions appeared to be. He knew more about robbery and violence than they ever would, but eleven people they didn't know! It might have been oneself! Besides, he sometimes had a feeling that in the end he'd not be sorry to make a clean breast of it all, to find an old black-skirted priest who didn't know him, to hear *'absolvo te'* – why not? When he'd cleaned up and settled down, maybe? Such weakness could never be mentioned to these two, but it was human, surely?

Carla replied,

'Not necessarily. They were strangers, of course – casualties in a war. You don't know the enemy soldiers your artillery shells kill in a war, do you, you don't feel anything about them.'

'I don't know. I'm not a soldier.' Vittorio had dodged military service, it went without saying. He was a statistic on no census, no electoral roll.

'It's obvious. And you see, this is war, everybody, *everybody* is at war, is part of the system of society, just by existing and not struggling against it.'

'So everybody's due to be killed!'

'Of course not. The point is to shake those who manage the system, shake them by spreading fear and insecurity throughout it. You see, the people in power are responsible for maintaining the laws, maintaining security, protecting life and property. When they're shown to be incapable of doing so, the sense of insecurity spreads, the system is weakened, confidence in it starts to go.'

'And you cause that loss of confidence, spread that fear by knocking off any sort of people, eh?'

'Targets,' said Carla primly, 'need careful selection. They should be chosen for maximum public effect. A robbery, or a kidnap, or a murder which was virtually unnoticed by press and TV would achieve little, except locally. The media help

34

us, of course – they spread the word, it's inevitable. Our word, our deeds. So, you see, they promote insecurity.'

Vittorio nodded and Carla said,

'The more notable the target, obviously, the better. The more anger, alarm, outrage the better. The more reaction the better. You can understand?'

'Certainly, and the more notable the target the tougher to hit it, that's bound to be so. What about the little ones, Carla?'

'Little ones?'

'Not all your Rome eleven were notable, I imagine?'

'Vittorio, it's what I said just now, you have to think of it like a war. It *is* a war. Now any war is caused by people at the top, by greed, by misgovernment, by the whole rotten set-up, right?'

'I suppose so,' said Vittorio, who had not devoted much of life to study of the causes of war.

'So the people at the top are responsible, but the wretched soldier in a tank or a trench gets killed, right?'

'Right.'

'And yet he *has* to be killed, if the war's to be won. It's not his fault; if you like, he's a casualty, a victim, but you can only shake the system that employs him if you kill enough of him.'

They looked at each other and she said quietly,

'And I regret it. But it has to be done.'

'Does Reno regret it? Regret killing the ordinary soldiers?' He added, probing what he thought was flesh not altogether healed, 'Like your Rome eleven?'

'Certainly,' she said, her head high. 'Reno is a deeply conscientious, high-principled man. He suppresses many things in himself because he recognises his duty towards the future of humanity.'

Vittorio thought it was all a long way from knocking an old antique dealer on the head and making an aborted attempt to scoop his safe. As if sensing his mind and making a connection, Carla said, almost gently,

'And war needs technique, Vittorio. These things need expertise. You have much to offer.'

Vittorio decided to broach a different subject on which he had cogitated long without any clear deduction.

'Carla, what do you do for money? You're not short.'

For the first time she seemed embarrassed. Mistaking her, he said,

'Not my business! You've obviously brought off a decent job or two, and good luck!'

'That may be necessary. We've – well, we've had to do one or two jobs, as you call them. We all help each other, of course.'

'All?'

'The organisation. We've told you we're not alone in all this.'

They had, although reticent on the subject, and Vittorio prudently reckoned that the less he knew of their associates the better. Carla said,

'Some groups are – well, they're strongly supported. Financially. And we help each other, like I said.'

'I see.'

'Still, we may have to help ourselves again, one day soon. Just now we've had luck. One of the comrades groups may have got some money from England, believe it or not.'

Vittorio nodded and Carla said, 'Still, one day – we've often talked about – well, you know, a bank –'

A bank, thought Vittorio, you must be joking! This couple hadn't the beginnings of bank work in them. You could tell that from their curiosity, their questions to him, the things they didn't know. Banks needed professionalism. On the other hand, Reno was clever. Given the data he'd master anything, and he had nerve, no doubt of that.

Carla was talking rather disjointedly. 'Of course we manage the ordinary day-to-day stuff not too badly. Reno, you see – Fascist, bourgeois background – he's always been in revolt against it – but there's money, you see –'

Vittorio did see. Reno was rich! Easily believable – but why on earth live in a wretched, bare-boarded attic funk-hole in a Perugia suburb? Couldn't revolutionary war be plotted from somewhat more stylish quarters?

36

Carla, no doubt discerning his feelings, said again,

'He's a very high-principled man.'

Vittorio smiled at her tenderly and sympathetically, feeling irritation and little comprehension. But he knew that he needed time, more time. And while he was like he was, a bit feeble and dependent, he needed a base. Reno and Carla provided that base and he fell, easily, in with their peculiar way of life, their jargon, their raw sensitivities. It wouldn't, he thought, go on very long.

The weeks passed and, encouraged by Reno, Vittorio began cautiously exploring the city and countryside. Getting confidence back – it was curious how the enclosed régime of a wounded man lying up and in the hands of others sapped the nerves. Then came the day in early July, soon after their drive in the country, when Reno looked at him and said,

'Vit, I want you out of here for a few days.'

There was a touch of nervous excitement in Reno's voice. Vittorio sensed it – sensed, too, that he, Vittorio, might be involved in whatever was brewing.

'Out of here for a few days, Vit, OK?'

'OK, Reno.'

# CHAPTER 3

'You've got plenty of time, Mr Langenbach,' said the driver, opening the car door and wearing a broad, charming smile. 'Lots of time, sir. Yes, sir.' He'd often driven Franzi from hospital to airport and had always enjoyed doing so. He liked Mr Langenbach, and Franzi, in turn, liked him. Franzi had never lost the habit of liking most people.

'Thanks, Sam. No rush. How are you?'

Franzi's English, fluent from long training so that he thought now in English and knew New York as well as any other city, retained an attractive touch of the stranger, the interested, alert newcomer. Franzi had once learned a stilted English in school in Westphalia and had first visited England in 1958; and America several years after that – 1966. Six years ago. Whether in America or England people found themselves smiling response at Franzi, but knowing – 'He comes from elsewhere. Perhaps from far away.'

Sam said he was well, white teeth flashing a grin in his dignified, black face. They had an unusually quick run from Manhattan across the East River, on to the motorway, and Franzi, as predicted, had a leisurely half hour to spend in the first-class passenger lounge. He still enjoyed this flight, a flight he had made now many times. He enjoyed the sense of care and cosiness in the small lounge, the knowledge that now he would be looked after, need make no personal effort; and the air-conditioning was a relief after the heat of New York in July, a heat and a humidity which had marked the drive to the airport, for Sam's car, by some unusual economy on the part of the authorities, was not air-conditioned. Now Franzi could look forward to the relaxation on board the aircraft, to a good dinner with excellent wine, the sense of being wafted, cosseted, without responsibility. He would feel sleepy next day, with the clock betraying his digestion, but many carefree weeks lay ahead and it didn't matter. It was 5th July. He planned some days in England, then he would fly to Germany, do a little residual business at Langenbach, go to Arzfeld, see Cousin Lise. There would be affectionate conversations with Cousin Lise, cousin, spinster, surrogate mother; a long walk in the Arzfeld woods, a summer day in Lower Saxony. He'd pick up his new car, his new Mercedes. And then Italy, the long drive south across the Alps, temperature climbing with the car's descent to the great Lombard plain; and so to the green of Umbria, the old-gold colour of village walls and ancient cities, rounded red tiles on roofs, cypress trees darkly spearing the sky. But first England. And perhaps England meant Miranda, rediscovered after friendship in youth.

Franzi ordered a dry Martini. He had been in the operating theatre until four o'clock that afternoon and the stimulus of the cocktail was good, although one would be enough – his first alcohol for three days. It had been a tricky operation, a challenging case. And it had gone well. There had been that superb moment when he could straighten, nod to the others as if it had all been perfectly straightforward, all in a day's work, anybody could have done it. But he knew that they knew that anybody could not have done it. His stance – and their positions, acolytes, rehearsed, essential – would express something which needed no words –

'Good. Very good, I think.'

Franzi had his vanity. He realised that they spoke of him with a certain awe. He realised, too, that some of his older colleagues among the surgeons regarded him with a modicum of jealousy, not always well concealed. Success had come early. He was always referred to as having shown exceptional flair – flair he had known from the beginning he had in his fingertips, in his speed of perception, his innate love of what he was doing. He supposed, without particular concern, that the general public might be distressed that medical men, saviours of life, healers of humanity, should be as capable of vanity, envy, spite and lack of charity as any. But a man's or a woman's profession, Franzi knew, however beneficent, did not immunise a person against weakness – every sort of weakness.

He sipped his Martini with enjoyment. On the whole everybody, of every generation, was kind to him and always, or almost always, had been. Thirty-two years old, something of a prodigy, his reputation in heart surgery was already international. 'Langenbach's the man we ought to get,' specialists would say to doctors, to their patients, to the relations of patients, nodding gravely, whether in Paris, Vienna, or London. 'It's worth the journey. He only operates in New York, and of course there's an inevitable queue of American cases. But I think we could manage it. It was in the States he made his name, you see,' they would explain. 'They were definitely ahead, over there.'

It was indeed in the United States that Franzi had made his name and America would always hold a large slice of his affections. He had known for certain that medicine was his vocation at the age of twenty – late by the standards of most of his dedicated contemporaries. He had been at Marburg University, studying philosophy and modern languages. He had changed horses, ignorant of what was involved, careless of how many steps he had already missed, of how complex and long the path to qualification. He had gone to Göttingen. At the age of twenty-five he had qualified. That had been followed by a year in a hospital in Hanover. Junior house doctor Langenbach.

The others had whispered, sneered sometimes, when he came on a group of them in those days.

'Have you time for a few hours in the wards this Saturday, Langenbach? Or will you be fully occupied going round your farms?'

Everybody knew he had inherited the lands and the ancient Schloss of Langenbach, although it was also accurately rumoured that most would need to be sold, there were taxation problems. Franzi Langenbach, the knowing ones told the others, had inherited as a child; his father had died before he was born. His mother – there were different stories about his mother, but it was generally known that she, too, had died when he was very young, some said 'during the dictatorship' – their way of referring to the National Socialist epoch, the Nazi time, the Second World War, that experience already remote from the young, the memories of hungry children now mercifully erased; and other memories by their elders suppressed.

'She died when he was a kid. He came into everything.'

He would smile gently, conquering with his smile, his unaffected kindness of heart, his manifest devotion to medicine, his dealing with all and every sort of person as a trusted friend. They knew he kept the various parts of his life in separate compartments, but after a while they ceased to resent it. He was a good companion, a good comrade, a decent fellow whatever his origins. And, they grudgingly admitted to each other, he was good at his job. In fact the more perceptive among them said,

'You know, Langenbach – there's something extraordinary about him! He's so quick – and he's – he seems to understand a body with his eyes and his fingertips, almost before properly examining, working it out, you know what I mean –'

Then, after a year in Hanover, he had spoken very respectfully, very quietly and modestly, to the hospital authorities.

'I wish to go to America. To seek a position in America.'

They had told him, with a bullying scepticism which he thought entirely fair, that he would find it very difficult. Perhaps impossible. There were strict regulations – and what had he to offer the United States? He had bowed. His mind was made up.

He had contacts. People guessed that. Toni Rudberg had provided the first. Few people knew all the twists and quirks of the Langenbach, Arzfeld, Rudberg story (and there was an English dimension to that story, surely, people reminisced to each other) but there was a general awareness that Toni Rudberg, who lived with that English wife in England, had some sort of close connection to Franzi Langenbach. Toni, Austrian, man of business, ex-prisoner of war for long years in Russia, survivor, had come to know the United States particularly well. Toni had friends.

41

'I'll write to Malzen. He's a Viennese by origin, very clever doctor. We made friends again last time I was over there. Malzen knows everybody. I'll explain –'

Toni had written. And, after interminable complications and delays, Franzi had gone to America.

Instantly he felt fully alive there. He had loved the friendliness, the immediacy of Americans' reactions. Europeans, half-supercilious, half-envious, spoke sometimes of the simplicity, the superficiality of American attitudes. Franzi saw it otherwise. To him the sheer energy was an intoxicant. And, brought up under the shadows of tragedy both national and domestic, he warmed to American optimism and confidence. Instead of the jaded experience of so many of those among whom he had hitherto lived, he found a readiness to rise to challenge, a sort of courageous innocence which might irritate some but enchanted Franzi. 'What's the problem?' the people seemed to say. 'We'll lick it!' And he grew accustomed to the fact that so much ebullience was, on occasion, succeeded by equally immoderate self-criticism and depression.

He had always dreamed of experiencing America and few things disappointed him. It was necessary, he had learned, to qualify again there, to show his paces, prove his basic abilities, spend another apprenticeship year, this time in an American hospital. He did so – Toni's friendly Dr Malzen was as helpful as anybody could have wished. Malzen said to him, looking at Franzi very hard through enormous spectacles,

'And I'm told you want to be a surgeon!'

'Well – perhaps one day I may –'

'Yes. Perhaps one day you may. But just for now you are going to carry on at the bottom of the ladder. And if you don't like it, get out and go back to Germany!'

He started again at the bottom, as Malzen promised, working at a hospital in New Jersey, some of the routine of a house doctor familiar from his time in Hanover, some of it astonishingly different.

After some months he saw Malzen again at a purely social gathering. Toni's contacts were widespread and Franzi did not lack introductions or hospitality.

'Well, Dr Langenbach?' Malzen's smile was friendly though his voice was ironic. 'Is America still worth a doctor's time?'

'Very much so!'

'I'd like you to meet another colleague of ours. James Foster.'

Dr Foster – the name had been Anglicised in 1920 – was by family origin another Viennese, Franzi discovered, but a second-generation American. His father had arrived before the First World War. He looked at Franzi in a penetrating way, not unfriendly.

'Malzen's spoken of you. You've got ambition, I hear.'

'Yes, I have.'

Nothing more. But, out of the blue, he had found himself invited to dinner by the Fosters. And by that time he had made enquiries, and understood that James Foster was regarded as probably the most brilliant young – or comparatively young, at thirty-eight – heart surgeon on the east coast of the United States. They liked each other. Foster's wife, a quiet, shrewd little woman with dark hair and enormous brown eyes, said to her husband after Franzi left them on that first occasion,

'He's got something, that one.'

'I think so, too. It's pure hunch, of course.'

'Your hunches tend to be good. So do mine.'

And so, after his year in the hospital in New Jersey, he found himself studying surgery, and working, by an arrangement Foster initiated, in a hospital in New York.

With Foster. He was twenty-eight years old.


'London passengers boarding in five minutes,' said a pretty air hostess, giving Franzi a special smile. She saw a young-looking man of thirty-two, slim, brown-faced, blue-eyed and taller than average, with a face full of laughter, a face that looked at you as if you mattered and life was fun. She added,

'Would you like another quick Martini, sir?'

'No, thank you very much. No quick Martini!' And he gave her, in turn, his smile, which made her reflect that the job was appreciably more pleasant on some days than others.

Franzi's mind was still in the operating theatre. On such occasions there always came to him, a memory half fearful, half exultant, that extraordinary moment a few years back when he had realised that he was, this time, entirely and solely responsible; James Foster was nowhere near. He was alone – alone with a man suffering from a very serious heart condition, a man who would die if he, Franzi, misjudged by a fraction of a millimetre, the merest portion of a second in time, what he was attempting to achieve. Alone with a man whom – as he severed his heart from the arteries it served, as he replaced that heart by an artificial pump and then worked on the natural heart itself, inserted into that heart a new valve preparatory to restoring it to its proper function – a man whom he would kill and then bring back to life again.

Alone with this man, the patient, the victim, the unconscious, supine creature over whom he held, for long moments, power of life and death. Alone with this man – yet not quite alone, for also surrounded by experienced eyes and hands; the theatre staff, watching, wondering how it would go, sceptical of young Langenbach, curious, helpful, competent, and some, perhaps, in the deepest, deepest levels of their souls, ambivalent about what they hoped, really hoped, as to how it would turn out.

And it had turned out well.

And afterwards Foster had said to him,

'It wasn't the easiest job, actually, Franzi. I know you knew that. Well done.'

A year later he had, completely inadvertently, heard James Foster speaking on the telephone as he was about to go into Foster's office.

'Frankly, Langenbach will do it as well as I could. I wouldn't say that of another man on the East Coast, you know that.'

He couldn't resist hovering unseen. He heard,

'Yes, I agree. It's a phenomenal career. Of course he's young, but he's got everything. He's a natural.'

Franzi slid away. Later the same morning Foster said to him,

44

'We've got a rather tricky one, or so it sounds. I've been speaking to Evetts.'

Evetts was a renowned heart specialist, a man at the top of the tree. So the telephone conversation had been with Evetts!

'I've talked to Evetts. Tricky – it's a Congressman, too! Not that it matters, but there's always publicity and so forth!'

And room for nerves, Franzi thought. If one has them. Foster took his arm.

'Franzi, I want you to do it. I've absolutely promised to take Maria away for three days. It's a quiet time. I've told Evetts everybody can relax if Congress are operated on by you, en bloc!'

He smiled. James Foster had no conceit. Brilliant in his line, Franzi's talents and success gave him as much pleasure as anything in life. Their relations were not only professional. The Fosters had no child and Franzi was at home in their house in a way which warmed them.

And so it had gone on, and it had gone on remarkably fast. Reputation flourished, responsibilities multiplied. Every year Franzi took a long, long holiday in Europe – 'Not long enough,' Maria Foster said. 'You mustn't burn yourself up, like these Americans!' He relished life, restless though it was. His few remaining responsibilities in Germany were settled without too much difficulty by correspondence, by activity during the European holiday, by sensible delegation to the beloved, the trustworthy, the ever-sensible Cousin Lise von Arzfeld. There was grumbling from Germany here and there but on the whole it worked, and it came to be accepted that Dr Langenbach was a medical man of great brilliance and distinction, albeit young; and that for such as he there were exceptions to life's rules.

His many friends wondered whether and when he might marry.

'Soon perhaps. But what girl would want so obsessed a fellow as me?'

Many, they thought. Very, very many. He had had a wealth of casual encounters, was photographed often with some lovely girl or other. But so far Franzi, charming everyone, talented beyond all justice, essentially generous-hearted and astonishingly unspoilt, had remained unattached, distanced from others however admiring, attractive or intelligent, by something indefinable. A solitary man. Now, as he settled into his seat in the front of the aircraft, accepted a glass of champagne, wriggled feet out of shoes and pulled on the oversocks provided by the airline, Franzi thought about the next few days and he thought, as he had a lot during these last months, about Miranda Wrench, his letter to her and her reply, and the telephone call he'd made deliberately casual two days before, finding her in bed (midnight English time, Franzi careless of rude awakenings) and fixing a dinner date in London. Tomorrow, Franzi thought, heart astir.

Franzi dozed.

'You'd like eggs, sausages, bacon for breakfast, sir?' said the stewardess, leaning over him, succulent smells surrounding her. Franzi swallowed some orange juice. An admirable dinner had been finished only four hours before.

'Just coffee, please.'

'A croissant, sir?'

'No croissant. How long to go?'

And the Captain's voice came over the address system at exactly that moment, advising them that they were about to begin the descent to London airport.


'Thank you for your letter.'

The letter had given Franzi something of what he thought he wanted – something but not a lot.

'You told me flattering, rather puzzling and certainly most undeserved things,' Miranda had written. 'I'm a rather ordinary person.' Deliberately damping and unromantic, in a vein which did little to deter Franzi who was perfectly used to some reserve and defences in a woman, and preferred it – but the letter had continued, 'I loved our talk. I've not felt so happy for a long time,' and that was good. There had been one sentence which needed challenging and was perhaps intended to provoke.

'I'm afraid I'm also rather an unresponsive person,'
Miranda's letter had ended, 'and destined to disappoint.
I've been rather bruised by some things in life and I've
been slow and stupid about recovering. It's made me a bit
useless. But it will be lovely to see you when back in
England,

Miranda'

'Rather bruised'. Franzi knew that she had suffered an unhappy marriage and to a rich American, people said; it had
been a failure from the word go. He looked across the table.
Miranda had suggested for dinner a small and agreeable
restaurant between the King's and Fulham Roads, near her
flat. Miranda had olive skin, straight dark hair gathered at the
nape of the neck and superb eyes. Slender and delicate-boned
she was wearing black and every man's eyes had lifted as she
walked across the room. Franzi felt immense joy as he looked
at her. He was still uncertain whether this joy, in being
with so exquisite a creature, in the fun of talk with such a
sympathetic intelligence, in the throb of desire for a physically
entrancing woman – whether all this, familiar and delightful,
was beginning to equate to something stronger, something
troubling, something deep. Sometimes recently when in
America he'd thought of Miranda, heard her voice in the
mind, said to himself, I rather think this is really important
to me. It might work. At other moments – and the nearer he
had been to seeing Miranda the stronger had these latter
reservations appeared – he had thought, No, one would have
no doubts if this were really one's destiny. When she's with
me she gives me an extraordinary feeling of uniqueness, she's
like a picture, an illumination. I see nothing else. But I hardly
know her, and I don't think I'm what is called 'in love'.
Yet, Franzi's musings would run, how do I know? It's never
happened to me. And this was true, despite the fact he was
thirty-two. Franzi had enjoyed many love affairs. He was
successful with women. He was sorry for the pain that he
sometimes inflicted, for his heart was generous and he knew
that he had never been able to return the degree of emotion

47

he often aroused; but beyond a certain point, that point, he said to himself a little ashamed, that good manners and the time-honoured language of love demand, he had never been able to pretend.

Was it different now? He said,

'Thank you for your letter,' and Miranda smiled coolly. Her own feelings were to some extent a reflection of Franzi's. He's immensely attractive, she thought, but the trouble is that I might, I just might start to feel a lot more, really a lot more, and then I'd find I didn't after all, that it was a false alarm – or, rather, another disappointment, with everything still hurting, no good done at all. Harm, in fact, a sore place badly scratched. The thought terrified her. Miranda's wounds were four years old but still unhealed.

Franzi knew that there were difficulties ahead. Her letter had conveyed, after all, little encouragement and a lot of warning. He said,

'Some words in your letter were puzzling and rather intriguing –'

'I didn't mean to be intriguing.'

'I'm sure you didn't, but you couldn't help it. You wrote a little sadly. You wrote that some things in life had made you a bit useless! I know that's nonsense, by the way,' he smiled across the dinner table, 'but it's quite clear you've been hurt.'

A waiter poured some more wine into Miranda's glass. There was enough hubbub in the restaurant for their words to be audible to each other and only to each other.

'I suppose that's clear. It's certainly true.'

There was no self-pity or self-absorption in her voice, and Franzi said,

'Your marriage – forgive me –'

'My marriage was unhappy but it has left no mark. Lasting pain was the result of different – different events.'

'And persons.'

'Of course.'

He inclined his head very slightly and said,

'Please say no more. I wouldn't intrude for anything – please –' How beautiful his voice is, Miranda thought, it's gentle, musical, and I could listen to it for ever. For ever? Miranda took a strong mental tug at herself.

'Franzi, you're not intruding and anyway I asked for intrusion by what I wrote. It's really quite simple. I was in love with someone and left my husband for him. Then I discovered he wasn't what he seemed. He was a – a betrayer.'

'Other women, you mean.'

'Nothing like that. He – my family had been good to him. My father, mother – he owed us a lot and he did terrible things, a sort of treason. He turned his coat. Do you understand that expression?'

'I think so.'

'It was a shattering, a really shattering experience. I can't bear to go into detail, and I don't expect you'd want it anyway. Have you ever had a dream where you're with people you know, people you love, familiar surroundings? And then one of them suddenly, as you watch, becomes somebody else, something else. Becomes evil, ugly, menacing, terrifying.'

'I have,' said Franzi, 'had exactly such dreams.' It was true.

'It was like that. Shock. Angel into devil.' But, she said to herself, much worse than that shock, that horror, is that I love him still and I can't get rid of his awful trespass on my heart, damn him to hell!

Franzi murmured, always watching her, that he could believe it had indeed been bruising. 'You will, in time, be healed,' he said softly, 'I know it.'

Miranda smiled and sighed, without affectation.

'You're a brilliant doctor –'

'I operate on the heart, don't forget!'

'Some things are a little harder to treat even than *your* patients' trouble, don't you think?' But wishing now to end this she said,

'Enough of me. I want to hear your plans. You're off to Germany.'

'I am off to Germany. I have already mentioned my relative there, my cousin, Lise von Arzfeld, who brought me up, she is like a mother. I spoke to you before of my own mother.'

'You did.'

'Lise is my mother's cousin. A wonderful woman. One day I hope you will meet her.'

Miranda let pass this easy assumption that in Franzi's domestic future she would play some part. She said,

'Apropos of nothing, that's a charming bracelet, Franzi. Didn't they comment on it in that Italian illustrated article?' Miranda had decided to lower the temperature.

'Ah! You saw the *Oggi* article! Vulgarity!'

'Let me look.'

Franzi wore a slender gold circle on the left wrist, a small vanity without a touch of effeminacy, yet somehow reinforcing the sense he conveyed of a young blade from an earlier European age, from the court of Charles V perhaps. He said rather formally,

'It was my mother's. She always wore it. She had a number of charms on it.'

'You've just got these two.' One was a small shield showing a falcon with a ring in the beak. He told Miranda it was the Arzfeld crest.

'And the other?' She held his wrist gently.

'The other is a little medal of St Anna. A lady gave it to me in New York – I had mentioned my mother's name. It's rather beautiful.'

It was indeed beautiful, a delicately etched head. So this bracelet, thought Miranda, must have survived search, confiscation. She always wore it, he said. But she must have removed it before being taken away to a place of torment and death. And now he wears it, and remembers her; and ladies in New York give him charms to wear on it.

'I've been told you own land in Germany. Is that where you're going?'

'No, I've sold now almost all – it was at Langenbach. There was Schloss Langenbach, a big house, impossible these days. And the last parts of the village and farmland have almost all gone. There were legal problems, tax problems.'

Yet Franzi had received much of the proceeds of the sale. From youth he had been rich; and now, a very high earner, he was extremely rich. Langenbach, anyway, had been haunted for him by his beloved mother. She had brought him up there. She had been arrested and taken away from there. He couldn't bear it.

'You're sad?'

Franzi didn't answer that, but explained he was going to pick up a new car near Arzfeld, near Cousin Lise's home. 'And drive it,' he said, 'to Italy. Where your brother Harry is coming to stay in my new house, a most beautiful, exciting house. And where you, I hope, will come too. I invite you! Now!' And, Franzi thought, Harry's said he only intends to stay a few days and Miranda surely, surely will then remain. And in that lovely place *if* this is really going to be important (even in his own silent anticipation he shrank from the word 'love'), *if* there is something here beyond the ephemeral, however enjoyable, then we can discover it and it can flower in that most harmonious environment. Meanwhile –

Meanwhile, Franzi said to himself a little uncertainly, this had better follow the pattern of any other courtship. Miranda was asking him about the Rudbergs.

'I've met them,' she said, 'I stayed once in their pretty house in Sussex. Bargate. What's their connection to you?'


Franzi's connection to Marcia and Toni Rudberg was a subject taken up at their next meeting, for when he said goodbye to Miranda that evening – a lingering kiss, no more – he told her that since he was in London for only four days – 'Flying to Hanover on Sunday as you know' – he wanted to spend every minute with her that he could. Every evening was free – he was visiting Bargate for the day on Saturday. Would Miranda dine again? And again? And so on Friday she did. 'He's the most charming and the best-looking man I know,' she admitted to herself, 'and I'm not sure he's not about the nicest, too. Perhaps '– But the perhaps ended in the usual tangle.

Miranda had, however, decided that if anybody could loosen the knot of her previous emotions, exorcise the demons, cut out the cancer, it might be Franzi. Whether it was fair to cast him in the role of exorcist she was less sure; but

51

while refusing to admit to herself that he might actually and sincerely come to love her – as he was so obviously close to declaring – she was enchanted by his company and found him so physically attractive that she couldn't help wanting to go some way further down the road. One thing, however, she told herself fiercely. She would not pretend; she would only express emotion when she could truly feel it. And an easy and unimportant affair of the senses wouldn't work in this case. Not with Franzi.

They dined again in the same restaurant and Franzi, ground neutral, said,

'You asked me about the Rudbergs. Marcia was English, originally called Marvell. She fell in love with him, Toni Rudberg, Austrian, in Germany where, astonishingly, she spent the Second World War. She was there when it started, engaged to von Arzfeld, brother of my Cousin Lise I've talked about. He was killed and then she fell for Toni. Then they met again here after the war – he was a prisoner in Russia for years and years – and married. Happy ever after. Marcia knew my mother.'

'That's the connection then – the von Arzfelds.'

'Partly. There's another.'

When he said, 'There's another', Franzi started to breathe deeply, and moistened his lips before next speaking. He looked at Miranda once or twice and looked away as if uncertain whether he could share something with her, even her. When he began to talk Miranda sensed that she was being admitted to one of his secret places, perhaps his most secret place; that she was being honoured. At the same time she knew it was something he wanted to impart, creating a bond between them. The knowledge alarmed her.

The other connection, Franzi told her, talking with difficulty now and in a different tone from the usual easy, sympathetic, rather melodious Franzi, the other connection was that his own true father was none other than Anthony Marvell, Marcia Rudberg's brother, who had been killed in a car with young Franzi at the wheel. Fourteen years ago.

'He was going to tell me – I knew it. I could feel he loved

me and that he had loved my mother. They had an affair just before the war – Langenbach was not good to her. But of course it was kept secret.'

'Who did tell you, ultimately?'

'Marcia Rudberg.'

It had been winter at Arzfeld, Franzi said, Arzfeld under snow, Franzi on holiday from the first phase of his medical studies at Göttingen. The Rudbergs had paid a visit – Marcia and Lise had spent the war as nurses together and were devoted. And during that visit, three years after the accident in which Anthony Marvell had lost his life, Marcia had told Franzi of his parentage. Walking together through the Arzfeld woods, through the snow. She had said there was something difficult to say; spoken almost inaudibly.

'My brother Anthony, Franzi. He was your father.'

His answer had been simple, automatic.

'Yes, I know. And I killed him.'

As Franzi told Miranda this, quoting himself very softly, making her feel the scene vividly in the snow-laden Arzfeld woods, air crisp, words spoken which turned his world upside down, his eyes were on the tablecloth, not holding hers as usually they did. She knew they were full of tears. It was better, however, to respond.

'How had you known, Franzi?' Perhaps Marcia had asked the same question. Or wanted to.

'From the first I knew he loved me. And I knew I loved him. It was like nothing else. When Marcia told me there was no surprise.'

Much later they walked back together in silence to Miranda's flat. Everything now seemed inevitable, sanctified. They had talked and talked – again of Franzi's mother, the beautiful Anna Langenbach, a little of Miranda's unhappy marriage and loves, even of Franzi's new house in Umbria whither Miranda had now promised to come with Harry shortly.

'And stay longer, of course!' Franzi said softly. 'Harry only intends two days before going to Rome and onwards.'

'Perhaps.'

And perhaps, she thought, perhaps this really is a first step towards recovery. Is my heart strong, as well as my body? I do pray so. I really do pray so. It's been too long and I'm not a girl. But I can't pretend.

'Perhaps.' And Franzi, excited and very ready to be convinced, thought to himself, This is it. This is different to all the rest. This matters. And time and Italy will prove it. Meanwhile, we're not children. Inside the flat he took her instantly into his arms, and his mouth found hers. And several minutes later Miranda, freeing herself, held him at arm's length, looked at him, her eyes laughing, and said,

'All right, darling Franzi.'

She felt light-headed, fearful, and extraordinarily happy.


'Sorry.'

'No need. I have perhaps not –'

'Nothing to do with you, Franzi. Really nothing to do with you. You are a wonderful man. I told you I was useless to anybody. The trouble is, you see –'

'Your lover of four years ago. He is the trouble.'

Miranda was silent. She felt wretched. To reject, in effect, so considerate, skilful and attractive a partner made her sure that she was emotionally twisted beyond repair. Franzi said again,

'He is the trouble, that one. Of course.'

'I told you he was a betrayer, an enemy, a contemptible creature who did my family irreparable harm, unforgivable, beyond –'

'Yes. You told me so. What you didn't tell me was that you are still in love with him.'

'*No*,' said Miranda fiercely. 'It's a complex, a psychological twist, a mess – all that. And I hate it, not least for hurting you as well as spoiling my life. But it's not still love. It can't be.'

Franzi said, very low,

'It can be, you know. It can be, my darling.'

'I still want to come to Italy. I want to terribly.'

'Do you want to? Or do you just want to want to?'

'I really want to. And Franzi –'

'Miranda?' Troubled, he loved speaking her name.

'Give me time. I don't see why you should, but give me a little time. It's the start of a cure, Franzi, and you're the doctor. But it's not instant. May I come to Italy?'

Franzi kissed her very gently and said that he would live for that day and that now he must go. As he took a taxi back to his hotel he decided that he really loved this woman, that the physical rejection which had surprised and wounded him was no more than might be expected from someone so complex and so valuable. The fact of her wanting, despite it, to come to Umbria surely meant that her heart was moving as he desired. The body cannot lie, thought Franzi, but it can take time in some circumstances to apprehend. When he flew to Hanover on the Sunday his usual confident optimism was almost restored.

# CHAPTER 4

'Out of here for a few days, Vit. OK?'

'OK, Reno.'

It was the first Tuesday in July and Vittorio had by now made a number of exploratory visits to other parts of Perugia. His health and strength were recovering fast, and in a bar near the Carducci Gardens he had struck up what looked like turning into an agreeable acquaintance with a tall girl called Edda. Edda had dark red hair, a sallow complexion, a cynical mouth, enormous sunglasses and very good legs. It was quite a smart place and Vittorio had gone there in search of temporary relief from the squalor of Reno's and Carla's apartment. Not that he intended to desert them; Vittorio, unlike many of his kind, was capable of gratitude, and he was grateful. They'd been good to him and he knew that he was, at the moment, dependent – Reno was a source of immediate funds and Vittorio reckoned he was unlikely to be within reach of the sort of exploit which could produce money, real money, for some time. Vittorio was also, despite the uncomfortable feeling they often gave him, intrigued by the peculiar pair, by their seriousness, their fanaticism, their apparent ruthlessness combined with a readiness to assume what in others would be regarded as a high moral tone. Vittorio could express little of this to himself and was not given to analysis, but Reno and Carla were creatures strange to his experience and he found them both fascinating and disquieting.

Furthermore – ashamed, not admitting it to himself – he feared Reno. Reno was so infernally still. So concentrated. He was like a hand grenade with the pin half out (or so Vittorio, not a military man, could imagine). You might, he could suppose, know perfectly well that it was safe unless some fool did the wrong thing but you couldn't resist glancing at it quite often. To make sure. And there was reason, too, to be cautious and more than a little fearful about the organisation of which Reno and Carla formed only a part – seemingly a pretty independent part, but in touch, nevertheless, with nameless, unseen others. This organisation was clearly able to provide funds; and able, doubtless, to seek out and punish a renegade, a backslider. Vittorio was watching his step.

Conditions in the apartment, however, were austere to say the least. Reno and Carla were content to read, read, read, talk, argue, drink a little – in Reno's case a very, very little – and eat some pretty nasty food. Carla cooked them a pasta now and then, but extremely badly and with such ill grace that it removed appetite. Reno hadn't got her under decent control, Vittorio often reflected. Once he said,

'We might go to a bistro, eh? Have something hot? I'd like to stand you something –'

Reno's cold eye was on him and he said feebly, 'I know it's your money, Reno, but it's a loan, you'll get every lira back, I promise you!'

But as a rule they didn't like bistros. They didn't much like bars, although Reno had one or two places he was prepared to visit, throughout north Italy, it seemed. Once they all visited Bruno, he of the garage on the Assisi road. Bruno had a lined, ravaged face, smelt of oil and smoked without ceasing. Next door to the garage was a small, rather dirty eating place in which Bruno seemed also to have a financial interest. He took them in there and they sat down to tagliatelli. Apart from this outing – and Bruno had looked at Vittorio with undisguised suspicion – there had been nothing one could exactly describe as a social life, and Vittorio was bored most of the time. He was, however, careful to play up to them. He sensed they were assessing his value to them, and putting it reasonably high – he knew the ropes, he could do the rough stuff, he despised the law, he owed nothing to society. He had no political affiliations, no dossier on that side – and, although Vittorio did not mentally explore their reactions to his own reactions to their revolutionary talk, it was an advantage that he had no previously acquired intellectual lumber to clear away, no conventional left-wing credentials to scorch off before painting on him the pure, fiery colours of their own anarchic beliefs. Always, without any sort of inner articulacy, he sensed something like this.

He was sure, therefore, that he had much that Reno and Carla thought they needed; and what he had he was prepared, on terms, to give. He was also sure that they must think him rash, intemperate, a gambler – indeed it was the self-portrait he had given them. They probably reckoned he might be likely to bolt unless kept on a tight rein. So he was wary. He wanted their trust. He needed their acceptance. It was astonishing how quickly Reno's first instalment of cash had gone.

A good deal of it had gone on Edda, whom he had wanted to impress and whom he had told he was a freelance photographer. Vittorio had always been fascinated by cameras and was sufficiently skilled to talk the jargon, to bluff his way. He was now planning, he explained to her, some Umbrian scenes – young, young people, old, old buildings and so forth. He had quickly established that Edda knew nothing of the subject so it wasn't a difficult part to play. She said, off-handedly,

'Where are you living?'

'Nothing settled. I'm a wanderer by nature.'

He knew she liked his smile, his aura of feckless adventurer. Once she said,

'You're walking stiffly. Are you hurt?'

The soreness of his belly scar still cramped him. He looked at her, grinned and shrugged,

'Bit of a quarrel! He's in a worse state than me. Don't let's talk about it!'

Edda excited him. She wasn't easy, she would need playing with care, a succulent, high-spirited fish.

When Reno said, 'I want you out of here for a few days,' his mind went to her at once. He'd established where she lived, her telephone number. He would say to her, lightly,

'I need to move for a bit. Bored with my lodgings. Know anything?' His heart beat a little faster. It was all coming together.

'OK, Reno.'

58

Then he said, 'A few days? A week?'

'Less. We've got another guy coming. For various reasons I'd prefer you didn't meet.'

'OK, Reno.' It suited, it might suit well. He was, however, intrigued. Reno seemed to think some explanation not unreasonable.

'You see, Vit, we may have a rather important operation coming off. The fewer contacts between those with a part to play in the action, the better. Nobody should know anything – or anybody – more than absolutely necessary.'

'OK, Reno. And I've a part to play, eh?'

'Yes,' said Reno gravely, 'you have. If you're prepared for it.'

'And this other guy –'

'You can speak of him as Josef. Also with a part to play. After all, you've been busy, I told you you were on duty, you've been under orders –'

Vittorio nodded. Since that afternoon's drive, ten days earlier, that drive at the end of which Reno had made that odd, incomprehensible remark about them being on duty from then on, he'd been out almost every day, driving Reno's car for miles with Reno or Carla sitting beside him, learning the way around the Umbrian roads, becoming familiar with the streets of Perugia and other Umbrian towns. Reno had said to him,

'You must never have to hesitate, not for an instant. Day or night, you must be able to take the best route from one place to another. If you suddenly have to switch, if something unexpected happens, you must be able to find an alternative way with no delay or doubt whatsoever.'

'I'm the car man, am I?'

'Part of your job. Probably a big part.'

Vittorio knew better than to press him. Reno shared planning with none, detailed planning not even with Carla. Once Vittorio tried to extract a little more from her.

'Carla, I know you and Reno – well, you're dedicated people, I admire you, you know that.'

She looked at him ironically.

'Do you, Vittorio?'

'Yes, I do. I know you think I'm just a small-time crook, someone that's maybe done a few hard things. I understand all that. But believe me I want to – well, help the – the cause.'

At such moments it was almost true. Vittorio felt his own intrinsic nobility. He eyed Carla, who said,

'Do you understand it?'

'I reckon so. What's life given to me? I want to crack the whole rotten system into pieces, as much as you do. But – well, you don't tell me much, don't help me to know what's in your mind. I might be able to help more than you think – with the planning, you know.'

She didn't reply. Later in that same evening, 5th July, the evening in which he told Vittorio to 'get out for a few days', Reno said,

'Are you feeling *completely* recovered, Vit?'

'Pretty good.' He'd now been with them two weeks and it was almost true.

'You might have to drive a great many hours without a break. Are you up to that?'

'You bet.' Vittorio was proud of his skill at the wheel of a car. He said,

'What sort of car?'

'Up to you. Bruno will help. You've got to find a car. Maybe not from Perugia, but not too far away or it will get too complicated. Treat it so it won't be recognised for several days, that's all that will be necessary.'

He said again, 'Bruno will help. That all right?'

'Of course. And then?'

'Then you'll have to drive it several hundred miles. I'll explain later.'

Reno was talking in his low, precise voice and Vittorio sniffed appreciatively. This sounded better, although it also sounded small-scale, risks unlikely to be balanced by anything yet hinted at by Reno in the way of rewards.

'Big job, Reno? I'm not inquisitive, it's just that if I'm to clean a car I'd better know –'

'Know what?'

Vittorio said, feebly, 'Well – as much as possible.' As ever, he wished Reno's eyes were less penetrating.

He said, 'For instance, this drive – you mean I'll be alone?'

'Yes, alone.'

'All right, but there'll be some merchandise, something in the boot, something in the wheels? Something important, obviously.' And suddenly Vittorio felt nervous. The financing of revolution – he knew no word to describe to himself Reno's and Carla's strange, determined obsessions, their boasted, destructive actions in which he could still hardly believe, as he listened to them conducting their intellectual and incomprehensible duologues – it all must entail access to considerable funds. Reno had admitted as much. He might be a rich kid in origin (Vittorio tried to nourish contempt for this, but without much success; envy came more easily). They might be supported, as they'd indicated, by those others in the organisation – but no bunch of anarchist nuts was going to keep Reno and Carla going, just to sit about and talk, Vittorio reasoned. Of course, Vittorio supposed, there might be other groups who funded them, really big stuff – international agencies? Secret services with an interest in destroying Italian society?

Vittorio felt out of his depth. He told himself that it only made sense if they, themselves, now and then, went for money to finance their operations as well as their beggarly lifestyle. What did they do? From what Carla had said, as well as from the logic of the situation, he'd decided pretty early that something like a bank job or a shop with a big cash turnover must be the chief reason for their help and hospitality to him. Vittorio could help in that sort of direction. Their incessant probing of his experience of violence was beginning to bore him – and his responses, he suspected, were sounding less convincing with repetition. For the truth was that Vittorio had used a knife, skilfully, on one occasion during a burglary. The man had died and Vittorio in retrospect regretted the fact, although he'd struck with a purpose, no question. The only instant killing in which he had been directly involved had been done by another, a real hard case who'd snapped a girl's neck when she found them at her mother's jewellery safe and

61

started screaming. Vittorio had got clear away and the hard case was in a Turin gaol, doing life. He had greatly exaggerated his experiences. Still, he'd been around. And it was perfectly true that he'd always been good in a fight, while preferring to avoid trouble if possible.

But when Reno talked about a car and a drive *alone*, Vittorio reckoned it was consistent with what he suspected of their needs. And – to his secret shame – he found himself nervous. Their sort of plans would need a lot of money, he supposed, and if he knew anything there'd be a load of heroin or worse put into that car, possibly put into it by some bloody amateur like Reno, and he, Vittorio, would stand as much chance of persuading the Italian police that he thought only engines lived under car bonnets as of thumbing a lift in a spacecraft. Or, God forbid! there might even be a load of explosives in the car! He could hear the police preliminary observations. And the little matter of the Florence dealer would no doubt obtrude into the conversation at some early point. Vittorio knew that his recent incapacity had harmed his nerve and was determined not to show it, but he felt the sweat dribbling down his spine.

If he was going into this one it had to be with open eyes and the price had to be right. Not for the first time he swore silently at his predicament, mixed up with a pair of bloody nutcases, amateurs. They might know something about letting off bombs and killing a bunch of inoffensive onlookers, but a skilled operation – Mother of God! He could always walk out, he thought. Why not? They'd no hold on him and pocket money wasn't everything. And yet –

'Some merchandise, something important? Reno, I'm not prying, you're right to keep –'

'The car will be empty.'

Vittorio did not believe this.

'I could help, you know. I've experience at packing – delicate substances, all that –'

'No delicate substances. Empty.'

'What, then?'

'Details later. And before you start your drive there'll be

62

another job – a quick, expert job to do. Right in your line. Think about the car, you've got some time. And now I want to say a little about Josef, who is coming here soon but whom you will not see.'


Reno asked quietly,
'Plenty of call boxes in that area, no problem?' He knew this sort of checking was unnecessary with Josef. Josef was Josef.
'No problem. But widely separated. Not like the streets of Perugia!'
'You will advertise in the *Tiroler Tageblatt*, on Tuesdays.'
'On Tuesdays. And *you* will ring on Sundays.'
'If I wish to. I or, it may be, Carla. At three in the afternoon. No call, no message.'
Josef's memory for detail was perfect. Reno had never seen a letter written by Josef, and had no evidence the little fellow could even write; but he was admiringly familiar with Josef's astonishing power of recollecting sentences, numbers, verbal instructions, with absolute precision. In early days he had said,
'Now repeat that back to me.'
Josef had stared.
'Why?'
As if humouring a child, with ill grace, Josef had done so, never less than perfectly. Reno soon took his effectiveness for granted. Josef needed no paper, no paper at all, no paper ever. It was a valuable gift.
Josef was five foot four inches tall, forty-four years old, a native of Linz in the Danube valley. Carla had found him. She had broken down in Reno's car in the outskirts of Milan three years previously, had managed to get towed to a garage and had been struck by the face of the little mechanic, as well as by his speed and skill. Carla had found something instantly sympathetic – indeed recognisable, like the echo of a vibration of her own – in his frowning absorption. This was Josef. She had tried, as if facetiously, a remark with revolutionary

63

undertones to one who had the key. Josef had responded. She'd slipped him their telephone number. At the time she and Reno had been living rather comfortably in Bologna.

'Come and see us.'

And Josef had come into their lives. He had once been a soldier, a boy soldier, conscripted into the Wehrmacht at the age of sixteen. He had served throughout the last year of the Second World War; had finished it sandwiched between the Russians, who were blasting their murderous, rapacious way through Lower Austria, and the Americans, drunk with triumph and the easy pickings in wine and women, who were driving east up the Danube valley. Josef was, remarkably, very near the point at which he had started both military service and life.

'I went home.'

Josef's father had disappeared when he was an infant. On slipping away to Linz from a defeated and disintegrating Wehrmacht, he found his mother dead. She had suffered some sort of internal haemorrhage in April, people said. He found neighbours indifferent, each concerned with private terrors, private anxieties. The war itself had stopped. The local Nazi bosses had disappeared as if they had never existed. The aftermath looked as if it was going to be as uncertain, dangerous even, as the conflict itself. Possibly more so at times.

Josef had never loved his mother. She had beaten him without mercy throughout his childhood, had drunk too much when she could scratch together the money, and had a bad reputation in their impoverished quarter of the city. He'd felt no pangs at leaving her in '44, whipped off into uniform, grim though the army had turned out to be. Now he examined his circumstances and appreciated that, at seventeen, nobody cared a fig for him, he loved nobody, he owed nothing to anybody, he knew of no country or institution to which loyalty made the smallest sense and he had no affection for Austria in general or Linz in particular. Survival meant work, and he made himself useful in a small garage, teaching himself all there was to learn there. As a mechanic he had flair, with strong, sensitive fingers, a logical mind and an ear for engine sound. He moved from job to job, gaining experience, as life in post-war Austria began slowly to lurch back towards normality. In the winters he often helped out on the ski lifts and mountain railways and cable cars – he loved the mountains. He was at home in both country and city, in Austria, Germany or Italy; a naturally adaptable man. He worked twice in Bavaria and, for a little, tried Bolzano, and then Milan. Then back to Austria for several years and then Milan again; where Carla found him.

During these travels Josef listened, and asked questions, and sometimes talked, although always with brevity. He found people – not many, but a few – who, like him, were filled with enormous disgust at a world which gave to him and millions like him no natural dignity, no status, no background, no memories of happiness, no pride. He was decently paid, for he enjoyed hard work and he was skilful. He was never hungry. Most people laughed at him.

'What the hell are you grumbling about?'

But Josef despised them. Life should be more than a full belly. Life should be dignified and rational and just. Society should be a community of free, equal creatures, liberated from the economic necessity to pander to the spoilt tastes of the undeserving, the exploiters. In Linz there were plenty of old-style Communists these days, but Josef found them unattractive and their philosophy mechanical and repetitive, with its stale jargon and surrender of independent thought. And what had it produced? Josef thought. The Red Army, for God's sake!

One day a young man came to work in the same garage as Josef, which at the time happened to be in Salzburg. The young man was several years Josef's junior, with a frowning, worried expression and brilliant eyes. He worked almost as fast and skilfully as Josef himself, humming classical motifs very tunefully. Josef made one or two sour observations. On the second morning the young man turned to him and said, very softly,

'It has all to be destroyed, you realise that, I'm sure.'

'How – all destroyed?'

'This system. We're like insects, you see. Our liberty can only come if the actual structure round whose rim we crawl is smashed. Like a cup.'

'Who's going to smash it?'

'There are a few,' said the young man cheerfully. He talked late to Josef that night. He talked of a community with which he'd been living in Wiesbaden.

'They understand. Fantastic, marvellous people. To the bourgeois world they're mad, they're murderous criminals – oh yes, they are prepared to take life. To the bourgeois world they're creatures to be exterminated, although the system's so rotten and flabby now it doesn't dare exterminate anything! The reality is that *these people alone* have the courage to see and to act.'

Josef stared at him. He sounded extraordinarily confident. He had the faith. The young man continued,

'It's always comfortable to close the eyes. And even if the eyes are open it's comfortable to do nothing, leave it to others. These people don't want comfort. They're prepared to suffer. To die – die as outcasts, hated, lonely. They realise they may see few results in their time. But they *know*, you see, that the system can only start to be smashed by the extreme actions of the few. And that until it's smashed nothing will ever change, nothing good can ever grow.'

'They're Communists?'

'Not of the orthodox kind, the disciplined party and all that. These people I'm speaking of don't believe in large-scale organisation.'

'What do they do?'

'You remember Werber?'

Fedor Werber, a rich Karlsruhe industrialist, had been found murdered in a wood in the Neckar valley the previous year, after his family, distraught, had refused to pay a huge ransom. Nobody had been arrested.

'That was my friends. The Government wouldn't let the family pay up.'

'What had Werber done?'

'Werber was a symbol. But the point was the drama, the

66

publicity. You remember, it was in the papers every day, maybe the Austrian papers too.'

'Something about it,' said Josef, not a great devotee of current news.

'It was on TV all the time, too, with the wife and the police and the Justice Minister all appealing. It created insecurity. That's the first step.'

'And the second step?'

'When enough people feel frightened,' said the young man, 'they start to lash out. Then they antagonise a lot of the so-called innocent and the cracks gradually widen. The cracks in the system.'

'Did that happen in the Werber case?'

'Maybe not, but you must remember this is still only a beginning. And when something like that happens and the police can't do a thing or make an arrest people feel insecure, they start to distrust authority, criticise its competence, feel unprotected. That all helps too. The key is violence – well-advertised violence. Headlines. Fear. It's hard but it's true.'

'It's going to take a long time.'

'Of course. But, historically, things sometimes move at an amazing speed, unforeseen. The Bolsheviks in 1917, tiny numbers, nobody knew what was going to happen next.'

Josef felt sceptical but excited. There was something brilliant and selfless about the young man. Josef felt no doubt at all that he would sacrifice himself – or anybody else – with complete cheerfulness. This one had seen a vision, and knew that to bring in a new world the destruction of the old must be accomplished. Old parties, established institutions, large organisations would never manage it, however extreme or strident their language. Only individuals, probably small in number, an élite, dedicated, would face the brave, lonely choices. Josef sensed the truth in all this. A few isolated, condemned and certainly young human beings would not change the world in his time; but they might make a beginning. They might blaze a trail.

Six months later Josef moved to Milan for the second time. It was easy to get work there that year and he liked Italy.

He knew all parts of his native Austria and much of southern Germany well but he didn't care to stay anywhere long and he never felt in the least attracted by domesticity. Truth to tell, he disliked feeling that anybody knew him particularly well. A vagrant by temperament, a skilled man with his hands, a nihilist, perhaps, by something like rather muddled conviction, Josef moved south once more. And in Milan he met Carla.

'No idea when, you say,' Josef remarked, reflecting rather than questioning. Reno's instructions were perfectly clear but there were one or two things to prepare. Reno said,

'It's 10th July today. I've established the pattern – the pattern of possibility. No more.'

'And that is –?'

'It can't be before 20th July. Any time after that for, say, three weeks. I can't say more. All right?'

'All right. First call, 16th July, next Sunday?'

'To the first number you gave me. Thereafter I'll watch the *Tiroler*. First ad. Tuesday 18th, OK?'

Josef nodded. 'OK.'

'You're going back tomorrow. Money all right?'

'I earned a hell of a lot during the winter. I spend nothing.'

Reno knew, with appreciative admiration, that this was almost true. He murmured,

'You'll have some expenses. Are you sure –'

'If I want money I'll tell you. Just now I'm all right.'

Josef looked round the bare apartment. In places like this, dusty, secret and impersonal, he felt as much at home as he did anywhere. He said,

'Carla –'

'She'll be in again later.'

'You've got a boy here. This Vittorio.'

'He's going to be useful. He's a young thug, no morals, no ties, on the run from the police – or, to be more exact, keeping out of their way, there's no hunt for him or anything like that.

68

It's just he got hit in a shoot-out in a robbery and he's lying low. Florence.'

'I don't like crooks.'

'Nor do I, I sympathise. But Vittorio's tough, he's quick, he knows what he's doing when it comes to –'

'Comes to what?'

'Well – the rough stuff,' said Reno rather awkwardly.

Josef thought, with as near as he ever got to amusement, how unnaturally such expressions came from Reno's lips. Reno could contemplate – could, indeed, execute – murder on a large, impersonal scale. Josef was unsure of his own feelings when he heard of the Rome bomb. But, at the same time, Reno was ill at ease with the casual, expert brutality, the underworld slang and habits of the experienced criminals from whose skills he needed to learn. Now he said,

'Yes, Vittorio will handle that side well. Not that it will be difficult.'

Josef detected a false note in the voice and looked at the other with admiration. He – and, he presumed, Carla – knew the iron control Reno exercised over his own highly nervous system in order to carry out an operation with the necessary degree of calm resolve. And he never failed.


Angelica Fantini climbed out of her small black Fiat in a quiet side street in the outskirts of the town of Umbertide at four o'clock in the afternoon on Saturday, 22nd July, 1972. She locked the car, patted her hair, gave a sharp glance up and down the street and moved to the door of Number 41 Via Tevere, an itch of delightful anticipation quickening her step.

Umbertide sprawls along the valley of the Tiber twenty miles north of Perugia. Perugia was Angelica's home. Nobody knew her in Umbertide. There was no chance of a casual encounter, a word subsequently passing –

'I saw young Signora Fantini in Umbertide on Saturday. I suppose she's got friends there –'

Nevertheless, Angelica wasted no time in ringing the front door bell at Number 41. Her impatience was rewarded. The door opened immediately – indeed her finger was hardly at her side from pressing the bell button when she found herself pulled quickly into the dark hall, and the next moment held tightly in Stefano's arms. Stefano had heard the car. Stefano had been watching.

Stefano said not a word. He was gasping, chuckling, kissing her mouth, her eyes, her ear, her nose, his hands busy with the zip fastener at the back of her dress. Next moment Angelica found the dress slipping off her shoulders. Under it she wore nothing but some black knickers with lace edging, donned in Stefano's honour.

'I'm entirely conventional,' Stefano had muttered to her last time, with a grin, 'entirely normal, conventional, you see! But indefatigable.'

Now she found herself pulled down to the hall floor.

'Stefano, Stefano darling, wait, wait, we mustn't –'

Stefano had no intention of waiting.

'Stefano – ah, beloved, beloved – we should go upstairs – ah –'

'Later,' said Stefano. It was his first speech, mumbled through the flesh of her breast.

Later, in bed now, Stefano said,

'How long?'

'Cris is away in Turin until tomorrow evening. Like I told you.'

'So you're with me until then. Angelica, you're adorable, you're a tormentor, you fill me with longing every second my hands are not –'

'Stefano, I must be back in Perugia by midday Sunday. Midday tomorrow.'

'So soon?'

'Darling, it gives us longer than we've ever had before. I've arranged things so nobody will suspect a thing if I'm back by then. Longer might be difficult.'

Cristoforo Fantini, a dull, jealous man, had never been given reason to suspect his wife. He was, however, both quick-tempered and a generous provider; Angelica had no desire to provoke the temper or place at risk the generosity.

Stefano nodded, his eyes moving, lazy, gloating, over Angelica's body. She was delicious: a slender girl with skin like satin and huge brown eyes. The suspicion of a moustache on her upper lip might give a problem one day – at present it only sharpened the sense of fine bone structure and narrow, elegant head. And as for the lower half of her – Stefano stretched out his right hand and caressed the inside of Angelica's thigh. She smiled at him.

'Longer than we've ever had before!'

'But still too short! Never mind, there's food and wine in the house. No need to go anywhere. And no need to dress!'

Angelica stroked his hair. Then she found herself again held by strong arms, lips moving over her body, enthusiasm unquenchable.

It was, therefore, not until five minutes past eleven o'clock on Sunday morning that Angelica whispered,

'Sweetheart. Sweet love. Stefano.' Stefano was asleep.

'Sweetest, I must dress. I must go.'

He woke and was instantly alert, like a wild animal.

'Time?'

'Time I was gone.'

She looked at him with much contentment. He was, she knew, a most undeserving citizen. Three years younger than she, recently emerged from an idle and undistinguished stretch of life at the University of Perugia, he appeared determined to do as little as possible. Sometimes there were 'plans', 'projects', which invariably came to nothing. He lived with and on his widowed mother, a rich, spoilt and spoiling parent now undergoing an expensive cure in Switzerland for some imaginary ailment. Angelica had met Stefano by purest chance in a shop in Perugia, near the University, a few months before. He had eyed her and then she found that he had followed her to her car. She had pretended outrage, affecting to fear an attack on her handbag.

'Yes? I see a police officer on the corner –'

'So do I, Signora,' he'd said agreeably, 'but don't let's invite him to join us. It would spoil everything.'

She was bored with Cristoforo Fantini, and her

71

temperament craved excitement and got little of it. Soon Stefano supplied it. Her visits to him were always risky, had to be arranged with a care which added spice to pleasure. Now the absence of both Fantini and Stefano's mother was a delicious conjunction. Angelica was always anxious about Stefano's discretion.

'You'd never mention –'

'Of course not!'

But she didn't believe him. She guessed – and guessed correctly as it happened – that Stefano's vanity led to a good deal of sexual boasting in the bars he frequented, whether in Perugia, Umbertide or elsewhere. Even before this present enchanted interlude he might have said,

'A friend of mine has her husband away – and I've got our house to myself! What a woman! You ought to see her!'

And a drinking companion might chuckle and say,

'How long has her man left her alone?'

'Just Saturday and Sunday – but we'll not waste many minutes, I assure you! She's really keen –'

The pictures formed by Angelica's imagination were by no means far-fetched. Stefano, lying back head on pillow, looked at her and yawned.

'When next?'

'I can't say.'

'Do you want me to escort you to the door? Or are you prepared to say goodbye just like this?' He grabbed at her, swinging naked legs off the bed. She giggled and dodged.

'No, no more. Really no more.' She kissed him quickly, wriggled into her knickers and dress and ran downstairs. Stefano smiled at the ceiling. It had been good – very, very good. She knew when to ring him and he was sure that within days she would do so. Poor old Fantini! Stefano heard the front door close and decided that another hour's sleep would be agreeable before seriously thinking how to spend the rest of Sunday. It was still cool in the bedroom. He closed his eyes.

The front door bell rang.

Stefano cursed, and pulling on a silk dressing gown ran downstairs. Angelica again, presumably? Forgotten something? She'd brought nothing to forget. Perhaps she couldn't start her damned car!

It was indeed Angelica. She looked distraught and pushed past him into the hall.

'Stefano, my car –'

'Won't it start?'

'It's gone.'

He whistled, seeing the problem clear and quick. He muttered,

'Stolen! I heard nothing –'

'Of course we heard nothing! I can't report it to the police here!'

'You must.'

'I can't possibly. Why am I here?'

'You came on an expedition to Umbertide. You left it for a while, went shopping –'

'On Sunday morning?'

'It was stolen last night. You were shopping on Saturday –'

'And reported it on Sunday morning, having walked the streets looking for it all night? Don't be absurd. Anyway, Cristoforo knows perfectly well I never shop anywhere but places I know in Perugia.'

'You came here this morning, on a sightseeing visit.'

'Incredible!' Angelica was shaking. She couldn't control her limbs and her mouth was dry. 'Incredible! Cristoforo would never believe in a casual, curious visit to Umbertide! Of all places!'

'Umbertide's not too bad!' said Stefano facetiously and a little cruelly. He was thinking that fear suited her. His gaze travelled down her body. There was little to prevent a last, quick coupling, and it might concentrate the mind. Angelica had no such action in view.

She said, 'You've got to take me to Perugia. At once! When Cristoforo comes back this evening I shall tell him that the car's been stolen when parked there, in Perugia, this morning. I'll report it to the Perugia police. Take me to the University quarter – I'll pretend I left it there early, went for a short walk to get some air.'

'It's not very convincing.'

'I'll work it up a bit. I'll think about it as we drive.'

'It doesn't give the police much chance to track the car!'

'To hell with that,' said Angelica. 'The insurance people will look after that. Fantini will be furious and won't give me another until they pay up in full but that's not what I mind about. I don't want the police finding the damned car, getting some thief to confess pinching it from outside your house, do I?'

Stefano nodded. She'd summed it up perfectly correctly.

He said, 'Nor do you want the police to find it was probably stolen twelve hours ago –'

'And fifteen before being reported. Misreported. Now for God's sake get dressed and let's go.'

# CHAPTER 5

'I hate airports. Really hate them. Hell would be like this.'

It was 23rd July. Other passengers glancing with approval at Miranda Wrench saw a dark, slender woman of thirty with delicate limbs and fine eyes in a pale, beautiful face, a woman who conveyed a certain rather elegant serenity. Her brother, two years older, was also dark-haired but a contrasting physical type in every way except in the natural grace of his movements; although there was about Harry Wrench an ebullience, an atmosphere of instant, extrovert friendliness which set off and emphasised the somewhat guarded personality of Miranda. They were an attractive pair.

'As you say, Hell will be like this.' Harry smiled agreeably at the crowd in the departure lounge of Number Two Terminal at London airport. His enjoyment of whatever he was doing, his habitual conversion of any occasion into a merry experience, a party, belied his words. Airports might be Hell, but Harry might find Hell a friendly place. They sat in silence for a few minutes not looking at the magazines on their laps. The Rimini aircraft had been delayed.

'I long to see that bit of Italy. Franzi said the house is still fairly primitive.' Miranda was maintaining, not without success, a certain detachment of tone.

'I don't expect so.' Harry's voice implied he didn't much mind, but he added,

'Franzi's standards are high, I suspect. A few rooms to decorate still, even some building going on. No swimming pool yet! But I doubt if we'll be living rough. Not that I care – I simply want sun. We've had no summer at all.' England had been cool and wet since emerging from a glorious spring.

The clock's hands moved slowly. Harry yawned. 'Do you want a drink?'

'No thanks. I'm glad Franzi's going to meet us. It sounds a long way.'

'Quite a long way. We're due to arrive at four o'clock, Italian time. We're bound to be late.'

'I'm not sure where the house is, exactly.'

'Franzi said one can go down the coast by *autostrada* some way, and then turn into the hills. I'm sure it'll be lovely, late or not.'

Harry yawned again, and at that moment they heard the welcome call of their flight number. Relieved by the possibility of movement at last, people heaved themselves to their feet throughout the crowded departure lounge.

At about the same time, one o'clock in the afternoon of Sunday 23rd July, Franzi Langenbach ran down the steps of his house, twelve miles north-east of the ancient mediæval city of Gubbio. It was a substantial farmhouse, a place with something of the dignity, the aura of historic continuity which might be conveyed by the word 'villa' in the Roman sense. Certainly the house had no aspirations to grandeur, no pretensions, but it solidly dominated its immediate surroundings. It had been built upon the site of an earlier dwelling by a rich farmer (a local phenomenon) in the year 1900, but in style, texture and atmosphere it was ageless, melting visually into the Umbrian landscape as if conceived in a quattrocento painting. A short avenue of cypress trees led to the house from a narrow road which first curved and then twisted upwards from the valley floor. The mountains rose steeply only two miles from where the house sat, four-square, orange-tiled, main door framed by a substantial stone-built verandah. Behind the house parallel walls ran back at right angles to the main front, enclosing a patio, beyond which were extensive outbuildings. Franzi was in process of constructing a wall to enclose the patio further, to make it smaller, more private. All these walls, and the house itself, were washed white and dazzled the unprotected eye.

He had bought the place for its setting. The house faced

south-west, towards where, in the far distance, the road ran south through a broad valley to Foligno, to Terni, to Rome. To the north and east rose tree-covered mountains, rock faces showing here and there through the forest, dark green in all weathers, all seasons. Beyond the eastern mountains lay the Adriatic.

Franzi felt a sense of being protected by the high, encircling hills. He could look towards the valley, to an outer world which need be visited only when he chose. He was secure, a king. He had fallen in love with the place when first he saw it, driving by chance from Gubbio into country unknown to him, exploring without conscious aim. He had made some local enquiries, then visited an agent in Ancona – to find the astonishing, the fantastic news that the house and a small parcel of land could be bought. He knew that he had paid more than the strict value, and might be locally despised for it, but he had no time to bargain or negotiate. The thing had to be done quickly or not at all; and the Ancona agent recognised the fact with complacency.

Since then Franzi had paid two visits, set some work in hand, written frequent letters, been agreeably surprised by some things – notably the workmanship of a local builder – and infuriated by others, including the dilatory way with correspondence of his appointed agent. But they acted, at least, as if glad to see him when he arrived now; and he often telephoned the house from America, England, Germany or wherever he happened to be – the installation of a telephone had taken much time – succeeding, if lucky, in making contact with Beppo, the gardener, caretaker, tender of the few vines the place boasted. Beppo seemed content, was exuberantly complimentary about Franzi's growing vocabulary of Italian, and was as yet unspoiled by a comfortable salary. Beppo had the wit to know that he could be idle about a good many things without disturbance provided that Franzi was made happy during his infrequent visits, provided the vines pro-duced a few grapes for the local wine manufacturer, provided the house did not fall down. And in fact Beppo was not particularly lazy by nature, and had taken a liking to Franzi;

a liking which transcended by some way his sense of obligation to an employer, a liking which increased with each contact. Maria, Beppo's wife, broad, dark, loquacious, also liked Franzi. Maria cooked, swept, washed, chattered and complained about the workmen, who were in and out of the place too frequently for her liking, concerned with Franzi's building projects and alterations.

Yes, it works, said Franzi to himself, half incredulous at so much good fortune and enormously contented, as he turned on the bottom step to look back at the house before walking round to the back to take his Mercedes from the outbuilding converted to garage behind the patio. It works, he thought, and it's wonderful. And each time I love it more. He sniffed the air. Franzi was wearing a pair of thin, russet-coloured trousers and a dark blue shirt. His skin was golden brown. The day was very hot but the aromatic scent from the forest was strong and delightful today, for the light wind was south-easterly, brushing the hills. The sun struck like a sword.

Beppo was doing something apparently aimless with a hoe, under the shade of the trees which hemmed the short drive.

'Beppo, I'm off to collect the English Signor and Signora, the *Famiglia* Wrench, from Rimini airport.'

Beppo nodded and smiled. Franzi had told him and Maria a dozen times about these English friends who were due to arrive. In fact it was the first thing he'd explained when he'd turned up in that wonderful car of his nearly two weeks ago. Everyone knew that an Englishman and his sister were coming to stay, were arriving this Sunday! The young boss was as excited as a child. Perhaps he'd got his eye on the lady! These were Signor Langenbach's first guests at the Villa Foresta, as the house had been somewhat pretentiously named by its previous owner. Maria had been grumbling for days about extra work but was in fact pleasurably and inquisitively looking forward to the Wrench visit.

Franzi paused. He never neglected conversations with Beppo, never appeared to have insufficient time for them.

'It'll take me two and a half hours.'

Beppo greatly admired the Mercedes but he suspected that

Franzi underestimated how long one could take, in any car, negotiating the narrow roads through the mountain spurs which ran down to the Adriatic. Franzi had gone for a run down the coast the other day, called to Maria, 'Back about eight,' and driven in at ten-fifteen!

'More, Signor!'

Franzi had always arrived by car. Beppo didn't expect he'd ever been to Rimini airport. A long way.

'I asked at the garage in the village last week, explained I was going there today, on a Sunday, in case it made a difference. The man reckoned two and a half hours. He gave me a short cut for the bit before the Fano road, said it would save a lot.'

Beppo screwed up his eyes. He left the village seldom and the Fano road meant little to him but he had a low opinion of the man at the garage, an outsider, from Ancona he thought.

'Maybe, Signor. But I think you'll need longer.'

'Well, I'd better be off. I've got plenty of time now and aeroplanes are always late. We should be back about eight, maybe before.'

He smiled at Beppo, his warmth like the sun itself. He acknowledged to himself that he had been living, impatiently and nervously, for this visit. He had taken much trouble with Maria over what, from her limited repertoire, they were going to eat – eat on a table in the patio, eat in the evening beneath the stars, one great candle illumining them, illumining Miranda's face as they drank the full, heavy red wine of the district. This visit might, if anything could, change his life. His heart lifted as he climbed into the Mercedes. From his first car at nineteen, that car of tragedy in which Anthony Marvell had died, a car of bitter memory, he had always driven a Mercedes. He touched the accelerator and the dark blue machine bumped over the short, irregular drive beneath the cypress trees, swung right on the village road and sped towards the mountain.

One and a half hours later Franzi reflected that Beppo's scepticism about the time needed to reach Rimini might be damnably justified. For the last part of the run he'd be on the *autostrada* but these first miles! He'd driven at fifteen miles an hour for a long way behind a giant piece of machinery no doubt bound for major road-widening works and denying him any opportunity to pass. And on a Sunday! He already knew that he'd have no time in hand. A few more mishaps and he'd certainly be late. The Wrenches would wait, of course, and it was unlikely their flight would be on time – but he'd hungrily looked forward to seeing Miranda's face emerging from customs, her smile, her watchful pleasure at arrival, the gentle, outwardly non-committal contact of their hands, the first, casual kiss. To be late was bad.

Franzi turned on the car radio, hoping for something to distract his irritation at this snail's progress. He glanced at the road map, open on the seat beside him; with luck he'd soon be approaching a turn to the right by a small lake, the turn the man at the garage in the village had told him he must take –

'Small road, Signor, but it will save you twelve kilometres.'

And at that moment a turning came into view. The man had explained that a narrow road climbed along the steep side of the mountain, with forest on the lower side and sheer rock face to the driver's right hand.

'But it's not a bad surface, Signor. And you can't mistake it!' He had used his hands to depict the sort of road Franzi would recognise. And here, without question, it was – indeed, he saw, gratefully, that a rough, wooden sign, with 'FANO' and an indicating arrow painted on it, had been stuck beside the road. Fano was where he wanted to head, no question. Indeed, Fano was beyond the *autostrada*. There was some other wording on the board which he saw as he swung the car round: '*Deviazione Stradale*'. So something was, in any case, closing the main road. Praying that he would not again meet a bulldozer, Franzi settled behind the wheel of the Mercedes and started to climb, his slender hands caressing the wheel, his bare arms hot in the sun. The man had been right, certainly about the first mile – the surface wasn't too bad and at least

80

he was going in the right direction. He reckoned from the map that in about five miles he'd start to descend. The road was climbing steeply and curving to the right. Then Franzi cursed aloud and braked. His prayers had not been answered. God knew how long this would take!

In front of him, perceived suddenly after rounding a sharp right-hand bend, was a wooden barrier with a red and white notice bearing some sort of picture. The message was perfectly clear. Ahead there was blasting of rock, and the road was closed. Franzi cursed again. The notice in the valley had marked this route as an authorised diversion; how could both roads be closed? Unless, and the thought gave him a spasm of sick frustration, horrid possibility – they were both, indeed, closed and a completely new route would have to be negotiated! He looked quickly at the map which lay open on the seat beside him. Could it be that he'd be forced to a much longer and more circuitous journey, by San Michele? Good grief, it would take a further hour! And why the hell hadn't there been an earlier notice?

Franzi felt a spasm of angry certainty that all of this had applied only to the previous days and had no relevance on a Sunday, but that the damned Italians had been too idle to remove the notices or the barrier. Meanwhile it was impossible to pass it.

The first step must be to return as fast as possible to the valley he'd just left and this was going to mean a long journey in reverse, for there was no room to turn the Mercedes where he was, nor at the barrier, no room at all. Three hundred metres back, the far side of the last bend, he remembered that the right-hand rock face had receded and there'd been some sort of flattish space holding some thick bushes, a disused quarry or something like it. Space to turn. He shoved into reverse and went back as fast as he dared, forest slope precipitous to his left, vertical cliff to his right. Poor Harry, poor, beloved Miranda! He handled the car lightly and expertly and reversed round the corner beyond which, he thought, was a turning place. Then he swore again, with astonishment as well as annoyance.

In the middle of the road was a sizeable boulder.

It must, he supposed, have rolled down from the upper slope to his right and failed to continue on over the sheer edge to his left. It must have done this in the last two minutes. Franzi's irritation was too great for him to reflect that had the boulder behaved in this inconvenient way a shade earlier it would have hit his car, and hit it hard! Now he could see that it certainly left no room for the car to skirt it, and as he raced back towards it in reverse he grimly suspected that it was going to be a hard job to shift singlehanded. It was a lonely spot and he supposed there was no hope of help. Unless Franzi Langenbach could clear the road by himself he had the prospect of a long, long wait or a long, long walk. Possibly both. He slammed on the car brakes, jumped out and ran to inspect it.

It was a large boulder but not as large as he had first imagined when he saw it, with horror, in the Mercedes' mirror. He braced his legs, getting as firm a foothold as he could in the gravelly surface of the road, and applied all his strength to the boulder – it was slightly higher than the level of his knee.

No movement.

Franzi exerted his muscles mightily. Sweat poured off him as he grunted and groaned. Then, suddenly, he was rewarded. He was sure it started very slightly to roll a little, a very little. One more heave, surely, and he'd be able to keep up the momentum, get the damned thing over the edge and clear the road. One more heave and he'd be able to reverse, turn and drive like hell down to the road junction, to the wooden sign saying 'FANO, *Deviazione Stradale*'. Goodbye to any hope of a short cut! Franzi replanted his feet in the road and bent for another supreme effort.

The boulder began perceptibly to move. Then it began to move more easily. Then, triumphant, he felt it starting to roll. The road surface tilted slightly towards the precipice and the boulder was beginning to roll with the slope. He straightened, gasping aloud before stooping for a final effort. He knew he'd won. The wretched thing was almost moving now under its own momentum. A final, moderate push and he'd be under way.

'*Grazie,* Signor!'

The voice came from immediately behind him, very close. As he swung round, astonished, something like a clap of thunder seemed to explode inside his head and for a second he felt his body spinning, falling, spinning, falling. Then darkness.


'There's no message. We were nearly an hour late as it was. I'm going to telephone.'

'Good luck, Harry. How one wishes one could speak better Italian!' Miranda was determined not to show exactly how disappointed she was. She, too, had been thinking throughout the flight of the moment when Franzi's face and smile appeared beyond the customs barrier.

'There's a charming, English-speaking girl at the Information Desk, I'm sure she'll do it. If he's had a breakdown he'll get word to us sooner or later, but we'd better try the house, just in case. There'll probably be no reply.'

There was indeed no reply. The girl was friendly but cool. There had been no message from a Signor Langenbach, no message for a Signor Wrench. The roads through the mountains were very slow, perhaps Signor Langenbach had been held up by road works, or an accident, or a puncture? It seemed likely.

'We were due here at four o'clock. He knew that.'

She shrugged prettily, and said she would ring the house at intervals, to check, when she got an answer, on when their friend had left home. She talked rapidly in Italian to a colleague. Harry suspected, accurately, that she was saying that these foreigners and their host, another foreigner, had most likely made a muddle of their arrangements.

At six o'clock he approached the desk again.

'I think it must now be extremely probable that Mr Langenbach has had an accident of some kind.'

The girl sighed. She was bored by him.

83

'*Momento –*'

Harry walked back to Miranda, seated in another part of the large lounge. He knew that, as she had emphasised at Heathrow, airports afflicted her with something like neurosis. Today would be unlikely to diminish this. As he approached she nodded, indicating something behind his shoulder, and he turned to see the girl from the Information Desk had left her post and was approaching, smiling and accompanied by a uniformed figure. The girl said,

'This is Captain Morsini, of the Carabinieri. I have told him about your friend. If you like I translate now. Captain Morsini would like to have particulars, please.'

'Thank you,' said Harry. He shook Morsini's hand. Morsini wanted to know Franzi's address. He wanted to know when they had last heard from him. He wanted to know what sort of car Franzi would be driving. He wrote everything down. He talked fast and without smiles. He seemed efficient.

'Captain Morsini,' said the girl, 'would like you to stay here please. He will return. If your friend arrives I will tell him.'


Marcia Rudberg said,

'I can hear you perfectly well. It's a good line. And thank you so much – it was thoughtful of you. How did you think of us?'

'My sister reminded me of how well you know Franzi. We felt we should get in touch with somebody – I think his family, his nearest family are in Germany, isn't that right? The von Arzfelds? Perhaps I should –'

'You're talking from an airport, that's not always easy,' said Marcia. 'You're perfectly right that if anything's happened, an accident or something awful like that, Lise von Arzfeld should be told. Leave that to me at present. I'll telephone her – keep in touch with me if you can.'

A minute later she said,

'Yes, yes I agree. One always worries, and it's always a simple and harmless explanation but one can't help it. Will you keep me informed? I'll be in this evening and all tomorrow.'

She joined Toni in the garden at Bargate, their Sussex home. It was six o'clock on a fine Sunday evening. 23rd July.

'That was Harry Wrench, Franzi's friend, on the telephone from Italy. Franzi's not turned up at Rimini airport to meet them. Nearly three hours late and no word.'

'He's broken down in that grand car of his.'

'Three hours, Toni. No word.'

'If there's been an accident the police will find him.'

'Of course. Harry Wrench will ring again. He said the police seem quite helpful, but that no accident has been reported. The Wrenches are going to an hotel in Rimini. The police will keep in touch with them.'

'How did Wrench have our number?'

'The local police,' said Marcia, 'were asked to visit Franzi's house. They saw his gardener, the man who works for him, who said Franzi left to go to the airport at one o'clock. Apparently it couldn't be more than a three-hour run.'

'Six o'clock now –'

'Seven o'clock there. The police asked about family and looked at Franzi's telephone pad and found our number – and others of course. They told the Wrenches and asked if they knew of Franzi's family. Of course the Wrenches knew our name and would anyway have tried to make contact.'

'I suppose one should tell Lise Arzfeld –'

'I'll ring Lise,' said Marcia, 'but not quite yet, I think. I still believe in a harmless explanation.'

She went back to the house, feeling rather sick.


Rimini, Miranda decided, was not a place she wanted to visit again. A holiday town with numerous hotels fronting on a great sweep of the Adriatic, a plethora of package tours much in evidence to jade her overstretched nerves, organised jollity mocking private terror. There was, the guidebook had explained as she had leafed through it at the airport, another Rimini, an ancient, gracious Rimini; but she felt she was unlikely to return and explore it. Rimini was loudspeaker announcements steering expectant bands of red-faced northern Europeans to waiting buses from airport to hotel. Rimini was exhaustion, a long search for somewhere that had rooms for the Wrenches, worried, unbooked, unbidden, a late, nasty dinner, a night without rest. Rimini was not knowing what had happened to Franzi.

She had not slept at all when the telephone by her bed rang at half-past one in the morning, Monday morning, 24th July. Canned music was still coming from some haunt near the beach which their hotel overlooked. It was Harry. His bedroom was on a different floor –

'M, they think they've found Franzi's car.'

'Where?'

'Apparently it had gone over the edge of a road in the mountains, a minor road, they suppose he was trying to take a short cut.'

'Harry – is he dead?' Miranda felt cold and sick.

'There's no sign of Franzi at all,' said Harry. 'Look, I'll come down to your room.'

A few minutes later he told her there was no doubt it was Franzi's Mercedes. The police had checked the number with Beppo at the Villa Foresta.

'It crashed over a steep edge, down quite a way, then was stopped by the trees.'

'Smashed to bits?'

'Not at all. Knocked about by the trees but nothing else. No sign of Franzi. No blood. From what the police told me – they've been very good, got someone on the line who spoke passable English – Franzi can't have been in the car when it went over the edge. Both doors were bashed in.'

'Perhaps he jumped clear. Then started to walk to get help and got lost.'

The police, Harry said, had been adamant that Franzi could not possibly have jumped clear, and had made it clear that they were unlikely to modify that view when they came to examine the place in daylight. Circumstances made that explanation incredible. They had told Harry that it was surprising the car had been discovered so comparatively quickly. It was a tiny road, unfrequented. The local police, knowing Franzi's starting point and objective, had done some deducing. There was an employee, too, who spoke of Signor Langenbach intending to try a short cut.

Miranda said very quietly,

'Then where is he?'

'The police reckon he must have somehow been got out of the car. Or got out of his own free will. Then the car must have been pushed over the edge.'

'Why?'

'They think it's a kidnap. They're treating it as a kidnap case. They asked me if Franzi might have had a complete breakdown and shoved his own car over the edge and walked off, done a disappearing act. I said of course not.'

'Of course not.'

'There've been a good many kidnaps in Italy. Of course they're pretty worried about it, particularly because Franzi's a foreigner, a very distinguished foreigner in his own line. They thought we're closer to Franzi than we are, might know a lot of things about him we probably don't. I said we'd go to Police Headquarters in the morning. Nine o'clock.'

'And then fly back to England.'

'Of course. I must telephone the Rudbergs. I'll do that now.'


At Bargate, Marcia said,

'I don't know whether to be glad they didn't find his body. I'm not sure this isn't going to be worse than death.'

At Arzfeld, Lise von Arzfeld said,

'Where there is doubt there is hope. Is that not so?' They told her it was so. Everyone at Arzfeld loved Franzi, known from infancy, known as a little brown-faced, bright-eyed boy, always laughing, never still.

The Wrenches, back in England, were assured by the Metropolitan Police that if they heard anything – and they would hear, they explained, terrorism acknowledged no frontiers, and the international co-ordination of counter-measures was

87

becoming more sophisticated every year – they would keep Mr Wrench informed.

'We quite understand the worry this must be to all Mr Langenbach's friends.'

'We weren't very close friends, although we'd known him since we were all children. But we'd met again recently and, of course, were just about to stay –'

'Very unpleasant for you and Miss Wrench, sir. That sort of thing brings it close, doesn't it? I gather Dr Langenbach has a great reputation in the States?'

'Everywhere, I think. As a heart surgeon – top of the tree.'

'So I believe. Well, sir, we'll keep you informed if we hear anything. And Mrs Rudberg down in Sussex too, of course. The Italians are good friends of ours.' Harry was in daily and often hourly touch with Miranda, and knew from the silent touch of her hand in his during their return flight to England from Rimini that here indeed was shock and suffering greater than warranted by the sort of casual affection for Franzi they'd pretended to each other at the start of the journey to Italy. Here was trouble, Harry knew, and his heart went out to his wounded sister. Nothing goes right for her, he thought, nothing at all. And as the days passed, as the first Black Monday was succeeded by Tuesday, Wednesday; as days elapsed with no word, no sign, no message reaching police, or newspapers or ministries in Washington, London, Bonn, Rome, where people who had never heard Franzi's name heard it now; as the heavy black headlines matched each other: 'Top surgeon disappears'; 'Playboy prodigy leaves no trace'; '*Beruhmte Chirurg entfuhrt*' (the German newspapers treated kidnap as a fact from the start: such cases had become unhappily familiar to them in recent months); as time passed, doubt persisted, but hope began to die.


Vittorio settled comfortably into the corner seat of the express. He'd moved by bus, attracting no attention he was sure, and then spent a few hours in Bressanone where he had caught a train south to Milan and to another agreeable hour or two.

Reno had told him not to waste time but, truth to tell, he felt no particular urgency to get back to the constrained life of Perugia. Except that Reno, speaking in a serious voice, had remarked,

'You will receive a generous bonus, an acknowledgement of what you'll have done for our cause, when you get back, when you report that it has all gone correctly.'

Vittorio was surprised that Reno's philosophy admitted such a concept as a bonus! He could not suppress the feeling that this was Reno's concession to a less exalted set of motives and type of person. But unlike working with crooks, Vittorio sorrowfully acknowledged, it was possible to rely upon Reno absolutely in such matters, for all that the fellow was cracked and dangerous. A bonus would be his if all had gone correctly.

And, he thought complacently, it had indeed gone correctly. There had been one or two strokes of luck, but luck favours the skilful and the bold, those who know how to recognise and grab an opportunity. There had, for instance, been that conversation overheard by Vittorio in a Perugia bar; he'd known neither of the two and had sat in the shadows, listening. They were talking low and with enjoyment, and he could hear every word.

'I've got her to myself the whole weekend!'

'Lucky man! I saw her once, you told me where she buys bread, remember? I had to have a look. A beauty!'

'Husband's away – this Saturday. I'm on my own, got our house to myself! Her husband's bought her a little runabout, a Fiat, she's independent –'

The two had chuckled, one lecherous, the other envious. The first, the fortunate one, had left the bar first. Vittorio approached the other on his way out. Casually, he said,

'Excuse me – was that Giovanni Taliani?'

'No –'

'Funny, I thought his face was familiar –'

'That's Stefano Bastico. Lives in Umbertide.'

'Ah,' said Vittorio wisely, 'Umbertide! That must be it! I've seen him somewhere. I go there often. Must have seen him around.'

89

'Stefano lives in the Via Tevere. Big house. He's got a rich mother.'

Vittorio nodded, uninterested, and slipped away. The Umbertide telephone directory gave him what he needed. Reno wanted a car cleaning, given a new identity to last several days, to cover Vittorio on his long drive and immediately afterwards. Any delay in reporting a loss would help give time, and Vittorio felt happy to bet that a pretty girl who wasn't meant to be in Umbertide wouldn't report a theft instantly and accurately to the police there. Besides, he thought with an inner grin, she might be too busy to notice the loss for quite a time, a time during which Bruno would help, as promised. And all this – which was not, of course, essential to the project, Vittorio told himself he could have lifted a car any day of the week – all this was a refinement, an adornment, something which turned out almost as if designed by Providence. For it would, of course, have been no good at all if it meant keeping the cleaned car under wraps with Bruno for too long. But when he returned to the apartment that evening, the evening he'd heard them talking in the bar, talking women, laughing, anticipating, that same evening Reno looked at him immediately he walked in. It had been July 18th, a Tuesday.

'Five days.'

'Eh?'

'Five days. Sunday.'

Vittorio had heard him, incredulous. It was all coming together, and when Reno explained more of the routine he was impressed and felt, as ever, awe for Reno's imagination and grasp. He reckoned his own contribution was not bad either. Reno said,

'That all right?'

'All right.'

'Car, I mean.'

'Of course you do. I said, all right.'

He'd been firm about one thing with Reno.

'I want to go over the roads with you. In your car. Tomorrow.'

He'd have to work hard through the Saturday night, but there was advantage in getting straight on with it. With luck he'd have done the main job before anybody even knew the car was missing! He'd already had a word with Bruno about paint and number plates in a general sort of way, and noted with satisfaction that Bruno knew his way around.

Timing, fortune, all had been favourable. Perhaps Providence was on the side of the Revolution after all.

And then there'd been the snatch.

Well prepared of course. He'd persuaded Reno, talking to him earnestly as they drove the circuit, to play a minor additional part, impressing Reno by his, Vittorio's own prudence.

'It's just in case he doesn't turn up that side road.'

'He will. I've told you he was advised, he talked to our friend at the garage the day after he got here, last Saturday. There'll be the notice board –'

'He might not. In that case he must be flagged down. You need a red flag at the bend, a kilometre on –'

Vittorio pointed out that at a certain point, ideal for the purpose, Reno could park his car and, on hearing from Vittorio (who would be positioned to observe) that the Mercedes had, regrettably, passed the sign '*Deviazione Stradale*' without paying attention, should emerge with a red flag, check the car and tell the driver that the main road was closed and traffic being diverted. It was possible at that point for the Mercedes to turn and turn it would. There would, it was true, be face-to-face sighting which would be a pity if they had to abort; but Reno would be dusty, dark-glassed and neckscarved and it wasn't a major snag. They certainly didn't want to involve a third person at that juncture.

Reno had acquiesced.

'Suppose there's another car behind him?'

'Then the show's off, we've agreed that. He's got to be alone, either way. The signs won't go out more than a minute or two before. And when have I seen more than one car in half an hour on that road? Odds are strong on success, Reno!'

'Yes,' Reno had said slowly, 'I think so.' His had been the concept, Vittorio's, now, much of the details.

'I think so. But –'

'If it's called off Bruno will get rid of the Fiat. No problem. A waste, a pity, but no problem. We start again.'

Reno had breathed in deeply.

'We start again!'

They had not had to start again. Reno's red flag had been superfluous to requirements. On hearing the signal from Vittorio's radio, Reno had driven straight back to a point on the Perugia road to prepare for the next stage. The snatch was to be Vittorio's alone.

And that, too, had gone perfectly. Vittorio smiled to himself. A steward came along the train corridor with an assortment of drinks on sale and Vittorio bought a can of beer. Yes, no hitch at all. Reno had said, 'Don't hit him too hard. We need him in one piece,' and Vittorio reflected that he'd got it exactly right, precisely judged, neat. He almost laughed aloud when he thought of it, thought of the poor sod straining to shift the boulder from the road! Strictly speaking it was unnecessary and he could have clocked him immediately he bent over, but (and Vittorio frowned, for it had been a minor piece of inexact planning on his part) the best place for the Mercedes to go over the edge was the near side of the point where he'd brought the boulder to rest. So it was best to wait until the guy had got it rolling! He'd strained and heaved, and later it had only needed Vittorio's finger touch to get it crashing over.

Yes, nice-looking young fellow, straining and heaving! 'Grazie, Signor'! Vittorio, remembering, tapped the knuckles of his right hand into the palm of his left, content. The only bitter moment had been running the Mercedes over the verge. What a car! How he'd enjoyed that fleeting moment at the wheel! And the little Fiat was no great ride – especially with Langenbach in the back, starting to moan as they neared Perugia for the transfer.

He sipped his beer and remembered the transfer. Reno hadn't exactly been dexterous. Then, just as the exertion was over and Vittorio was keen to get away, to start the journey north, he'd been shocked.

'Reno, what the hell's wrong with you?'

Reno had gone greyish white, his hands to his temples.

'What in hell –'

'It'll be all right.' Reno sat down beside the road, head in hands. 'I – I sometimes get these blinding headaches.'

'Well, take your headache home. I'm off.'

'No, Vittorio, just wait until I'm all right. It'll pass in a minute or two. I can't drive until then, it's, it's –' he was gasping, it was almost as if he was having a fit! Hands to temples, writhing, dust-coloured face. Vittorio felt impatient. Nerves! And he'd done nothing yet.

After a little, Reno said quietly,

'All right.'

'Carla there all right? You'll cope?'

'Of course.' Reno tried something like a smile. 'We'll steer him up between us. Place is ready.' They'd given Langenbach a knockout jab. He'd be out for six hours at least. And if Carla wasn't up to getting the poor brute of a doctor upstairs there were always the two minders, Berto and Aldo, who did nothing much, lived on the floor below and seemed generally under Reno's thumb for minor tasks. Vittorio thought them poor quality but Reno had said, 'They're safe,' so presumably he knew. At least they could help lug Langenbach upstairs; although Vittorio knew that Reno wanted to keep it as close as possible between Carla, Vittorio and himself. He said,

'I'll be off.'

And as he'd driven north then, and now, as he gently travelled south again, Vittorio reflected that Reno's ideas were good, no question. Reno had assessed that the ditched Fiat would be discovered – soon. But not too soon. Reno knew that after a little, when they'd crawled all over it, it would be linked with a theft near where Langenbach lived – but not too near. There would be a credible connection, and in time the connection would be made. Reno knew that the gold charm would be found, identified; and that then, but only then – five days? four days? – they would know

Langenbach had been in the car, that the car had been stolen for a purpose, and that a day traveller, crossing from Austria, had probably been tasked to pack a kidnapped surgeon in the boot of an Innsbruck-bound vehicle. Yes, thought Vittorio approvingly, they'd get there in time. Reno's time. They might even have got there by now – it was Wednesday, 26th July. No doubt Reno would say the sooner the better, now Vittorio was clear. The woman sitting next to Vittorio asked him whether they were approaching Perugia, since the train was slowing, and he told her with a charming smile that he believed it to be so.

On 27th July, four days after Franzi's disappearance, the telephone rang at Bargate at nine o'clock in the evening.

'Marcia, you have heard anything?'

It was Lise von Arzfeld. She and Marcia had spoken almost every day.

'Nothing since Tuesday evening, Lise.'

The authorities, sensible, busy and humane, knew that negative information was better than silence and kept regular touch with those they knew were suffering.

Lise said, 'They have spoken to me from Bonn. I expect they will be telling you the same in London.'

'What is it?'

'They have found a car. They have found a small Fiat car. Near a place called Masseria.'

'Where's that?'

'It's in the mountains, the Alps. Very near the Austrian frontier with Italy. The car had been pushed off the road and left. The Italian police have identified it. It was a stolen car.'

'Well?'

'It had been changed, you know, painted and different numbers and so forth. But there was no doubt it was a car stolen from a different part of Italy. From not so far from where Franzi's house is.'

'What else, Lise?' Marcia's voice was raw. Lise had always to tell a tale in precise chronological order, every detail clear and recounted before moving to the next; or, Marcia thought sharply, to anything like a point. There were probably hundreds of cars stolen in Umbria every month and no doubt some were driven towards the Alpine passes. Why not?

'The police think the car was abandoned and the people in it picked up by another car coming over from Austria for the day.'

'Lise, Franzi –'

'They found a little gold sign in the car,' said Lise. 'They described it to me. It was the little gold badge Franzi wore on his bracelet. The von Arzfeld falcon. It was on the floor, under a seat. They had taken Franzi there, in that car.' Her voice was even. She was a courageous woman, who had suffered much over the years.

Yes, thought Marcia, he must have been taken in that car. Dead or alive.

'What do the police think now, Lise?'

'They are sure,' said Lise. 'There are other things, too, which make them sure, I think. They are sure he has been taken across the frontier. Into Austria. Now Austrian police are very busy. There is to be a television notice, with details, shown in Austria, in Italy, in Germany. Maybe in England. Perhaps even in America. I think it will be this evening. Asking for information. Giving a telephone number in each of those countries which a person having information can ring. Even without giving a name. Also an address to which they can write. It is usual, I think.'

Marcia said, 'You feel sure he's alive now, Lise, don't you? I can hear that.'

'Yes,' said Lise. 'I know now that he is alive.'

# CHAPTER 6

'This is a special announcement,' said the fair-haired girl in the BBC studio. 'A similar message is being shown on television screens in a number of European countries and also in America, and there will be a radio broadcast during this evening in the same terms.' She looked serious and stern, her pretty face and rather protuberant blue eyes expressing regret and disapproval as at some lapse in the person she was addressing. It was a Thursday evening, 27th July.

'Four days ago, on Sunday 23rd July, Dr Franz Langenbach disappeared from his holiday home near Gubbio in Italy. Dr Langenbach is a world-famous heart surgeon and there has been widespread public concern for his safety.

'The Italian police have reason to believe that Dr Langenbach may have been abducted. It is possible that he has been taken out of Italy to a neighbouring country, and it is likely that, for at least some of the time, he travelled in a small black Fiat car, registration number Pe 55-77-04. I will repeat that.' She did so.

'If anybody, particularly anybody who has recently travelled in Italy, Austria or West Germany, has seen any circumstance which they believe might throw light, however remote, on Dr Langenbach's disappearance they are asked to contact New Scotland Yard.' The girl gave a telephone number and an address. Miranda Wrench watched the screen in frozen silence. There was more to come.

'In the studio with me is Dr William Baxter who has worked with Dr Langenbach in New York. Dr Baxter, presumably the whole medical fraternity are deeply concerned about Dr Langenbach's safety?'

Dr William Baxter had enormous horn-rimmed spectacles and the impressive face of an Edwardian actor-manager.

96

Silver-haired, he looked grave, formidable and successful. His voice was deep and musical, an American voice with certain attractive inflexions derived from his Central European origins. He nodded.

'Deeply concerned.'

'Dr Langenbach is German is he not?'

'He is. Like many of us practising in the United States – or principally in the United States – he came from Europe some few years ago.'

'And he is brilliant, would you say?'

'I would say Dr Langenbach is near the top of his profession. He is a young man – no more than thirty-three I am told – and has made a very great reputation in this difficult, challenging world of heart surgery. In America, primarily, although his name is now known throughout the world by those who are familiar with such things.'

The girl asked if Dr Baxter had known the missing surgeon personally and Dr Baxter said that he had, indeed, known him, 'as a colleague – a very charming colleague'. Had he a family? she enquired. Dr Baxter said that Dr Langenbach was unmarried. He supposed his relations were in Germany but he knew nothing of the family. 'He is a man,' he said, 'who is utterly dedicated to his calling. We must all hope that information will soon be forthcoming –' He shook his fine, silver-crowned head and sighed. The girl thanked him with a sad, grateful smile, turned a strict look on the viewers and gave them again the address and telephone number which should be used by anybody with news of Franzi.

Miranda telephoned Harry. Each was in, and each alone.

'Did you watch?'

'Franzi – yes, I saw it. M, I can't believe in people spotting car numbers. Doesn't it mean they've now got the car in question?'

'I suppose so. And I suppose they can trace it, or have traced it now, traced where it comes from.'

Reno deposited a copy of Tuesday's *Tiroler Tageblatt* in a municipal dustbin. He had marked an advertisement in the personal column.

'Bernhard. Try 41-97-78-01 on Sunday. As ever, D.' Reno had added to this run of figures the paper's date – 25th July, the seventh month of 1972. By adding 25.07.72 he had eight digits. He moved into a telephone booth, closed the door and looked at his watch. Two minutes to three o'clock in the afternoon of Sunday 30th July. It wasn't a part of Perugia he frequented. Next time, he reflected, he'd use a different booth, some way away. Always different.

He dialled the Austrian code followed by 42.22.85.73 and was rewarded by Josef's voice, non-committal. Reno said,

'Go ahead.'

'OK.'

Just that. Josef waited for a half-minute in case Reno wished to say more. He didn't.


'This was sent by telex to Vienna at once,' said Georg Venner, the police officer in charge at Villach, in the Carinthian Alps. 'Of course it was sent to us in the first instance as the nearest place of any size – the presumption is they're in this district – look at the postmark –'

'Surely too obvious a presumption,' said the detective officer studying the letter. 'Unless they're stupid, they wouldn't hold him in a mountain hut and write to the local cops. I expect they've picked Villach at random. He may be anywhere.'

'It was posted locally. Yesterday.'

'So what? We live in the age of the automobile.'

'Vienna will have to handle it. The television angle – it's stuff for the Minister.'

'Of course. And Forensic in Klagenfurt will give us what they can on the letter. It doesn't look as if it will be much. Printed characters cut from a variety of Austrian newspapers, whole words in some cases. You can tell the paper concerned, as often as not, just by looking at it. And I'm no great reader.'

'An old trick.'

'But safe.'

They both peered again at the sheet of paper, torn from a standard, child's exercise book, on which printed characters had been gummed. It was a long, explicit message, without redeeming ambiguities to which hope might attach.

We hold F. Langenbach. Response to this demand must be public, broadcast on television and radio at intervals during Wednesday 2nd August. Details of this demand should be broadcast at the same time. This transaction must be enacted before the eyes of the world.

F. Langenbach will be released, unharmed, when Klaretta Barinski is released from custody by the authorities of the Federal Republic of Germany and enabled to travel by air to a destination of which you will be informed. At present it is only necessary for the agreement in principle of the German authorities to be conveyed. Details will follow.

If Barinski is not released Langenbach will be executed.

'Why not send their bloody messages to Bonn, or somewhere in Germany in the first place?' said Venner. 'What do they think the Austrians can do? The Germans will make up their own bloody minds. Release that Barinski bitch? I ask you!'

Klaretta Barinski, arrested the previous month, was awaiting trial in Kassel, in the Federal Republic of Germany, on charges of arson (at a factory of IG Farben), of murder of seven persons the preceding November, blown to pieces by a bomb in the railway station buffet at Fulda, and of various other activities connected to the wave of terrorist violence which had appalled Europe during the previous three years. She was one of eleven defendants, all variously accused.

The detective officer was looking meditatively at the unwelcome message Villach had received two hours earlier. His eyes were on a photocopy – the original piece of paper was on its way to Klagenfurt.

'They can't give in – the Germans, I mean – about Barinski. I agree. Of course not. They'd never get away with it politically. But they've got a problem. Langenbach's a very well-

99

known man. He's got friends. A lot of people will be talking to Bonn as well as Vienna.'

'Vienna's a post offfice.'

'Of course. I mean the Americans, primarily. They'll certainly be talking to Bonn. Today.'

'Still,' said Venner, 'the Bonn Government can't do much. They'll simply bleat, and ask our people why the hell we haven't found him. Anyway Langenbach's still a German citizen,' he added, without obvious relevance.

'So I believe.' They looked at each other, anticipating long hours of almost certainly fruitless work in their district of Austria. Checking, checking, checking. A long, long way from the high-speed chases and dramatic discoveries of television drama police work. Venner said grumpily,

'You'd think the bloody Italians would have come up with some leads from the car. They must know all about it by now. They've had it for nearly a week, for God's sake!'

The other sighed. He had little sympathy with Italians. His family had once fled north, across a suddenly shifted frontier, to avoid compulsorily becoming Italians. From what they called Alto Adige. From Sud-Tirol. He said, with more generosity than he felt,

'Once they get the car's history, they'll probably get some ideas, and then they'll pass them on to Vienna. And to Bonn.'

'It's only speculation,' said Venner, 'that he's in Austria at all. Or ever was. And they've got to shift themselves if they're to make sense in a TV broadcast on Wednesday! I ask you! We're all at the mercy of these bloody people. We're so bloody soft! I'd shoot them down without a second thought!'

'You'd have to catch them first!'

They nodded to each other and picked up the threads of the day's other work.


The Langenbach case received extended radio and TV coverage in Germany, Austria and Italy; more cursory mention in other countries including Britain, where Toni and Marcia Rudberg watched the news on the evening of Wednesday 2nd

100

August. It was read by the same fair-haired girl who had told audiences about Franzi six days before. She spoke with a pained familiarity, as if someone called Langenbach, always regrettably likely to end up in trouble, had now done so; and that viewers deserved some apology for being pestered about the matter.

'The affair of the heart surgeon, Dr Langenbach, took a new turn today, when a message received by the Austrian authorities was read out on Austrian, German and Italian television. The message purported to come from people holding Dr Langenbach prisoner, and, in return for his release, it demanded that the West German authorities free Klaretta Barinski, who is awaiting trial in West Germany on charges connected with terrorism. The West German authorities say they are studying the message, which was originally sent to a police station in Austria.' The girl paused, and seemed to be studying a new document slid towards her, from which to read. Then she said,

'A new development has just occurred in the Langenbach case. The West German authorities have issued a statement to the effect that Klaretta Barinski cannot be discharged, under German law, until she has stood trial to answer the accusations brought against her; and that, meanwhile, it is hoped that those claiming knowledge of Dr Langenbach's whereabouts will take immediate steps to restore this distinguished and respected benefactor of humanity to his family and friends.'

'In other words,' said Toni, 'no deal. I suppose they can't say otherwise. How was Lise?'

'Brave, as usual.'

The Bonn announcement and the earlier news item about the letter of demand had been seen on German television two hours earlier, and Lise von Arzfeld had already been on the telephone to Marcia.

'Bonn still keeping in close touch with her?'

'Certainly. She said they were being very thoughtful. But she knows, of course, that they can't release this Barinski woman. Not only would it be unjust and illegal but there'd be

101

an appalling political storm. Lise's perfectly realistic about that – besides, she's such a principled person that she'd think such a deal actually wrong – whatever her misery.'

Toni said nothing. He had learned to respect von Arzfeld correctitude and moral strictness but he wondered whether, on balance, it was worth keeping a vicious young woman locked up for twenty years if the price of doing so was the killing of a brilliant young surgeon who might save many lives. And, as it happened, whom one loved. He knew that it was improper to reason thus in a matter to which principle, above all, had to be applied. As if reading him, Marcia said,

'I don't care a damn what happens to the Barinski female. But I suppose the precedent is what matters. Once give in and where does it stop? Kidnap, demand and win. Kidnap, demand and win.'

'No doubt. There have been surrenders in the past.'

'Which is why we are where we are.'

Of course that was true, thought Toni, the only problem being where, when and at the sacrifice of whose life to draw the line. He gently kissed his wife's hand, from finger to wrist, understanding almost all the reasons for the tears reflected in her eyes.


Franzi was sure that he was still in Italy. They had spoken to him from the start in curt Italian sentences, of which one of the first had been to enquire if he knew anything of the language. He had said '*Si*,' adding in hesitant Italian that he understood and spoke a little. He had stared at them, the two of them, as he answered. He would never forget that first confrontation.

Franzi remembered nothing of how he got to wherever he was. His last, blurred recollection was of starting a journey in his car from the Villa Foresta, although disconnected pictures of road, possibly on that drive, came back to him with difficulty. He had recovered consciousness, with an appalling headache, to find himself lying on a mattress stretched on bare boards in a tiny room with a low sloping ceiling and one skylight. His hands were tied behind his back and his ankles were bound to each other but not tightly, giving discomfort rather than pain. A few wriggles showed him that there was not the smallest chance of loosening the knots or freeing his limbs. One of the most irritating immediate circumstances was a pronounced itching on each side of his head between the corner of the eye and the ear; he realised afterwards that he had been blindfolded when first brought to this place and the bandage, of some rough stuff, had been wrapped tightly and left an itch which he longed to scratch and could not.

Facing him as he lay on the mattress was a heavy wooden door. He could hear the sound of traffic, some way below as far as he could tell, but persistent. He supposed he must be in a town, and on one of the upper floors of a building in that town. Added to his headache and itch was a raging thirst. Franzi tried to assemble his wits, which seemed to be working slowly. Then there had come the noise of the door creaking and opening. And then he had seen them for the first time. The first confrontation.

They had stood, one in the doorway, one just inside the room. One was short, the other about his own height as far as he could judge from his prone position. They both wore crimson masks which entirely covered the face except for eye slits and openings through which they could speak. The impression was inhuman and sinister, as of creatures with whom natural contact was impossible and from whom any cruelty, however barbarous, must be expected. The shorter of the two was holding a pistol in both hands, covering Franzi. The taller, incongruously, was clutching a mug. Franzi looked at them both with a sense of nightmare. For a long time there was no word. They gazed at him and he looked back and snatched at thoughts to steady himself. They're human beings, he forced himself to remember; behind those beastly, wicked-child-like criminal masks each has a face, and behind it there's a mind, stuffed with evil, no doubt, but perhaps not entirely. The tall one had asked whether he could speak Italian.

They had both come into the little room then, and examined the cords on his wrists and his ankles, and satisfied themselves

103

– or, rather, the tall one had satisfied himself for the short one kept distance and held the gun – that he was secured, safe, no threat to them. And, carefully but a little clumsily, the tall one had started to undo the bonds and free his wrists. Then the mug had been pushed at him and he had drunk so fast that he coughed and spluttered, so fierce was his thirst; and they watched him.

Franzi then had tried to ask one or two questions. In a curious way he sensed that they wanted this. They wanted to tell him certain things, and to establish some bizarre connection. They wanted to hear him speak, to play his own part in the communication. Franzi, on that first occasion, had asked the obvious questions. Where was he? Who was he speaking to? What had happened? He had been informed, in few words and without elaboration, that he was a prisoner of the European Liberation Movement, that when certain conditions had been met he would be released, but that meanwhile he had to be held in complete security.

After that first exchange he had said, absurdly, 'I was struck on the head.'

'It was necessary. It was not severe. The wound has been dressed.'

Franzi had no reason to doubt it. There was soreness but not the angry throb of infection. The voice of the tall one, a quiet, rather clipped Italian voice – in a peculiar way a gentle, even an attractive voice – said,

'We will now give you something to eat. We will free your hands to eat but will remain with you and tie them again afterwards. It is necessary.'

'I am not hungry.'

'You must eat.'

The short one had lowered the gun. While the tall one watched, the short one left the room and reappeared with a plate on which there was a piece of bread and slices of sausage meat. They watched him while he nibbled something and drank some more water. They were, he reflected, already taking more chances with him. Some hero of the cinema would have seized the opportunity when alone for a few moments

104

with the tall one, alone and apparently uncovered, to grapple with him, break his neck no doubt, get rid of ankle bonds in a second or two and apply the same treatment to the short one on reappearance. Franzi knew that he had not the slightest aptitude for these sort of acrobatics. He was bemused, exhausted, and, without doubt, frightened. For the sort of moral and physical effort which escape would demand he would need to make a considerable recovery. At present, he felt it beyond envisaging and he knew that his kidnappers' increased confidence and easiness in not covering him at all times painfully reflected this reality. As they left him on that first evening – he knew it was evening from the failing light through the tiny roof window – he tried to read something from their eyes, fixed so curiously on him. Through the eye slits of the tall one's awful mask he fancied he could see enormous concentration. This one seemed the boss, undoubtedly was the boss, from his postures, his brief words of command to his silent companion. And this boss was in total control.

Franzi tried to get something from the eyes of the short one. Disturbed and, as he lay alone afterwards, hoping that the impression was mistaken, he thought he saw hatred. Real hatred. Directed at him, Franzi. And as they tied his wrists again and first one, then the other went through the door (gun not now in evidence) he heard what sounded like a question shot from the tall one, though he could not make out the words. And the answer, also incomprehensible, told him one fact which the mask and his confusion had hitherto obscured. The short one was a girl.


Every day for the first two or three they came to him together. It was always the tall one, the man, who spoke; and he said the minimum. Franzi heard himself trying to reach some sort of human accord, some relationship, be it of prisoner to gaoler, which showed that life existed, that time existed, that their situation was not a static, unchanging, frozen, repetitive mummery, a nightmare fixed until death and beyond.

'How long have I been here?'

'Three days.'

'When do you propose to release me?'

'When your friends agree our terms.'

Franzi said, 'Can I write something to my friends? How do they, how does anybody know you are holding me?'

'They will know. If you are to write we will decide.'

The cords had been checked, the door slammed. The mug of water was regularly replenished. There was a bucket in the corner into which he urinated and over which he squatted. Every day they pushed a basin of water along the floor to him, loosened his cords and indicated he could wash himself if he wished, and he did his best. He found he had to ask for this.

'*Lavare. Per favore.*'

Silence. Then, sometimes, the basin. These bodily functions had to be preceded by shouts to attract attention. Shouts were followed by a pantomime as, covered by the girl's revolver, his cords were removed and he was left to himself, and then, after cautious, covered re-entry by his gaolers, he was tied up again.

For the first few days the physical misery, the squalid discomfort, dominated his mind in a way which became, in retrospect, almost a relief. There was nothing else to think about but the body's wretchedness, and concentration on how to alleviate it made the time pass. He grew hoarse with yelling, his only way of attracting attention. Somebody usually came, opening the door carefully, revolver ready; then seeing him lying, bound, relaxing a little, would snap a question,

'What now?'

Franzi tried to detect something human through the eye slits of the masks. Dimly aware that he would, probably, deceive himself intentionally, that he would invent imagined characteristics to suit his hopes, that he was in a state not far from delirium, he thought the tall one, the man, had eyes which were intelligent, and by no means bad. In the eyes of the smaller kidnapper, the woman, however, Franzi continued to find that he could discern actual loathing. She never spoke in those first days, but he was appalled at the malevolence he saw, or grimly believed he saw, in the green eyes framed by

106

that obscene, crimson mask, made of what looked like nylon. He felt, and did not doubt they wanted him to feel, that these people would not shrink from anything.

On what he was almost sure was the sixth day – counting the day of kidnap as the first – the tall one came to him alone, revolver not in evidence. It was morning, a sliver of brilliant sunshine striking through the tiny skylight window. Franzi had slept better when dark came than on the two previous nights. His head was less sore, his feeling of near-delirium less pervasive. For the first time he felt, together with fear and discomfort, terrible, stupefying boredom. This had, hitherto, been smothered by physical discomfort, by the small reliefs afforded by their visits, the loosening of cords, a plate of salami, the mug, the use of the bucket. Now these things had become routine and the great enemy, solitary boredom, had joined him. He knew it could be a tough enemy indeed. The tall one (but only about my size, thought Franzi) was looking down at him. He spoke, slowly and carefully. Franzi watched the lips moving in the mask slit; Why red? he wondered. Politically symbolic, as simple as that? Terrorists usually wore black masks, didn't they?

'Langenbach, we are making certain requests to your friends so that you can be released. When these requests are met you can be free.'

'So you told me. I don't know what you mean by "my friends". I know nobody who can do anything for you. I imagine you have asked for money. Why do you not talk to me about it?'

'No money. The request is not for money.'

'What, then?'

The other stood, silent, considering, but made no move to leave. Franzi found himself desperately needing to prolong the conversation, somehow. It was contact, it was sanity, whatever the words used. He stared up at his gaoler.

'Please tell me what I can call you.'

'You can call me Reno.'

'And the other? I have only seen one other, always the same, the short one.'

Again a pause, thoughtful. Then, almost with regret, misgiving –

'That is Carla.'

'A woman,' said Franzi, who knew it. He nodded his head, never taking his eyes from the slits in that scarlet mask above him, 'A woman.'

'A comrade.' Still no movement.

Franzi said, 'Can I be untied? It is absurd to suppose I can be dangerous to you, attack you, or try to escape. You have guns, I'm locked in. I don't know where I am. Is this tying of ankles and wrists necessary to you?' He spoke in as reasonable a tone as he could. In no way did he wish, at any time, to sound angry, or hectoring – or excessively fearful. A reasonable request between reasonable men. After a minute he said again, without particular emphasis,

'Reno, can I be untied?'

Reno said, 'It is what I have come to tell you. I am going to untie your ankles and your wrists. If you try to use this freedom to be violent in any way, or to do damage to this room –' (Like what? Franzi thought. The place was bare. He supposed he might be presumed capable of smashing skylight or denting door) '– or try at any time to escape from us you will be executed. As you say, we have guns. And not only guns. And there are enough of us here, enough of us in this building. All the time.'

Franzi listened, uncaring how much he believed, only joyful, incredulously joyful, that soon his cords would be removed. Each time, each day they had loosened them so that he could use the bucket it had been more painful to exercise the chafed, cramped limbs. Now he said,

'Thank you. I understand.'

'If, at any time, there is need you will be tied up again. And if you try to attack us or behave badly you will be executed.' He used the formal word – '*giustiziato*'! Franzi only understood later that it implied not simply punishment but death. Reno's stern tone, however, conveyed a good deal.

'I understand.'

This conversation followed one between Reno and Carla the previous day. Carla had said,

'I'm getting fed up with being a nurse, and a gaoler. Bathing his head. Untying him to eat. Untying him to shit. Looking after him like a baby.'

'I suspect we could let up on that a good deal. He thinks there are plenty of us. He's no idea where he is. As long as we take care, I think we could lock him up and leave him. As long as two of us are always around and don't take any chances.'

They had made the tiny cupboard where Vittorio had once lain an effective cell. Reno had nodded to himself and said,

'We'd tie him up when there was a special need. Besides, I think it may be necessary to talk to him.'

'Well, what stops you talking to him tied up?'

Reno found this difficult to answer. He knew, however, that he wanted to speak to Langenbach and hear Langenbach speak, not as a bound, prone figure, but as one who could be addressed and could be led to respond, could take part in a rational exchange, could even be brought to comprehend, perhaps, the motives and the compulsions of those who would probably soon have to kill him. Reno felt this more strongly each day that passed. They had now held Franzi Langenbach seven full days and to his, Reno's, surprised shame he was beginning to find it personally intolerable. He had anticipated all things, he had supposed, but he had not expected that his own reactions would be so impatient, so frustrated.

When he now stooped and undid Franzi's bonds, it was he as well as his prisoner who felt relief. Not for the first time Franzi asked,

'How long have I been here?' He asked in a conversational, not especially interested tone as Reno, watching him carefully, slackened the knots and then removed the cords. Franzi heard a sneeze outside the door. The other, probably, Carla: told to be ready at this critical moment in case Langenbach tried something. Holding a gun and grumbling that it was surely unnecessary to put on a mask, she'd come in fast if wanted. These surmises were, in fact, pretty near the mark.

109

'How long have I been here?' He drew his knees up to his chin, remaining for the time being hunched up on the mattress. The time for exercise would be later. Alone.

'Seven days.' Reno's voice was rough but not entirely unfriendly. Franzi, immensely sensitive to tone, thought it possible the roughness was assumed and far from natural. In this perception, too, he was near the truth. Seven days! So he had missed one – he had thought it was six. He began to realise what every account of captivity had always stressed – how important and how difficult it would be to mark the passing of time. Just now the most desirable thing was, somehow, to keep Reno talking.

'Reno, as I have said, I don't know what friends I have who could do anything for you. You say you have not asked for money.'

'No. Maybe later I explain to you. Just now we have to wait and see what the response to our request will be.'

'To whom has this request been made? I don't understand.' But Reno had already moved, shrugging his shoulders, and Franzi realised with sadness that the conversation was over.

That day and for the next two, Franzi concentrated on strengthening his limbs, on walking, walking up and down, up and down, on moving his fingers, his hands and wrists, his arms and shoulders. After twenty-four hours his body felt better and he began, cautiously, to do some of the keep-fit exercises to which he was accustomed, steadily at first. These had, normally, to be increased in duration and intensity each day and it helped his sense of the passage of time to concentrate on them. Tomorrow, he thought, I'll be running on the spot not thirty-five but fifty-five times. A healthy man with a strong frame, he felt relief at something like normality in his body's reactions to this régime. And at least the cell – for he thought of this dingy little attic as a cell – was cool. He stripped for these exercises. After them he lay for a little, cooling off. On the second occasion, still naked except for a pair of pants, he started shouting. The door opened and the smaller kidnapper, the woman appeared. Carla.

Franzi smiled politely. '*Acqua*? *Lavare*? *Per favore*.'

110

Carla stood gazing at him with what Franzi felt tolerably sure was resentful hostility. She went out, slamming and bolting the door. There were bolts on the outside. They always sounded heavy.

No *acqua*. No *lavare*.


'I want to tell you certain things, Langenbach.'

'I am glad to hear it, Reno. How long have I been here?'

'Twelve days. We will be very glad, believe me, when our conditions are agreed and we can release you. Langenbach, we have made certain requests to the authorities, the West German authorities as it happens. If these are granted, we have told them you can be freed.' Reno heard himself with wry self-knowledge. He had said 'we have told them' which was true. It was not, however, the whole truth for he had reached a certain and a different conclusion. Earlier that day, 3rd August, he had said to Carla,

'He'll always be a threat to us. You realise that.'

'We've always worn our masks –'

'Yes. But even without seeing us he'll always be a threat. Voices. Circumstances. Small things that could come back to him. A blindfolded man has other senses sharpened. It's the same. He can't see our faces but every other characteristic will be sketched in his mind more precisely.'

'To prove identity, you must have sight.'

Reno had said, 'I don't agree. He'll always be a threat,' and Carla had looked at him a sharp question. She knew that expressionless note in Reno's voice when he had wrestled with himself about a difficult decision and had reached certainty, the way ahead clear. He had said, almost inaudibly,

'We must never let him go. Alive.'

'And Barinski? Klaretta, whose release will shake *them* to their foundations?'

'I don't think they'll agree – which will make the decision for us. But if they do – well, I've got the transfer mechanism worked out, at least in general terms, details later. First she gets out. Then they get Langenbach. Dead. After all, if they

111

agree – and I don't think they will – we hold the cards in the transaction.'

Carla had continued to gaze at him, fascinated.

Reno put this conversation and all associated thoughts from his mind as he now looked at Franzi and said,

'Yes, certain requests to the West German authorities.'

Franzi asked for a mug of water and was given it. He said,

'What requests?'

'There is a comrade of ours, held by the Germans. We have asked for her release, in exchange for yourself.' Reno spoke carefully as he always did, appreciating Franzi's lack of fluency in Italian. Franzi nodded.

'And I suppose they have refused.'

'They have not,' said Reno, 'yet shown much understanding. Of course you have friends, and no doubt your friends have done their best to persuade the German authorities. Friends, as is widely known, in many countries: America, England, as well as Germany. Langenbach, have you a family?'

'Not an immediate family. No parents. No brother. No sister. No.'

'Or anybody close to you, who might be – persuasive – to the German authorities?'

Franzi stared at him. How should any who loved him – Lise, Marcia, dear cynical old Toni Rudberg, New York friends and colleagues (he pushed Miranda from his mind) – how should they be expected to influence the German Government? Or have one chance in hell of doing so? Why should the liberty to practise surgery of Dr Franzi Langenbach – German citizen, now in practice mainly in the United States – why should this, so precious to him, Langenbach, be thought sufficient to distort the path of Federal German justice? Reno was watching him.

'When you were first brought here, Langenbach, you were delirious for a while. As you know, it was necessary – your head –'

Franzi nodded. He said, 'So you have told me.' He tried to feel cold hatred and found he felt nothing.

112

'You spoke a name, in delirium. Several times. The name was "Miranda Wrench". We have friends in England who have identified the lady. And we understand this young lady to be particularly close to you.'

Franzi shook his head. His mind flickered and he felt sick. He said, trying to sound steady, 'You're mistaken.' He sensed that it mattered a lot.

'I am afraid I cannot accept what you say about Signorina Wrench. We know that she was about to arrive to join you in your house here in Italy.'

'Well? She was coming out with her brother, as my guests.' But Franzi knew that in spite of effort his voice trembled. He thought of Miranda, that beloved, enchanting, girl. He supposed knowledge that the Wrenches would be anxiously awaiting him at Rimini airport had surfaced in delirium from his subconscious. He had not, if Reno were to be believed, called out 'The Wrenches', or 'Harry Wrench'. He'd named Miranda. Reno was watching him closely.

'No doubt Signorina Wrench will be concerned at your disappearance.'

'Presumably all my friends are concerned.'

'They know,' said Reno, conversationally; 'they know what has happened. Our request for the release of our comrade has been shown on television. In several countries. At our demand. It is the only way we are prepared to negotiate. We wish all this to be with full publicity, you see.'

At that moment the door opened and Carla came in.

Franzi said, without particular concern, 'I suppose it's Barinski you want.' It was a shot in the dark, the most recent name he remembered in the news.

Carla looked at him and looked interrogatively at Reno. Then she looked at Franzi again. Franzi shrugged his shoulders. He said,

'Reno, I have a request. I think it may take a little time for your friend to be released and I have a request.'

'Well?'

'You have a lavatory here. May I use it instead of that bucket?' Franzi carefully kept disgust out of his voice. Carla started to speak but Reno held up his hand and she stopped.

'It would mean escorting you. It would place more of a burden on us.'

'I have a suggestion.'

Again Reno said, 'Well?'

'I suggest I give you my word that I won't try to escape. Or attack you or Carla or anyone else. I'll stay where I am and do as you say.'

'You give me your *word*?' said Reno staring at him.

'I give you my word. And in return you let me use the lavatory. Lock me in afterwards, by all means.'

Reno was silent, looking at him. After a little he said, 'Why would you expect me to believe your word?' but he said it without conviction from behind the red mask.

'That's up to you. Obviously it wouldn't be easy for me to make a break, I don't know where we are, I don't know how many of you there are, I'm not in a very strong condition, you've taken away my money, my shoes, my belt.'

These had, indeed, been taken into Carla's custody.

'But that's not the point,' said Franzi, 'I agree that, although it might be stupid, I might try something, I might be desperate. The point is, I promise not to.'

'Why?'

'Because if we're going to sit here together waiting for the response of the German Government to your request it may be a long time. And I suggest we would be happier if I were not kept to this rather – insanitary – routine.'

'*You* would be happier, Dr Langenbach. The rest of us are perfectly content. Your happiness, I regret to say, is not our primary concern.'

'Naturally not,' said Franzi, and he managed a smile; that smile which had always, from childhood, conveyed so much love to almost everybody. 'Naturally not. But please think it over, Reno. I'm prepared to give my word. And I think that with some changes of that kind it would be less disagreeable for all of us.'

Later Reno said, 'They don't really believe we've got him. "Claiming knowledge of Dr Langenbach's whereabouts" – it's what I guessed would be the response to the first demand.'

'What's the second message?'

'Easy – it gives them a deadline: another week. 12th August.'

'Isn't that a bit feeble?'

'I don't think so. They've got a hell of a lot of arguing among themselves to get through. I think it's realistic to give them that sort of time. And I think it's convincing.'

'Suppose they show they still don't believe we've got him. Your second message isn't going to persuade them just because you set a time limit.'

'It was,' said Reno, 'expressed in emphatic terms. Barinski or else.'

'Reno,' said Carla, 'Reno, *carissimo*, do you think the Germans will really release Klaretta?'

Reno shook his head.

'I doubt it. As you know, I've always doubted it.'

'Then what?'

'Then we execute him, of course. We have always been ready for that. The world is waiting for it.'

'And meanwhile?'

'Meanwhile they've had the second message. Deadline. And they'll soon get an indication with it.'

'The indication –'

'Certainly. Vit's here. I want it done tomorrow.'

Carla said to him, despising herself for saying it, for thinking it, 'Wouldn't it be better to send a letter from him?' and heard without surprise Reno's answer, that a letter would simply confirm that they held Langenbach, that this was unlikely to be in doubt, that what was needed was an indication of their resolve, their implacable determination to put threats into effect.

'It must be done,' Reno said. 'They must be given that chance to see sense. If they want to save Langenbach.'

'Which you are already determined they won't succeed in doing.'

'Which I am already determined they won't succeed in

115

doing, and over which our comrades, generally, agree with me. But we want *them* to surrender. To come crawling, pleading. To admit to the world our strength. If we can manage it.'

'But, *carissimo*,' said Carla once again, 'you have said that you doubt if we can manage it. Doubt if they will release her. And so do I.' She looked at Reno, a very straight look. She knew the strain under which he was living.

'Reno –'

Reno sat down with a sharp cry, both hands clapped to his chest. Carla put her hands to her temples, aghast. It had happened twice in the last month and Reno had assured her that for this sort of violent indigestion there was nothing to be done.

Now he muttered, 'It's crushing me! It's crushing me!'

'Reno, you must –'

'Shut up,' he said, his face now grey. 'Shut up. It'll pass. It'll pass. One of those pills –'

'You know there are none left! I'll go out now –'

'No! It'll pass.' He slumped to the floor, sweat pouring down his colourless face. Again he gasped, 'It's crushing me.' And the blinding headache, the familiar blinding headache that came over his temples like a cold, stinging tide of acid, now made him close his eyes, groaning and shuddering.


'This happened over two weeks ago,' said the very senior official in the Federal Ministry, 'over two weeks ago, and the first of these demands was a week ago. The response of the Federal Government was prompt and correct. True?' His voice was a-tremble with rage.

'True, Herr Frenzel.' The voice of the less senior official in the State Prosecutor's Office of Land Hesse was also unsteady, although not with rage.

'And now you – you dare –'

'Herr Frenzel, it has taken some time for the legal opinion to become absolutely definite on this point –'

'"Taken some time"! And, when the first response to these

damned terrorist demands was drafted, was it not discussed with your office?'

'It was, Herr Frenzel.'

'And was there any suggestion, *any suggestion whatsoever*, of what you are now telling me?'

'None, Herr Frenzel.'

'And again, when this latest threat was uttered, and again the statement of response prepared and broadcast to the world in three or four languages, was there any such suggestion?'

'No, Herr Frenzel. The definitive opinion was only submitted this morning – the minute is dated 6th August. I read it this morning.'

'"Only submitted"!' roared Frenzel. 'Have your people been sitting for a year in some Trappist monastery, beyond human communication? This Barinski case is intensely political, you know that, your miserable lawyers know that, the women who clean lavatories at Kassel railway station know that. So the Federal Government is closely involved. And the ramifications are international.'

'Precisely, Herr Frenzel.'

'And yet – having permitted the Federal Government to say, correctly, courageously, inflexibly, on two occasions and with maximum publicity, that in no circumstances will there be concessions to terrorism and that the woman Barinski will stand trial –'

Frenzel paused, out of breath. He was gripping the telephone as if to crush blood out of it.

'– you now tell me that your office are advised the evidence against her is inadequate. And that her defending lawyers are likely to succeed in submitting that there is no prosecution case needing response.'

'That is so, Herr Frenzel. I hope I make matters clear. There is no suggestion that the woman is not, almost certainly, guilty of – well, on at least two charges. The difficulty is proof in court. The witnesses are totally inadequate.'

'Yet your people are sure she did these things.'

'Morally sure. But they have assured the Land Minister that a conviction is virtually impossible.'

'And so,' said Frenzel, 'the Federal Government has two choices. It can watch you release Barinski and drop the case against her, having just announced that it will never do so. It will then stand before the world as incompetent, cowardly and unprincipled. Nobody alive will believe in your damned jurists preparing their convenient legal opinion at exactly this time. They'll believe – the whole world will believe – we're trading her for Langenbach. The other choice –'

He began coughing, unable to prevent exasperation near choking him. He took a gulp of water. There was silence from the Kassel end of the line.

'The other choice is to let the prosecution go ahead. Even if she's acquitted – which you tell me is certain – we'll at least have been consistent. We won't have capitulated to terrorism.'

There was a gentle and apologetic clearing of the throat which came through perfectly from the other end of the line.

'In that case, Herr Frenzel, one imagines that the unfortunate Doktor Langenbach –'

'One does indeed imagine,' said Frenzel, grim and calculating, the minute of advice for his Minister starting to draft itself in his mind's eye, 'one imagines. A dead surgeon, of a distinguished German family in other times. Killed so that a murderess could be tried, acquitted, and save Bonn's face. One imagines indeed.'

He could now see, without difficulty, newspaper headlines as well as the main sentences of his minute to the Minister. Without further courtesies he slammed the telephone down.

# CHAPTER 7

Franzi lay back on the mattress and gazed at the skylight through which it was possible to see the pale blue of the sky which he knew was Italian sky. He wondered, always, exactly where he was. They had refused to tell him that, although, since they had explained their demands on the German Government, and since he had won his concession over the lavatory (the day before) his relationship with both Reno and Carla was almost cordial. Reno adopted the line that a little flexibility shown by Bonn would soon open doors for Franzi. And, curiously, Franzi felt that his own stated assumption that Reno could accept his word, would understand that concept, had made a bond between them.

'We'll have to take you to an agreed point, give ourselves a clear get-away, have some safeguards. You can understand that.'

'Yes, I can. Where are we now?'

But they wouldn't tell him. He could calculate, within very broad limits, from what he knew of timings. Once he said,

'After all, it was night when you brought me here?'

'Night? Not a bit of it. Not a minute after seven o'clock in the evening.'

He knew, or could work out, at what hour he'd been hit on the head, and if a journey thereafter (which might have been circuitous) had culminated at seven o'clock that set a certain radius of possibility. He had no idea whether they'd taken him north, south or west, but he reckoned that he must be somewhere east of the Appenines and north of Rome. And what did it matter, he thought, as bravely as he could. He had said to Reno that morning, the fourteenth day,

'When the German Government refuses to liberate your friend, Reno –'

'Comrade. Not a friend. I do not personally know her.'

'Ah! Well, when they refuse, what are you going to do?'

Carla was in the room at the same time, silent. Reno said, 'I am sure something will be arranged.'

The hint or possibility of some alternative negotiation? Franzi supposed, with a sick absence of illusion, that his life was on the line. They had not spelt that out to him. He did not want them to spell that out to him. He wanted no threats, no dark silences. He wanted communication, to encourage a sense of sharing, patiently, a vigil. Taking advantage of what seemed an easier atmosphere he had said to Reno,

'Would it not be a good thing for me to write a letter? To explain I am being well looked after, that I hope an arrangement can be made?'

Inane perhaps. Cowardly perhaps. But anything to get and stay on some sort of terms. Reno had shaken his head. Insofar as he could judge time, Franzi thought by the light it was now evening. He heard the outer bolts slide noisily back. Reno and a companion came into the room.

This was another one. Taller than Reno, slender, lithe, a good mover. Franzi could get nothing from his eyes and never at any time heard him speak but thought that the lips through the mouth slit of the mask were curved in something like a grin. Reno spoke.

'We're going to tie you up again for a short time, Langenbach. Then I will explain. Lie down.'

Franzi did so, watching not Reno but the other all the time. There was a reason for bringing him in and it could not be a welcome one. Reno retied Franzi's ankles and wrists.

'Now it is necessary to give you an injection.'

The word was so similar, *iniezione*, and Reno's gesture so emphatic that there was no mistaking the meaning although Franzi's vocabulary was still limited.

'An injection?' he said. 'Why?'

'Langenbach, it is necessary to perform a small operation on you. The injection will –'

'I understand injections,' said Franzi, trying to keep voice steady, 'and I understand operations. What operation?'

But the other man, the new man, had stepped briskly forward, a syringe in hand. Afterwards Franzi reflected that they had done that well, in the circumstances. Sense had certainly been dulled although he'd never lost consciousness, and he remembered, with regret, giving a drugged sort of scream or screech. But they'd thought it all out with care; they'd freed his wrists, separated the fingers of the left hand and placed them on a low block which the new one, as Franzi thought of him, had produced from somewhere. Afterwards Carla had materialised, and worked briskly and efficiently at what must have been the considerable feat, in a place like that without equipment, without training (he supposed), of stopping the bleeding. And later – how much later he didn't know, for the effect of the injection was again to blur the mind and obscure the passing of time – later the pain began, sharp, throbbing. And worse than pain was the sense of being helpless in the hands of creatures without pity. He had thought, only the previous day, that some sort of communication had begun, some sort of contact between fellow human beings, however opposed their interests, their aims, their understanding. Words had begun to produce exchanges, even something like cordiality despite those ghastly crimson face masks that blotted out and were intended to blot out humanity. And now they had done this to him.

As it happened, on exactly the same day as Franzi suffered 'the injection' and 'the small operation', on Sunday 6th August, Battisto Ponti was sitting at his desk for what he hoped was only a half-hour Sunday visit to the police station, not one mile from where Franzi was lying on his mattress. Ponti, police lieutenant in Perugia, was temporarily performing the duties of his immediate superior in that city, and he afterwards regarded the events of that morning as one of those breaks which come seldom and generally never in the life of a police officer of the detective branch of the service, in any country. Something which came not as a result of patient routine enquiry, ceaseless trawling of turbid waters, but unexpectedly, out of the blue. Ponti was told an elderly woman wanted to speak to someone 'about the Fiat car'.

'What Fiat car?'

His sergeant shrugged.

'She's a funny old soul. Said it had suddenly occurred to her. Not in Perugia. Lives in Umbertide. Signora Delmonte.'

'Bring her in.'

Things were quiet. She was dressed in black, respectable, not in the least poor, a widow probably. Ponti said, politely but with the air of a man averse to having his time wasted,

'Signora?'

'Signor *Tenente*, it's about the car on the television last month. The one when the American surgeon was kidnapped.'

'Ah,' said Ponti, 'that car.' He didn't feel cheered. Every Perugian who fancied wasting a bit of police time had spent the week following each TV notice explaining that they'd seen a Fiat, it *could* have been the one – all leading nowhere, of course.

'That car,' said Ponti, nodding, 'stolen in Perugia. In which it is likely Dr Langenbach was taken to Austria, as the newspapers have permitted themselves to speculate. Yes, Signora?'

'I don't notice car numbers –'

'Of course not, Signora.'

'But I noted the numbers it gave on the TV. I always do. My husband was a police officer, like you. In Umbertide. He died two years ago.'

Ponti looked at her with increased respect. Sympathetic respect. An excellent woman, clearly. And retaining sensible instincts, noting things down. Just in case. He nodded his head, a gesture of understanding, admiration, interrogation and deference. He couldn't recall a Delmonte.

'Signora?'

'There were two different numbers given on TV – two announcements – separate –'

'That is so, Signora. Let me explain – there's no secret about it. In the first announcement, we gave – the authorities gave – the car number as it was when found, and the description of the car when found. That is when it was – as we suppose

– driven from this area, where it had been stolen, driven to north Italy. Driven, it is probable, with the kidnapped Dr Langenbach. We traced this car – there had been effacement of the engine number, false number plates, new painting –'

The woman nodded. He could see she was enjoying the semi-professional detail, the sense of complicity in the pursuit. It reminded her of her husband, no doubt. She was being treated as something like a colleague by the '*Tenente*, someone a man could speak to and be instantly understood. That was good.

'– but we traced it. It had been stolen, without doubt, from a Signora Fantini, here in Perugia, on the Sunday morning, 23rd July. It was found in Masseria, in the Alps, days later, disguised. But of course we got the car's true number and appearance from Signora Fantini and we put that out in what you've referred to as the second announcement. The car might have been noticed, you see, in its proper condition, between theft and disguise. Or, of course, after disguise.'

'Thank you, Signor '*Tenente*. I quite understand. What I want to say is this. In the second announcement it referred to a mascot, a bird, stuck on the bonnet.'

'That is so,' said Ponti. Sharp old girl! The silly Fantini creature hadn't mentioned it at first. When they'd gone back to her and told her they'd found her car, that it had been almost certainly used in the Langenbach kidnap, that it had been sprayed, doctored, but was hers all right, she'd taken it calmly, identified it without doubt. Her husband had said,

'You told the police originally about the *rondine*, Angelica?'

'I think so.' She'd shrugged. Ponti had raised his eyebrows.

'*Rondine*, Signora?'

'Yes, it was a mascot, a *rondine*, a swallow, with wings spread. On the bonnet. I think I mentioned it.'

'I think not, Signora. I have your statement here. You gave us number, colour, type, upholstery. No swallow.'

'I had it fixed.' It had been knocked off, of course, and had not been found. Now Ponti said to Signora Delmonte,

'Perhaps you noticed a car with a bird – mascot of that type, at that time, Signora? You were in Perugia yourself?'

'No. I come to Perugia quite often but this was in Umbertide and I didn't see it myself. I've a young niece, a good girl but not very quick. She came to see me two days ago and we were talking about this and that. We were saying how dreadful this kidnapping is, and now this American surgeon –'

'German surgeon.'

'Yes, and taken from here in Perugia. Or the car was, which they used. They're everywhere. Devils.'

'And your niece?' prompted Ponti.

'She said, "I expect there are lots like that with a swallow". The car, she meant.'

'Certainly.'

'She said, "I saw one sitting for hours in the Via Tevere, here in Umbertide. It was there at seven o'clock on the Saturday evening when I went to visit Isa Montini for supper that weekend. And still there when I returned at eleven." She said, "Funny, to hear one described like that a few days later. But I expect there are plenty." She was talking about the same weekend, you see, the weekend it happened.'

Ponti did not think there were plenty. His attention had been held, and he said,

'It is a pity your niece did not instantly report this to the Umbertide police.' He spoke courteously but sternly. Signora Delmonte sighed.

'Just what I said to her, at once.'

Ponti noted down the niece's particulars and asked a few questions about where they lived, about the Via Tevere, the young lady's reliability, the car bearing the swallow. He thanked Signora Delmonte warmly. Half an hour later he spoke on the telephone.

'Signora Fantini? Lieutenant Ponti here. It's possible we might have further information relevant to the theft of your car. Could we have a few minutes' conversation, do you think?' He was exaggeratedly polite, tentative. She told him it would be easy to come to the police station.

'With Signor Fantini, if you and he wish it, naturally.'

'No, my husband's away for the day. He'll be back this

124

evening. A business trip to Turin, he stayed on over Saturday night.'

'Then if you would please come, Signora. I regret – a Sunday – but –'

'Of course.'

Later he sat looking at her with enjoyment. A theory was beginning to form in his mind. He was pretty sure she was nervous, more nervous than the circumstances warranted. He let a few minutes' silence lie between them, having given her a chair opposite his desk with careful courtesy, then sat pretending to write for a little. He affected to look carefully at what he'd written and then looked up.

'Signora Fantini, something rather curious has happened. Your car was stolen from near the University quarter in Perugia.'

'Yes.'

'On the Sunday morning, 23rd July.'

'As you know. A quick job, while I was having a short walk.'

'It was the car's first outing that morning?'

'Certainly. From our house. Not far away.'

'You went out in it the previous day?'

'I told you. I was shopping in Perugia, I took the car. In the morning. Again for half an hour only, around two. That was all.'

'Signora,' said Ponti, softly. 'Can you explain to me how your car was observed in Umbertide, in the Via Tevere, on the Saturday evening?'

Angelica looked at him with her mouth open. Ponti knew fear when he saw it. He knew that there was something here, something to go for. Where it might lead was uncertain. He said,

'Signora?' and Angelica shut her mouth and opened it again like a fish, a sweet, shapely little fish, he thought. And no sounds came. Ponti pretended to look at a paper on his desk and said,

'On Saturday evening, Signora Fantini.'

Angelica began to cry.

125

Ponti said, 'Perhaps this can all remain confidential between us, Signora. It depends. It may have no bearing on the kidnap itself, you see. But I must be told everything, you understand. Everything. You have a friend in Umbertide, Signora. Signor Fantini was away and you visited a friend in Umbertide.' He pulled a notepad towards him with relish as Angelica sobbed away.

Reno came into the little room without apparent motive. The bolts were clanked open, the heavy door thrown back and Reno entered. No companion. No gun. No tray or mug. As far as could be seen, no syringe or implements, no presage of further 'injection'; 'small operation'. He stood looking down at Franzi who was sitting as usual on the mattress with pain in his hand and something like despair in his heart. Reno said nothing and Franzi looked at him steadily.

'Why have you done this to me? What you did yesterday. You and that other one.'

Reno was breathing heavily. Franzi supposed he had run up the stairs. His voice was higher than usual.

'It was necessary to send evidence, convincing evidence that you are not only held by us but are in physical danger. Sometimes it has been necessary to amputate an ear, a hand even. We –' He paused, still breathing deeply.

'Thank you. I know what you did.'

'I regret the necessity.'

Curious, Franzi thought – but was it simply a spark of hope, however feeble? – curious that I almost believe in his regret. He said quietly,

'You know I'm a surgeon.'

'Of course.'

'My hands are important to me. And to others.'

'I know that it will not affect your ability to carry out surgery, Langenbach.'

Reno remained, staring at Franzi. He had not enjoyed the previous evening. Vittorio had followed him from the little room with something like a swagger.

'I'd be a competent butcher! The great thing is to make sure one's got the right tools. I had! Cleaver and clippers!'

'There's not too much mess?'

'Nothing to speak of. Carla will manage. I want a drink.'

And Reno, too, had a drink on that occasion and then showed his firmness by attending to the packing of a little box. He wanted Vittorio on the road as quickly as possible. Vittorio's strength was entirely recovered now, and the long journeys as courier between Perugia and the Austrian border were a positive relief for Reno. They absorbed some of Vittorio's energy.

Now the place was, once again, temporarily clear of Vittorio. Yet Reno knew that Vittorio might, probably would, have another, all-important, grim part to play, a part they knew he might play better than they.

Franzi was, as usual now, untied. His left hand was bandaged and Reno was looking at Franzi's face, not his hand. He seemed about to say something but it wouldn't come. The moment was full of tension and dread as Franzi continued to sprawl on the mattress and look up at his kidnapper, gaoler, mutilator.

And, perhaps, executioner.

For want of words, continuing from Reno's last remark about his surgical ability being unaffected, Franzi said,

'I hope so.'

Suddenly, Reno stepped back with a cry from behind the mask, a wholly unexpected cry. He clapped his hands to his chest. Unbeknown to Franzi it was a gesture Carla had learned to recognise and to dread.

'God! Oh God!'

God, formally disowned by Reno, showed no disposition to help him much. Reno sank to the floor, his neck beginning to turn to the ghastly colour of grime-stained putty.

'Oh God!'

Franzi's response was instinctive. He leapt up, moved sharply to Reno and looked down at him.

'Reno!'

Carla had heard Reno's cry, Reno's groan – heard and recognised. She came through the door as Franzi bent to Reno, ran through the door, maskless, calling out, oblivious of Franzi,

'Reno, Reno!'

Reno muttered, 'Carla, out of here – this is nothing to do with – with –' He tried to say 'Langenbach' but groaned again. Franzi took no notice at all and continued to look down at him. When he spoke his voice was different from that they both knew. Carla looked at him, lips parted, breathing rather fast. She seemed unconscious that she had not put on her mask. Reno made no move and hugged his chest. He knew that the sound coming from his lips was dangerously close to a whimper but he could do nothing to affect it. The pain was lasting longer than on previous occasions. He did absolutely nothing to impede Franzi who, with a swift gesture, pulled off Reno's face mask. I suppose, he thought afterwards, I had the upper hand and could have made a break. They were muddled, unarmed and one of them was having a seizure. I'm a poor man of action! But the thought had never crossed his mind. Instead he addressed Reno with authority.

'Reno, has this happened before?'

Reno nodded. He said, 'Indigestion!' and tried to twist his mouth into a smile.

'Perhaps. Please answer these questions, Reno. The pain always attacks the chest?' Franzi paid no attention whatever to Carla.

Reno nodded.

'Does it come on particular occasions? After eating, for instance?'

Reno felt a little better. The violence of the attack was fading. He croaked,

'Seems to come if I – sometimes when I – exert myself – run upstairs for instance – something strenuous –'

'I see. Reno, have you had any severe headaches recently?'

Reno had indeed had severe headaches, he admitted.

'Same thing. Stomach trouble. Everyone knows it gives you headaches.'

Carla started to speak. It had been only four days previously that he had been convulsed and she had said,

'You *must* see some doctor –'

And Reno had snapped, gasped,

'Shut up. It'll pass.'

Now she said – 'Listen, he's had this trouble, it's not the first time –' and Reno summoned strength and snarled at her,

'Shut up.'

Franzi said in a matter-of-fact way,

'I'd better examine you.'

'Nonsense! Who the hell –?' Reno was feeling a very, very small degree better.

'Better examine you,' said Franzi, 'but let me ask one more question. Have you, as far as you know, ever had any sort of –?'

He guessed, correctly, they had an Italian-English dictionary and he asked for it. Carla ran from the room and fetched it without a word. Franzi found the word he wanted. It was very predictable – '*convulsione*'. A fit.

'Any *convulsione*, Reno? At any time?'

Reno was, Franzi could see, nervous about the answer but he gave it. There had been, a doctor had said some years ago, a slight, a very slight tendency towards epilepsy.

'He said it was so slight it wasn't worth recording,' Reno lied. 'That it'd probably pass as I got older.'

Franzi said again, 'I see. Well, I'd better do my best to examine you. It would be good to take your blood pressure but we'll do our best with your pulse and my ears. Take your clothes off.'

'Now listen, Langenbach –'

'Take your clothes off. You never know, I might be able to help you. I want to listen to your chest as well as to take your pulse.'

And later he said,

'We'll see if there's any pulse in the groin,' and listened and shook his head, face serious, hands active.

Carla immediately assumed the role and appearance of a

nurse. It was a bizarre scene. It seemed to Reno to go on some time. At the end of it Franzi said, cheerfully,

'It's pretty clear, I think, what's causing these attacks, Reno. I don't think you're epileptic.'

'That's good!'

'On the other hand you've got very high blood pressure, which is causing the headaches.'

'So. You get me some pills? You tell Carla, here, what I need?'

'You need more than pills, I'm afraid. I think – I'm pretty sure – that I know what's happening, what's causing your pressure to build up, what's giving you these pains. It's not indigestion.'

'What is it?'

'I suspect you've got what we call a stenosis, a partial blockage of the aortic valve. That's a valve from the heart through which blood passes by artery to the lower half of the body.'

Franzi used the English anatomical words, realising that Reno couldn't possibly understand them literally, but using such emphasis and miming that he aimed to convey something of their significance. He thought, hoping desperately, that he had a degree of success. Reno looked puzzled and mulish.

'The pains are in my chest.'

'They would be.'

'So,' said Reno, trying to wear a contemptuous smile as he pulled on his clothes, reminding himself that this man, who now spoke as if he had knowledge of life and death, was in his, Reno's power. That Reno had had his small finger sliced off yesterday and could do more, and worse. That Reno intended to kill him, probably quite soon.

'So! I need more than pills! What, then?'

'You need surgery. Complicated surgery, of the kind I perform. You need it rather urgently, Reno.'

'And if not?'

'If not, these attacks will happen again, each time worse. And quite soon you will die. How old are you, Reno?'

'Twenty-five.'

Franzi looked for the first time at a young man with a high, intelligent forehead, a face which might well be attractive if it were not distorted with pain, grey, twisted. An interesting face, perhaps. Franzi had previously guessed Reno's age as a good deal more. His captor was a boy! Twenty-five! Franzi sighed and said,

'Then it would, I'm afraid, be an early death. But quite certain. A man with your condition cannot last long.'

Reno looked at him – 'You are trying to frighten me.'

'Yes, I am. In order to help you.'

'How?'

'By persuading you,' said Franzi, 'of the necessity of surgery. Soon. And that raises a lot of questions which are certainly of importance to you. And perhaps they may or might be of importance to me.'


Miranda was not a woman who affected horror at the prospect of spending August in London. Her gallery, although visited now and then by some from the hordes of visitors who thronged the capital in summer, depended upon the sharper, the discriminating end of the buying market, and that end came prowling round London more frequently in the autumn and the spring. Miranda did not do a great deal of business in August. But she was generally content to feel that life in the hot weather – and August 1972 was certainly hot and generally humid – was ticking over, that people felt under little compulsion to answer letters because 'everybody's away', that a sort of genial inefficiency was accepted as all-pervasive and was almost robbed of the power to irritate. 'August's no good of course,' her associates would say (even though their office staff holidays were scrupulously arranged to permit some sort of continuous manning), 'let's be in touch in mid-September.' Once, long ago, the fashionable world had found it degrading to appear anywhere in August but in Scotland or abroad – certainly not in London. That world had ceased to exist, or at least to have the smallest significance, but its shadow now fell over all society, whether or not their official holidays were

131

due. August, it was agreeably accepted, was a dead month. Either you went away or behaved as if you had. Miranda, plans to spend weeks in Italy miserably frustrated, did not find London itself especially vile; although, since Franzi's abduction and the horror which had followed, everywhere was vile. She had renewed acquaintance with the Rudbergs – it was a relief to be able to talk about Franzi to his friends and she knew that if they heard anything or received any approach they'd tell her. She maintained daily contact with Harry and saw him a good deal. She did her best to think about the gallery and business. And all the time she felt sick at heart – and suffered a good deal of physical nausea too – wondering what secretive, sinister exchanges might be in hand between 'the German authorities' and the evil devils who were holding Franzi.

One of the minor, unworrying eccentricities of August in Chelsea, where Miranda lived, was the lateness of the first post in the morning. Miranda assumed that half the postman strength was on holiday and that deliveries were reduced and delayed accordingly; or something. No doubt it need not have happened and she could have made a fuss, demanded some remedy or improvement, but she felt not the slightest urge towards that sort of agitation. Let the post come when it felt inclined. On Thursday, 10th August, it felt inclined at about half-past ten in the morning. Miranda, after one telephone call to the girl who minded her gallery when she wasn't there personally, had dressed slowly, walking about the flat, drinking a cup of coffee, looking out of the window, leafing through her morning copy of *The Times*, after a quick glance at the headlines of the *Daily Express*. There was nothing much happening today.

The front door bell rang. It was, as ever in August, an unknown postman; and a different one from the last week – the last occasion when they'd met because he was delivering something which wouldn't pass through the letter flap. Miranda smiled.

''Morning.'

''Morning. Thought it'd get through, but it won't, quite.'

'It' was a miniature parcel: brown paper wrapped round something which looked like a small box. Hard corners. About three inches long, two inches wide and two inches deep. It was the depth which had defeated the letter flap.

'Bit too thick, love. Hot morning again!'

'Thank you so much.'

The accompanying letters looked dull: circulars, one newsletter, perhaps a bill. She inspected the parcel. It carried a collection of stamps which proved to be Austrian and a postmark which looked like 7th August – quick work! Tearing away the brown paper she found a neat, rectangular box which might once have held a piece of jewellery, although no jeweller's name was inscribed thereon. The lid was secured by small strips of sellotape. Miranda pulled this off and opened the box. Cotton wool. She frowned. No note, as yet. An anonymous present from Austria hiding deep in cotton wool. She parted the top layer carefully. Then she sat down very suddenly; got up, equally suddenly, and rushed to the bathroom; and retched her morning cup of coffee into the basin.

On a layer of cotton wool, carefully disposed and undisturbed by its travel from Austria, was the tip of a little finger. Severed below the top joint. Exactly one inch as she was later, sickeningly, informed. Attached to the finger by an elastic band was a small, circular gold badge with a head delicately etched upon it. Round the head could be discerned a saint's halo. The finger was bloodless, colourless. Some of the cotton wool seemed to have stuck to it at the point of severance.


'I know it was posted in Austria,' said Venner irritably. International attention had made life in the Villach police station intensely disagreeable in the last few weeks and it was worse now.

'I know that,' he said. 'Everything pointed to Austria. Everything has been designed to point to Austria, and these people aren't such fools as to spoil the story. And I'm not saying he's not in Austria, I'm only saying that because his damned finger was posted to London from here it doesn't prove he's here.'

'Of course not. It could have been sent here, or brought

over the border from Germany, or Italy, no problem. For onward transmission. Still –'

'Still, what?'

'There's a natural presumption –'

'"Natural presumption"!' said Venner explosively. 'What's that got to do with detective work?'

'What else in hell is there to go on?' said his companion sulkily. 'There's the message. And this bloody finger. And the car. If the bloody Italians were any good they'd have got somewhere with the car. And they gave – the terrorists gave – today as their deadline.'


The discussion with the little Fantini and what followed took time. Ponti had instantly reported that the Langenbach snatch car had been taken not from Perugia but from Umbertide, probably on the Saturday evening. It hadn't led to anything very dramatic – 'So what?' in official language, had tended to be the reaction. Yet Ponti was a pertinacious man. He told himself that it had all gone too conveniently for the conspirators. A car belonging to a faithless wife, enjoying herself while her husband was away, lying about when and where her car was stolen because it compromised her, and losing the police some useful time because of that lie. It was all mighty convenient for them, Ponti said to himself, a very, very lucky break. A very happy coincidence.

He'd had several long talks with young Stefano. He envied Stefano. The Fantini piece was an appetising little number, no question. Ponti had been entirely honourable in keeping his knowledge between the three of them. Of course if it were all needed in evidence one day the world and Cristoforo Fantini would know the lot, but meanwhile –

They'd both been grateful – Angelica with tears, Stefano, less concerned, with a shrug. Ponti had dealt with him on a man-to-man basis. Frankly. And, of course, separately.

'I'm only concerned to find out who could have known she might be visiting you. Who could have known of your relationship.'

134

'Nobody, Signor *'Tenente*. I was naturally discreet. It's a man's duty –'

'Of course. But I wonder whether anybody might have just managed to suspect something, to gather an idea from a word you let slip –'

Stefano admitted, at the second interview, that a friend in Perugia, 'had an idea about it'.

Ponti nodded. 'Naturally, after all Signora Fantini is a very beautiful woman. Any man would be envious. You must have been proud of her. Do you think you ever spoke of her with this friend – in Perugia, you say?'

'Yes, in Perugia. Nobody in Umbertide knew. I protected her, always.'

'Of course. But this friend in Perugia – do you think he could have spoken about her, about Signora Fantini and you, been overheard?'

'He's a good friend. Loyal.'

'I'm sure. Did he know she was visiting you this week-end?'

Stefano hesitated. Ponti, expert, knew he was deliberating whether to tell the truth, and knew at once what it was. He waited patiently.

Stefano said, 'Yes, as it happens I told him.'

Ponti nodded as if it were of little importance. Then he shot out one word–

'Where?'

'Where?'

'Yes. Where did you tell him?'

Stefano affected vagueness but Ponti knew the young man could entirely recall the conversation. He said, 'I doubt whether there'll ever be the slightest need to trouble your friend, by the way,' and Stefano said,

'I think it was in a bar.'

'Ah,' said Ponti, and there was quiet again between them until he said, 'Which bar?' And nodded again at the answer.

'Stefano Bastico?' said the Bar Baglioni proprietor. 'Yes, certainly I know him. He used to come in pretty often when he was here at the University. Only once or twice recently. As a matter of fact last time he was here must have been mid-July. With a friend of his, Giovanni Arosto, I remember it because, funnily enough, another fellow, the only other in the bar, asked Arosto who Stefano Bastico was. Thought he was someone else. Arosto told him Bastico's name, that he lived in Umbertide.'

'And this other,' said Ponti, 'this other who asked Bastico's name, who thought he was someone else – have you seen him since? Can you describe him?'

He had soon established that Stefano's loyal friend, Giovanni Arosto, could have played no possible part in the kidnapping of Dr Langenbach. Arosto had left for a holiday in Greece on 20th July. It had been the first check he had made after the latest conversation with Stefano.

The man thought. He said that the young man had certainly been a stranger to Bastico and to Arosto; and Ponti said to himself that Arosto would be unlikely to recall more than did the proprietor. It was a small place and this seemed a shrewd, observant fellow.

'Has he been here since, this young stranger?' It was 8th August by now.

'I'm not sure. I think maybe once. He was a good-looking lad. I can see him now, a bit pale, big eyes, gentle voice. He asked about Bastico. I was here, behind the bar.'

'Had Bastico and Arosto been here long?'

The other chuckled. 'Quite a while! Talking women! I could hear them, muttering away, talking women! They were always the same! Always after some girl or other! Specially Stefano Bastico! And he liked the world to know!'

'He did, did he?' said Ponti. 'And that evening?'

The bar proprietor shrugged.

'Can't remember anything particular. He'd got something lined up which he was boasting about, but I can't say I heard what. I could have heard, so could anyone who tried, but I didn't listen. One such story's just like the next, truth to tell.'

'How true,' said Ponti. 'How very, very true. If this young man who asked about Stefano Bastico that evening – if he came in here again, you would recognise him?'

'Certainly.'

Ponti said that it would be desirable to inform him, Lieutenant Ponti, without the smallest delay if the strange young man appeared again. He assured himself that this was all a very slender chain of probability but one never, never knew. The odds were that the conspirators, the terrorists, the utterers now of appalling threats unless that German murderess were freed – freed very soon according to the last broadcast news – the odds were that these people had stolen a car from Umbertide which by pure chance was the adultress Angelica Fantini's car, had removed the distinguished Dr Langenbach after ambushing him in the Appenine mountains, had taken him to Austria. The odds were that Lieutenant Ponti, tabbing round Perugia in the August heat, was pursuing a wearisome irrelevance. But one never, never knew.


It was immediately after his diagnosis, in extraordinary circumstances, of Reno's illness that Franzi realised he was looking at Carla and seeing her, as he had just seen Reno, as a creature maskless, recognisable. He saw a girl below medium height, with reddish-gold hair and green eyes. The reddish-gold hair was a shock – it was rich and good to look at, and since it had hitherto always been covered by Carla's mask it now hit Franzi's eyes with the force of surprise as well as beauty. He had not envisaged Carla having hair of burnished gold. In fact he had not envisaged Carla at all. All he had previously noted, with disquiet, had been the animosity of her eyes, through eye slits. Now he made himself concentrate on Carla's face and hold her eyes with his own. If the woman had persuaded herself to hate him she had better look him in the face.

What he saw now in Carla's face, however, was not malice but puzzlement. There was suspicion, but not particularly hostile suspicion. Reno had left the little room, Franzi's cell, calling something over his shoulder which Franzi didn't catch. Presumably he was telling Carla to lock Langenbach up again. It all seemed wholly unnatural. Roles had been turned inside out and behaviour was unpredictable. Franzi went on looking at Carla and found he could not help smiling. Carla didn't smile back but there was a touch of relaxation around her mouth, and her frown was fading. Franzi saw, also with surprise, that Carla was exceptionally pretty. She was wearing jeans and a shapeless grey blouse but her scruffiness detracted in no way from her looks. He could tell from her slender wrists and ankles, the set of her head and the neatness of her that she had an excellent figure. Carla's was a delicate face, her expression curiously gentle and in no way brutalised or sneering. She had a small, pointed nose, a wide mouth, straight, thin eyebrows above those green, green eyes. And above it all that mass of truly splendid hair. She moved with grace – in his subconscious mind he had noted this before. Franzi remained standing, motionless, smiling at Carla. To have met these two face to face now was extraordinary. It was some sort of return from the dead. Sooner or later, probably sooner, they would, he supposed, be agitated by the self-betrayal of their inadvertent unmasking. That might be a dangerous moment. He would take it when it came. Meanwhile, concentrate on Reno. Helping this decision, Carla said,

'I should go.' She meant to Reno. The absurd, the almost social, half-apologetic 'I should go' to excuse disruption of a tête-à-tête, was so out of character with all that had happened between the three of them in the last fortnight that Franzi found himself smiling even more broadly. Instead of speaking to a masked gaoler who covered him with a gun and mopped his blood after they'd taken a butcher's cleaver to him he was addressing a charming-looking girl who was saying 'I should go' and didn't mean it. It needed adjustment.

'Carla, I was speaking the truth about Reno. I believe his condition is very serious. I understand these things, you know that.'

She nodded. He knew she believed.

'He needs, he probably needs, an operation. It might save

his life. There need to be tests, of course, but I do not think I am wrong. If he is simply left as he is this condition will kill him. The flow of his blood will be interrupted – you understand me?'

'Yes.' It was different, completely different, hearing her speak without the mask and he thought how attractive her quiet, serious voice sounded. 'Yes, I understand you. I have read books on medicine, too, books about the body. I understand what you say, understand what can happen. But Reno will not agree.'

'Then he will die, Carla. Perhaps very soon, perhaps a little later. But he will die.'

She sighed and said,

'*Momente*,' and darted from the room, not bothering to close the door behind her. Franzi heard her voice talking rapidly to Reno. She came back to him after a few minutes.

'I have been telling Reno, you are explaining to me the best treatment for him. I tried to teach myself to be a nurse once, he thinks I understand these things a little. He understands nothing. But I must tell you –'

She looked at him, apparently considering. 'There are others – friends of Reno – on a lower floor here. There is always somebody – watching.'

He nodded. 'Carla, you're warning me not to take advantage, not to try to get away. Don't worry. I know I wouldn't get away. And I gave Reno my word, remember?'

She shrugged her shoulders, as if despising such absurdity. She said,

'They would kill you and the outer door is always locked and bolted except when we're going in and out.'

'I understand. Now let us talk about Reno.'

'Reno will not agree to treatment.'

'I'm speaking not of treatment, Carla, but of an operation. A rare, difficult, dangerous operation. One which might have a chance of saving him.'

'What chance?'

Franzi could not say 'An even chance' in Italian and moved his wrist expressively to indicate a balance, a possibility.

'He could not do it. Who would carry out such an operation? On one of us? You don't understand – we have to live secretly. Besides – it's not an ordinary operation, is it? It must be a matter of money, publicity, arrangement! Such things are impossible for us. For Reno.'

Franzi said,

'Well, when they release Klaretta Barinski, I hope we will be saying goodbye to each other. At least I have told you what I think Reno needs. Urgently.'

'When they release Klaretta Barinski.' Carla stared at him. She could hear Reno's voice when she had asked 'Do you think they will release Klaretta?' and he had said, 'I've always doubted it.' That would mean they'd be saying goodbye, all right! Somebody would have the job of killing this tall, brown-faced young surgeon with the laughing eyes who was talking to her so easily. And if the Germans *did* release Barinski, and announced they would by the deadline, 12th August, under a week away? She could also hear Reno's voice,

'First she gets out. Then they get Langenbach. Dead.'

She moved her mind away from those recollections, those images, images she suddenly found disturbing in a way she had not been disturbed before. She heard, instead, Franzi Langenbach's voice. He was acknowledging her point about the improbability of managing such an operation for Reno. He was saying,

'Carla, you realise *this is something I could arrange*. If I had your agreement. And if you can get Reno's agreement. Carla, Carla, it can be done!'

For Franzi, too, doubted whether anybody would ever agree to exchange Barinski for Langenbach; and he reckoned, as he had always reckoned, that his life was on the line. But there was another thing now – a grey, twisted face, an intelligent, concentrated face contorted by pain, also under threat of death. Dr Langenbach might save him, knew how to try to save him. Roles were, or yet might be, reversed indeed.

# CHAPTER 8

Reno was in conference. Franzi had noted that on some
occasions Carla was excluded, and if she had no other duty
she would find her way into 'the cell' where she might change
the dressing on his wretched finger stump or find something
else to do.

And Franzi found that he now looked forward to Carla's
appearances. She was always cautious, always bolted the door
on departure, always opened it at first with circumspection,
making sure he was not about to attack, going through the
forms, almost, of earlier days when she had thrown it open
and covered him with a gun while Reno entered. But those
days seemed remote, and although Franzi knew that it must
be possible to devise an escape plan (despite the alleged,
unsleeping presence of Reno's 'friends' on a lower floor, in
whom he entirely believed) it would involve violence, risk,
and a most uncertain outcome. It would, furthermore, involve
breach of an undertaking to which he was now committed.
An undertaking which it was reasonable to hope might also
lead to liberty. An undertaking agreed four days before. An
undertaking which could save life.

Carla was dressing Franzi's wound, the unsightly stump
which embarrassed them both, evidence of a brutal, deliberate
mutilation. He had come to admire her skill, hands gentle,
deft, sensitive.

He watched the top of her head, bent over her task. Her
hair always gave him pleasure with its dark golden colour,
almost red, its curls cut very short, near-masculine, devoid of
adornment. This left her neck uncovered and Franzi noted as
ever how smooth her skin was, all of the same creamy colour
and texture, no mark, no line, no surplus flesh. She was
speaking very softly.

141

'It is true what you told me, that this – to lose this – does not matter to a surgeon?'

'True. It doesn't matter.'

He'd noticed that in the last few days she'd increasingly spoken about his work, his life, even his future. She must, unless she was a consummate actress which he doubted, believe he had a future. Or was he clutching at a straw?

He knew she had needed hours of painful argument with a Reno whose conscience was at first appalled by the idea that he was betraying the Revolution for personal survival. Franzi had left persuasion to Carla. His own personal survival was, he suspected, also so bound up with the success of her attempt that he knew Reno would pretend to regard any words of his simply as an exercise in self-preservation, would sneer and dismiss while secretly longing to assent and to hope. Reno, thought Franzi, had probably been through all this endlessly with Carla. He would have said,

'Langenbach just wants to save his own skin! He guesses they won't release Klaretta! He's in a funk! With reason!'

Sometimes Carla was able to join him in the cell and tell him, nervously, disjointedly, how her debate with Reno was going. He helped her. He could guess at Reno's pride and private agonies. He recognised in Reno a man of principle. Carla, needing relief, was able to blurt out a few of her words used to Reno when he spoke of betrayal. She had actually said,

'Why "betraying", Reno *carissimo*? You are ensuring that you can live and continue to work for the Revolution. And your action, our action, will have freed Klaretta Barinski and got the bourgeois pigs to come crawling. It will be a triumph! Why talk of betrayal?'

For Reno still insisted – and Carla, too, was insistent – that Barinski must be released as part of the deal. And Franzi, who thought this improbable, could only hope that as they got more and more accustomed to the idea that there *could* be salvation for Reno, so they would be more and more loathe to lose all because of German intransigence on this point. Nevertheless the hope was a slender one and he knew that if

142

Bonn refused all demands the odds must still be that they would both die. He and Reno. He by Reno's hand. Reno by God's. In spite of their talk he knew with cold fear that they must have threatened to kill him if their demands weren't met, and he knew very well about Reno's chances – that had been no exaggeration. Meanwhile, he had at least shown them another way, and to each other the peculiar pair pretended that the Barinski release was likely to be 'just a matter of procedure' for the threatened German authorities who must, Reno told Carla, be under considerable pressure now the Front had shown itself determined and implacable. Bonn knew they'd kill Langenbach all right, Reno said. Bonn must be scurrying around to find a way of letting Klaretta go and save its own face. But he doubted, Carla knew. And she knew that, by now, he did not in the least wish to kill Langenbach. He wished to fly with him to the United States. He wished for 'the undertaking' to come into effect. He wished to live.

'Have you always been a revolutionary, Carla?'

Since first mention of the 'European Liberation Movement' neither of them had spoken to Franzi of politics, motives or ideals. They had left him to guess. Carla considered.

'Since I could first understand anything, yes.'

'Why?'

She looked at him very seriously.

'Because there is no hope of decency or justice until the world is utterly changed. That makes necessary the destruction of this social order in order to rebuild another. You would not understand me saying "there is no hope of decency or justice". You probably think it's a good world, just one or two imperfections. It's been a good world for you. It's not a good world for millions of others. I'm one of them. Unlike most of them, however, I'm not meekly accepting it. That's why I'm what you have called a revolutionary.' She looked at him very directly, a challenging, uncompromising look. Then she sighed and left, abruptly, as if out of patience.

Franzi gazed at the patch of sky and rubbed his chin where

143

three weeks of captivity had produced the beginnings of what might be a handsome beard in time but was at present a grubby-feeling stubble. His mind was on Carla. 'You probably think it's a good world,' she'd said. There could have been angry bitterness in that, the pent-up expression of everything which gave her power and dedication. But there had not been bitterness. She'd said it as if from an enormous depth of sadness. It was not a good world, but sometimes, perhaps, she was visited by a reluctant dream of how things might be if it were. When Carla returned a few minutes later, apparently again dismissed from conference by Reno, Franzi said to her,

'You interest me greatly, Carla. You've known despair, to talk like that.'

'I used to live with despair. But since I've begun to understand the Revolution – the certainty of revolutionary change even if I never see it – I don't despair any more.'

'You knew despair as a child?'

'Yes,' she said gravely. 'Yes, I did. My childhood – it was not good.'

'You had a father and mother? Parents you knew?'

'I knew my mother. I loved my mother. She was – wickedly treated –'

'So was mine.'

She looked at him without much interest, her mind on a suffering, savage woman, once beautiful, always wretchedly poor. Her mother.

'So was mine. My mother was killed in a concentration camp.'

Carla nodded, her attention unwillingly engaged.

'German?'

'Yes, German. She had broken the law – indeed she'd broken several laws.'

'In that war?'

'In that war. My father was English – they weren't married, you see, nobody knew about it, people thought I was the son of my mother's husband who was killed in a flying accident – and he, my real father, was a prisoner of war in Germany.

He escaped, and my mother looked after him and helped him get away.'

'So he had a happy time, this escaper,' said Carla, 'and you were born. Later.'

'No, I was already there, you see my father and mother – their love affair had been earlier, before the war. It was a coincidence that they found each other again when he was escaping. I was five years old already.'

'And they caught him. And took your mother away?'

'Yes,' said Franzi. That was about how it had been, he thought. They caught him and took my mother away. He thought of his mother, Anna Langenbach, of a voice that held a caress in every sentence uttered, of eyes which seemed to know so much, a smile that held all love in it.

'Yes. They took my mother away. I never saw her again. She was shot in the place they took her to.'

'And you?'

'I was taken to a farm where a lot of children were lodged, children of people in concentration camps. When I arrived there they took my clothes off me straight away and gave me a sort of overall cut out of sacking. I expect all decent clothes were cleaned and sold.'

He lay, looking at Carla, remembering. Small for his age, he had stood, shaking with fear, crying. The farmer and his wife were grumbling to each other about another burden put on them without warning. The woman had turned to Franzi a red face contorted with irritation.

'Take those shoes off.'

'Excuse me, I –' Franzi had, as it happened, a bad blister on one heel and had been told by his mother to take off shoe and sock with particular care as it would need dressing again.

'Do you understand *orders*?' the woman yelled. Franzi had said, 'Yes, but I should –' and next moment, overall pulled up over head, found himself bent over the trestle table in the kitchen. Then came the first whipping. He never knew how long it went on. He heard himself screaming and remembered afterwards the shame of the tears streaming down his face, tears that he hated to recall, while indifferent to the memory

145

of blood trickling down the backs of his thighs. He'd been bundled out to a barn, cold, dark and smelling filthier than anything he'd ever experienced. There had been about twenty of them.

'They fed us by pushing a trough in. We used it. They kept us alive.'

'They beat you again?'

'Often. The place was – well, we slept in it, used it as a lavatory, vomited – several of the kids were near dead from stomach troubles. Sometimes they'd come in and pretend to be angry at the mess. Then there'd be whipping. And some sort of cleaning out. By us. With our hands.'

'Yet, you stayed alive!'

'Yes, in fact we *all* stayed alive. No child died when I was there.'

'How long?'

'I found out afterwards that I was there for three months. We were found at the end of the war. By the British.'

Carla said nothing, staring at him. There were voices just outside the room and the sound of a heavier door shutting, followed by silence. Reno's conference seemed to be over.

Franzi smiled at her.

'Anyway, you're right, Carla. For most of life I've been lucky.'

'What happened to your father?'

'I killed him.'

'You –'

'I killed him. In a car smash. I didn't know he was my father at that time, although I think I guessed. He was a wonderful man, and his sister was a friend of a relation who'd brought me up.'

('If he ever speaks about family,' Reno had said, 'do not seem over-interested but note it, remember and tell me. It may be useful later.')

Carla gazed at Langenbach, famous heart surgeon, prisoner of revolutionaries. She said,

'Well, you've certainly –'

But at that moment she heard a call from Reno, turned abruptly and left Franzi contemplating his patch of sky.


With Reno, too, communication had become possible. Reno eyed Franzi suspiciously, fearing, no doubt, pressure from the surgeon about his medical condition. Franzi avoided the subject. Instead he did his best to discuss, for the first time, the terrorist's philosophy.

'Reno, you are part of a large organisation?'

'Not your business.'

'Of course not, but "European Liberation Front", or "Movement" – it's a big name. Rather a lot to do just for you and Carla!'

Franzi's smile was sufficiently friendly, he was sure, to remove sarcastic inflexion, even in the ears of Reno. And he managed to make his stumbling Italian help the impression of sincere enquiry rather than smooth irony.

Reno responded, 'We have friends.'

'Yes, I know. You have said so. On the lower floor.'

'Not that,' said Reno contemptuously. 'I mean other groups.'

Franzi nodded, interested.

'A large organisation.'

Reno's natural reserve, his obsessive discretion, struggled with a determination to explain to this man that he, Reno, represented considerable forces. They might now blow up a street-load of passers-by here, kidnap a well-known surgeon there: but there was more to come. He said coldly and precisely,

'There is better co-ordination all the time. Many groups have had particular injustices with which to deal and have only thought in their own terms so far.'

'Like Palestinians,' said Franzi encouragingly. 'Like Basques.' Reno ignored this.

'All the time co-ordination will improve, year by year. And all the time experience is gained. And one day, perhaps soon perhaps not, more groups, each more experienced, will work to a completely co-ordinated strategy.'

147

'I suppose,' said Franzi, 'that a co-ordinated strategy means an agreed aim. Will you get that?'

'We will get that. When each group, with its individual wrongs to put right, realises that those wrongs spring from the general system which rules the world. And will only be put right by the destruction of that general system. And when that point of co-ordination is reached, I can tell you, the authorities everywhere,' he spoke the word 'authorities' with indescribable loathing, 'will be attacked directly. Not just people like you, Langenbach, who are a symbol, but the authorities and their instruments of power, of oppression, their police, their armed forces. Attacked directly. Co-ordinated attack.'

'Co-ordinated internationally.'

'Of course.'

Franzi, against part of his mind's judgement, referred now to 'the project', 'the undertaking'. To the possibility of saving Reno's life.

'Reno, I realise it wouldn't be an easy thing for you to come to the United States, to agree to the operation by me. I realise that you would need, perhaps have already needed, to consult colleagues.'

Reno looked at him, and Franzi regretted opening the subject. But Reno simply said, without expression,

'It is done. Provided it is arranged as I have proposed. They agree.'

'I'm glad.'

'But first Klaretta Barinski must be promised her release. That was our first demand. There could have been others.'

'Of course.'

'It was a single, a simple demand. And before you, or I or anybody else –' he paused and shrugged his shoulders. Franzi knew, at that moment, that they both hoped the same thing.

'– It must be agreed. Klaretta Barinski must be set free.'


The Rudbergs had flown from England to Hanover, a sudden decision. Marcia knew that although telephone contact was almost daily her actual presence with Lise von Arzfeld would

148

provide support of a very particular kind. It was 12th August, the day the world knew the terrorists' ultimatum expired.

Marcia and Lise had shared much, much of it sorrow. Her mind went back to another terrible day somewhere in what was now called the German Democratic Republic, an evening in 1945. Snow on the ground, an icy village street, Lise exhausted, Marcia exhausted after hours of breaking, sickening work in the hospital. An east wind whipping up the village street, bringing the sound of Russian gunfire. German troops emaciated, dead-eyed, shuffling through the village, pouring like grey driftwood from a sack into the hospital. Lise's eyes wild, her grip on Marcia's arm fierce, her voice without expression.

'They've done it!'

The People's Court had condemned Frido, Lise's brother, gentle, honourable, sweet-natured Frido, whose last letter, a declaration of love, was at that moment in Marcia's bag. The girls had known what to expect since a visit, agonising to remember even after twenty-eight years, from Frido's and Lise's father, Kaspar von Arzfeld. That visit had taken place some days before. The old man had left them in no doubt. Frido would die for what he had attempted.

'They've done it!'

And the authorities had indeed done it, hanging Captain Frido von Arzfeld by the neck until he died, writhing and twisting on a hook in Plötzensee prison. He had been a small fish in the dark lake of the conspiracy, but the court had agreed that almost the worst aspect of his guilt was his contemptuous refusal to be other than proud of it. 'What I did, I did for Germany,' he had actually said, pale, absurd-looking in his braceless trousers, unshaven. 'I did it for Germany,' he had said. 'It' had been participating (in a minor capacity) in the futile, botched attempt on the Führer's life. 'For Germany.' No shame.

The girls had shared that, shared the next terrifying weeks of flight and evasion of the Red Army that was by then raping and sacking its way through Poland, Prussia, Saxony, Silesia. The bonds around them were like no other bonds. After the

149

war, after some sort of return to normality in Europe, Marcia came often to Arzfeld. Lise had never married: her love, with both her brothers dead and old Kaspar gone two years before, was concentrated on Franzi. Orphaned cousin Franzi, cherished from infancy when brought by his mother Anna Langenbach on frequent visits to her cousins at Arzfeld. Franzi brought up, since 1945, as a son by Cousin Lise; a beloved son.

And now a son without the little finger of his left hand. On the previous day, the newspapers had given gloating coverage to the atrocity. Miranda had somehow managed to escape TV interviews, God knew how, Marcia thought. Poor girl, Marcia had said to herself, sick with horror, she's not even part of the family, why pick on her? And because they, too, could not answer that question 'Why pick on her?' the newspaper story writers had hinted, no more, that Miranda Wrench must be a 'close friend' of the missing Franzi Langenbach, so that a little salacity could be stirred into the August story, the off-season story of blood and flesh and pain and mutilation. Marcia had said, strongly and impatiently,

'She's a charming person and how good it would be if she and Franzi have fallen for each other. Miranda hasn't given that away although she's in a terrible state about him, poor girl, and there's *something* there. Meanwhile we owe Lise some support. Franzi is the world to poor little Lise.' Toni had insisted on accompanying her.

Lise met them at Hanover airport. When they were driving south towards the Weser valley above which her home sat, a place of memories for both Marcia and Toni, Lise turned her head. Marcia was sitting on the back seat.

'There's going to be another TV announcement this evening. Thank heaven you're going to be here. Toni too. I can't bear looking at that screen and listening to a stranger talking about Franzi as if he were dead. Or as if it were all an interesting detective story.'

'Anything new?'

'They've talked to me from Bonn, from the Ministry. They've been very good about it.'

150

'So you've always said.'

'Very considerate. They're going to make a statement which makes it sound possible – at least possible – that the Barinski woman might be released. They think that will seem to be meeting this so-called deadline of these terrorists, these people.'

'But surely that's hopeless, unless she *is* going to be released! And surely, as you've always said, it would be politically, as well as juridically and morally impossible to release her?'

'I think they will release her.'

'Lise! Why? Why do you think so?'

'Because they don't think they can convict her. The man was very cautious on the telephone, but that's my impression.'

'That's extraordinary,' said Toni, frowning. 'Every paper has painted her as being proud of herself. A blatant, self-confessed, self-glorifying, terrorist revolutionary. And now you say Bonn thinks a court wouldn't convict?'

Lise said, 'He hinted it's the evidence, the witnesses, which won't be adequate.'

They drove on in silence for a little. Marcia looked at the back of Lise's head, fine-spun straight hair drawn tightly back, narrow shoulders set square. A back of uncompromising principle, whatever the strength of love. And it was indeed strong. To Lise justice mattered.

Toni said, 'It will be difficult for them. Difficult not to let it seem to be a surrender.'

'Of course. I think the announcement this evening on TV will be quite vague. It's a question of preparing public opinion, using words which will make it look less like a surrender when it comes.'

'And it *won't* be a surrender; and mustn't look like one.'

'Exactly. That is how I understood.'

'What the hell does it matter?' said Marcia explosively. 'While they're fooling about, bit by bit, saying things to prepare German public opinion, what are these monsters going to do to Franzi? They've given their ultimatum. They've said it expires today. If your Government are going to accept it in the end –'

'It is not to accept an ultimatum, Marcia. It is to act as the terrorists demand but for different reasons. Correct reasons.'

'Well, for God's sake, at least let them do it, correct reasons or not, quickly enough and clearly enough to save Franzi! What's the point in going through all this and not getting the benefit in the end?'

'It is a political question –'

'Of course it is! But for Bonn to show itself standing firm against terrorist demands isn't the only political point. There's also the point, or the possibility, of them making such a muck of it that a great, a *great* heart surgeon gets murdered because the German Government couldn't make up its mind to say the terrorists' conditions would be met! For whatever reason!'

Toni smiled round sadly at his wife. She had never been one for equivocation. He said,

'I'm sure the Government here will have that very much in mind, darling. I don't for a minute expect they'll risk that. I wonder what their latest communication from the kidnappers actually is?'

'Perhaps,' said Lise, 'we'll hear that too. They seem to have made it a condition from the start, that everything is to be done in public. It's part of the game.' Her voice was steady but high-pitched and Marcia recognised the strain under which her beloved friend was living day and night.

That evening they watched a calm TV announcer say that the Federal German Government reiterated its only concern in the case of Klaretta Barinski, like all such cases, was with justice. No pressure, however humanitarian, no other considerations could outweigh that. Of course the evidence in all these cases was complex, and the German people, indeed people everywhere, could rest assured that prosecutions would not be brought unless the authorities were totally satisfied that the evidence merited such prosecutions. Meanwhile, . . .'

'Yes,' said Toni, 'I agree. There can't be much doubt about it, they're going to release her. And let's hope that will be the end of the matter, and quickly.' He spoke more cheerfully than he felt, and realised his words, with their note of rather

152

hearty confidence, were inappropriate. Both Lise and Marcia were unsmiling.

'Why fool about, if they're going to release her? Why not make it clear?'

'I think maybe – politically it will seem better –'

'Oh, *politically* it will seem better! But are the terrorists going to understand these nuances?'

'I think so,' said Toni, 'I really think so. Evil they may be but not fools, and it's pretty clear what Bonn means.'


'Josef?'

'Here is Josef.'

'Next in the sequence as follows.'


'If broadcast on 12th August on German TV indicates readiness to release Klaretta Barinski, then broadcast clear confirmation of that fact on 16th August and arrange parallel broadcasts in neighbouring countries. Thereafter, transfer instructions for Barinski and Langenbach will reach you within two days.'


'OK?'

'OK.'

'Got any problems?'

'None. Reno, this transfer?'

'Well?'

'You want me to help?'

Reno said, 'Vit's on his way to see you. Usual place. He'll explain.' He rang off. It was 13th August. A Sunday.

Earlier that morning Reno had done an astonishing thing. He had appeared to lose control of himself, not from anger but from triumph. He had swept into the attic apartment and seized Carla round the waist.

'We've done it!'

'Reno, Reno –'

'We've done it! The announcement last night, the Bonn statement –'

153

'Yes? Yes?'

'It was just an indication that they've surrendered. They can't say it all at once, there'd be uproar in Germany, giving in to terrorists, all that. So they've used weasel words, no prosecution of anybody without proper evidence, only justice will be a consideration, all that. There's no doubt about it. They'll release her. What's more, they'll say so in a few days' time.'

'Reno, *carissimo*, why are you so *sure*?'

'I've talked to Hel!'

'Helmuth' was the code name of a very highly placed comrade inside the German bureaucratic apparatus. Reno – and, he thought, one or two other groups – were permitted to contact Helmuth 'in emergency'. Unsure of exactly why the present circumstances counted as an emergency, but assuring himself that they did, Reno had spoken on the given telephone number. He had no idea of 'Helmuth's' identity, nor of what he looked like. The contact had been immensely worthwhile.

'Helmuth's had a bit of difficulty finding exactly what they're up to, but it's clear now, he says. No question. Just what I thought – their statement was deliberate fuzz. There'll be another within days. They'll release her. We've done it! Our last message, telling them to broadcast again, wasn't really necessary – they were going to do so anyway! Never mind – we've kept the upper hand, shown who's giving the orders!'

He was enormously excited. Carla looked at him with a smile, but with a relief in her eyes which was as deep as she had ever known. She said with a matter-of-factness she certainly did not feel,

'We'd better tell *him*!'

'Yes,' said Reno. 'We'd better tell him. And tell him we're now putting the next demand in! A free flight to New York, eh?' But he laughed, confident for the moment that those who had agreed to release notorious terrorist Barinski would not jib at further conditions. Still, these had to be sufficiently exacting – 'colleagues' had insisted on that. There must be no slip. Reno had been told his life and freedom mattered to the cause.

He did not, however, want to appear triumphant in front

154

of Langenbach. Langenbach might ascribe it to Reno's relief at the chance of his own survival, whereas Reno's overwhelming joy was at the success of the kidnap operation at getting Bonn – and no doubt others – to crawl. He said,

'I've got to go out. There's a lot to be getting on with. You tell him.' Still with a sense of huge exhilaration he left the apartment.


Carla's eyes had shone as she told Franzi the news. She pretended that her visit to 'the cell' was for daily changing of dressings on his hand but he knew that she was in a state of high excitement and soon she told him why.

Franzi, unaware of Helmuth's authoritative information, tried not to hope too much. It still sounded improbable. Release Klaretta Barinski without trial! To Carla, however, he said smiling,

'Well, I'll soon be operating, in that case! In business again!'

She finished the bandage and sighed. Franzi misunderstood.

'It doesn't matter. I'll be able to operate perfectly well. I need the first two fingers and thumb of my right hand, little else.' He smiled again and said, trying to joke, 'Don't tell that to Reno and his comrade whom I never saw. They might decide to send some more mementos of me to my friends.'

'Don't say that!' Carla said fiercely. She had finished the bandaging and had straightened, standing facing him and very close.

'A joke, Carla. *Beffa.*' Franzi's Italian had come on faster than he would have thought possible.

'I don't like such *beffa.*' Carla's eyes were wide open, sparkling. Pretending uncertainty as to her mood, Franzi said,

'I'm sorry, Carla. I know how much it matters to you that I make a success of my operation on Reno. If all goes well, and it happens.'

'Of course it must happen!' She was breathing quickly.

'I know it will. From what you've just told me they've agreed Klaretta Barinski will be freed. So it must be only details to fix about movement and so forth. Of course everyone

– they, Reno, you – will be suspicious. And I quite understand that every detail has to be passed to the other side very laboriously, so that nobody finds you all here.' Franzi had given all this a good deal of thought. 'You don't want suddenly to hear the Italian police on your stairs in a bid to rescue me, I understand all that! But we'll be fixed up soon. I'm sure everyone will agree to what we propose, about the operation and so forth.' Franzi was far from sure, but certainly the extraordinary decision she'd just told him about the Barinski woman cleared the chief obstacle out of the way. What an absurd situation, he thought. She's my gaoler, and I'm reassuring her, telling her not to worry too much, that of course I won't be rescued!

Suddenly he found that his right arm was round Carla's shoulders, and she had not moved away. Next moment he had put his other arm round her also, and said very softly, 'Carla.' And then Carla's head was on his shoulder and she was crying. Breathing very deeply and crying. Franzi found words, a mixture of English and Italian, were coming to his lips without any volition on his part. He also found his heart in an extraordinary state of turbulence.

'Carla, Carla! You are beautiful! You are like an adorable little wild animal, a gazelle, part gazelle, part girl from an Italian landscape, in a cinquecento picture. Do you understand?'

'Not a word!' she gulped.

'Carla, I'm in rather a feeble state, a prisoner, a poor creature, but you're making me feel strong. And, do you know, happy!' He pressed his lips to her forehead, her cheek, her ear. Hunted her lips, but she turned her head, to and fro.

'Carla.'

She whispered, 'I'm so frightened something will stop Barinski's release.'

'Frightened because then there'll be no exchange, and Reno won't be operated on, and will die?'

She gave a long sigh. Then, almost inaudible, she muttered, 'Frightened, because if the deal's off you're to be killed.'

'I've always supposed so, Carla.'

'And if they don't agree to this flight to America, to giving

156

us immunity – even if Barinski *is* released you'd be killed.'

'I see.' Franzi's head spun. But he knew she was telling the truth.

'It's arranged. And I deserve to die, too. I've betrayed a secret, betrayed the Revolution. You'd be killed because you'd be too dangerous to us. You'll only live if you can operate on Reno.'

Franzi said, very low, 'And the thought of them killing me frightens you?' He caressed the back of her neck with the fingers of his right hand.

'Yes. I want to prevent it more than anything.'

'Why?'

She said, so low he had to repeat the word, carefully, incredulously,

'Love, of course.'

This had come to Carla very suddenly and very blindingly. Her emotions had moved with frightening violence. First had been triumph at the successful seizure of young playboy surgeon Langenbach, class enemy, frivolous and spoiled embodiment of the exploiting classes despite his medical skill – which had been used only for the rich, only to accumulate further riches while Carla and the millions for whom she felt herself embattled suffered on, suffered, starved and died. Then there had been curiosity – curiosity aroused by his beauty, his charm, the atmosphere of the man. Was it not unjust, was it not irrational that so deceptively enchanting an exterior should surround so corrupt a creature? Was he, conceivably, better than Carla supposed?

A mask! Carla said to herself contemptuously, a pretty mask! He is part of the system and the more dangerous for his attractions! But she had then found a sort of pity. The young man did seem extraordinarily generous-hearted and open – it was unfortunate that he must –

Or must he? There were so many others who deserved to die. And at that point Franzi had become the possible saviour of Reno.

Carla cared for Reno, felt protective towards Reno, and at the same time revered Reno's cleverness, dedication and

157

strength of will. She was a disciple of Reno; but she was also in a sense maternal. Reno, in practical matters, needed Carla's support and Carla was proud to give it while playing her part, too, as an equal, a comrade. She felt responsible for Reno, and she immediately told herself that if Franzi Langenbach could save Reno's life (which she didn't question) then it was a clear revolutionary duty to save Franzi. And with this understanding came, more slowly, and faced by Carla reluctantly, the realisation that she was trembling with relief at the discovery of this revolutionary duty to save Franzi.

Why? Carla's life had been harsh, her memories chiefly wretched, her bitterness a poison until it found outlet in revolutionary belief, action and violence. Until it found a channel provided by Reno. Why be relieved that it was right for Langenbach to live? And when Carla asked herself this her other transcendent quality surfaced. For Carla was completely honest. She hated lies. She loathed humbug and pretence. She could be savage at evasion. Now she said to herself with astonishment and anger and confusion, I'm glad he must live – not because of Reno, but because I want him, myself, Langenbach. I contrive excuses to go into that room where he is. I treasure the moments when I change his bandage. I hear his voice at every moment we are apart, with its gentleness, its teasing, its music. I see his face when I close my eyes. And when Reno's arms are round me I pretend to myself they are Langenbach's! She could not yet say 'Franzi's' to herself though she knew, the world knew, that that was how he was known. And then, like a sword piercing her, he had asked 'Why?' Why did she want to prevent his execution? And she could say absolutely nothing but the truth, and faced the word and the reality for the first time.

'Love, of course.'

Franzi, too, was trembling. His condition was, he knew, extremely weak still. The only light in a great darkness in recent days had been when this small, beautiful, solemn girl had come to him; and when the hatred he was sure he'd first discerned in her eyes had been succeeded by something else.

'I think I love you, too, Carla.'

158

'Don't say it. I don't believe it. But I love you. Perhaps I always will. And I deserve nothing; and will get nothing. And I know I've only known you just over a week, but I don't want anything to happen to you. I despise myself for saying this, feeling this, do you know that? I believe in our cause – absolutely. But now this thing, suddenly! Oh –!'

'Carla,' said Franzi, 'I suppose we might both escape, together. Only I've given my word! Still, if Reno plans to kill me –' he tried to smile. Miranda's face flashed before his eyes for a second, and then disappeared, the vision fading. Everything would be comprehensible and perhaps forgivable one day, if one day ever came.

Carla hissed, 'Only if the deal's off –'

Then she said, 'We'd never get away from here, I can tell you that.'

'Not by a quick dash to the nearest police station?'

'Never! There are others, you know. And you know that in the rest of the building Reno has friends. Besides – I couldn't betray Reno.'

'Yet you love me, Carla.' He held her very tight and kissed her hair and her eyes.

'Oh I do, I do! But I've been – well, I've been with Reno a long time. I've been his comrade. I couldn't just quit and hand him over. Never! And that's what it would mean.'

Franzi said, 'I understand.'

A little later, the most natural thing in the world, he drew her down beside him on the mattress, loosened her blouse, ran his hands over her naked body, unzipped her jeans.

'Carla, Carla!'

Carla gasped 'Ah-h-h!', and her own hands were busy and soon Franzi found what he had almost given up hope of experiencing again, the sharpness of pleasure in another's body and the luxuriant relaxation of his own.

After a long while, satisfied, she muttered,

'I *won't let* them kill you! If the deal's off. If it comes to that I'll threaten them, tell them you've got to be released or I'll, I'll –'

159

'They'd kill you, too, Carla.'

She turned her face up to him and he pressed his lips to hers, tongue finding hers, hands moving over back and shoulders and buttocks, relishing the slender limbs, the silken skin. Again he said,

'I think I love you, Carla,' and knew he was near to meaning at least something. But 'love', Franzi thought later, with a small cold piece of his mind, what lying nonsense! People say my mother was 'full of love'. I believe they even say it about me, so I've heard. Yet I don't think I've ever known what it is to 'make love' in my life! I've said it often enough. I've gone through enjoyable movements often enough. I've taken pleasure in hearing a girl say she loves me often enough – and this little one, this pathetic, criminal little one uses her voice and body in a way that almost convinces me she means it. But love? To make love? It's not within my experience, alas, alas. He thought again fleetingly, painfully, of Miranda. That might have been love, but now? Wasn't it simply doomed? Again, with certainty, the thought came to him that Miranda would understand how he was behaving now and would, extraordinarily, not regard it as betrayal.

'I think I love you, Carla.'

Later she whispered,

'And I will come with you. To America. It was Reno's own idea.'

'Little love –'

'Yes, I will come with you!' She twined arms and legs round him once again.

Later again he murmured,

'Where are we?'

'In each other's arms. What more do you want to know?'

'I want to know the name of the place which has given me so much pleasure – as well as so much pain.'

Carla sighed. 'We are in Perugia.'

'Ah!'

Two days later, Reno appeared to be suffering from one of what had become recurrent fits of remorse. He had by now explained fully to Carla the details of what had been proposed to the German authorities by way of the latest demand, and about transfer. She was, he said, most certainly not to discuss these with the prisoner, Langenbach. As if to remind her and himself of their continuing relationship as gaolers to Franzi he had taken again to referring to him with a certain rather hostile formality.

Reno said that 'they', the enemy, would make much of Reno apparently seeking to save his own skin. Carla, knowing her man, bent every effort to reminding him that the first 'conditions' offered after Franzi Langenbach's kidnap were being met in full. The German Government had agreed to Barinski's return. Granted they were pretending that she would have been released in any case, but that would fool nobody. Barinski was being released under pressure of the European Liberation Movement, and the entire Western world, following every step on TV, was aware of the fact.

'It's a triumph!' Carla said repeatedly. As to Reno's safe-conduct (and her own, for Reno had made it a condition that she would accompany him under similar safeguards), 'they' might well dishonour that if they could.

'But we'll have that woman,' said Carla. 'The Wrench woman. I'm sure of it. They won't break their word *and* sacrifice her. No charges, from any quarter, on any matter,' Carla said.

'Listen, Carla, they've not agreed any of this yet. You're talking as if it's all sewn up. It isn't.'

'Reno, you've been so confident up to now. Surely –'

'Surely nothing. It'll be as hard for them, in many ways, to agree not to have our blood as it must have been to release Klaretta. And don't forget they've got to hand the woman over, to make sure there's no double-cross. And to make sure your surgeon friend doesn't forget his skill!' He spoke with deliberate roughness. Carla chose not to notice 'your surgeon friend'.

Reno said, 'Then we must start again, as soon as possible.

As soon as all this is quiet and we can establish different identities, a new base –'

'Yes, of course. And you will be well, at last. And the slate will be clean.'

But when she said this a second time, Reno said,

'Carla, you have not lost faith because of any of this, have you?'

'Lost faith?'

'In the Revolution. Been corrupted.'

'What could have corrupted me? The prospect of a few weeks living, isolated, in America? I dread it.'

Reno shrugged his shoulders and said he didn't know what could have corrupted her, it was simply that she didn't seem the same. He never mentioned Franzi Langenbach to her except in severely practical terms, planning. Once, the day before, he had felt something rising within him and knew he was about to shout,

'You're not in love with that playboy doctor, are you? If I thought that, I'd call the whole thing off and kill him! And you!'

But he knew, from certain awful indicators, that such exertion, such emotion would bring on an attack. He said nothing.

'We've got to make it all clear now,' said Rudolf Frenzel, very senior official in the Federal Ministry in Bonn. 'We've done our best, implied in our last broadcast that the case was a difficult one, that the State Prosecutor was deliberating carefully on the chances of a successful prosecution. We said, "Naturally, the German authorities would not be inhibited from discontinuing prosecution by spurious fears of appearing to bow to pressure. The only principle to be followed is that of justice." We said all that. I doubt if a single viewer throughout the Federal Republic believes a word of it. They think we're running scared.'

'And we're not.' His immediate subordinate removed his spectacles and polished them.

'And we're not. But the fact is Barinski's not going to court, because the evidence has collapsed. And this evening we've got to make that clear, utterly clear, on TV. This evening, 16th August, just like those bastards said. Then we sit and take what's coming. We get called every name in the book – cowards, betrayers of fellow nations threatened by parallel acts of terrorism, unfit to govern. The lot.'

'But we also sit and wait to be told what to do with Klaretta Barinski. And how to obtain Dr Langenbach.'

'That's right.'

'Provided, Herr Frenzel, that the terrorists mean what they say.'

Frenzel said that they might try to double-cross but that there was an escape clause in the planned announcement which would delay the physical departure from prison of Klaretta Barinski.

'We're going to say, "When certain investigative formalities have been completed". At least that'll hold her until they've made the contact.'

'I wonder how they'll make it?'

'As before, I expect. Patched-up printed message to a police station in Austria. Tracks are covered pretty well, I must say. Every message has been posted from somewhere different in Austria. Austrian forensic have got absolutely nowhere with the documents themselves. And nothing to go on about who-ever posts them, no leads at all. Let alone leads to Langenbach. Anyway, we'll hear from Vienna within minutes of anything coming through. At least that line of communication is working fast.'

That line of communication did indeed work fast, for on the second morning following the news to the world that no prosecution of Klaretta Barinski would take place at Kassel in the Federal Republic of Germany as anticipated, at eleven o'clock on that morning of 18th August, Frenzel stared at a telex on his desk which contained the text of a message, constructed from cut-out letters from Austrian newspapers as previously, and delivered by ordinary post to Villach police station one hour before.

Frenzel asked his immediate subordinate to come into his

office, using a voice of deceptive mildness. He looked at the telex as if his eyes could scorch it out of existence. He did not look up when the other entered. He said in a low voice,

'It's come. The terrorists' response. It's come.'

'Details of the proposed transfer, Herr Frenzel? Barinski to fly to Libya? Something original?'

'Original!' said Frenzel. 'They've got a completely new demand. They want one of their own bastards to come out with Langenbach for medical treatment, provided Barinski's freed. And to make sure he's safe, and the medical treatment works they want another hostage.'

'Named?'

'Named. And English. So now London's in on the act.' He stared at the words in front of him. The name Miranda Wrench meant nothing. 'I'll show you the telex. And they demand that the whole matter be completed by a given date. 29th August. Ten days from now.'

# CHAPTER 9

'Marcia, it's Harry Wrench.'

It was 19th August. The Wrenches, brother and sister, had come to rely a good deal on Marcia and Toni Rudberg in these dementing days. They sensed, although without knowledge of detail, that the Rudbergs, middle-aged and now seemingly so placid, so secure, had come through a good deal in life and the sense was reassuring. These people, both Harry and Miranda felt, had strength, and they were close to Franzi.

'Harry!' Marcia said, affectionately, easily. There had been frequent telephone contact.

'Have you heard this business? Seen the latest on TV?'

Marcia, as it happened, had not. They had been away until evening and would probably watch the ten o'clock news. It was now seven-thirty.

'They've put in another demand. They want Miranda handed over as a hostage.'

Marcia, astounded, could hear the effort Harry was making with his voice. 'They want *Miranda*! But Harry – how on earth does your darling sister come into this?'

'They must,' said Harry, after a small, painful pause, 'have got her name from Franzi, mustn't they? The Barinski woman is going to be freed, the Germans say, and yet Franzi is still being held – in other words these beasts are going back on their side of the deal. Unless Miranda's handed over. There's some business about one of them needing Franzi to operate on him or her. It's all insane.'

Marcia, stunned, said, 'Harry, it mustn't happen. It can't happen. These people are capable of anything. Franzi himself would be horrified to think that this – this was being demanded.'

'I daresay,' said Harry, 'I daresay. But my sister is a very strong-minded lady.'

'You mean she wants to do it?'

'Yes,' said Harry, 'that's what I do mean. She wants to do it. In fact she's sure that – well, that it's what she *must* do. She's had the people from the Embassy on the telephone, and various – various others. Official people.'

'Who've persuaded her.'

'No, they've been completely fair, but they made contact before she could see it on TV, you see. Warned her. Since then they've explained, no obligation, up to her, all that.'

Marcia could imagine. Something a little more comforting moved in her mind. Maybe the German – or Austrian, or Italian, or British – authorities were being more ingenious than the world could suspect. Maybe they were thinking, planning. Maybe a trap could be set.

With Miranda as bait! The idea was revolting. Harry was saying something:

'. . . I don't know her, but I wonder how she feels about all this, she's his closest relation I know, it must be hard for her –'

'You mean Lise von Arzfeld. I'm going to talk to her on the telephone right away now. We went over to see her for a day or two. Lise is likely to be horrified at the whole idea, however much she loves Franzi. Let's keep in touch, dear Harry. Is it possible to talk to Miranda, though God knows what I'd say?'

Harry said, carefully, that Miranda, at present, could not be contacted, and that he'd keep the Rudbergs informed. And it was not until after watching the next television news that Marcia made contact with Lise, so that when she heard that thin, confident voice on the line she already knew the complex, indeed the fantastic details of what was now being demanded in return for Dr Franzi Langenbach.

Klaretta Barinski was to be freed and put on an aircraft flying to Tripoli in Libya. As viewers throughout Europe and America learned with scepticism, the Federal German

166

Government had decided that there was no case against Barinski which could go to prosecution for the various acts of terrorism with which her name had been linked in the previous two years. It appeared, therefore, that the Barinski part of the kidnappers' conditions raised no problems as far as Dr Langenbach was concerned.

The second part of the deal was composite. Two persons, one male, one female, would be with Dr Langenbach on his release, release which would only follow information that Klaretta Barinski had emplaned safely. These persons must, with Dr Langenbach, be flown to New York where a surgical operation was to be performed by Dr Langenbach on the man; Dr Langenbach had agreed to this. No investigation was to be made, no prosecution initiated of these two persons. While this was happening, and until the safe return of the two to a place of their choice after the operation, an English woman, by name of Miranda Wrench, was to be transferred to the custody of the European Liberation Movement by whom she would be held, safe and unharmed, as surety of the deal.

'Their problem,' Lise von Arzfeld called down the telephone in her clear, penetrating tones, 'is political. There is a political storm here. People are saying the Government are giving in to terrorism, and telling lies to pretend they are not doing so. Can you hear me?'

'Yes, of course, Lise.'

They had stayed three days at Arzfeld and been home now for a dragging forty-eight hours.

'Now it is very political. Those people in Bonn who oppose the Government say they are weak, unfit to rule, that there will be more terrorism because of this.'

The criticisms of weakness of governments for yielding to force and thus encouraging terrorism as an epidemic had been rising throughout 1972. These things provoke imitation, too, people said, whether referring to Franzi's kidnap or earlier outrages, and whether speaking of Italy, Germany or Ireland. Only three days before four people had been killed and two wounded in Sardinia in an attempt to kidnap a local doctor.

These things are contagious, people said grimly, fearfully, their anxieties and expectations fixed on governments.

'I can imagine, Lise. It's being pretty fully reported in the English papers too, you know.'

'Yes, and the people who attack the Government from the left say they are doing this because of pressure from the Americans. They even say, would you believe, that if Franzi was not a distinguished man, it would all be different.'

'It *would* all be different, Lise. If he were not a distinguished man he wouldn't have been kidnapped.'

'I mean, they pretend to think the Government is influenced by Franzi being a Langenbach and so forth. The reverse, I should think! With our Government! But it all becomes more stupid all the time.'

'Of course, Lise. Very hard, especially hard for you to hear all this sort of comment. But what do *you* think?'

'Think about what?'

'About why they've agreed to release Barinski?'

There was a pause, and Lise said, slowly, 'I believe the Government. I think they do this because it is true. Because they cannot argue a good enough case against her, from the evidence they have. As I said when you were here.'

Marcia wanted to talk quickly of Miranda but she knew that Lise had to expound a subject in her own time and she said,

'The timing, in that case, was bound to make them – the authorities – vulnerable, wasn't it? Vulnerable to the accusations of weakness everyone's now making?'

'Of course. But what could they do? Make it look better by waiting till Franzi's been murdered, and then dropping their case?'

'And what do you think of the other conditions, Lise?'

'It is terrible that they have involved this girl, this Miranda Wrench, is it? I don't understand it. Is it Franzi's girlfriend? He's never spoken of her to me.'

'A lovely girl. We know her.'

'They must have got the name from him, Marcia.'

'Yes, we don't know about that – she and her brother were going to stay with him as you know. People there, in Italy, in the house and village, may have known her name.' But it sounded improbable, she knew, and said again, 'Anyway, what do you think of it?'

'As I say, terrible. It is me they should demand, me they should hold. I would be prepared.'

'I know you would. Anyway, I suppose the police find communicating with the brutes, bargaining with them, rather difficult. It all seems to be done through public announcements. Both ways.'

'It is that which they want. It is the public attention which they want, this European Liberation Movement. Ach, they make me sick! Spoilt children, I expect, playing at grievances and revenge, pretending they are oppressed so that they can smash things and kick people like naughty children. I could tell them about European Liberation! I could tell them what real tyranny, real terror, real atrocity means! Liberation indeed! I could tell them!'

'Yes,' said Marcia, 'you could, couldn't you. And so could I. And now this poor, wretched girl, who I suppose is under some sort of guard, who's presumably got some protection from publicity, who's living under arc lamps already, ever since they sent her –'

After renewed assurances that they would keep in touch at all times Marcia rang off. This was a nightmare of a kind she supposed she had long outgrown. Outgrown in 1945, in fact, when all had been pain and terror and flight. Mutilation, threat, murder, hostage, incarceration! These things, common currency for long, dreadful years, were now again being used, were again disturbing the decency and normality of everyday life. Not used by the ostensibly powerful now, but by those who proclaimed themselves in revolt against power. And there didn't appear to be a damned thing anybody could do about it. She stared at the blank television screen in the inner hall at Bargate as if it was an enemy.

During the BBC one o'clock radio news on the following day, 20th August, they learned that,

169

'It appears that details for the safe delivery of Dr Langenbach, who has been held by kidnappers, have now been
settled. Dr Langenbach is expected to be released shortly.'

'It means,' said Toni Rudberg, 'she's agreed to go. I suppose
she's being briefed, and that our people don't intend to stop
her. The price of Franzi. She's agreed to go!'

Reno was very busy. There was a great deal to organise, consul-
tations which necessitated long absences from the Perugia
apartment, cryptic telephone calls. He had to arrange additional times for calls to Josef, a thing he disliked. Frequency,
emergency – all these things could disrupt security. Reno was
careful of himself now – he knew, the doctor-prisoner Langenbach had emphasised, that exertion could bring on the sort of
attacks which he dreaded, which knocked him out.

Which the doctor-prisoner Langenbach could cure. A cure
which would restore him, Reno Vanetti, with full strength
once again, to the prosecution of revolutionary terror in
Europe. Meanwhile there was much to be done. He told Carla
a certain amount of what was planned, watching her carefully.
It was inevitable that he had to leave her to her own devices
a good deal. She was very quiet these days; he refused to think
about her and Langenbach. Telling her about the transfer –
enough detail, not too much – was a relief, a linkage, a restorer
of confidence.

'It's like this. We've reached the stage where, just for once,
there has to be direct telephone contact between Josef and
the Italian police. Of course they'll put the Austrians on to
the call, trace the call and so forth. They won't catch Josef.
He's got clear instructions. He's asked, in his last letter to the
Austrians, that the Milan police main headquarters be ready
to respond to a telephone call, code name Rosa, at a particular
time and day, when details will be given of how the exact
transfer's to be done. The Italians will put it around all right.
The whole world is watching us!' Reno's eyes were bright.

Carla said, 'Why Milan? All correspondence has been with

170

the Austrians! And it's Bonn that has to release Klaretta! And the English girl will presumably –'

'Milan, because we're flying to America from Milan. You, me and him. And we're going to move to nearby, to near the airport, the day before. I've got it fixed. First they deliver the Wrench girl to an hotel in Vienna, right?'

'Right. On what day?'

'On Friday, 25th August. Four days' time. It's an ordinary sort of hotel, and the Austrians were told to keep that bit to themselves, not broadcast it. You can have too much of a good thing, and nobody, not even Josef, wants the girl on TV at every stage! So she's told to wait for a message at the hotel. She gets it, a telephone call. Next morning.'

'And it has to be traced. Any call to Signorina Wrench at that hotel has to be traced.'

'From a call box in Munich, no problem. Josef has that fixed: the comrade melts away into Munich. The Wrench girl is told by the telephone call to – to obey certain instructions. In Vienna.'

'And she'll be followed, of course, from the hotel. The police will watch her day and night.'

'Naturally.' Reno chuckled. He seemed to Carla in a better humour than for many days. He said, 'Really, Josef is a wonderful fellow, truly wonderful. Ingenious!' He chuckled again. Carla knew better than to question further at this stage. For the moment Reno's face wore its pleased, secretive look.

'Then, when we know Josef's got her, provided we know Josef's got her, we turn up, the three of us, two days later, at Milan airport. Where our tickets to New York will be held in Dr Langenbach's name at the Pan Am desk.'

'And where he's met by his devoted family, while you and I are led away by the Italian police.'

'Not a bit of it,' said Reno, still in an excellent humour. 'Not a bit of it. They've been told, and one must hope that our doctor friend's finger helped convince them, that when we say a prisoner's life – and limb – depends on their keeping strictly to their bargain we mean what we say. And we'll still have a prisoner.'

Carla had been looking at him, frowning.

'Reno, all this happens after they release Klaretta, right?'

'Right. That's the first step. That's agreed. She flies to Tripoli from Frankfurt. That was all announced publicly. No problem.'

'It's a precondition.'

'Of course. No Klaretta, no deal. But why –'

'Reno, suppose something happened to stop that? Fresh charges against her, or something?'

Reno stared at her.

'Why on earth suppose that? I never thought we'd get her, as you know, but now they've agreed, they've given in to our first demand, we've won that game, the other side are being abused for surrendering to us, it's wonderful! I didn't think it would happen, but it's happened. Why should they go back on it? She'll be flying on 27th August, Sunday – two days after the Wrench girl turns up in Vienna.'

'And if she doesn't?'

'Doesn't turn up?'

'No, Klaretta. Doesn't fly.'

Reno sighed impatiently.

'I told you. No Klaretta, no deal.'

Carla looked at him. 'And if no deal, then you're going to die, Reno. I know that now, and so do you. Die quite soon.' She kept her voice as steady as she could. Reno shrugged his shoulders and avoided her eye.

He said, 'Yes, die. I suppose so. And someone else will die, too. You know that.'

He preferred not to watch her face for indications of which contingency disturbed her most particularly. He said, apparently without direct consequence,

'Vit will stay here. He's doing a small job now, in Vienna. Part of the preparation. Then he's coming south. He'll stay here. Mind this end. In real emergency I've told him how to make contact with Josef. But only in real emergency. He's never met Josef, remember?'

'I know. What sort of emergency?'

But Reno had shared his plans enough for the time being

172

and, indeed, to an unprecedented extent, even with Carla. He said shortly,

'You can leave that to Vit. It's unlikely to arise. And we'll be in America, under the good Dr Langenbach's protection. We leave here with him on Friday, Carla. This Friday, 25th August.'

Carla nodded. He had indicated that it would be soon. She had no idea how one prepared for the extraordinary, disturbing adventure of flying with Reno and with Franzi into enemy territory, flying to America. Carla supposed she would simply take her few small possessions in a holdall Reno had bought her. Reno, and Reno only, held money. Papers? They never possessed such. Reno would see to all. Now Reno was looking irritable again. He said,

'Langenbach will get a nasty shock when he sees his friends and learns he's free but his girl has been handed over to Josef, to make sure I'm looked after. You and I.'

'She's not his girl.'

'How do you know?'

'He's frank about it.' But Carla was pretending. Franzi had never mentioned Miranda.

'I said he is *not* to be told what we've stipulated about the woman! He'd start to make a fuss –'

'I know, and I've not told him. But he's spoken about her – you know, in conversation. Like when you mentioned to him that he'd called out her name.'

She lied calmly, not looking at him. Reno eyed her grimly. He felt less in control than once he had been. Carla, Vittorio, Josef, all these people had formerly moved exactly as he had prescribed. His had been the directing intelligence. Now it was still so, but more and more the others interposed ideas, made conditions. All this had come about since he, Reno, had become a sick man, a problem, one whose life was to be saved as part of a deal. And because the single, pure aim of revolution was now vitiated by this device to save his, Reno's, miserable life it was as if his fire was being quenched and the others were no longer warmed by it; or scorched by it. The virtue had gone from him, he felt bitterly.

173

'Nonsense,' Carla said when it was necessary to respond to his self-accusations. 'There's no difference between using revolutionary means to save Klaretta Barinski from a bourgeois gaol, in order to carry on revolutionary work, and using revolutionary means to save you from dying, to do the same. The aim's identical.'

But Reno did not believe her.


Miranda found, as they had said, that a room was reserved for her in the Hotel Donau Ufer. Some way from the Danube, despite its name, it seemed clean and unsinister, a small place in what, in her taxi drive from the airport, she thought she could identify as the eastern suburbs of Vienna.

They had said to her in London,

'Naturally, Miss Wrench, try to note everything you can, everywhere you go. So far as that is possible.'

'Naturally.'

'You can rest absolutely assured that our Austrian friends will be watching you all the time. Of course that must not appear to be so. For Dr Langenbach to be handed over – or, rather, brought over by these two persons, terrorists as one must call them – for that to happen, it's obviously essential that they must assume they have you in their custody, without the authorities having any knowledge of where you are.'

'Obviously.'

'But you can be confident that the Austrian police will, in fact, be in absolute control of the situation, unseen. If we, ourselves, were not sure of that I know that our people here would never approve your – er, volunteering – as you have.'

'I suppose not.'

'May I say, Miss Wrench, how much everybody admires what you're doing? It won't be nice, and we've tried to prepare you as much as we can. But it won't be nice. For instance, they'll blindfold you. Bound to. We – everybody, including the Americans of course – have agreed to the terms of the last message, which made absolutely clear that unless you are well

174

treated these two thugs can expect nothing but a very long prison sentence.'

Miranda had said nothing. She was unimpressed by talk of threat and counter-threat but she supposed they had to say all this.

'And, of course – as I've explained – we hope it won't be very long. But that must be left to our Austrian colleagues. Meanwhile, do everything they tell you. Don't argue. Just do as they say. At all times.'

It had been a shattering moment when a call from the British Embassy in Bonn had interrupted her evening what seemed like a decade ago but was in fact six days.

'Miss Wrench?'

'Miranda Wrench, yes.'

'Miss Wrench, this is to warn you of something very extra-ordinary, which is bound to be given a lot of publicity in England, starting from this evening. It's already broken in Germany. I'm afraid it will be rather a shock to you. I know you're a friend of Dr Langenbach and of course everybody knows of that horrible, horrible thing that happened to you – in that connection.'

Miranda kept her voice calm. 'Yes. I am a friend. Have they killed him? Is that what you want to tell me?'

'No, it's not that. It's the latest demand from these extra-ordinary people who say they're holding him. It concerns you . . .'

And she'd learned, and then learned to live with the sicken-ing information that for some unguessable reason the kidnap-pers of Franzi had said they wished her, Miranda, to surrender as a hostage. In return for Franzi. While he carried out an operation on one of them in America. To make sure it went well and they, the kidnappers, weren't molested but let go free at the end of it all, to fade unchallenged into the murder-ous twilight from which they had emerged.

'This is just advance warning,' the voice from the Embassy in Bonn had said. 'Somebody will come round to see you in the next hour. But it's bound to be on TV. Picked up from here.'

They'd been enormously scrupulous after that. They'd told her she had no conceivable obligation to run risks ('and however extensive the steps taken, Miss Wrench, it is only honest to say there *must* be risks') on behalf of anyone. And Dr Langenbach was in no way her responsibility. And she'd known they wanted her to do it. Everybody wanted Franzi out, safe; she knew that. And she saw they thought it might, just might, work.

Miranda had no doubts of what to do. She recognised that her motives were mixed. There was the plain challenge of taking a personal risk to help Franzi survive. There was the knowledge that whatever they said to her about 'no obligation' she'd never be able to live with herself or face the world if she refused. They'd been decent about that, she thought grimly. They'd said that *if* she said 'no' ('and to be frank, Miss Wrench, that would be what we should advise') it would be made publicly clear that the British authorities had intervened to *prevent* her doing what the terrorists demanded. 'Powers could credibly be invoked,' they had said, primly and somewhat obscurely. But Miranda knew that she could do it if she willed: and that they hoped she would.

But there was more. She thought about Franzi a good deal of the time, his face, his voice, his sympathy, his body, his poor mutilated hand, the possibility of his love. And just as she had desperately hoped that a holiday in Italy with Franzi would have thawed her still pained and half-frozen heart, so she now dared hope that in agreeing to be some sort of hostage for Franzi she was taking a step which would bring all to the truth in the end, and that the truth would be that he loved her and she would come to love him. She wanted this desperately. She was near believing in its possibility. And she heard herself saying to them, quietly,

'I'm ready to do it.'

She put aside their ritual protests.

'I'm ready to do it. Please tell me what I have to do next.'

The briefings, the explanations, the agonised and obvious attempts by those representing authority to pre-empt outcry if things went wrong – these seemed to go on for ever. Now, at last, the flight, the airport, the taxi, the Hotel Donau Ufer. Far from the Danube, or at least not within sight of its banks. In the eastern suburbs of Vienna. A decent-looking place. Miranda had never in life felt so lonely. 'They will, they have said, make almost immediate touch with you.' And after that, what? Captivity, of course. Physical hardship? Torture? Humiliation? Rape? In spite of their assurances?

One of the aspects to which most attention had been given both in London and Vienna was how to shake off the media. In England they had persuaded her to move to a special place near London, to cut off communication with friends 'except in personal emergency, naturally'. They had relayed messages to and from her brother, Harry. They had clearly, she thought, done some brainwashing of him too, after his initial outrage, persuaded him that all would be well, that her act of heroism would turn out to be comparatively risk-free, because Harry had sent words of love and support but had not attempted to raise hell, to get the whole thing called off. In one message, he had said,

'The Rudbergs and their friends, Franzi's relations, are against you doing it. They want you to know that. But they want me also to tell you how much they love you for it.'

She had asked if it was really essential for her to be kept so isolated during this period of waiting.

'We know it's hard for you, Miss Wrench. But it's really better.'

They'd been considerate, done all she asked to ensure that life went on, that the gallery ran properly.

'There's been such publicity, you see, Miss Wrench, that's the way these brutes have chosen to play it. It would mean you'd have reporters on the doorstep, TV cameras on you every minute. It's hard for you, but it's really best you disappear.'

She'd understood. And perhaps the terrorists, the kidnappers, who presumably watched television, also understood. There had even been a certain thrill, a certain exhilaration in putting on a sort of mask of invisibility, in disappearing and yet being there. The agreeable, albeit slightly sinister man who had briefed her had given confidence of a kind. He had said to her once,

'We'll beat them, Miss Wrench, don't worry. But I wish I could get my hands on the sort of people who, from stupidity or weakness, give in to them and put them in funds! Without a good deal of money they can't keep up games like this.'

That had been England. Then there had been the journey, well managed, anonymous, the sense of protective eyes and arms all round her, unseen. Then the Hotel Donau Ufer. They'd assured her that the Austrians had co-operated fully in continuing the charade to keep her whereabouts private. It had been pointed out to the Austrian media that the terrorists could easily be scared off contacting Fraülein Wrench (a critical step in the procedure leading to Dr Langenbach's release) if she were accompanied by TV cameras and reporters at every step. Most of the press and so forth would play fair, Vienna said, most would take the point; but you always got some, you know how it is –

And additionally, therefore, they'd had a deception plan, for media benefit. Very discreetly they'd also booked Fraülein Wrench into another hotel, not the Donau Ufer; and on a specific day – not 25th August but two days later. To the Donau Ufer she was 'Fraülein Jackson' and for the journey she had also been Miss Jackson, with passport to match. It had all been efficient. She was told to inform the Donau Ufer that she was 'Wrench-Jackson' and a message might come for her under that or either name, and the Donau Ufer management, so the Vienna police swore, were trustworthy; it had been necessary to place certain confidence in them, but they wouldn't sell information to the media. It had been as well that the terrorists had privately named that particular place without giving it publicity, it had a decent reputation, no complications. As far as the thing could be done, Miranda had been assured, it had been done.

When she checked that Fraülein Jackson was expected at the hotel, she smiled at the man behind the reception desk, wondering whether he was really one of the gang who had seized Franzi, whether the whole place was a terrorist lair.

178

He looked very ordinary, very correct. Franzi, she supposed, might be somewhere quite near – most of the world presumed he was held in Austria. She filled in the particulars required by law and provided her passport. The man spoke English with a slight American accent.

'Your passport will be available whenever you want it.'

'I shan't be going out. I shall dine in the hotel.'

'Of course, Fraülein Jackson.' Did she imagine a slight smile at the corners of his mouth? She explained about her name.

'Thank you, Fraülein Jackson. I will ensure the telephone exchange and the porter understand.'

'There may be a message –'

'Of course, Fraülein Jackson. And if you want a taxi at any time, just tell the hall porter over there.'

'I will.'

She took her key. A neat-looking boy had her suitcase and was summoning the lift. The reception clerk smiled politely and then, as if near forgetting something, said,

'Ah! Fraülein Wrench-Jackson, there was an envelope.'

'Thank you.'

Miranda waited until she reached Room 36 before opening the envelope. A rather large envelope addressed 'Miranda Wrench'. Her stomach heaved at opening packages whose contents were in the least mysterious.

The envelope held a brilliant scarlet headscarf. Printed upon it was a striking representation of the Arc de Triomphe in Paris. Vulgar, colourful and redolent of the tourist trail down the Rue de Rivoli. Certainly not of Vienna. Miranda fingered it. No note was enclosed. She was, predictably and belatedly, very much afraid. What would happen now? She knew desperately that she wanted air – the hotel bedroom already felt like a prison – but to go for a walk, explore Vienna, was unthinkable. What would happen now? Would she be called down by message to the street and bundled into a taxi? Struck on the head and wake up bound hand and foot in a cellar? Have a chloroformed handkerchief stuffed over her face and be dragged into some alley? When? What? And what was the significance of the headscarf – if, indeed, it had any significance? 'What does it matter?' she said to herself, and found, with worried embarrassment, that she had said the words aloud. Indeed, what did it matter? She had come to be kidnapped. She was offering herself, a sacrificial object, for taking as a hostage. All she desired was to get it over. She unpacked and tried to read the paperback thriller she'd bought for the flight.

At exactly seven o'clock the telephone rang.

'Fraülein Wrench?'

'Fraülein Wrench-Jackson, yes.' Miranda spoke passable German.

'There is an outside call for you. Wait, please.' A click, and a man's voice. Quiet and inexpressive.

'I will soon have instructions for you, Fraülein Wrench. You are expecting them, I think.'

'Yes, I am.'

'You speak German, I know.'

'A little.'

'Instructions will be given to you in detail at eleven o'clock tomorrow morning. Please be in your room at that time.'

There was a click and a buzzing sound. He, whoever it was, had rung off.


At about the same time that Miranda arrived at the Hotel Donau Ufer, a telephone conversation was going on between Rudolf Frenzel, very senior Federal Ministry official in Bonn, and a less senior official of the Hesse Land Government in Kassel. The former thought that never – absolutely never – had such a series of disasters been described within the covers of one file as in the Langenbach-Barinski case. Everything, everything without exception, had been sheer horror. It had started as an unwelcome, but comparatively straightforward, affair of standing up to terrorism. It had then been infected by a confusion of factors and events that made it almost impossible to pick a safe way through the political minefield, however delicate the tread.

180

First, of course, those bunglers of the prosecution service had discovered at the worst possible moment that the Barinski female was unlikely to be convicted, so that the firm decision of the Federal Government to stand on principle in the matter and have no truck with the terrorists was undermined. It had been a question of either trying to save Langenbach and admitting that Barinski could go free – amid a chorus of contemptuous scepticism, of accusations of yielding to terror – or, on the other hand, of going ahead with the Barinski trial, appearing to stand firm, and then seeing her acquitted; and Dr Langenbach dead. Just so that Bonn could escape embarrassment! Ghastly! And there was no doubt that the fact of advice having been given earlier about Barinski's likely acquittal, in time, had the Government willed it, to agree to her release and save Langenbach – that fact would have been sniffed out by the press, no question.

Although Frenzel was sure that the Government had been perfectly correct in choosing the first alternative, the immediate aftermath had been most disagreeable. The opposition parties and press had enjoyed themselves. The Government had been described as unprincipled, cowardly – and dishonest, since nobody believed the truth, which was that the impossibility of convicting Barinski had only just been raised. It had been a bad week. Needless to say, and not unreasonably, ministers had demanded why they had been so poorly served by the official machine, why they had been put in so idiotically embarrassing a position. And Frenzel, feeling the injury badly, had experienced this ministerial indignation more personally and more strongly than most.

Nevertheless, he knew that it was the right as well as the least damaging of the two alternative courses of action. Barinski would be freed 'after certain formalities'. She would be flown to wherever it was they'd demanded – Libya was the latest. On the same day an English girl would be meekly handed over by the British authorities to be held as hostage (and, by God, they'll be attacked if *that* goes wrong! Frenzel said to himself, not without grim relish) and, with luck, Dr Langenbach and a couple of murderers would be flown as

181

a convivial little party to New York, so that the celebrated young surgeon could do his best to save their wretched lives – or the wretched life of one of them. Frenzel sighed.

And now!

'When was it discovered?' He snapped at the telephone as if he hated it.

'At two o'clock this afternoon. At present the knowledge is restricted to those immediately concerned. But obviously we wish to agree the terms of the public announcement, as well as discuss –'

'Obviously!' said Frenzel. He felt he could take little more of this. The implications! And there couldn't be much time before they'd need to put out an authoritative version, to pre-empt rumour. He replaced the telephone as if in a dream. Almost without volition he found he was starting to move a pencil across a sheet of paper:

> The Land Government of Hesse regret to announce that at two o'clock this afternoon Klaretta Barinski, against whom all charges had been withdrawn, and who was about to leave the Federal Republic by international flight this evening, was found . . .

Heidi Bormann had been working at the garage as a pump assistant for seven months when the young man with dark hair and a nice smile had said to her,

'Ever watch football?'

She laughed. She was filling his tank with 'Super'.

'It's my passion!'

'Do you know, I guessed that.'

'I can't think how!'

She was intrigued and came round to his window to collect the money. She'd never seen him before, she was positive. A foreigner. His German was terrible but his eyes were lovely. She said,

'Why ask about football, anyway?' It wasn't a busy time.

'I've got a spare ticket for the pre-season friendly against

Anderlecht Brussels on Saturday week, 26th.' Anderlecht would be playing Rapide Vienna, Heidi's heroes.

'Well?'

'I'll probably be going. I wondered if you'd be able to get away.'

'I'd love it!' Heidi was fervent. Tickets for that match were already fetching high prices. She was sure she'd be able to swing some story to get an afternoon off. And he really was a charmer!

'I'd love it. But why me? You must –'

'I've been here before, filling up. I guessed you were an enthusiast. I heard you talking about the game once, when another girl was at my car – you know.'

'I don't remember,' said Heidi, prim but flattered. He'd obviously had his eye on her and she couldn't imagine how she'd failed to notice him before. Then he told her that it was possible – unlikely but possible – that he'd miss the match himself.

'In that case a friend of mine will have my ticket – and yours. But I'm pretty sure I'll be there myself.'

'How will we meet?' said Heidi, pleasantly excited. He told her the gate to approach.

'I'll be in the passage with your ticket. Just by the door into the "ladies". And if I'm not there Otto will be. Most unlikely.'

'How'll he recognise me?'

'Easy,' he said, with a beautiful smile. 'Wear this.' He handed her a scarf.

'You don't know I'll be there.' She looked at the scarlet square with pleasure. It had a picture on it, which she thought she recognised as French. Very elegant! She'd suspected he might be French himself. She smiled and said,

'I might disappear, scarf and all!'

'I'll risk it,' he said, laughing. 'See you then. Come early. I'll be around from one o'clock. What's your name, by the way?'

She told him. And two days later there was an envelope at the garage for her which showed his complete good faith. A note – and a ticket.

Heidi,
I think you'd better have the ticket in advance – just in
case one of us gets held up. But I don't expect we will.
Same place, same time. Wear my scarf please! I'm looking
forward to seeing you – and the football, of course!

He'd not signed it and she realised she didn't even know his
name. It was rather an adventure! Anyway, she'd got a ticket
for a game everybody wanted to see.

'They may,' said Reno, his voice firm but low, his face paler
than ever and his whole being expressive of the tension within,
'they may, at once, take the Wrench girl away from Vienna.
They may think this negates the whole agreement.'

Carla looked at him, feeling confused but feeling little for
Klaretta Barinski.

'Why do you suppose she did it?'

'How can I know? They may have killed her. They – the
Germans – may have decided they simply weren't prepared
to see her go free. Some underlings may have hated her,
hated all of us, hated the Revolution so much that they were
prepared –'

Carla said flatly, 'We'll never know. She's dead.'

'Yes. She's dead. Hanged. A brave woman, a great woman.
Hanged.' There had been rumours within the movement that
Klaretta might be suffering from some very grave medical
condition but Reno said nothing of that, and turned his mind
away from such things.

'Reno, I don't see that this will stop *them* going ahead. They
want to get Franzi –' Reno looked at her grimly.

'They want Langenbach. Yes. But what do *we* want? They
have now failed to meet our first, our original, our greatest
demand, to free Klaretta. Instead they've killed her.'

'Reno, we don't know that. She may have killed herself,
like they say. Anyway, why should it make a difference to the
deal? It seems to me that they *agreed* to free Klaretta, that's
the great thing. We won. And now the rest goes ahead as
arranged.'

184

Reno said, voice sounding strangled,

'So all we get for this playboy doctor, for whom governments have been running round in circles it seems – all we get is a little medical attention! That's the end, is it?'

'Reno, don't say that, don't feel like that. We're still getting everything, *everything*, do you hear? A climb-down in the first place. Now this Wrench girl to make sure they don't rat on their word. Is she in Vienna now?'

Reno looked at his watch, nodded and said,

'She will get full instructions tomorrow morning. If *they* let her stay there. If *they* decide nothing is changed and it goes ahead. And if *I* decide it goes ahead! I – and others. I shall talk to the comrades today. For it to go ahead without having got Klaretta alive could be represented as a setback for the movement, without some further concession, you realise that? In spite of everything, you realise that?'

'Reno *carissimo*, of course it must go ahead.'

He looked at her intently, breathing deeply. Carla was standing beneath a skylight and the evening sun shone through it on the burnished gold of her head and made a small pool of light on the smooth skin of her neck. He said, very low,

'God, how you want to save that bastard's skin, don't you!' Then he moved swiftly from the room.

Reno did not return until the evening. There was a grim set to his mouth and he avoided Carla's eye.

'Well?'

'What are you talking about?'

'You know, Reno.'

'Ah! The doctor.'

'The doctor and you, Reno.'

'They've agreed we go.'

'I'm glad,' said Carla, keeping her voice steady. 'I'm glad.'

'But they agree it's not enough. We must demonstrate a further success.'

'If you're restored to health. By *them*. And –'

'You know very well it's not enough. What they've directed is this. The Wrench woman will be held until we're freed, and

185

I'm clear of this damned operation. Then we'll abort the transfer.'

'But they'll be holding us. They'll be able to call the tune.'

'Not entirely. Anyway, you leave that to me and others, there's a lot of work to be done in these next two or three days. The point is the woman won't be released unless the authorities agree to free Branca.'

Giovanni Branca was held by the Italian authorities for complicity in a series of kidnappings and murders in north Italy.

'The Italians won't release Branca! When will they be asked to do so?'

'Only at the last minute. When we're clear.'

Carla stared at him. 'And if they won't?'

'Same thing,' said Reno with a show of indifference. 'I've agreed to brief Josef and Vit. If they won't let Branca go, the Wrench woman is executed. Instructions are perfectly clear.'


'Fraülein Wrench?'

It was exactly eleven o'clock in the morning of Saturday 26th August. Miranda had deliberately drunk a little too much wine at her solitary dinner and had slept fitfully, waking often. A *café complet* in her room. A bath. Now the voice, a man's voice, soft and gentle, different from the evening before.

'Fraülein Wrench, this afternoon there will be a football match in the stadium in Vienna. Please attend that match. We have a ticket for you. Here is what you must do. Are you understanding me?'

'*Verstanden –*'

'Take a taxi from the hotel at one o'clock. It is necessary to go early because of the crowds. Enter the stadium at Gate Fourteen. In the passageway at Gate Fourteen keep well to the right.'

'I understand.'

'As you approach the barrier where they will take tickets, someone will give you your ticket. Please watch the match and leave by the same gate, Gate Fourteen. Is that clear?'

'Perfectly clear.'

'Fraülein Wrench, one more important thing. You have a red headscarf, it was left for you at the hotel, a French scarf.'

'I have it.'

'Please wear it on your head, so that the person with your ticket recognises you easily. Take nothing, not even your handbag in your hands. That is all.'

Two hours later Miranda, sickness in her stomach, climbed into the taxi outside the Hotel Donau Ufer. Trying to achieve an inward smile she wondered whether to take a small package with her, whether a hostage about to be kidnapped should go packed for the experience. 'Take nothing, not even your handbag,' the voice had said. Might she, nevertheless, not get away with a few personal things in a paper bag? Better not! Her heart sank. Even in hospitals and prisons one was surely admitted with some articles of one's own, some reminders of identity – or was that true of prisons? Hospitals yes, but prisons? She didn't know. She looked out of the taxi window without interest.

'I want Gate Fourteen.'

The taxi driver said something obscure in his soft Austrian voice. Then she found herself paying him and standing in a huge crowd which eddied round her, past her, all moving in the same direction. There were, it was clear, a large number of gates to the actual ground. The taxi had only been able to put her down at the main entrance, through which what appeared to be a hundred thousand people were surging. The driver had whistled when she'd said she wanted to go to the stadium. A foreign fan, of some kind, she supposed he thought her. He'd talked about the match.

'A friendly. Pre-season. Should be good.'

'I hope so.'

She had no idea who was playing. If she asked he'd think he had a lunatic in the taxi. He was unintentionally obliging.

'The Belgians are good. Our people –' he shrugged his shoulders and made several remarks critical of Austrian football management. Miranda said nothing. To hell with everyone! Why had she any interest in playing a part?

187

Anderlecht, Brussels. Rapide, Vienna.

So much tumbled out of the driver's conversation. Clearly he was a fanatic. She saw the huge figures indicating gate numbers and moved towards Fourteen. A long covered passage, full of slowly moving people. A ticket barrier, as the voice had said, at the far end of it. On the right, ahead of her, was a sign and a door. '*Damen*'. On the left '*Herren*'. How considerate, she thought, and no doubt duplicated in every passage! She moved slowly onward, pressed near the wall. Somewhere before the ticket barrier, somewhere in the next twenty yards, someone – that soft-spoken voice on the telephone? – would press a ticket into her hand. Otherwise she'd feel pretty foolish arriving at the barrier – all around her tickets were held grimly in hands, ready for display. There was no purchase, no payment – she'd seen queues forming at windows outside for that purpose, and no doubt many would be disappointed. Miranda shuffled on.

'Fraülein Wrench.'

It was a murmur, so soft as to be almost unheard. She could not immediately tell from which of her neighbours it came. She turned her head and said,

'*Ja?*'

'In here, please.' There was no doubt, it was a woman's voice. Why not? And 'In here' meant into the '*Damen*'. Again, why not? Miranda, still uncertain of who was speaking to her, pushed through the public lavatory swing door, passing a young woman who emerged from it at the same moment. A young woman about whom something was familiar.

She felt hands, gentle hands, pushing her, propelling her towards one of the lavatories, a murmured voice, '*Entschuldigen*'. Then a handkerchief, a hand, a strong hand at her shoulder blades. Then nothing at all.


'How's it going?' said the Milan police captain. He had to keep in touch with every stage of the bizarre sequence in which their part, at Milan, would follow in a few days' time. Meanwhile the action was in Vienna. He approved of the

188

German authorities' decision – indeed, the decision of all the relevant governmental authorities, Italian, German, Austrian, British – to press on with this peculiar deal, in spite of the suicide of the German terrorist, Barinski. Suicide before release, presumably as mad as her actions. But they were all on tenterhooks as to whether the other side, the kidnappers, would go ahead with it now that Barinski was dead. It depended, when one thought about it, on how much they valued their own lives. This kidnapped doctor was, allegedly, capable of saving one of those lives. If he was released.

'How's it going?' He'd been told to keep direct contact with Vienna.

'All right.'

The young English girl, Wrench, was in Vienna. They – the other side – had called her at her hotel the evening before. Call box somewhere in Upper Austria! Nothing to go for there, and anyway there must be no interceptions, no attempt to interfere with the kidnap plan. It had to be left to go ahead, or the smart young doctor with a missing finger wouldn't be allowed to turn up. Nevertheless it was vital, absolutely vital, to keep tracks on the girl. Then, when they'd come to Milan with Langenbach ('And why the hell come down to Milan?' the Italians had said to each other, irritably. 'Why not fly to America from Frankfurt or Munich, or Vienna? Just because they snatched him in Italy why involve us again?'), with Langenbach safe, the Austrians could lift the Wrench woman and everybody around her. And then, bother the brute's heart operation or whatever it was. He and the bitch with him could be taken in by the New York police. After which there'd be a long, long investigation.

In which we'll be involved, we Italians, the police captain thought. They must have had Italian helpers, to pinch that car at Umbertide and lift him from Gubbio before running him north. There's an Italian end.

'Going all right, eh? She went to the football match?'

'That's it. She's there now.'

The line from Vienna was very clear.

'Who gave her the ticket?'

189

'Not sure. There was a hell of a crowd of course. But it doesn't matter. She's watching the game and there's an empty seat beside her so whoever it was didn't decide to be escort. We've got four men around her.'

'Four men of yours watching a football match,' said Captain Bastini. 'Police work is certainly tough in Vienna!' The other laughed.

'I'll tell you one thing – they're reporting every ten minutes, and it seems the young English woman is mad about the game! Cheering her head off, jumping up and down! So it's not turning out a bad way to be kidnapped!'

'She's a cool one,' said Bastini, admiringly. 'But nobody with her, you say.'

'Nobody. They'll pick her up again when she leaves, obviously. It suits us just as well. We'll have people all around her still. Follow her up.'

'Any idea where they'll take her?'

'My guess,' said his Austrian colleague, 'is that they'll keep her somewhere in Vienna. Some place they'll have ready in Vienna. They'll lead us straight to it.' He sounded contented.

'And then –'

'Watch and wait. Watch and wait. Till you tell us the doctor and his two terrorist friends are airborne. Then we'll go in – that's the idea at present.'

'Of course if they've decided not to go ahead, not to produce Langenbach because Barinski's done herself in – they may leave this girl alone. They know you're tailing her, they won't want to run pointless risks. If they're not going to turn up and fly to America it would be a pointless risk.'

'Of course. But we know they're still playing. She's got her ticket, you see. And they told her it would be given to her. Anyway, why call her, why make contact at all if they're not going to lift her?'

'Of course,' said Bastini, 'of course.'

'I'll keep you informed.'

'I'll be here late this evening.'

It was not until seven o'clock that evening, however, that

he had another call from Vienna, and he knew at once from the tone of voice that all was not well.

'Anything new?'

The other's voice was curt and unfriendly.

'We've lost her.'

'*Lost her?*'

'Lost her. There was another girl – same scarf. Some story about it and the ticket being given her by a young fellow at a garage, days ago. We're working on her, but she seems genuine. Silly but genuine. Some story about another fellow meeting her, steering her to the *Damen* while he did the same, he'd meet her in two minutes. And disappeared. So she watched the match alone!'

'Decoy?'

'It's hardly likely to have been a coincidence. Our boys – well, they're in trouble, but it was a pretty obvious scarf and –' There was a gloomy grunt down the telephone.

Bastini wondered whether to say, 'I suppose, anyway, they enjoyed the match,' and decided against. Instead he asked politely,

'Any ideas?'

'Of course, we're trying everything, everyone and everywhere. Without much optimism. So it looks as if, from their point of view, everything is going exactly according to plan. Have a nice party at the airport on Monday!'

# CHAPTER 10

It was Monday, 28th August, when Reno Vanetti, Carla Rosio and Franzi Langenbach were due at Milan airport to meet Italian police, authorities from various other national embassies, and the television cameras of several national corporations. Discretion had been decreed and had failed utterly. The transfer, Reno's brainchild, was to be a public affair – if it happened. But in every mind was the same question, 'Will it really happen?' Everybody knew that Klaretta Barinski's suicide must put the whole matter in suspense. Everybody knew that the heroic Miranda Wrench had disappeared. 'You can bet we know where she is,' people said importantly to each other, 'the Austrian police will be watching her all right.' But everybody also knew that people who had cut off Franzi Langenbach's finger, who boasted of murder and mayhem, might simply be exulting in having acquired a fresh hostage – without the risk or trouble of kidnap; and be formulating new demands without intention of handing over the missing surgeon. The extraordinary condition that Langenbach was being released to perform an operation on one of his captors was recalled but discounted. 'They don't value their lives,' some people said. 'They're playing with us. They won't hand over Langenbach.'

'I'm not so sure.'

TV reporters, well briefed and sceptical, gossiped to each other at the airport. It was a hot day, and the authorities had been unhelpful about the exact time at which the peculiar delegation with its prisoner was expected to appear. The latest rumour was that it would not be until the early evening, to catch the overnight flight to New York.

At ten o'clock on the same morning, far away in Perugia, the proprietor of the Bar Baglioni telephoned Police Headquarters and asked for a particular officer.

'Signor *'Tenente?'*

'Ponti here.'

'Signor *'Tenente*, it's Crespo. Bar Baglioni.'

'I remember.'

'He's been in.'

'He –'

'The young man I told you about. He's been in.'

Ponti frowned. A good deal had happened, in other cases, in the intervening period. Was this important? Then he remembered.

'I'll come round later.'

'I've got a photograph of him.'

*'A photograph?'*

'Yes. Bit of luck. Some of them were having a party on Saturday night, taking pictures. I'm in several. He's in one. Instant development, you know the sort of thing. Colour. They gave me one. He's in it – the young man I told you about, the one who was asking about Stefano Bastico. Like to see it?'

Ponti said he would; and one hour later was passing the photograph to the appropriate record office for rephoto and check. These things went quicker than they used to, he reflected, and people said they'd soon go so quick, and internationally too, that previous generations would regard it as a miracle. As it was he looked at a signal of response from records at three o'clock that afternoon with a sense of profound, of near incredulous satisfaction. It might – of course it might – still all be coincidence. But, 'Well,' he said to himself as he looked now at name, record and photograph, knowing that others at that moment would be doing the same, 'Well, it was I who put them together.' It had, indeed, been he, Ponti, who had inspired the guesses which had put them together. It was early, yet, to tell how it might turn out, but –

'Bravo, Ponti,' he said to himself. And if that young gentleman was around Perugia he'd soon be having a chat. It must,

193

if it were of the significance he suspected, be very soon indeed. 'Bravo, Ponti, Bravo, bravo!' Photograph on the desk before him, he started summoning a few energetic subordinates for conference.

'They've passed the first gate. They're travelling exactly as agreed. They're on time.'

The small private lounge at Milan airport was generally reserved for high dignitaries of state or airline; sometimes of commerce where wealth had been considered sufficient to earn such recognition. A large reproduction of a print of Milan Cathedral occupied one wall. The room was air-conditioned, the atmosphere cool. A white-coated steward approached Marcia Rudberg with a murmured offer of some refreshment.

'Thank you, nothing.'

Lise von Arzfeld smiled and silently shook her head. The two friends had flown together from Cologne to Milan the previous evening. They formed Franzi's reception party, to greet him with love and trepidation before his flight to New York to perform his part of this bizarre bargain. If it took place; and if he now arrived.

Marcia had been impressed by the sympathy of the Italian authorities. She and Lise had been met the previous evening and escorted to their hotel. They had been assured that everything was in order, the *terroriste* had done nothing to cast doubt on their intentions. The terrorists had obviously now travelled to near Milan, to within reach of the airport – or were proposing to do so in the first hours of the following day, Monday, 28th August. If the police had any notion of where these, the self-styled European Liberation Movement activists, were holding Franzi, whence or whither they were bringing him before appearance at Milan airport, they did not disclose it. To the agreeable young police officer in plain clothes who had explained matters to them Marcia said,

'Do we know where he – where Dr Langenbach is now?'

He shrugged his shoulders. He talked a mixture of Italian, in which Marcia could stumble along with difficulty, and a passable German distorted by a curious accent, although Lise, mercifully, spoke Italian well. They understood that the doctor and the two terrorists agreed in the negotiation would arrive at Milan airport at six o'clock on Monday evening. There they would be escorted to the private lounge, would be passed, with appropriate papers, to the airline people; and would be flown on an evening flight to New York.

'Where, of course, the United States authorities will receive them. As you know, Signore, one of these persons is ill.'

'And Dr Langenbach has agreed to operate. Yes, the whole world knows.'

'Precisely.' The young man seemed hesitant, to have more to say. Lise said bluntly,

'Is there anything else?'

'You should know, Signore, that it has been made a condition by – by these people – that there shall be television coverage of their departure.'

'I suppose so,' said Marcia, nodding. 'From the beginning they've been determined that every move must be conducted with maximum publicity.'

'That is so, Signora. There will be cameras allowed into the lounge. The lounge where you will meet Dr Langenbach. And where,' he added with a half-smile, 'the Italian police will meet the people who kidnapped him. Or who have been holding him, at any rate.'

'TV cameras!' said Lise. 'After a few moments of comparative privacy, I hope.'

'We hope so, too, Signora. It will be difficult. There will be a number of people. Perhaps a little confusion. Naturally these *terroriste* have to be under strict surveillance even though we are not permitted to arrest them. They are mad, after all. They might do anything.'

They smiled at him, grateful, uneasy, envisaging the following day, the lounge crowded with police, representatives, no doubt, from Austria (where Franzi had been held? was still held?), from Germany (so unwillingly and unfortunately involved by the linkage to the wretched Klaretta Barinski), from Britain (why? thought Marcia with disgust, because they sent

195

his finger to London? Then she remembered Miranda, British subject, volunteer hostage, the sacrifice). All these and TV cameras too. She and Lise could imagine. They murmured thanks for the young man's helpfulness. Marcia took his hand to say goodbye.

'Is there anything to be said about Miranda Wrench? You know – Signorina Wrench, the English girl who has placed herself in these people's hands to assure them they will not be harmed?'

He said he knew little of that, but they were watching him and suspected this was less than the whole truth. That had been yesterday.

'Thank you, nothing,' Marcia said once again to the white-coated steward. They had been sitting for forty-five minutes in the small lounge. The day had passed with terrible slowness. It would have been possible to postpone arrival at Milan from Cologne until that morning, but they had dreaded the possibility of flight delay and decided to over-insure in time. Franzi *must* see them, they both felt. The weeks since 23rd July had been very terrible. They talked to each other, inconsequential remarks in low tones. Not since 1945 had they felt so close; 1945 and fleeing together before the Russians, living with another sort of terror. Despite the air-conditioning the atmosphere in the airport lounge was oppressive – not hot but entirely without freshness. There were about fifteen people in the small space, some of them in uniform. One of the latter appeared now in the doorway and spoke aloud, it appeared to nobody in particular.

'They will be here in two minutes.'


Marcia registered with part of her mind the fact that nobody seemed to know exactly how to behave. The social conventions, ancient or modern, were inadequate to regulate manners between a group of officials and two young people who had undoubtedly perpetrated appalling crimes and were now accompanying another, whose finger they had hacked off, and who had undertaken, by surgery, to try to save the life of one

196

of them. Nor did Marcia find it easy to know what the reactions of Lise and herself should be, could be; they who loved Franzi, and should desire nothing but retribution on his captors and assailants. She looked now at a tall, pale young man, with a high, intelligent forehead and wearing spectacles, who was being addressed quietly by one of the police officers and was nodding his head. Behind him stood a girl with fair, reddish hair; a short, pretty girl with very green eyes which she darted in all directions like a nervous, trapped animal. Marcia saw, without for the moment noting it, that the girl's right hand seemed to be clutching the hand of the person immediately behind her in the doorway as she edged further into the room. There was a low clamour of conversation, no doubt conveying to the *terroriste* the facts about tickets, documents, about aircraft timings, about the imminent arrival of TV cameras.

Do they have luggage? Marcia said to herself, with something like an attempt at inner flippancy. How did terrorists under safe-conduct travel? What about visas? Then she saw Franzi.

He was standing in the doorway looking solemn. At first she didn't recognise him. Then she realised that the pale face with its fringe of newly grown beard, its restless eyes, was indeed Franzi's. An important-looking man had taken his hand and was shaking it with what looked like emotion.

'Franzi! Franzi!'

Lise pushed violently forward towards the door, Marcia immediately behind her.

'Franzi!'

Marcia could see it was a shock to him. There had presumably been no way to warn him that people who loved him would be there, so soon. Those things need preparation, gradualness. Marcia knew. She had experience.

'Franzi!' Lise's arms were around him for a long time before she released him. Then she found that the three of them, Franzi, Marcia and she, were standing in a small group, isolated, surrounded by the beaming faces of most of the other people in the lounge, policemen, officials, whoever they were. The light was suddenly much brighter and she saw why. TV

197

cameras! The hubbub was now considerable. Franzi said to them both conventionally, rather stiffly,

'You shouldn't have come all this way.' Lise seemed incapable of speaking and Marcia took him up.

'Franzi, darling Franzi. You're thin, very pale, but you look marvellous.'

'Do I? I haven't been able to shave this thing off. I can't look marvellous!'

'Yes, marvellous.' The lie was for something to say. 'We'll see you very soon. We know you've got to go to New York.'

'Yes, that's right.' His eyes were moving about the lounge, screwed up. He said,

'Where's Carla?'

'Carla?'

'Ah, there she is. With Reno over there.' He half-raised a hand, as if reassuring others as well as himself. Lise followed his eyes.

'Ah, those!'

Conversation in any ordinary sense was impossible. Marcia supposed that very soon some reporter would ask Franzi for a few words to be relayed to the viewing world. God knew what he'd say. Lise fixed her eyes on his face and devoutly wished that she could accompany him to New York, to care for him in what must surely be an extended period of recuperation. Surgery indeed! And on one of these wretched animals! He shouldn't be allowed that sort of effort for months! With a sudden, silent resolution she said to herself, I'll go! I'll go to America just as soon as I can arrange it! Of course he must have *family* near him, not just affectionate friends but family. And that must be me. But I won't say anything now!

Marcia whispered,

'Franzi, don't worry about Miranda. They've kept their word about you. It will be quite all right. Everybody has promised us that.'

'What do you mean?' Franzi stared at her blankly.

'Miranda Wrench, you know –'

'What about her?'

'Well – she had to sort of hand herself over, it was one of

198

the conditions, didn't they tell you? To make sure these – these two aren't prosecuted, you know –'

'*Miranda handed herself over!*'

Franzi was now looking beyond her to the outer rim of the circle of chattering, uncertain people, glancing at watches, murmuring to cameramen. A reporter, microphone in hand, had been speaking to a burly police officer and was now moving towards Franzi. Franzi took no notice of him and called out,

'Reno!'

Heads turned. There was a check in the hum of forced, unnatural conversation. The tall, pale, young man standing with the girl within a little knot of police officers looked impassively through his spectacles, looked in interrogation across the small lounge. Said nothing.

'Reno, what is this about Miranda Wrench? You have told me nothing. Where is she?' Franzi was speaking loudly, apparently oblivious of the small crowd about them, of cameras, of reporters, of everything.

Reno – everybody now began to think of him, quite naturally, as Reno – shrugged his shoulders and spread out his hands, palms upwards.

'I don't know! What do you mean?'

'You're a liar,' said Franzi, still loudly. '*Menzogna!*' To the senior-looking official who had first taken his hand and was now standing next to him, looking deprecatory, he said,

'What is this about Signorina Wrench? I demand to know. Before I move from here I demand to know!'

'Dr Langenbach, of course, in one moment! The cameras!'

'Damn the cameras!'

The man with the microphone had managed to elude a restraining official hand and was now standing next to Franzi.

'Dr Langenbach, welcome!' He spoke in careful, deliberate Italian. He had been told Dr Langenbach spoke the language, but perhaps without great fluency.

'Welcome! Everyone will be delighted to see you here safe and apparently in good health.'

Franzi looked at him as if noticing him for the first time and said,

'Did you know about Miranda Wrench?'

The interviewer was unready for this. Film might need to be cut. On the other hand –

'Certainly, Dr Langenbach, everybody knows how Signorina Wrench has agreed to stand as, as –'

'As a hostage.' Franzi spat the word at him and at the viewing millions if permitted later to share the scene. 'A hostage. *Ostaggio*. Is that right?'

'One could indeed say so, Mr Langenbach. May I now ask you one thing, very briefly –'

'I will tell you one thing, very briefly,' said Franzi. 'It is that I was never a party, I never agreed to this involvement of Signorina Wrench. I never would have agreed to it. And I am not bound by any negotiation which involved this lady, without my knowledge or consent.'

Far away in Sussex, Toni Rudberg was watching the television screen, absorbed. The scene in the small lounge at Milan airport was being relayed to British viewers only one hour after it took place. Uncut. Toni watched Franzi's face as he called out, 'Without my knowledge or consent', and said to himself, The boy's in a terrible state, why not get him away somewhere? Fools, why expose him to this sort of thing? They've been holding him for five weeks, probably given him a bad time. Toni, himself, had been a prisoner of the Russians for thirteen years, eight of them in solitary confinement. He knew something about it.

Then the cameras ranged over the small and crowded room. It was possible to see a pretty girl, identified now by viewers as the female terrorist, waving her arms. Fascinating! Toni thought he heard her shout something. At Franzi? Toni's Italian wasn't bad but he could distinguish no words. Then the camera was on the young man again, presumably the principal thug, the clever-looking one. He appeared to be wagging his finger at the girl. The scene faded and the very cool English voice of the neatly groomed girl who had been reading the news told Toni it was understood that Dr Langenbach and the two persons who had accompanied him and surrendered themselves were now flying, as agreed, to New York. Toni switched the set off and sat, thinking.

It's all very well, he said to himself, Franzi yelling he's not bound by any deal because he'd never have agreed to the Wrench girl's involvement. Poor fellow, he can't be in a condition to understand anything or work anything out. But he must pretend to go along with the deal. To operate, and so forth. To agree that these two brutes shan't be prosecuted, although it's not for him to say, and I must admit, thought Toni, the girl really looked enchanting! But still – but still, he *must* go along with it. And so must everyone else. Otherwise they'll do in Miranda Wrench.

Toni watched the scene at Milan re-enacted on a later version of the news. He tried, unsuccessfully, to telephone Marcia at an hotel in Milan. Then he tried to telephone Harry Wrench. Toni wasn't good at friendly initiatives of that kind – he still felt the English, among whom he lived happily now, found him over-effusive and he left much to Marcia, but in these last weeks they'd both had a lot of contact with the Wrenches and he imagined Harry must be going through hell – he loved his sister very deeply, everyone could see that. Toni knew that Harry was putting on a brave face, that he was hinting – accurately? one didn't know – that he knew more than he could say, that the authorities had matters under control, that Miranda would be all right. But there was no answer from Harry's flat.

Toni slept badly. On Wednesday, two days later, Marcia would arrive at London airport at one o'clock in the afternoon and he decided to meet her. She had told him that she would go from the airport to London and take a mid-afternoon train to Sussex. But no, he thought, I must meet her. It can only have been a ghastly, ghastly time. A muddle, too, although it might work out all right in the end.

He turned on the car radio as he drove through Sussex towards Heathrow two days later, and learned from the eleven o'clock news flash that Dr Langenbach and the two terrorists who had surrendered themselves with him at Milan airport were in New York, had arrived the previous day. 'It is understood,' the announcer said, 'that, contrary to earlier reports, serious charges are now likely to be brought against them.'


Vittorio looked at Lieutenant Ponti, looked at the ceiling, the floor, his own hands and Lieutenant Ponti again.

'Can I smoke a cigarette, Lieutenant?'

'No. You cannot smoke a cigarette, Vittorio. We haven't got far enough yet with our conversation.'

Ponti was making notes on a pad in front of him, on his desk. He looked relaxed, a man with all the time in the world. He had worked hard that Tuesday morning, he had assembled a good deal of what he needed for a protracted conversation with Vittorio – including assent and even a certain amount of guidance from his superiors. Ponti supposed that he knew most of the implications of this curious affair by now. His immediate job was to break this pretty little brown-eyed crook sitting on a hard chair six feet away. He knew the type and thought it would not take long. They had said,

'You realise timing is crucial! The whole thing needs fingertip timing. It must be controlled from here, you understand?'

'I suppose so.'

'There is the international aspect.'

'Of course.'

It was of little use, Ponti had reflected sourly, their wasting his time with chatter about how important and subtle the business was; beyond the comprehension of a simple Perugia police lieutenant, no doubt. It was a Carabinieri matter, naturally, but they'd at least had the grace to acknowledge his part and continue to depend on his co-operation. They would have got nowhere without his hunch, his painstaking deductions, his professionalism; and it sounded as if they'd needed a break! Losing a girl in a crowd, indeed! Austrians!

Still, the quicker things went with Vittorio no doubt the better. They'd picked him up within twenty-four hours, given the photograph and the knowledge he was likely to be in Perugia. Completing a scribble on his pad Ponti remarked,

'I'm afraid my colleagues in Florence will give you a hard time. That old antique dealer was well respected, a decent Italian citizen. Now he's a cabbage. No mind, no feeling. That's not the sort of thing people like.'

'I've told you –'

'Yes, you've told me about your friend, who's due for twenty years. But you helped him. You helped him a lot.' Ponti added, 'Your friend is rather angry with you, as a matter of fact.'

Vittorio expected it was nonsense, he'd given nothing on that, but he was badly frightened. He knew that it wouldn't be hard to pin the Florence job on him if they really started trying. So far, of course, it was police presumption, police guesswork, police bullying, police bluff. But this bastard seemed to look right through one, with his dark eyes and his contented smile. Now Ponti said very suddenly,

'I want to talk about something else, Vittorio. You nicked a car, a Fiat car from the Via Tevere in Umbertide, the property of Signor Cristoforo Fantini, on Saturday 22nd July.'

This was totally unexpected and Vittorio knew, a split second later, that he had reacted wrongly. He had started to shake his head, with a shrug of the shoulders expressing incredulity and puzzlement, but he had, he knew, done so too quickly. Ponti had spoken sharply and fast. Vittorio's speed of response betrayed familiarity with the circumstance, the car, the place, the time. He should have said,

'*Car*, Signor '*Tenente*? Please repeat that – I was nowhere in the area.'

Too swift and automatic! Ponti had been watching beneath his very dark, thick eyebrows, with his unnerving grin. Now he continued,

'It was a good idea to watch for the car and nick it from young Bastico's place. You knew his girl wouldn't report it in a hurry. It gave you a few hours you didn't deserve. Well done, Vittorio!'

Vittorio stared at him and said as strongly as he could,

'I don't know what you're talking about.'

'I think you do. I also think you're capable of understanding that it might – it just might – be possible to help you over that Florence business. You may have been led astray; that friend of yours is a hard man, we know that. One would have to be assured you could help us a little in the other direction. Perhaps even help us a good deal in the other direction.'

Vittorio said nothing and Ponti nodded in a friendly way to him and said,

'The direction of the Signor *Dottore* Langenbach. Whom you most unwisely struck on the head and drove to the Austrian frontier last month . . .' 'Struck on the head' was a guess, unimportant but probably right, Ponti thought. He added, gently, 'Or *was* it, in fact, to the Austrian frontier?'


Miranda remembered only the latter part of the journey. She supposed that there'd been some way of drugging her at the football stadium in Vienna – she remembered arriving there, but not much more. A blurred picture, which might have been a dream, of white walls, water taps, a lavatory? A public lavatory? Then nothing, until waking on the back seat of a small saloon car whose engine was particularly loud. There was a bandage over her eyes, and the fact that she could see nothing was bad, very bad; but they had warned her of this, she remembered that. Obviously she mustn't be enabled to recognise places or people. She wondered how long they'd been driving.

Circumstances came back to her slowly, gently. The taxi drive to a football stadium. Why? She remembered – the telephone call, the quiet voice telling her to be at Gate Fourteen and to wear a scarf they'd left for her at the hotel. She wriggled her head for the scarf. Gone. She moved her limbs a little – they were stiff but not painful. She was, she discovered, wedged not uncomfortably, lying on the back seat of a car with rugs beside her and a rug round her legs. She moved a hand, a wrist. Bound?

Bound. But loosely, albeit efficiently.

So this, Miranda thought without yet registering fear or even concern, was kidnap. She tried to fasten her mind on the reason why. Franzi! They'd asked for her, to hold her as a surety, to make certain –

Make what certain? Miranda, still drowsy, was aware that she knew but couldn't exactly recall, and for the present didn't greatly care. One thing mildly puzzled her, although she expected it would all fall into place one day. Why, since she was a willing hostage, a volunteer, why go to such lengths to drug her (as she supposed), to spirit her away in secrecy? It was, she remembered now, all a well-publicised affair – she could have presented herself anywhere, packed for the occasion.

'Well, here I am!'

So why the conspiracy, the violence? If it was violence. Why? Then she remembered, it was the same reason as the blindfolding, it must be; she was never to be enabled to recognise, to identify later. She felt sleepy again, and as she closed her eyes she realised, with an easy sense that obvious things were returning one by one for her to recognise and arrange in her conscious mind, a further answer to her own question. They had had to make sure she wouldn't be followed, they had needed to shake off surveillance. From what seemed years ago she remembered a voice telling her that she would be watched at all times, that protective eyes would be on her, protective hands ready to reach out to her assistance at any time; invisible to her custodians, at any time, any time. It was to escape the watch of those protective eyes, the reach of those protective hands that she had been drugged and spirited away. So that now, perhaps – and the first stirrings of something like a former terror came, to animate her still drowsy senses – now, perhaps, nobody knew where she was. Perhaps she really had disappeared.

Conscious again of the loudness of the car's engine, she realised that they must be climbing steeply, and that their road twisted every hundred yards. After a little she fell asleep again. She only awoke when the car stopped. She seemed to be surrounded by an enormous silence. Then it was broken by a voice, a soft, rather gentle voice speaking slowly in German. The voice was very near.

'Fraülein Wrench, I am now going to take the blindfold from your eyes and release your wrists. I am sorry both were necessary.'

Miranda said nothing. She heard the car door open and felt a rush of surprisingly cold air. Then hands, dexterous but gentle, took the cord from her wrists and after a tiny pause lifted the bandage from her eyes. Blinking, eyes painful, she first focussed on the person who had been driving her and who now stood looking at her as she moved her cramped wrists, opened and shut her eyes, stared back at him.

Miranda saw a very small man, several inches shorter than herself, a small man with very brown, slender hands and exceptionally piercing blue eyes. She at once felt she was with one who valued expertise, who would concentrate absolutely on any task, who would despise the slovenly. One who both thought and felt. Impossible, she thought later, absurd to form such impressions. Such information comes from faces, not hands, not even just eyes. But the impressions remained.

For the small man wore over his face a black, woollen mask in which eye and mouth slits had been cut. It covered face, back of neck and top of head. This man appeared to be of middle age. Over forty, Miranda thought, but under fifty. Probably. He now said,

'I am Josef, Fraülein Wrench.'

Josef was standing by the rear door of the car, for all the world as if he were a well-trained and solicitous chauffeur. He helped her out, and supported her elbow as she first set her feet on the ground. They appeared to be on a small tarmac parking place, a sort of platform just large enough to turn a car or truck, a platform levelled at the termination of a steep, bumpy track through forest. Above their head cable stretched both upward and down at a steep angle. Adjoining the platform was a square wooden hut, raised above ground level with three steps down to the tarmac. They appeared to be standing in thick fog which Miranda soon realised was low cloud. All around were the tops of tall trees etched against the mist. Suddenly there was a patch of sunlight, a temporary thinning of fog, a glimpse of blue sky. Then Miranda saw that they were in the middle of high mountains. They must have been noisily climbing for a long time, climbing through cloud.

Josef spoke again. His voice was entirely consistent with his appearance – soft, almost deferential, but with a note of confident assurance in it.

'Fraülein Wrench, we will wait here a few minutes. It is better to walk up and down a little, after the time in the car, to use the legs.'

Miranda stared at him. The time for questions, if such a time ever came, would be later. Now she said,

'I agree. *Einverstanden.*' She stamped her feet and felt circulation returning. She looked around her, at the shapes of trees dimly seen through swirling cloud, at the slopes falling away steeply beside the track the little car had laboured to climb, at the mountain rising higher above them, where cable moved mysteriously into the omnipresent cloud, into the silence. Josef said, 'Excuse me,' and mounted the steps into the wooden hut.

The cable above Miranda's head began to move. Josef reappeared, saying again,

'Excuse me.' He threw a quick, professional eye at the moving cable.

'One minute, please. One minute to wait.'

Miranda said, 'You work here?' She said it with a smile, an effort to make some sort of natural response to him. It was, she supposed hazily, important not to seem too inquisitive, not to become a menace; on the other hand, questions are essential to the opening of human contact.

Josef shook his head and said, 'Sometimes. I know them well. Sometimes I help.' Then the cable car, silent, miraculous, appeared climbing out of the cloud immediately below them, and came to a halt by the little hut. Josef said, 'Please,' and gestured Miranda to follow him up the steps into the wooden structure. The inside constituted a mounting platform for the cable car. On one wall were a number of switches and a display panel; the hut was both landing stage and control point. Miranda, as if in a dream, stepped into the cable car, seeing with a vague sense of familiarity the racks for the

207

upright skis of those who would use the car at other times. Then, noiselessly except for an occasional clank of cable, they slipped upwards, further into the engulfing clouds.

After what seemed an age, they alighted at another hut, a much larger hut, far, far above where Josef's car was parked. Later Miranda learned that Josef's contacts, which were extensive, enabled him to help with the frequent summer running and testing of the cable and cable car on this particular slope. Then they started to talk quite naturally, Josef's mask apparently inhibiting him not at all. It was a decently appointed hut: there was water, a lavatory, a huge window and several tables and chairs. The cloud cleared for a few minutes as Miranda first approached the window and she could guess from the sun's position that it was early evening. She had not until that moment thought to look at her watch and now did so. Eight o'clock. Could it still be the same day, the Saturday which had started in the Hotel Donau Ufer? Or had she lost days along the way, days never to be recalled?

Josef nodded to one wall with something like a smile.

'Bar! In the winter!'

'Of course.' Miranda smiled. It was a peculiar place of incarceration. Josef, performing a holiday job while a regular attendant took his annual entitlement of leave, was in control.

'The fellow who's really my boss is down in the valley. As long as I assure him all is well here and at the two intermediate stations he never stirs! He lets me time the tests, the switch-ons. No problem.'

'And your car?' Miranda asked, forcing herself to take an interest in their bizarre circumstances.

'Stays at the middle station. Where we got on. You will be perfectly comfortable here, Fraülein Wrench.'

Miranda said,

'You've gone to a lot of trouble. Of course you realise that I'm not going to try to escape, even if it were possible! I'm here willingly, for a little, because you've asked for it as a condition of releasing Dr Langenbach. I'm your guest.' She smiled. She had early found, to her great relief, that, whether rationally or not, she was unafraid of Josef. In spite of that

208

sinister mask. Indeed, his presence was rather comforting. He said, seriously,

'Yes, certainly, a guest. I do not know about the other things. I only know that a young lady was to travel in my car –'

'A drugged young lady was to travel in your car!'

'Perhaps. I was to have the car ready and the young lady, Fraülein Wrench, was brought to it. Then the others left and I was to bring you to a comfortable place here and look after you. All very confidential.'

'And to keep me – a prisoner!' But Miranda smiled again as she said it. Josef bowed his head.

'True, we can only go down together, because I control the *skibahn*. There is no other way. It is too hard to walk, to climb. But they told me you would not wish to leave.'

'They told you absolutely right.'

'So I do not think "prisoner" is right, Fraülein Wrench. I am here to see you are comfortable.'

She looked at him. What risks they must be running, she thought, how very strange it is. Despite what he says he must know all about Franzi, about the demands, about the deal, about the reason I'm here. He must be in the whole thing up to his neck. And here we are, with him acting almost like an obliging servant, no, not a servant – like a guide perhaps, a mountain guide. A masked mountain guide, chauffeur, provisioner, gaoler – yet reassuring, too. He showed her round the hut, the provisions, the water. Then he murmured something and left her, and the cable car went smoothly down the mountain.

Josef was away from the hut most of each day and all night. The first night he said,

'You will be all right, Fraülein Wrench? You will be alone here and I will return in the morning.'

'I will be perfectly all right.'

He had shown her a generous stock of tinned food, a tiny kitchen. In the winter merry crowds, stamping the snow from their boots, would crowd this place, eating *bratwurst*, drinking *glühwein*, boasting with laughter of ski runs performed. Now it was utterly deserted. Except for her. And, when he was there, Josef. In his mask, invariably donned before he entered the hut.

There was a bed with blankets. She was rather touched that Josef had also produced a small bag with such necessities as soap and a toothbrush. This was by no means part of his instructions. These touches were Josef's. Josef had his own, somewhat obscure, code of conduct. He said, rather shyly, on the second day,

'Is there anything you wish, Fraülein Wrench? I am going down to the village. I regret that my orders – you must stay here, unless you ask particularly, then I seek instructions. I hope you understand.'

'Of course I understand. There are one or two things – and I don't expect I will be here very long.' Miranda gave Josef a primitive shopping list of the sort of articles which even the village shop might have. What a fool I was, she thought, not to take a small grip with some underclothes, tights, another jersey to the football stadium. In spite of what they said about no bag! Still – it can't be long. In England they had said, 'A few days, Miss Wrench. A few days, we expect. But we must leave that to our Austrian friends. After Dr Langenbach is safe we don't think anybody will want to leave you, wherever it turns out to be, a minute longer than necessary.'

'I don't expect I'll be your guest very long, Josef. And as I've said and you know, I'm here entirely of my own accord.'

He said, 'There are magazines, here.'

There were indeed – old, illustrated Austrian and Italian magazines. In addition, Josef each day brought up a newspaper, from which Miranda knew that she should be able to deduce her approximate position. Unfortunately – but did it matter, she thought? – her recollection of Alpine geography was inadequate and the places familiarly mentioned in the local news meant little to her. Miranda had little sense of time and slept a good deal. It was a strange existence. Josef appeared punctiliously in the evenings, sometimes with supplies. On the second evening he brought a bottle of Austrian wine.

'Shall we have a drink together, Josef?'

He smiled, bowed, and shook his head.

'I never drink. Please enjoy it, Fraülein Wrench.'

Miranda thought his smile charming behind the mask's mouth slit, and his eyes sad.

Before Josef left one morning she said, casually,

'Tell me, how long have I been here? What is the date?'

Josef considered.

'It's 31st August, Fraülein Wrench.'

'And I came here when? 26th August?'

Josef shrugged and nodded as if it were a matter of no importance. 26th August, Miranda thought, the day I went to the stadium. If he's telling the truth we got here, cable car and all, in under seven hours from doping in Vienna. Well, that gives a pretty wide radius of Alpine ski resorts! But we've about reached the limit of 'a few days we expect, Miss Wrench'! And, as increasingly in the last twenty-four hours, she began again to feel extremely afraid. This was going on too long.


'All right, you were to call in emergency. I saw your notice, what emergency?' Josef's voice was sharp. He had not expected this to arise and he disliked it. He had never seen the young man whose voice now murmured in Italian to him down the telephone but he had felt distrustful from Reno's very first descriptions. Reno had kept them apart. Josef had said, 'I don't like crooks!' but he'd obeyed orders. Now what?

'What emergency?' Josef had acquiesced in the communication system and procedure, but he had explained to Reno that he was more vulnerable than he had been in the earlier stage of the operation. Then he had been able to range widely, using call boxes now here, now there. On this occasion – although he supposed that the odds against a call tap were extraordinarily long since, presumably, 'that young crook' was also speaking from some anonymous call box – Josef was circumscribed in his choices. There were not large numbers of call boxes to choose from in that corner of the Alps. Josef liked to be on the move during an operation, never long enough in one place to make a footmark. Now Miranda pinned him. One thing, he reflected with gloomy relish, Vittorio had not the slightest idea where he was. All 'that young crook' knew was that he, Josef, had the girl safe somewhere in the mountains.

'What emergency?'

'You saw the TV broadcast? Midday?' It was 31st August.

'No, I did not see a midday TV broadcast. I've not been told to watch, you must know that. I'll get my instructions –'

'OK, OK. So you didn't hear the radio broadcast either?'

'So, I didn't hear the radio broadcast either.'

Josef could imagine him from his voice. Vittorio indeed! No good would come of him.

'Well, they've double-crossed.'

'Who?'

'They. They're going to prosecute your friends.' The voice at the far end was like a hiss.

'Did it say so? On the radio?'

'Certainly. "Serious charges", that sort of thing.'

'They'll drop them.'

There was a pause, and Josef heard Vittorio say, 'I've got orders as to what to do in this particular case.'

'Well?' Josef found himself disliking the business more than he would have supposed possible. There was no reason – compared with some work he'd done for the Revolution this was hardly dirtying the hands. And yet –

'Well?'

'You can leave the details to me. They – you understand?'

'Of course.'

'They are to receive a reminder that a certain young lady's return to her friends depends on agreed conditions being honoured.'

Josef's distrust of Vittorio – whom he thought of not by name but always as 'that young crook' – was intensified by Vittorio's volubility down the telephone. He, Josef, spoke little, needed nothing to be explicit, remembered all. Who knew when a chance remark might put listening police ears on the alert and lead to God knew what? Now this young waster was making speeches about 'a certain young lady', about 'conditions being honoured' as if, as if – Josef glared at the telephone and longed to get the conversation done with. Vittorio, however, appeared in no hurry, although now he thought of it, Josef reckoned there was something nervous in the other's voice. He was glad of it. Vittorio's voice was continuing:

'Return to her friends *in one piece*, as they say.' Then there was a laugh. A nervous laugh but still a laugh.

'Well?'

'Well, there's to be a reminder sent, a, shall we say, physical reminder. I'm to do it. The instructions, the contingency instructions were left with me, you see. They're perfectly clear.'

'I don't believe it.'

There was a silence. Then Vittorio's voice again, sounding strained and indignant:

'I tell you I've got clear instructions what to do. I'll come north, we'll talk about that – something's to be sent to an address in England again. They'll start to –'

'I don't believe it. Not yet. You don't know they'll prosecute. He can't have meant us to start this sort of thing until – well, until it was clear they're for it – he and she, I mean. And I don't believe it. Why announce it so soon?'

'I told you, it said –'

'What did it say?'

'Something about "It's probable serious charges will be brought". Something like that. I told you.'

'That would have been for public opinion. That would have been to shut up those people who'll be saying "why let dangerous terrorists into the US, why make deals with these people?" That's all. They won't do it. And if they do, it'll be announced after the operation, all very leisurely. You know their procedures. There'll be plenty of time for the sort of thing you're talking about.'

Vittorio said, sulkiness as evident down the line as if he had been facing Josef, lips pouting,

'Anyway, if we have to take the big step, the final step, I've got the instructions.'

'You are speaking of the step which might be taken if there is a refusal to meet the further demand. Which has not yet been presented.'

'And won't be, yet. Of course that's what I'm speaking about. *He* told me to give you the details. You know I'm to be responsible.'

'I know that.'

'You can leave it all to me,' the same resentful, insolent young voice, a shade unsteady, went on. 'As you may know, I'm rather expert at that sort of thing. Now, here's what you would have to do.'

He talked for a while. Reno had told him the unseen Josef never forgot a detail, was utterly reliable. He concluded, 'So if we talk again, all we need mention is day and time, agreed?'

'Agreed.' Josef felt better. The young crook had said no more about 'physical reminders' – that was a try-on, there could be no need for it yet. Who was this immature lout, to presume that Josef had no experience, no powers of reasoning? As for 'the final step', Josef told himself it wouldn't come to anything, and he preferred it that way. Even the Italians wouldn't sacrifice this girl for Branca! But he moved his mind to the present again, from a future he did not particularly wish to contemplate.

# CHAPTER 11

'Carla, you are comfortable where they've put you to stay?'

'What do you mean, comfortable? Of course I'm comfortable as you call it. I'm in a hotel, sheets on the bed, food when I want it, nothing to pay. Nobody to speak to, nothing to pay. What more can I wish?'

Carla threw out her arms in a gesture of mockery and contempt. Franzi knew that she had spent much of the preceding four days in tears. They had arrived, the strange trio, in New York on the evening of Monday, 28th August, the same evening they had left Milan, gaining exhausting hours in flight before the remorseless path of the sun. Franzi had immediately been led by a posse of police officers, officials from various departments and welcoming friends, to a private lounge – yet another private lounge with yet more reporters and yet more cameras. Very tired, on edge, uncertain of what he thought or felt about anything, he only just managed to recognise the affectionate and enthusiastic friends who stepped forward past protective policemen to wring his hand.

'Franzi, it's great to see you. Have you had us worried!'

The hospital at which he operated was well represented. The senior surgeon, Dr Batley, managed to get a word in above the general confusion, the flashing bulbs.

'Franzi, Mary and I want you to stop with us a few days. Don't go back to that apartment of yours right away. You need a bit of a break, kind of looking after for a while. Mary insists.'

'Tom, that's very nice of you. But –'

'No, it's all fixed. We've got to get you in good shape and you can't win this one all by yourself.'

Franzi said that there were many things he would need to

discover, many aspects of his life he needed to unravel, tidy, adjust. It would need a lot of telephoning.

'Of course it will. Franzi, look on us as your base until you're fit, and until everything's fixed.'

'There's my house in Italy – the people there –'

'I guess things like that have been pretty well looked after, but why not call them there tomorrow? You'll want to call your friends, your relatives in England, too. And in Germany.'

'Yes. As a matter of fact the two people I care most about met me at Milan. I was so dazed I didn't know what to say. I still am.'

Then another hand had claimed him, and the assurances came fast.

'We'll get you away very soon now, Dr Langenbach. If you could just bring yourself to have a word with these boys here, just one word –'

He turned, exhausted, dazzled by strong lights. To someone he said,

'Reno and Carla. Where are they?'

The man was a plainclothes police officer who looked at him politely.

'Who exactly, Dr Langenbach?'

'Reno and Carla. They flew here with me.'

'You mean the two terrorists? The kidnappers?'

'Yes, of course. Where are they?'

He was told that both were in the hands of the authorities and special arrangements were being made. Suddenly Franzi felt not only fatigue but panic and something like anger. Who was in charge of all this? He said to the man, who appeared to have a certain standing,

'It was part of the arrangement that these people with me should in no way be harmed. Correct? Do you know that?'

'Yes, that is correct, Dr Langenbach. I think that tomorrow you will be seeing –'

'I daresay. But I want to know what is happening now. Reno – the man – is very ill. I have agreed to operate.'

Someone else who had heard the exchange interposed.

'Yes, we appreciate what was extracted from you, Dr Langenbach. Tomorrow –'

'There is no question of extraction. I have diagnosed for that man. I have undertaken to perform an operation. He is my patient.'

'Quite so. Well –'

'And it's urgent.'

Somebody else had come forward then, there had been telephone calls, conversations between twos and threes, murmurs, gestures. There had been repeated pleas to Franzi to come away, to join Dr Thomas Batley and leave for the latter's apartment. Reno and Carla were nowhere to be seen and eventually he learned that Reno had, by agreement, been taken to the hospital. Franzi, more out of bravado and a desire to assert personality, authority, than because he believed it likely, called out,

'I shall see him in the morning!'

To Batley he said, 'I should operate before the end of next week, Tom. It's an acute condition.'

'Maybe. They'll look after him. You've got to get fit before you operate on anyone or anything.'

Franzi knew this to be true. Conceding nothing he had said,

'Now, there's Carla –'

'The girl. Franzi, the police officer that seems to be handling it, this Captain Malone, you shook his hand first, a nice fellow, well, it seems they've got the girl fixed up in a kind of hotel. They'll keep an eye on her. It's a place where the police have some sort of an arrangement. But she's not in a cell.'


'What more can I wish?' Carla sighed deeply. Then she muttered, 'After all, it will be prison next.'

'Why should it be prison? You know that there has been an undertaking.'

'Yes. And do you know what they have told me? And what has been in the newspaper? That in spite of everything there is likely to be a prosecution of us! Of Reno and me! Now they have got you safe their promises are what I always knew they would be. Dirt! Do you know this?'

Franzi had indeed learned this with angry concern, two days afrer their arrival, a Wednesday of ceaseless interviews and reports made for the benefit, as far as he could see, of almost every police force and prosecution office in the Western world. For these, the Americans – long-suffering, wearied and less involved than most – were acting as proxy agents. He had spoken with great force to the most senior man he met, an official of the Federal Justice Department, by name Barrow.

'It is appalling that this statement was made, about a possible prosecution of these two after all. Appalling! It is against the agreement –'

'Quite so. Quite so.'

'I understand it was put out earlier today.'

'That is so.'

'It must immediately put at risk Miss Wrench, the English friend of mine who – a thing I would never have agreed – is a hostage in these people's hands. Their immunity is the condition of her safety, as I understand it.'

'Well, Dr Langenbach, I expect there was a good deal of bluff in that –'

'I see no reason to suppose so.'

'But we see your point, of course. As a matter of fact that announcement about a likely prosecution was the result of a confusion –'

'Then it was criminally irresponsible. Was it originated in Italy? In Austria?'

'I rather believe, Dr Langenbach, that the story originated in Italy. There was a misunderstanding some time yesterday. An Italian Minister was asked why terrorists were given immunity to leave the country in a deal which had no benefits for Italy and offended the principles of justice, that sort of thing –'

'I understand perfectly. And sympathise.'

'And, you know how it is, the Minister got emotional and started shouting that there was no immunity, that if ever they returned to Italy, they'd face justice for their actions, that the

218

question of extradition was not for him – that sort of thing.'

'Which didn't answer the question of why they'd been allowed to leave in the first place. I see. And what is being done to correct this impression, this false impression, that these people will be prosecuted? This false statement which may bring, or may have already brought great danger to Miss Wrench?'

'There has been a corrective statement made, Dr Langenbach. Most networks have carried the story. In most countries, I believe.'

'What did it say?'

Barrow had been imprecise. He thought the corrective statement had said that 'no decisions had been taken' to prosecute the two persons, Reno Vanetti and Carla Rosio, who had flown to New York with Dr Langenbach. An earlier report that they would now face charges had been based on a misunderstanding.

'You realise that my integrity is completely involved with the fulfilment of promises to these two people, Mr Barrow?'

Barrow had nodded.

'Sure, Dr Langenbach. And the United States will be glad to see the last of them, frankly. Our Government took a lot of persuading to let them in.' Barrow was one who thought America had been unreasonably generous in the matter. He said quietly,

'Problem is, where'll they go?'

'I thought it was agreed to fly them both to a place of their choice. Libya, perhaps.'

'Maybe,' said Barrow. Then he added,

'Of course our Italian friends would like to get their hands on them. The crime after all – kidnapping your good self, not to speak of what they did to you – took place in Italy. I guess the two parties to this now are Italy and the US. And the Italians reckon this pair were behind a lot of other things. So it's not easy, Dr Langenbach. We have very close relations with our Italian friends.'

'The Italians let them out, knowing what had been agreed.'

'They did. But there was no other way to ensure you got free. They couldn't just grab you and lift the other two at Milan airport, could they?'

'One could ask,' said Franzi, 'why not? If it is proposed to dishonour the undertaking not to prosecute.'

'I didn't say that, Dr Langenbach. I just said it's not easy, that's all. There's a lot of discussion going on. As to why they didn't simply arrest these two at the airport, well there's the question of Miss Wrench, isn't there? Naturally nobody wants anything to happen to her.'

Franzi had said, with irony,

'Naturally! Yet she must now have been placed in danger by a stupid and unnecessary announcement that there might be a prosecution. And she will be in certain, quite certain, danger if there is any question of returning Reno and Carla' – and he could only think of them by those names, Vanetti and Rosio sounded wholly false – 'to face prosecution in Italy.' He felt certain, but did not allow himself to think about it, that there would also be grave danger to Miranda if, under his expert hands, Reno died.

Now he looked at this girl who, only nine days earlier, had been lying in his arms.

Carla said again,

'Their promises were dirt! As I knew!'

'Carla, there was a mistake. You won't be charged. It will be like you, like Reno, told me was agreed. You'll be free to fly to wherever you wish. When Reno's well.'

'I don't believe you.'

'I'm sure of it.'

'They have told you so?'

'Yes,' exaggerated Franzi. 'Yes, they have told me so, Carla. It was a mistaken announcement you saw or heard about. It was always natural there would be some muddle, some confusion. It's been corrected. People know, now, that you and Reno will go free.'

They were standing facing each other, in the foyer of a small hotel on New York's West Side, an hotel Franzi supposed the police were able to use for this sort of purpose. Two other

220

people were hovering in the foyer. Carla would be watched, of course. All the time. He kept his voice at a conversational level, entirely unnatural. Carla was trembling. In a low voice she said,

'Why should I believe you? Any more than I should have believed you when you said what you did to me some time ago? About – about –'

She spoke so low Franzi had to bend his head. He caught the smell of her, evocative of a time of pain and fear and frustration. But of feeling too.

'A-About what you felt.'

Franzi was experiencing the acute discomfort which comes from seeing a human being in entirely different circumstances and from suffering, in consequence, totally different emotions from those felt, genuinely felt, on a previous occasion. He had once said, 'I think I love you, too, Carla.' He had said the words to a bowed golden-red head of hair, to the back of a smooth, smooth honey-coloured neck, to a slender body felt through a thin, shapeless blouse in a bare, sordid Perugian attic. He had said the words to a girl trembling, suddenly in his arms, a girl he had only been speaking to, had only seen (except behind a face mask) for the previous seven days; a girl who had joined in the planning of his kidnap, who had nursed him, co-operated in the hacking off of one of his fingers and then bandaged and nursed him again. To a girl who had said, 'I love you, perhaps I always will love you.' To a girl, damn it, who, whatever she was or had been, possessed that sort of terrible sincerity, that capacity for feeling, which compels belief on the rare occasions when such a one says, 'I love you.' What had she once whispered to him as he'd held her in his arms, Reno in the next bare room?

'It's like a candle flame that lights up a face in a dark room. One sees it and says, "I love you". I suppose it's the flame one loves, really, the light. It just falls on a particular face, suddenly.'

'Yes, Carla. And the candle flame is always there. It is love itself.' But then he had told he she was like a gazelle. And had said that he thought he, too, loved her; and had known

221

she hoped for that above all things. And then they had made love. Love?

Now he was looking down at her in the dark and depressing foyer of a third-rate New York hotel, unobtrusively watched by strangers, no doubt plainclothes cops. Nowhere to go – and another act of treason if he made it easy to find somewhere to go, even if it were allowed. Franzi was unsure what he had felt when he had once murmured, 'I think I love you, too, Carla.' All he knew was that he had no such emotions within him now, none whatsoever, only an enormous pity; and that it would be not kind, but wicked and weak to lead her to believe otherwise. And, at the same time, he intensely disliked himself for feeling as he did. Franzi was incapable of cynicism – incapable to a fault.

Carla said,

'Where are you in this city?'

'I'm staying with friends.'

'Can't I see you? Can't I be with you?'

'It's difficult. You see I've got to get myself ready, there's a lot to do. I can't just operate, just like that. I've got to be one hundred per cent. I must rest, get certain things sorted out, be very calm.'

Carla was looking at him intently. Still very low, she said,

'All right. I know you don't want me.'

'Carla, it's not that –'

'Don't speak. You don't want me. About whether these pigs put me in prison I don't care a damn. As to Reno –'

'Carla, I'm going to do my best, my very best for Reno. I've promised.'

'Yes. You've promised. And if Reno dies do you know something? Your rich bitch friend will probably die too. You know that?'

Franzi stared at her. They were standing very close.

'You know that, Dr Langenbach? You let Reno die and she dies. All arranged. And if not for that reason maybe for another reason. And you know something else? I hope it happens! You mind about her, I saw you, you made a fuss when you heard we'd got her. At Milan! You were emotional!

For the first time! You shouted at Reno! *"Menzogna"*, you shouted. Well, it's not *Menzogna* that she'll soon be knocked on the head. Why not?' She was talking still low, but very fast, breasts heaving.

'Why not? And I tell you, I hope it happens!'


Three days later, on 4th September, Lise von Arzfeld arrived in New York, faithful to the vow she had made to herself at Milan airport one week before. She and Franzi had spoken several times on the telephone. He had felt from her, who had been more like a mother than a cousin, ever loving, ever supportive – he had felt a depth of unspoken understanding which he greatly needed. She had always understood. Always gone to the heart of a matter. And she loved him, unpossessively but deeply. In a second telephone call, not arguing the matter, she had said,

'Franzi, I have never, as you know, been to America. Now I intend to give myself a little extravagance. I intend to travel on 4th September, early next week, and to spend two weeks in New York. Maybe we can see each other a little, although I know you are very busy. I have always wanted to see that place. Please reserve for me a room in an hotel, not too expensive but nice. I leave that to you.'

When Lise made a decision she wasted little time. 'Always wanted to see that place!' He'd never guessed it and smiled disbelief. Lise was coming because she knew instinctively that the presence of somebody, something, familiar, redolent of family, of boyhood, of home (for to Franzi, Arzfeld had long been home) – Lise knew that this might help. And it was not difficult to guess he needed help. He had had to fly to America – all the world understood that, and all the world knew why, knew the details of this strange bargain which had procured his freedom. But America was not his home, although he lived there much of the time. America could not give him the sort of peace he must need to remake himself, Lise was right to be sure. If there had been a woman in America, somebody for whom he felt something deep, then, maybe – But Lise was

223

sure she would have gathered a hint of such from his easy talks to her throughout the years, on his fleeting visits. Lise was certain there was nobody, nobody who really mattered. She did not find the knowledge satisfying, as some would have done. In her love for Franzi there was little room for jealousy. She longed for him to be happy, but she was perfectly clear that she was needed in New York.

Franzi met Lise at the airport. He glanced sideways at her as she sat beside him driving towards Manhattan. Straight grey hair parted in the centre, hair that had once been very fair, surrounding a face which still had much of the pretty and gentle girl she had been when Franzi's father had first known her, when Franzi's mother had petted her as a loved younger cousin. But Lise's face was strong and it held a severity, a firmness, which had come from suffering bravely experienced. Lise had never talked much to small Franzi or adolescent Franzi about the war and its aftermath, about the Nazi period, about the death of her brothers. She had spoken in a matter-of-fact way sometimes about her own experiences, about how she and Marcia Rudberg had nursed on the Eastern Front, had managed to get away from the Russians. But she never talked with self-pity or dramatisation. These things had happened. She, Lise von Arzfeld, had survived. That was that.

He showed her his apartment.

'Last week, you came straight here? Alone?'

'No, I'm still staying with very kind friends. The Batleys. He's a colleague at the hospital. I went to them – they thought I needed looking after!'

'They were quite right. It is a nice apartment but you should be with people, not sitting by yourself. You must have had too much by yourself. Oh, Franzi!'

She put her arms around him, crying quietly. That awful, unnatural moment at Milan airport! It had been necessary to go, to see him, to touch him, but how grim it had been! Of course, she had reflected often, I should have insisted on flying with him here to New York, straight away. As a nurse, that's what he needed. But she had not known just how things would be or would appear to Franzi; and there were those two, those

224

wicked two with him! A strange, strange situation. But now it would be all right.

'Oh, Franzi!'

Franzi said, 'Listen, you know I've booked your hotel room for three nights, to begin with –'

'I wish to stay more than that. I have seen it, it is a nice hotel. And not too expensive.' Lise had dipped deep into the Arzfeld financial reserves for the trip.

'Good. But Lise, I thought you might like to move in here, into the apartment and stay with me. If you'd like that, I'll move out from staying with the Batleys. He's my colleague, Dr Thomas Batley, they've been very kind but I must move back here sometime. And we'd spend the rest of your two weeks here. Would you like that? I can tell you where to go, what to see, while I'm at the hospital. I'll explain where I generally buy food and so forth. There's a woman who comes and cleans, whether I'm here or not –'

Lise was utterly delighted. It had been in her mind but she had wanted Franzi to suggest it first.

Much later when they were sitting companionably in Franzi's apartment, Lise said, without particular emphasis, naturally,

'Please explain to me how it is with these two people who came with you. Who – well, I don't know, was it these two who kidnapped you?'

'Yes, it was. They held me. There were others, of course, but these two were the bosses of this particular group.'

'And it is this man, Vanetti, on whom you are going to operate?'

'In a few days' time, that's right. He has a very, very serious heart condition.'

Lise was watching him closely. He said to her,

'Lise, love, you can understand me, can't you? I know you can. I must operate on this man, do my best to save his life, whatever he's done to me or to anybody else. He's a murderer – they tell me that and I believe them. He's been prepared to kill me – he was probably going to kill me if Bonn had not agreed to release Klaretta Barinski –'

225

'Ach! That business!'

'That business. I don't think he was bluffing. Carla – that's the girl – told me. They would have killed me. It's likely that they'd have killed me anyway – I was never sure – until this happened, this extraordinary chance that he's got a heart condition I was able to diagnose. And which I'm able to operate on, as not many can. Until then, I think they – or, anyway, Reno, that's what we call him, Reno – would have killed me, whatever concessions they obtained. I would have been dangerous to them. I owe him nothing, except revenge.'

'Well?'

'Well, but I must still do my best for him –'

'Of course. There is no question about it. I am sure nobody disagrees with you.'

Franzi was less sure. He smiled at her, gratefully and tenderly.

'Lise, there's more to it. You see there's the question of what happens to him, to both of them, after he's had his operation and recovered. It was the agreement. I've been through this very thoroughly with the people here, of course I knew little at the time, they told me very little in Perugia, where they were keeping me –'

'They were holding you there, in Perugia in Italy? Everyone thought it was in Austria.'

Lise remembered reading in the newspapers after Franzi's release that it appeared Dr Langenbach had been held not in Austria but in Italy throughout his captivity! She said again, 'In Italy!'

'Yes, in Perugia most of the time. Of course they've cleared all traces there, so that nothing I say can lead to other arrests, to any particular place or name. Reno's very thorough, very clever. As you can imagine it took him some time to arrange all that when he agreed to bring me out, to come to America himself –'

'I understand.'

'But the point is, what happens to them? It was the agreement that they, Reno and Carla, would certainly *not* be prosecuted. That they'd be free to be flown somewhere, anywhere they chose. An awful life, but no prosecution. No prison. That was the bargain.'

'So we have all understood. You know, Franzi, there has been nothing like this, I think, every move, every offer, every response has been reported fully on TV –'

'I know. That's part of Reno's plan. You see publicity is what these people want. But it was *agreed* that there should be no prosecution.'

'By whom, Franzi?'

'By the authorities – obviously here in America, obviously in Italy or they'd have been arrested at Milan airport. And now I get the feeling – I've had several long talks with the Justice people here, of course, and they're in touch with the Italians – I have the feeling that they're going to go back on it. Once this operation's over.'

Franzi shrugged his shoulders. The apartment was air-conditioned and the humid heat of New York's summer was comfortably at bay.

'I may be wrong, of course. I have the feeling that there would be criticism if the authorities reneged on their word to a man who's very ill. Everybody knows, you said so, that their word's been given. Whereas when he's better there may be hitches, diplomatic problems, you know the sort of thing. And they, Reno and Carla, will end up in the dock after all.'

'And you would be distressed at that?' Lise asked.

'Yes,' he looked at her hard. 'Yes. I would be distressed at that. Because although it was not my word that was given I feel my – my integrity is involved.'

'One can still say "honour",' said Lise very softly. 'That's the word isn't it?'

'That's the word.'

She took his hand in hers and held it tightly.

'You are your mother's son.'

'Am I wrong?'

'No. You are not wrong. As for me I wish these people were in prison cells for the rest of their lives. It would be justice. But you are not wrong. A promise was made.'

'To obtain my freedom. And, of course, there is another

227

thing and a more important thing. There is this girl, Miranda Wrench.'

Lise had supposed he would talk about that from the start. It appeared to her the most important factor. She nodded.

'It's incredible what she's done,' Franzi said in a low voice, his hand still in Lise's, 'it's wrong that she should have been allowed. But now everything, *everything* must be done for her safety. If they prosecute Reno and Carla she'll – well, Lise, they may kill her. Then I don't think – I don't think I could go on living.'

He said it near inaudibly but Lise was unsurprised. He added, still difficult for Lise to hear,

'And they may kill her, too, if the operation fails. Or for some other reason. I live with that knowledge all the time.'

'Franzi, darling, it's very, very important this. And the authorities must see it – must see that Fraülein Wrench will be in danger if they don't keep their word to these two terrorists. I understand your feelings about your own honour, and I agree with them; but others might not. This other thing, this danger to the girl is obvious. Surely it's very serious? Surely you must be mistaken about the authorities' intentions? I know there was an announcement that it might happen – but it was corrected. Why do you think what you do?'

'I can't get a direct answer,' said Franzi. 'I put the point to them all the time and they say "of course". So why aren't I satisfied? Well, they say the Italians won't issue a positive statement that there'll be no prosecution. In spite of my request. I would have thought the British would have seen the point, too, and pressed the Italians. I've talked to the Embassy people here – same thing, the point is well under-stood, Dr Langenbach, we are sure all will be well, no purpose served at this moment, our Italian friends, all that sort of thing. It still leaves me uneasy.'

They sat for a little. She stroked his hand and said,

'I expect they are right. They must have considered it very carefully, with Fraülein Wrench's safety uppermost in their minds. I expect they are right.'

She added,

'It's not easy for governments, darling Franzi. There is a lot of public indignation, you know, at these terrible things that are done. It's not easy for governments to say, "It doesn't matter, we'll strike a bargain, we'll let this evil person go free".'

'I understand that. Of course, public opinion is very important.'

Franzi gazed out of a window at the Manhattan roofscape. Lise felt, every moment, gladder that she had come to New York. Now she said,

'You have not said much about the girl.'

'About Miranda?'

'No, not about Miranda. I think Miranda is very important – maybe very important to you, not just because she's in danger and has done this thing for you, but because of something in your voice when you say her name. I don't talk about that, maybe you're not ready to talk about that. I ask about the other girl, the terrorist girl.'

'Ah! About Carla.'

'Yes, about Carla. I saw her in that room at the Milan airport. She's pretty. I saw her come into that room, not knowing what to expect, very vulnerable. And very pretty. More pretty than she appeared on television, I think.'

Franzi said, 'Yes, she's pretty.'

'And is she a murderess?'

'I suppose so. In a way. She has helped in – in outrages which have led to death, yes.'

'And,' said Lise, 'does she love you, my darling Franzi? And do you, perhaps, a little, love her?'

Franzi smiled at her gently. He said,

'Lise, I'm going to cancel your hotel room from tomorrow. I want you to move in here tomorrow, and we'll sit together, and be quiet and it will be like home. Sit and be quiet. Not say much. Like at Arzfeld. Watch television if we feel like it.'

'Ach!' said Lise. 'How I have come to hate that television!'

Next evening, however, Tuesday, 5th September, they were in Franzi's apartment, and they enjoyed a quiet supper and a sense, his first sense, of considerable peace.

229

'When will you do this operation, Franzi? Surely not yet? You are not fit, I think.'

'Next week. Today week. I'm getting better every day. And I'm much, much better today than yesterday.'

He smiled at her and, despite a muted protest from Lise, he turned on the television news which had already started.

'According to the latest information,' the announcer said, 'the terrorists climbed a security fence into the Olympic Village at Munich, West Germany, at around five o'clock local time this morning, 5th September. Soon afterwards shots were heard, and two Israeli athletes were shot while still in bed, while the rest of the Israeli team were held hostage by the gunmen, who demanded the freeing of two hundred Arab freedom-fighters imprisoned in Israel for other outrages earlier this year. Negotiations proceeded with representatives of the Federal German Government, as a result of which a helicopter was deployed to the open space in the Olympic Village itself.'

'My God,' Franzi muttered, eyes fixed on the screen where some film of the Munich Olympic village was now shown. 'My God, I've heard nothing of any of this.'

He had been taking little interest in current news and none in the Olympic Games. Lise was breathing fast and agitated. The announcer's voice continued:

'It seems the Israeli hostages, who were blindfold and bound, boarded the helicopter at gun point, together with their captors, at around 10 pm local time, that is about four hours ago. The helicopter, by agreement with the terrorists, then flew to Furstenfeldbruck military airfield, where it was supposed an aircraft would take both terrorists and Israelis to a destination thought to be Libya.'

On the screen was an airfield, photographed through what appeared to be a security fence. Franzi supposed it was Furstenfeldbruck.

'As the exchange from helicopter to aircraft was taking place the Federal German security authorities opened fire and a gun battle took place in the dark. According to the latest reports, there are nine dead, including four of the terrorists.

At least three persons are in the hands of the German authorities. Responsibility has been claimed by the Black September Group, which is thought to have connections with other terrorist groups in Germany and several Western European countries. This is New York –'

Franzi switched it off. He said, 'Bad. Very bad.'

'Horrible.'

They sat in silence for a while. Then Lise whispered,

'It will make a lot of publicity, a lot of indignation this. Even more than some other such things.'

'I know.'

'It will make it harder, all these things make it harder for the authorities to seem soft towards terrorists, Franzi. To give in to demands.'

'Yes. I know.'


Next day, Franzi had another interview with Barrow, of the Justice Department. He again spoke of the unfortunate announcement, later retracted, that charges might ultimately be brought against 'Vanetti and Rosio'.

'I really think there should be an unequivocal public statement that there will be no prosecution. I'm thinking always, as you know, of Miranda Wrench.'

This was to go over familiar ground. Barrow was always courteous and patient.

'Dr Langenbach, have you considered that it is not for the United States authorities to make such a statement? The crime or crimes which could be fastened on these people were committed in Italy.'

'Of course. But you have told me of the co-operation, the communication, that has taken place in the whole matter between the two countries. Could it not be suggested –'

Barrow said that was true. There was close touch, 'and no disagreement' between Washington and Rome. He said that nobody supposed, however, that a statement on the lines Franzi suggested would be helpful.

'Dr Langenbach, there is no reason to suppose it would

231

lead them to release Miss Wrench. Why should they? They are holding her to ensure Vanetti and Rosio are flown out of America to somewhere they choose. Why release Miss Wrench before that?'

Franzi said quietly,

'I think they are also holding her to ensure – if one can put it so absurdly – that the operation on Reno Vanetti goes well. Have the authorities thought of that? Have they reflected that if, *if*, this operation does not succeed, the sort of people we're dealing with are perfectly capable of convincing themselves the failure is deliberate?'

'I know, Dr Langenbach. I know these people are pathological, their capacity for self-deception is great, I know that.'

'And Miss Wrench – Miranda – is to them a hostage against failure. And would become a sacrifice. I know this sounds theatrical.' His hand was shaking slightly and he rested his chin upon it to steady and disguise it. He said, for what sounded to him the hundredth time, that while this latter danger to Miranda was one which he alone could do anything about, an unequivocal statement about amnesty for Reno and Carla might, just might, help Miranda's safety. 'It would, as it were, give them something more positive to look forward to. Something they wouldn't wish to place at risk.' He had been over this ground again and again.

Barrow said that he entirely understood. He looked carefully at Franzi and wondered whether this man would, in reality, be fit to carry out a difficult surgical operation very shortly. Of course, what he said about the girl was perfectly true – they'd always appreciated that and so had the Italians. There were, he thought with regret, things he could not explain to Franzi so that the conversation had to be conducted upon inevitably false premises. It was the third time Franzi had pressed him to seek from the Italians a new public statement that Vanetti and Rosio would not be prosecuted, could go free, and Barrow, as he nodded seriously and sympathetically to Franzi, thought of his last conversation with Rome.

His Italian colleague talked excellent American. Barrow had said,

'Of course he's anxious about that hint of prosecution! He fears for the Wrench girl, naturally, and he thinks his own word, his own integrity depends on there being no back-tracking –'

'Ah, that!'

'I'm simply explaining his state of mind. Perhaps if I tell him –'

'Not possible. You know the complications.'

'He's anxious about the operation on Vanetti, too. He thinks the Wrench girl is at risk, real risk in two eventualities – first if Vanetti doesn't recover, second if it looks as if Vanetti's going to be prosecuted.'

'Of course, of course. But *you* know –'

'It would be helpful if I could say something to help Dr Langenbach's peace of mind.'

His Italian contact said, very vehemently, that this was not possible. Some things must remain on the most secure and secret basis. 'He must try to be relaxed, Mr Barrow. He simply needs to think about his patient!'

'Then there's the girl – Rosio –'

'We don't care a damn about the girl! Is Langenbach sweet on the girl?'

'I've no idea,' Barrow had said primly.

He did not look forward to the post-operative period, when the surgeon, outraged, would accuse all and sundry of betrayal. Primarily the Italians, of course; but America in general and Barrow in particular would be prime targets of his attack. Now he said,

'You will also appreciate, Dr Langenbach, that governments have to take account of public opinion. When people reflect on the sort of dreadful thing that happened in Munich yesterday, they're not disposed to like the idea of terrorists going free.'

# CHAPTER 12

12th September. Franzi, masked, silent, using the first fingers and thumbs of both hands, dominated the artificially cool room. Several nurses and a junior surgeon moved anonymously in the background, responsive to Franzi's brisk indications. On the operating table was stretched a carcase belonging to a dedicated member of the European Liberation Movement, indistinguishable now from any other carcase, whose ribs had been neatly sawn open to expose the workings of the human machine within, the movements of liquid and matter which constituted the material aspect of what is known as life. The vital element, the pump which kept things going, that which whether in anatomy or poetry is described as the essential, the core of the person – this, the heart, had in Reno's case been disconnected and was temporarily serving no functional purpose. Instead Reno's arteries had been attached to an artificial pump, performing its task most efficiently, keeping something technically describable as life in the carcase technically describable as Reno Vanetti. Meanwhile Franzi – forefingers and thumbs holding instruments with a delicacy which absence and strain did not appear to have in the least diminished – Franzi gently, moving the points of his instruments like the artist he was, worked on Reno's actual heart, original heart, heart which presumably contained (at least in allegorical terms) all that revolutionary fervour and fire. Reno, no poet, would have contemptuously dismissed such fancies, pointing out that his adherence to the Revolution was a thing of the mind, not the conceit of some gobbet of flesh and gristle called a heart. But even Reno felt emotions when he thought of the Revolution and the world, emotions which were not purely cerebral. Even Reno felt what poets called a stirring of the blood – indeed he felt such more often than most. Reno's heart, now an object temporarily without purpose, stood for something as well as being a mechanical provider of necessary physical impulses. Would it beat again?

Franzi was still very aware of the stump where his little finger once had been. He had insisted that the mutilation made no difference to his operating capabilities, and in logic there was no reason why it should. Nevertheless, there was a soreness, a discomfort which he knew would take months to disappear. When he had first arrived in New York he had at once had the hand examined. The atrocity had, of course, received maximum publicity a few weeks earlier and he found people avoiding his eye when his left hand was too demonstratively paraded. Even at the hospital they had seemed to hesitate between sympathetic outrage and dispassionate professional attention. An incredible, a disgusting indignity! And to a surgeon of such distinction!

Carla had done a good original job, but of course the wound had to be treated thoroughly and it was going to take time for tissues to heal, skin to grow.

'It doesn't inconvenience me. In the least.'

'No doubt it's uncomfortable at times, Dr Langenbach?'

'Of course. But it would be absurd to suppose it puts me at any disadvantage.'

He had initially been told 'with respect, sir, but with firmness,' that he should not think of operating 'just yet'.

'Your experiences have been hard, Dr Langenbach. That sort of thing takes a lot out of a man. And nobody knows better than you in what fine condition a surgeon needs to be.'

Franzi said that he proposed to operate – and to operate on Reno Vanetti – on 12th September. The date suited the hospital.

'I shall have been in America over two weeks by then. I am already in perfectly good condition, rested, well.'

It was true in one sense. In another it was false. His mind was tormented throughout every day by the fact that Miranda was in the hands of God knew whom because she had volunteered to go into captivity so that he, Franzi Langenbach, might be free. To bring that fear and uncertainty to an end as soon as possible was the main motive for his haste to get on with the business, to operate. Of course, Reno's condition was extremely serious but it was unlikely to be affected by minor delay, despite the urgency he impressed on all. No, it was essential to drive this nightmare business through to its conclusion, to save this man's life if he could, and quickly; and end another nightmare for a brave, quixotic girl far away, a girl Franzi told himself, without knowing for sure whether it was true, that he loved.

On the other hand he heard Carla's voice, low, intense –

'She'll be knocked on the head! I tell you, I hope it happens!'

The other disturbing factor, that deprived him of peace all the time, was the presence and the future of Carla herself. Carla had said and very clearly meant that she cared nothing for Reno, that Reno could die because it meant Miranda Wrench would die as well. Carla loved and hated. She loved him, Franzi. She hated any woman who might mean a thing to him – suspecting Miranda of being in that category, in reality lashing out, wishing her dead, because she could see with cruel clarity that she, Carla, had no hope of Franzi's love. Whatever there had been was past.

Franzi was gnawed by compassion and understanding. He could perfectly imagine a sort of emotion which would so dominate mind and senses as to drive out all other considerations, all previous loyalties, all earlier feelings. He had never loved – nor felt any passion – with that kind of consuming force, but his imagination was lively and he could comprehend and ache miserably for Carla. He felt neither smugness nor self-congratulation in having awakened this; and he knew that any person, especially no doubt Carla, would be filled with bitter rage as well as unhappiness to be regarded as an object of pity. But pity Carla he did, from the bottom of his heart. Only he knew that to pretend to her, simulate hopes of a future in which he was sure he could play no part – that would be atrocious, more cruel than open indifference, must compound guilt. Nor was he indifferent to Carla – he remembered her sudden passion for him, their incongruous love-making, with deep gratitude. Astonishingly, in the midst of darkness and pain and fear, there had been gentleness, beauty, joy. And Carla had brought it. She was a lovely girl, and, for all her criminal record, a girl of spirit, a girl with a heart. But Franzi knew that by now, and in a different setting from a locked Perugian attic, his response to Carla could only be an act. And it could convince neither of them.

So what could be Carla's future? When he had successfully fitted a new aortic valve to Reno's heart, when Reno, no doubt surly and resentful but a man with renewed expectation of life, was flown to some sheltering destination, some asylum – Libya? Eastern Europe? – Reno would undoubtedly begin again to work for 'the Revolution'. He would probably, Franzi reflected without interest, conspire to re-enter Western Europe, although he could expect little mercy from the Italian authorities at least. Consistent with orders from his shadowy 'superiors' Reno would continue his savage, remorseless private work for the European Liberation Movement, drawing strength from the contacts with other terrorist organisations which he undoubtedly possessed, supported by the parallel 'groups' who sustained each other. He would live in that shadowy underworld of safe houses, casual robbery, occasional sensational and violent crime, to which he had dedicated his talents and his youth. That would go on until he was caught, something pinned on him; or until he was gunned down, his planning having for once failed, in a police ambush. That would be Reno's life, a life now about to be prolonged by Franzi's skill. Reno would, no doubt, kill again, kill innocent people as at the Rome railway station. They would die because the eminent Dr Langenbach had enabled their killer to survive, where nature had decided to end his destructive days. And why had Dr Langenbach so decided, and so procured their deaths, these future victims? In order that the eminent surgeon should himself be freed, to continue a life of wealth, ease and distinction! That was it, wasn't it, rather than highflown rhetoric about the neutrality of medicine, the healing of the sick? Franzi glanced at the artificial pump to which Reno's arteries were in process of being connected. It would perform the actions of the heart while Franzi isolated the true

237

heart and operated upon it. It might be possible, he had said earlier to himself, to place a new aortic valve in Reno's heart, but no surgeon in the world could implant pity and remorse where there was seemingly none. Yet Carla would no doubt accompany Reno on his destructive and ultimately self-destructive pilgrimage. She probably had, after all, absolutely nowhere else to go.

Franzi had seen Carla only twice since their first dreadful meeting, three days after arrival in New York. He had been asked – politely but firmly – to check any visits with the police before and after they occurred.

'Miss Rosio is not under lock and key, naturally, Dr Langenbach. She's not a convicted criminal. At present she's in this hotel we often use – of course, you know our immigration rules, there can be no question of free movement yet, officially she's in kind of quarantine –'

Franzi understood perfectly. Everybody wanted to get rid of Carla as soon as possible. Meanwhile she had to live a half-existence that would last until Reno was fit to travel. A bored, dispirited, unhappy prisoner in all but name. On his first of the two subsequent visits he had brought a number of Italian books and papers.

'Carla, I know this waiting is very dull, a wretched existence.' He had tried to act as if he were an ordinary friend, to make believe that the awful moment when she had hissed, 'I hope it happens,' had never been.

'I know it's boring and dull for you here.'

'Of course it's boring and dull. How could it not be?'

'You were determined to come.'

'I dreaded it. I told Reno I dreaded it.'

'Still, you insisted –'

'Of course I insisted. And you know why.'

'Yes, well I want to tell you about that, about Reno. Our present plan –'

'It was not about Reno. It was not because of Reno I insisted. And you know that.'

Of course he knew that. He knew that she had determined to follow him, Franzi, into that other unguessed-at, unregenerated world which the Revolution was dedicated to destroy; to follow him to where he was at home and she the eternal outcast. Enemy territory. And her determination had nothing to do with the health of Reno.

He explained that Reno was under observation –

'Our plan is probably to operate some time in the week after next.'

'Why not sooner?'

Carla was perfectly sharp and knew that if Reno's condition was as Franzi had once described, it was unlikely to benefit from a postponement.

Franzi said he wanted to be entirely fit himself. He said it lightly, and Carla sighed and said, 'Why cannot someone else do it?'

'They could, Carla. But I've – well, as you know, I agreed to do it and it's not really something I want to ask a colleague to take on.' For nothing, he thought. These things aren't free, little Carla. But that was not a leading consideration.

'I ought to do it. As you may know, it is generally agreed I'm good at it.'

He smiled, as if reminding her tacitly that it was the fame of the gilded young surgeon that had once brought him to the attention of the European Liberation Movement. Carla did not smile. They were again sitting in the foyer, half-lounge, on the street-level floor of her hotel. A dingy, depressing place, but the police were courteously insistent that this was where such encounters ought to take place.

'Carla, is there anything you want?'

'A great deal.'

He sighed. Soon afterwards he stood up to go, and took a step towards her to kiss her. Carla turned away.

The second interview (he now thought of them, with inner repulsion, as interviews) took place a few days later. He had told her of the exact date of operation, of Reno's condition and of the likely period needed for recuperation 'if all goes well'. Carla said absolutely nothing.

Reno's aortic valve had been subject to a stenosis. It had become partially blocked, and the blockage had seriously interrupted the blood flow through arteries servicing the lower half of Reno's body. The result had been an increase in his blood pressure, which had risen and fallen but which had produced, and would increasingly produce, the sort of serious attacks which Franzi had witnessed. Attacks which could, and sooner or later would, prove fatal.

The symptoms, inevitably, resembled acute indigestion. It was unsurprising that Reno had muttered that it was indigestion, all he needed were some more of those pills. In fact, his spasms of fearful, crushing pain in the chest, his ice-cold greyness of face, the stillness with which he had sat, moaning, were all consistent with the condition which Franzi immediately suspected and had seen remarkably often: a condition of the heart.

It was also consistent, of course, that Reno had grumbled of headaches. Any sharp increase of blood pressure could cause those, but in this case the increase had a definable and worsening cause: aortic valve stenosis. Franzi had witnessed it often, diagnosed it frequently, operated to remedy it a large number of times. It was consistent, too, that Reno had muttered, when questioned, that there'd once been talk of mild epilepsy. The sort of gripping spasm which an aortic blockage produced was sometimes taken for epilepsy. But, primitive though Franzi's original examination and diagnosis had necessarily been, he was in no doubt, no doubt whatsoever of what was wrong.

The answer had to be surgical – open heart surgery. And it could, of course, go wrong. Cure should be total if the operation was successful. But it was tricky – for Franzi, for anyone. It would have been better if diagnosis and treatment had been earlier, much earlier, young though Reno was. And, like all such operations, it could go wrong.

A nurse moved her head, indicating to her colleague exactly what she thought. It was good to have Dr Langenbach back in the theatre – very good. Everybody in the hospital had followed the case with appalled fascination. When they had read of the appearance of his severed finger in a parcel in London one nurse had had something not far from hysterics. She had decided several months before that she was in love with Dr Langenbach, a condition which her fellows did not find peculiar but with which they had little patience.

Now he was back! Back, and operating on one of these brutes! Perhaps the one who had, himself, taken a chopping knife and –

Now the criminal, the sadist was having his life saved by his victim! How saintly could you get?

Franzi concentrated on the television screen with the slight narrowing of the eyes he always showed at moments of tension. Within Reno's body, at exactly the angle and in exactly the position which would show the valve itself, was a tiny camera. Franzi watched the points of his instruments moving. The insertion and then the making good of a new valve, a brand-new piece of human equipment to replace Reno's blocked one – this was tricky. The whole thing – from first incision to final connection of arteries to heart once again – inevitably took a long, long time. So far Franzi was not conscious of exceptional fatigue. He had worried, worried more than he allowed anyone to see, whether he should not have waited longer before operating, recovered more of his own normality. He had decided that the pressures – of Reno's condition, of the dreadful uncertainty about Miranda, even the emotional situation of Carla – all these made further delay unthinkable. Besides, when, if ever, would he recover more of his own normality? Sometimes he felt himself deteriorating.

He nodded his head again. That particular moment had gone well. Behind his mask the junior surgeon watched, admired and, he hoped, learned.

12th September was a very beautiful day in Tirol, cloud free, dazzling. Miranda tried that evening to get something, some small hint of information from Josef. She kept track of time from the newspaper he brought most days. Not all.

'Josef, I've been here now two and a half weeks. I think that's right.'

'I believe so, Fraülein Wrench.' Josef, masked, was always enormously correct. She saw him twice a day on his visits to the hut. It was, she supposed, solitary confinement – not uncomfortable, but driving her back on herself, starved of sound or conversation. Once she'd asked him if a radio would be obtainable. He'd looked regretful and said it might be difficult. In spite of the newspaper she guessed he had instructions not to let her have any direct, uncensorable access to the news. She did, however, manage (surprisingly) to persuade him to bring a small German-English dictionary. She worked at it hard.

'Two and a half weeks is quite a long time,' Miranda said inanely. Josef said nothing. He was gathering up some empty tins.

'Have you ever been a prisoner, Josef?'

He looked at her politely, serious.

'No, Fraülein. That never happened to me.'

'What have been the worst things which have happened to you?'

'I expect it was the war. Like for most people of my age.'

'You were in the war, Josef? I didn't imagine you were old enough. It finished twenty-seven years ago, after all.'

Although she never saw his face, Miranda had formed an increasing impression of Josef's youthfulness, rightly or wrongly. There was something persuasively young in his voice, his lightness, his step. And he was so very, very small!

Josef showed a certain touch of animation.

'I was young. They took me into the army when I was just under sixteen.'

'Which army?'

His voice indicated mild surprise.

'The German army, Fraülein. The Wehrmacht. I was mostly quite near my home, here in Austria.'

'Fighting whom?'

'We had the Russians, east of Vienna. Then we were switched west. We never knew much of what was going on.

242

Then the Americans arrived. I went home. My home was in Linz.'

'So you weren't taken prisoner.'

'I didn't wait. I went home. Burnt my uniform. I was still only seventeen.'

Miranda made a mental note of the fact.

'Your parents must have been glad to see you!'

'No father. My mother died while I was in the army.'

'Oh dear, Josef. I'm sorry.'

'No need. She was bad to me.'

He had finished collecting tins, but paused for a little, no doubt remembering. Miranda said,

'What did you do next?'

'I worked. Mechanic. And in the summer, at places like this in the mountains.'

'And became a kidnapper!' She said it with a smile. '*Entführer*! Why exactly? Or can't I ask?' It might be imprudent, yet she had no fear of Josef. But now he sounded rather stern.

'Fraülein Wrench, this is a world which is a very bad, cruel place for a great many people. I saw that as soon as I saw anything. People treat other people worse than animals. Some people get on and grab all they can and don't care who ends up in the ditch. Other people are hungry all the time. It's not a good world. It's not a just world.'

Miranda stared at him. She had never heard him show anything like emotion. Josef was nodding his masked head.

'It's a pleasant world for some I daresay. And an unpleasant world for some. But that's not the point. The point is that it will always be so under the present system. It forces people to it. People will only have a motive to behave decently to one another if the system itself is entirely changed.'

'So you are a Communist, Josef, is that it?'

He considered.

'I know what you are thinking, Fraülein Wrench. You are thinking that if we travelled about one hundred miles eastward we would find a completely changed system, but people still behaving cruelly to each other.'

'Behaving much more cruelly to each other, I would say,

243

Josef. And without much chance to complain about it, let alone talk of entirely changing it.'

'I know. And we know the Russians, believe me. We've no illusions.'

'Who are "we"?'

He ignored this.

'No illusions, Fraülein Wrench. But that doesn't mean there shouldn't be the destruction of a rotten system and a real attempt to build something new. Really new. Really decent at last.'

'Can that only be done after destruction? Can't one build on what's good, adapt, improve, modify, progress?'

Josef shook his head slowly. Miranda was thumbing the dictionary, conversation spasmodic.

'Won't you sit down, Josef?'

He sat down on a bench delicately. Every movement of Josef was neat, controlled. Miranda thought she had never seen a body which seemed to waste so little energy, whose every gesture appeared so exactly right for the immediate purpose. Now he looked very directly at her, considering her last question. He sighed.

'No, Fraülein, unfortunately one can't just modify, progress. That used to be thought, of course. I know people used to suppose everything is getting better, it just needs patience. But it's not true. Of course *some* things are better – people eat better in Austria, almost all of them, than when I was a boy. But the *system* is still degrading, still leads to the wrong values, still makes men less than men should be. And that will be so until a new system grows. On the ruins, the total ruins of what went before.'

Josef paused, and then said, politely and rather absurdly,

'I regret it, but it is so!' Then he said, 'I expect life has been good to you, Fraülein Wrench. Perhaps you don't know what I'm talking about.'

'Good in many ways, very good, unjustly good. In other ways – well, life isn't only about being warm and well fed, is it?'

244

Josef acknowledged this sincerely.

'And I've had unhappinesses, like most people. Family things, personal things.' She kept her voice undramatic, unsentimental, carefully free from the smallest note of self-pity. This man has known poverty, she thought, real poverty, war, danger, death, brutality, misery. What are my small pains to those he must have known, seen, maybe felt?

Unexpectedly, Josef said, 'One can see in your face, Fraülein Wrench, that you have experienced sadness.'

Miranda was touched. She felt like telling him that she greatly missed the chance to read his face too, but it would have sounded foolish, even, God forbid it, flirtatious, provocative. Josef, hitherto the incarnation of propriety, might misunderstand her. And anyway, she recognised that he could never, because of self-preservation, remove his mask. She shrugged and said,

'I'm a lucky woman.'

There was a silence between them, companionable. She smiled at him.

'So a new system must be built on total ruins, Josef. And I am part of the ruins? Is that why I'm here?'

But Josef, who was aware that she knew perfectly well why she was in the hut and had no inclination to discuss her situation further, said that he must be going. And when he came back the following day, he was later than usual, and said little, and his usual courtesy was covered with something not far from surliness. And, for the first time ever, Miranda smelt alcohol on his breath although he had disclaimed ever drinking.


'Is that Miss von Arzfeld?'

'Yes, this is Lise von Arzfeld.'

'Miss von Arzfeld, my name is Thomas Batley.'

'Of course, Franzi has spoken of you, Dr Batley, you and your wife were so kind, you have been really wonderful to him.'

'Yes, well it's been a pleasure. We love him, we'd do

anything for him. Miss von Arzfeld, Franzi asked me to ring you. He'll be with you in half an hour.'

'Is it over, then, the operation?'

'Yes, it is over.'

'And did it go well?'

A pause.

'Dr Batley?'

'Yes, I'm here. Well, Miss von Arzfeld, unfortunately, it did not go well. These things are very uncertain, as I'm sure you appreciate. Of course Franzi has a wonderful name, he's sort of a genius we all think, but there are no cast-iron certainties in open heart surgery.'

'So?'

'So unfortunately the operation was not successful. There was a failure at a very critical moment in the patient's responses. It can, unfortunately, happen. It was, as I'm sure you would appreciate, in no way a thing Dr Langenbach could foresee. Dr Langenbach's – Franzi's – success rate has always been very, very high as I'm sure you realise, but there's nobody on earth who, every time –'

'Dr Batley, it was not successful. Does that mean the patient is dead?'

'Yes,' said Dr Batley. 'Yes, that's so. He died. A statement has had to be drafted, there's a lot of public interest of course. Kind of controversy, too. He died.'


Marcia Rudberg said,

'I've had a letter from Lise, Toni. She's full of joy at being with Franzi, you can imagine. I'm sure she's been wonderful for him.'

'How long is she staying in New York?'

'Till the beginning of next week.'

It was 13th September. Lise's letter had taken five days. Marcia was re-reading it, as they sat companionably in the evening peace of Bargate.

'Franzi did the operation on that creature yesterday. At least he was planning to – Lise says, "Franzi intends to do the

246

operation on the 12th. He is wonderfully recovered and says he is well enough and that it is important. I understand him although I wish it were later. But I also wish very much to have all this business finished!"'

'I know what she means, Marcia. The nightmare isn't over while those two are still, effectively, under the protection of Franzi in New York.'

'Exactly. I feel it too. I suppose it's possible something will be said about the operation on the news. The whole thing hasn't quite been forgotten. Almost but not quite. It's been overshadowed, in its own line, by that ghastly business at Munich of course.'

It was, however, at the very end of the news that the announcer – as it happened, Marcia remembered, the same girl who had once explained to them Franzi's kidnap and the first of Reno's demands – looked solemn and said,

'Reno Vanetti, the man involved in the kidnapping of Dr Franz Langenbach nearly two months ago, has died in a New York hospital. Vanetti underwent a heart operation yesterday, performed, as had been agreed as the price of Dr Langenbach's freedom, by Dr Langenbach himself. The operation was not successful.'

Toni and Marcia were silent. Then Marcia murmured,

'I can't weep. But I wonder what effect that will have on Franzi. Failure –'

'Shsh –'

The girl was saying something more.

'– Italian authorities have received a communication from a group describing itself as the European Liberation Movement. In this communication it is stated that in the light of Reno Vanetti's death the release is now demanded of Giovanni Branca, who is awaiting trial in Rome in connection with bombing outrages earlier this year. The communication, according to an Italian Government statement, threatens that if Branca is not immediately released Miranda Wrench, who, it will be remembered, is an English friend of Dr Langenbach and volunteered to be a hostage for the safety of Reno Vanetti, in return for Dr Langenbach's release –'

247

Yes, yes, Toni said to himself. Get on with it! We know that. And she didn't volunteer, she was demanded. By name.

'– will be executed.'

'My God,' said Marcia. 'My God. My God!'

The girl had not finished.

'The Italian authorities have issued a statement to the effect that there can be no question of releasing Branca, who must stand trial. The Italian statement demands the immediate release of Miss Wrench who was last seen in Vienna. The Austrian authorities have associated themselves with this demand. A statement from the Foreign and Commonwealth Office, London, reads,

> '"The British Government are in close touch with the Italian and Austrian Governments in the case of Miss Miranda Wrench and request her immediate release in accordance with undertakings given."'

The girl added – 'These undertakings, it is understood, refer to the promise that Reno Vanetti and Carla Rosio would not be prosecuted. Reno Vanetti died yesterday, and a statement made by the United States Justice Department earlier today has confirmed that there is no intention to prosecute Carla Rosio. And now, the weather –'


'Yes,' said Josef. 'I can hear you.'

'No doubt about it now. They were going to ask for him – Branca – anyway. Then they reckoned it was all the more important, with Reno dead. They've got to show some sort of win, haven't they? So they asked for Branca and they've been told no deal. So what can they do?'

Josef followed the reasoning perfectly. Prestige, the appearance of victory, was always important.

'You know what to do, Josef?'

Josef did not respond. It had been nearly two weeks, but at their last exchange it had been said that only day and time were necessary, so there was no cause for the young crook to start recapitulating or insulting him, Josef, by implying that his memory might have slipped.

'Hello?'

'Hello. I heard you. Well?'

Vittorio said, '16th September. Three days from now. Eleven o'clock. You said you needed three hours. So we say eleven o'clock –'

For Christ's sake! Josef said, 'OK,' and rang off. He was deeply unhappy. '*Befehl ist Befehl*,' he said to himself, 'there are others besides Reno. I've given my life, my word; without discipline the movement is nothing. There are men above Reno, I've always known that, I know something of them, not too much, not dangerously much but something. To step out of line now, or at any time, would be the end of Josef. Anyway, I hate disobedience, I hate treachery, treason, above all things, we deserve nothing unless we are true to each other and to the movement, true whatever the challenge, true whatever the risk, true whatever the temptation.' But he felt unhappier than for a long time.

# CHAPTER 13

Josef arrived earlier than usual that morning. She always heard his movements, of course, because the creak of the cable portended the arrival of the cable car, Josef in it. It was eight o'clock, a clear, bright, crisp morning. September in the Alps was lovely enough, thought Miranda, if not experienced by a solitary prisoner in an isolated mountain hut. She thought it was the 16th of the month.

'We are leaving, Fraülein Wrench.' Miranda's heart leapt.

'You are taking me back to my friends, Josef?'

He said curtly, 'Now we go down to the car.'

Miranda felt enormous elation. There were tears of relief in her eyes. She was unreasonably disappointed when Josef said,

'I must cover your eyes, Fraülein Wrench. You are not to see our road. Nor to see me.'

'I understand.'

Her imagination worked behind the bandage as they descended in the little cable car, for Josef had gently but firmly blindfolded her before they left the hut. Of course, she thought, he must take off his mask, he's got to drive and he could never risk being spotted in a mask, even up here. But she felt sharp disappointment. She was re-entering the world and she longed to see it.

Josef told her, in his usual courteous but businesslike voice, that it would also be necessary to bind her wrists and lie her on the back seat of the car. Again she thought, Of course. He can't risk being stopped, driving a blindfolded passenger, but she dreaded the cramped discomfort.

'Have we far to go, Josef?'

'Some way.'

She heard his reluctance to inform, to talk. He was on duty

now, more than ever, and she could only submit, rest in uncomfortable darkness until he said, 'We're here.' And whom would she first see? She tried to control her immense excitement and to create in her mind the sort of journey they were making, keeping a rough account of time, sensing descent and ascent, corners, speed. Josef had taken trouble to put her as comfortably as possible on the back seat, her knees drawn up, her body curled, some sort of light rug covering her. This was the path to freedom! And, she must assume, Franzi had been returned to the world. The few days she had been assured would pass before her own release had lengthened to three weeks, but all was now well. She had seen nothing of the matter in the local papers Josef had brought – there had been gaps in these, but they had anyway carried little beyond regional news and a great deal of sport.

'They' had told her in England that she would be carefully watched at all times. She found this hard to believe, unless Josef, in some obscure underground deal, had a retainer from the police as well as orders from the kidnappers of Franzi! But in that case they would surely have pounced, made him lead them to the cable car and the hut and freed her? She had puzzled at this a thousand times, and while she had desperately needed to feel that she was, in reality, under the protection of unseen, beneficent powers, she found it painfully hard to credit. The best she could suppose was that the exchange of Franzi was being harder to negotiate at the last moment. Perhaps he was ill? Obviously nobody would let her out or get her out until Franzi himself was in friendly hands.

Anyway, she would shortly know. All things would soon be made clear. Feeling unworthy, she had often said to herself, If I'd known the sentence would be as long as this I wouldn't have agreed.

Not even to save a life? another part of herself asked; *His*, Franzi's life? No, probably not even for that. The strain! – but there was no need now to play games with her conscience, tease out her motives. She was on the road to sanity, normality and freedom. She had often asked herself whether she had not been inspired by a dawning love for Franzi Langenbach.

251

It would be romantic, a happy ending, she thought, if I, his deliverer, now become his true love! But she knew, with a clarity which her strange captivity had made more intense, that this denouement would not be simple, whatever they were both like when they met again, whatever they decided they felt. When they met again – Miranda told herself it was natural to anticipate that, all must be going well, why not? But sometimes, feeling sick, she made herself think, *If* we meet again, and hardly knew whether her fear was for Franzi or herself. And often she said, and found herself saying aloud in the white silence of the ski hut, He's charming, he's got star quality, he's very attractive, he's a most sympathetic lover. But could I love him? Josef was right to have seen sadness in her face. How conveniently love can be lost and then rediscovered in another form in fiction, she thought, and for a lot of people in real life, too. But not easily for me. Not easily for me.

'Have we far to go, Josef?'

'Some way.'

Then he had again been silent at the wheel. His only remark, before first edging the car from the little parking platform at the start of their journey, had been to say,

'Fraülein Wrench, it is very important that you do exactly what I say now, all the time. It is very important for you.'

She nodded understanding. Then she closed her eyes and gave herself to imagination. Time passed.


'Far to go, Josef?' She thought they had been driving for something like two hours.

As if by telepathy, at that moment he swung the car off the road they had been following, twisty but with a decent surface, and started to climb on a rough bumpy way, perhaps a track similar to that down which they had driven at the start of the day. None of the journey, Miranda supposed, would be negotiable when snow came to the Alps – perhaps quite soon now.

She said, 'Josef?' and he muttered, 'Now, not far.' Then

Miranda heard the sound of water, the roaring of water falling from a great height. It seemed to be directly ahead.

Miranda said, '*Wasserfall*!' with what she told herself was idiot obviousness. She was feeling the need to keep some sort of contact with Josef.

The car stopped.

Except for the alarming roar of the water there was silence. Then Josef started speaking, in his usual soft voice. If anything, softer than usual, hard to hear.

'Fraülein Wrench, I am now going to remove your blindfold.'

She heard him get out of the car, and knew that he must be putting on his mask. So the place must be entirely isolated. A moment later a masked Josef uncovered her eyes. She blinked in the hard light, sun refracted off cloud, atmosphere both bright and grey.

They had climbed by a rough track to where it petered out at the edge of a meadow. A wooden house, obviously deserted and half fallen down, stood in front of them. Beyond the house the ground fell away as if it perched on the edge of a small cliff. Looking out of the passenger's window in the opposite direction from the house Miranda could see what looked like painted posts the other side of a steep gorge. Into the gorge, between her and those posts, was cascading a mighty mass of water, rushing down the mountain which rose almost sheer ahead of them. There was cloud now, and the mountain rose into it; and out of it came that huge, deafening mass of water, never ceasing, remorseless.

Josef said, 'For the moment just sit where you are, Fraülein Wrench. I will explain. We are in the mountains near the frontier with Italy. The Italian road comes to the other side of the *Wasserfall*. To where those posts are. There was once a bridge for carts. Now it has been swept away.' He added, 'That is the road people use who come to see the *Wasserfall*. You can walk across to Italy from here but not drive. Not now.'

'At exactly eleven o'clock,' Vittorio had said, 'I'll be there. Tell her to walk across the bridge. You leave beforehand, she'll have nowhere else to go, she won't run back. If she does I'll come across of course, and get her.'

Josef said, 'If she runs back I'll deal with her. I know it's not the way you planned it but I'll be ready to deal with her.' He had spoken quietly, as usual, but loquacious for him. He didn't like it but it seemed obvious where duty would lie. If she ran back. But why should she? Why should she suspect anything unless that young crook –

Vittorio had worked things out very carefully in his mind.

'No, best if you pull out a few minutes earlier.'

'I'm not sure.'

'Well, I'm sure. Just her and me, that's all we need. I know what I'm doing.' Curse you, he had thought to himself. If you know best you can take what's coming to you! Josef know-all! Again he said,

'Yes, you get clear a few minutes earlier. Got it?'

'Right.' It had been said very softly, almost resentfully. Vittorio was sure, however, that he'd do as ordered. He knew Josef's reputation.

'You can explain to her that it's the frontier. Which is true. Tell her to walk straight out on to the wooden bridge and she'll be among friends. Tell her that you won't see her again. Then drive to hell out of it.'

'And then?'

Vittorio had chuckled down the line.

'You can leave that to me. It's a long drop. Don't worry. They'll not find anything for ages.'


'Fraülein Wrench, please now pay attention to me very carefully. You are to get out of the car.' Hard against Josef's ribs was the long-barrelled Luger pistol with which he practised assiduously. This Luger was a residue of war. He'd lifted it from a dead officer – a capital offence if discovered – immediately before desertion in 1945. He'd always travelled with it, concealed but kept in good order. Josef was proud of his

Luger but it had always been his intention never to use it except in grave emergency. He hoped fervently today would not produce such an emergency. Why should it?

'It is now ten minutes to eleven. In five minutes, when your watch shows five minutes from now, you are to walk up that track. In about two hundred metres you will find a wooden bridge. It crosses the *Wasserfall*. Walk across it. Take care, it is maybe slippery. Walk across it.'

Miranda nodded.

'And then?'

'Then you will be met, you will maybe see someone straight away, the other side of the bridge is Italy. Here in the mountains there are no official posts except where a motor road crosses the frontier, you see.'

'You know the mountains well, Josef.'

'Just hereabouts I know every track, every tree.'

'The other side is Italy. And they will be expecting me?'

'They will be expecting you. Now get out of the car.'

'Will I see you again, Josef?'

'No, and do not turn round until you hear me drive away.'

'Well, goodbye.' She got out of the car stiffly and held out her hand. Josef, masked, was in the driver's seat. Josef nodded and said nothing. Then, which touched her, he lifted her hand to his lips at the unsightly mouth slit in the mask and nodded again and turned his head away.

Miranda looked at her watch. At exactly five to eleven she started walking up the track. A moment later she heard the sound of Josef's car engine starting, and heard him manoeuvring to turn the car and head back down the track. She waved, pointlessly, without turning her head, and started walking again. What she could not see was Josef switch off the engine, quit the car and himself start rapidly to climb the slope parallel to her own path but unseen by her because of the sheerness of the rock wall bordering it. Miranda's path was wet and stony; it was also steep.

Miranda felt utterly alone.

Josef had said two hundred metres. The track twisted and turned round what seemed like the walls of a cliff. The sound

255

of the great waterfall ahead of her was now deafening and Miranda could see spray rising into the air to her left. She hoped the bridge which Josef had described as probably slippery was in good condition.

Then she saw it. Rounding a sharp twist in the track she saw it.

A long, plank bridge perhaps twenty metres across. One handrail. Beneath it, far below, a great, foaming white cascade of water, plunging a sheer hundred feet beneath the planks of the bridge, blinding the eyes, shattering the eardrums, dominating every sense. Miranda suffered from vertigo, and she licked her lips. Never mind, she said to herself. Onward, onward! Italy and liberty!

She approached the first planks of the bridge. It did indeed look slippery and she swallowed. The noise was terrifying.

Miranda stepped on to the first plank of the bridge and put her right hand tentatively on the handrail. It felt thoroughly unsound. She fixed her eyes straight ahead and started to walk slowly and unsteadily towards the middle of the bridge.


'My name is Lise von Arzfeld,' said Lise. 'I am a cousin of Dr Franzi Langenbach and he has specially asked me to talk to you because you have refused to see him, you have said you do not wish to see him. As you know he has tried to see you, Signorina Rosio, several times since – since your friend died.'

Lise spoke a careful, correct Italian. She had always loved Italy, drawn to it on such visits as she could afford by the magic which the south often exerts on those from harsher, colder, northern climes, its softness of atmosphere acting like a skilful massage on stiffness and angularity of character.

Carla stared without emotion at this severe-looking, middle-aged woman with greying hair gathered straight back and tied at the nape of the neck, with a clear skin, slightly olive in tint, and with rather beautiful brown eyes which looked now very directly at Carla. They were, once again, thought Carla, playing out a scene in an airport – and once again in the small private lounge of an airport. Before arrival at Milan a few weeks before, Carla had never flown in an aircraft. Now life seemed a succession of flights, each one more futile and hopeless than the last. She had travel documents which would take her to Tripoli in Libya. They had told her that it was understood there might, after quite a short time, be the possibility of her return to Italy under some sort of amnesty. It was appreciated that her own part in 'all this' had been inconsiderable. The Italian Consul should be contacted – he would have been apprised of her case. At present, of course, any move to Italy must be followed by her being detailed, questioned, she no doubt understood that. For their part, the American authorities had explained to the Italian authorities that in view of the peculiar bargain struck over the release from kidnap of Dr Langenbach, a bargain honoured (if one could speak of honour in that connection) by Miss Rosio's associates, there would be no question of deporting her to Italy. The Italian authorities had naturally understood this. They remained, however, anxious to interview Miss Rosio.

Carla had heard all this without interest or surprise. Reno's funeral had taken place, quietly and impersonally, the previous day. Now Carla looked at Lise levelly. They were both small women.

'I don't want to see Dr Langenbach.'

'So you have said. But I must explain one thing which is very important to him, and very important to make clear to you. It is the most important thing he wanted to say.'

Carla put her head on one side, eyes narrowed, lips tight. She looked sceptical, contemptuous and bored. Lise had noted from the beginning that she was extremely pretty, despite having taken no trouble whatsoever with her appearance. Lise changed tack. They had, she knew, at least half an hour before Carla's flight would be called.

'I should explain I am a particularly close cousin of Dr Langenbach, of Franzi. I brought him up, in our home in Germany. His mother, you see, died in a Hitler concentration camp.'

Carla said, 'I know about that,' expressing all the lack of interest she could possibly convey.

'He has been like a son to me. Very close to me.'

'What is the important thing he wants to say? Not that I care.'

'He wants you to know that he did everything he possibly could for your friend Reno Vanetti. He has the idea that you – I'm sure you'll tell me he's mistaken – might think, might even suppose –'

'That nobody tried very hard to save Reno! Yes, that's what I do think. And it's what we – my friends in Italy, in Europe – will think, do think. We expected it. And why not? Why save Reno? He was the enemy of – of all *this*!' Carla's gesture encompassed New York airport, the United States, the capitalist system, Lise herself and much else besides. Her voice was strident and dramatic.

'You come and tell me he did everything possible – he! Why should he? Has there been such a failure before? No! I have asked! He chooses this time to have his failure! Just the little move of an instrument that might be done a bit more cleverly, maybe, eh? Something like that? But not when it's a millionaire, no, just when it's Reno Vanetti! Because Reno Vanetti had this spoilt, clever, rich doctor once in his power! And then let him go because he, Reno, was generous! So now this doctor can't bear to think of that, think of being in his power once, so he kills him!'

Carla was breathing fast and her voice which had started soft was now loud.

'And you know, too, why he killed him, another thing? Because Reno Vanetti was a revolutionary, because Reno Vanetti wanted a better world, because Reno Vanetti was prepared to destroy the rotten things he saw around him and build one day a new, a new –'

She looked at Lise, eyes flashing. She said, again, 'So he killed him. So they killed him.'

There was a silence. They stared at each other. Then Lise said calmly,

'My poor child. You have loved him, truly loved him,

Franzi. It is making you very unhappy, and I understand it. I understand it completely. But you will not help yourself by telling yourself nonsense about anybody letting Reno Vanetti die. Nobody did that. He was very ill and he died, as many people do after that sort of most difficult operation.'

Carla opened her mouth but Lise lifted her hand with such a gesture of silencing authority that the girl stood absolutely still and no word for the moment came.

'I know a little about you, Carla. I know you had a hard childhood and that your mother was treated cruelly. I know what it is when wicked things happen to people one loves. I had a brother once, whom I loved more than anything in the world. He was taken from us, tortured again and again, then hanged slowly on a hook by the neck until he died. And he had committed no crime.'

Carla gazed at her, frowning. 'You needn't be sorry for me. I don't know why you tell me this about yourself. I'm all right. I have friends, contacts, where I'm going!'

Lise continued as if there had been no interruption.

'Long before you were born I saw men dying, I saw, I watched men screaming because their limbs were half torn off, I listened to them asking to die, praying to die, to escape from what had become of life. And not only men. We saw women, girls, children, old women – raped, mutilated, then killed for the fun of it. That was the Eastern Front, I can tell you, in 1945. And we saw it, or saw the immediate consequences. I was a nurse, you see.'

Carla said, with a tone of bravado, a hint of a sneer –

'Well, what's that to do with me? Anyway, you got away!'

'Yes, I got away. And there were just as bad things – different but as bad – being done by people who called themselves our people, in the camps. At the same time.'

'Everybody knows that.'

'Yes, everybody knows that. And Franzi's mother died in one. Well, that was a lot of my life when I was young, Carla. And you ask what it's got to do with you. Only this. When you next start to feel sorry for yourself, just remember what a safe, pampered life you've had –'

'Me? We were poor, really poor! You and your sort can't begin –'

'A safe pampered life compared to a large part of the people of Europe who had the misfortune to be born twenty or thirty years before you were! European Liberation indeed!'

Lise had never raised her voice. Now she suddenly spoke louder, but as she did so she smiled, and to Carla's astonishment it was a smile of great warmth and sweetness.

'My dear, I know you have a great heart, that you long for the world to be beautiful and fair, that you hate injustice. And I also know that you will, *one day*, realise that people who believe cruel, violent acts to be necessary and justified, in order to rid the world finally of cruelty and violence, always end by creating something worse that what went before. It's not pure motives that produce heaven on earth. It's people refusing to behave badly to each other, however noble the cause.'

This was simplistic, bourgeois morality of a kind Reno had been used to demolish with sardonic savagery, thought Carla. It was, however, a relief to exchange a few words with another human being who took the slightest interest in her, however hostile. And this old one didn't seem hostile. Rather the reverse, Carla admitted unwillingly to herself. In spite of what they'd done to her Franzi in Perugia. In spite of the fact she was on the other side.

She heard herself saying,

'He will live here now, I suppose. Here in New York. Like before.' She could not bear to go away without some picture of Franzi's existence in the mind.

'He will move to and fro between Europe and America, I expect, as before. Just now he is going to England, next week I think. He is always restless. Carla, I've told you what Franzi was most anxious for you to know, that he did his best for Reno. I know you only half-believe it –' she held up that stern, inhibiting hand again as Carla opened her mouth to deny even semi-credulity – 'but it is so. I want to say only one thing for myself. It is that I'm very, very grateful to you.'

This at least had the effect of surprise, thus capturing attention. The sneer that curved Carla's lip was still there but less pronounced.

'Grateful! Why?'

'Because, my dear, I know perfectly well that you gave him love at what must have been a hard, lonely time in his life. No, you shouldn't say anything, I'm asking nothing but I know him very, very well. You gave him something precious – the warmth of human affection at a moment when all must have been cold, lonely, uncertain –'

Carla thought of a bare attic in Perugia. It was almost unbearable. She heard herself mutter,

'Did he say that?'

'He has said nothing. But I can see it in his face and his unhappiness about you, I can see it in your own anger and pain. You gave him something of infinite value. You saved him, in one sense. Something in me tells me you would, if it had been necessary, have saved him in all senses. I know that to have given what you did has left you suffering. I know you must, perhaps, have dreamed of another sort of future, in which there was Franzi. No –' again the gesture of command. 'No, don't say anything! People's emotions move on, you know. It doesn't destroy the validity of what has been, even if for a little while only. In that little while you saved, with your warmth and generosity, someone I love. And I think he was very, very lucky. I look at you, and I know what I say is true and I think he was very, very lucky. And I will be grateful to you always. Now I say goodbye –'

She took a rapid step forward and before Carla knew what was happening she found herself folded in Lise's arms. She also knew that, as so often during recent weeks, tears were rolling down her cheeks.

'Goodbye, Carla. I hope all will be happy for you in the end.'


Miranda moved slowly forward, planting her feet carefully, avoiding the fearful urge to look downwards at the mighty, frothing cascade of water visible far below the planks of the bridge.

Suddenly she felt not only frightened but a fool. Why on earth wander into the unknown like this? Why do what Josef told her? There must be, there absolutely must be something wrong. If it were a simple matter of releasing her, why go through this rigmarole, this absurd ordeal? Why had Josef not simply put her down in a village street, discreetly removed her blindfold, said 'Don't look round. Go into the police station. Say who you are! Give me ten minutes to get away, Fraülein Wrench! If you will be so kind!' Or put her down on a road and told her the nearest village was an hour's walk, no problem, you can't miss it. Why, if it were just a question of passing her back into the world in such a way that Josef could make a safe get-away, why this complex business? What really lay the far side of the bridge? Miranda, despising her nerves but also shocked by her own stupidity, hesitated. Josef had gone, he'd said so, she'd heard him. It would surely be best to go back, best to walk back down the steep path, then down the motor track they'd followed from the road. She had no idea where she was, but she reckoned they'd driven up the track from the road for only about ten minutes – climbing slowly. She'd walk back down it, she'd reach the road, any road, she'd start walking, she'd stop the first car – they'd passed several cars, it wasn't completely deserted – and get a lift to anywhere, anywhere. To a police station, to shelter, to communication, to people, to safety. Miranda, mind still concentrated on not looking down, turned round cautiously on the narrow slippery planks and faced the way she had come. The known way.

She took two hesitant, nervous steps back. At the third step her foot slipped and she gripped the handrail with a tightness which sickened her, and felt sweat start to run down her body.

'Signorina!'

The yell, just heard above the roar of the waterfall, came from behind her now, came from the Italian side of the wooden bridge, the side towards which she been walking until sense prevailed. She stopped. Slowly and carefully she turned her head again. Mistrustful.

'Signorina!'

She could see him now, a young man, dark, waving at her. Wearing a raincoat, shouting.

'Signorina. Signorina Wrench!' He was moving towards the other end of the bridge. He was waving his arms in the air, pointing towards the country behind him. She thought she could see, far behind him, what looked like the flat, shiny roof of a car, two cars, perhaps three hundred yards away. They were, her mind registered dully, near the posts she'd observed when getting out of Josef's car the other side of the gorge. They were parked at the end of the proper road on the Italian side, no doubt.

'Signorina, OK!' He was coming out on the bridge now, she could see his smile. He was extending a hand towards her. He moved confidently, easily.

'*Prego, prego!*'

Miranda could see his lips forming words although the noise of the waterfall was still drowning other sound, thunderous, terrifying. She found her whole body shaking. She realised that even if she retreated now to the Austrian side of the bridge he could follow her, run after her, do whatever he had come to do. And it would surely be best, therefore, to conquer her fit of nerves and do as Josef had said, cross the bridge – 'You are expected,' Josef had said. The young man was now only about ten yards from her, hand still extended. She could see his smile, a wide smile in a handsome face. She took a pace back towards him. At the same moment she knew with blinding clarity that she distrusted him totally. She took another pace.

Mirand would see until her death what happened next. First, for one incredible moment, she supposed the bridge had broken. She could hear nothing but the roar of water when, without warning, the young man in front of her, now five yards away, threw his arms high in the air with a screech which was the only sound Miranda consciously remembered afterwards, above the sound of the waterfall. It was a terrible screech.

263

'*Ay-y-y-y-y-y-*'

Miranda saw, in the same moment, that the whole of his throat had suddenly, without reason, turned scarlet. She was able to observe this for about three seconds before Vittorio's body, arms flailing, pivoted gracefully on one heel and crashed over the side of the bridge, falling exactly one hundred and ninety-five feet before hitting the first sharp rock, and swept on thereafter by gravity and water, down, down, down. By a useful circumstance, police officers told each other afterwards, it was still in Italy at the bottom, but the bottom was one thousand feet below.


Lieutenant Ponti had enjoyed the change from routine greatly. He had not at first supposed that they'd let him play much of a part: it was hundreds of miles from his own city and it wasn't his sort of scene. This was, basically, a Carabinieri matter and he was a Perugia copper, a man presumed to have only limited horizons. But, he thought complacently, they had been most enlightened. He had explained it to them without, he hoped, sounding bumptious or unprofessional.

'I've got his trust now, you see. I think he really ought to have me with him. It took a long time to get as much as we've got out of him. And I think he could remain a real asset –'

'That will take a lot of persuading the authorities!'

'I realise that.' Ponti was respectful. 'Even so, Signor *Capitano*, it's a bit of a break. It's not easy to get on the inside of any of these people. Providing he's not compromised he could lead us to quite a lot. And after all, without him – and without, er, my bit of luck in getting on to him and breaking him' – Ponti tried to sound modest – 'we'd be nowhere near this English girl, would we! Nor would anybody else, to judge from the way the Austrians lost her!'

'He's bound to be compromised. If this goes as it should.'

'I don't think so. We're going to ambush him – not that anybody will see! He'll get away, the worse for wear, and we'll have the young lady. You must remember that with this Vanetti being carved up in New York, and his girlfriend with him, there's an important link gone from the organisation. Vittorio reckons he can explain matters to the few others he knows – there's a garage man here in Perugia and two young thugs who do rough jobs for them, no talent at all, they live in the same block as Vanetti: where Langenbach was held. Vittorio reckons he can put it about in such a way as to get him acceptable again.'

The captain's silence was sceptical and Ponti said apologetically,

'Anyway, that's what he thinks.'

'So he might be an asset. So we let him go.'

'Escape, Signor *Capitano*!'

'People higher up in their damned organisation will see through it. They'll settle him. It's going to be a big bill to look after him, you know that? He'll end up with his throat slit, you mark my words!'

Ponti had shrugged that graceful, expressive Italian shrug which implied that even if Vittorio's throat suffered that fate it would not be a crushing disaster for the Italian State. And eventually they had told Ponti that he was to accompany Vittorio north, after setting up the whole thing, standing over Vittorio as he held his telephone conversations with Josef, going over every detail with the decidedly nervous, brown-eyed young man.

Vittorio said,

'I'll grab her. I'll start back towards the road.'

'Then we'll grab you. No worry. And in the muddle you'll get away. You're quite a rock climber I expect!'

Vittorio had smiled sourly.

'We'll let you have a burst or two over your head! Don't worry. The official account, of course, will be that, acting on information, we followed you, saw you'd got the woman who appeared to be crossing illegally from Austria, went for you, you pulled a gun –'

'And she turned out to be the missing Signorina Wrench!'

'Exactly! And as far as your friends go you were about to knock her on the head and chuck her over the edge, just like you were ordered, just like they expected after the

Government made it so horridly clear that friend Branca stays inside, regardless! But it just went wrong. We saved the young lady, nick of time, exciting really!'

Ponti chuckled with pleasure. Vittorio looked at him without amusement.

'Why didn't I?'

'Why didn't you what?'

'Knock her on the head.'

Ponti felt impatient, but to Vittorio he never showed it. I've been like an uncle to him he thought, almost affectionately.

'Well,' he said, 'you don't want us hoofing up too close behind you at the damned bridge because your friend Josef might, just might, see. So you've got to bring her back to us, haven't you? Stands to reason.'

'Yes, but they may say why should I do that, why not deal with her straight away, why –'

'Ah,' said Ponti comfortably but with an edge to his voice, for it had been a long day, 'you'll think something up, boy, won't you? I'm sure you will.'

The big problem, of course, had been for Vittorio to persuade this Josef to hand the girl over to his, Vittorio's, tender mercies. It was clear that in no circumstances was Josef prepared to tell Vittorio where he was holding the girl. There'd been the initial announcement that the two terrorists 'might be prosecuted'. That hadn't worked – it sounded as if the Austrian, Josef, wouldn't let his prisoner go without clear evidence that this so-called bargain whereby Vanetti and Rosio went free was a load of codswallop as far as the responsible governments of civilised countries were concerned. And nobody wanted to make that clear, for some reason, until the bloody murderer had his heart swapped or something. Then Vittorio had helped. He'd explained – and this had taken a bit of extraction but of course it was vital, it enabled them to time the whole thing, to orchestrate – that the bastards were going to double-cross when Vanetti had had his operation safely, or died which was the same thing. Double-cross and ask for Branca of all people! Or knock the girl off! But the beauty of it was that young Vittorio had been charged with

266

the job. And when the Government put out their tough statement that that sod Branca was staying right where he was, Vittorio knew, and convinced Ponti, that there'd be no further argument. Josef would reckon it his duty to deliver the girl.

For execution.

'It's been publicised, you see. The organisation would regard itself as losing all credibility if it didn't happen.'

Vittorio had been confident. Furthermore, the organisation would probably think that 'they' had engineered Reno's death; talk of medical ethics and the implausibility of such a thing being managed in an American hospital would mean nothing to them. It was another reason why they'd decide the young Wrench woman must die, chalk up their score a bit.

'And this Josef of yours. He'll take that line?'

'Yes, he knows it was agreed. That was a condition of the latest deal. No Branca, dead Wrench.' And, Vittorio thought sardonically but with a small touch of sincere sadness now, dead Reno, dead Wrench.

Ponti thought they'd be throwing away a live asset, it made no sense, but these people made no sense anyway – although Vittorio made sense, he valued his skin and knew the time of day. But in this, Vittorio had appreciated the comrades' reactions accurately. Josef had acknowledged the order. *Befehl ist Befehl.*

And now Vittorio was being scooped out of a mountain river and scraped off the rocks far from the scene of his single act of usefulness, thought Ponti, with something like sorrow. A colleague said to him,

'The young fellow miscalculated his mate, obviously!'

'He always explained he didn't know him personally,' said Ponti, 'but he was a wholly dependable man. And I think you could say that was right. After all, from their point of view, this Josef's point of view, he had reasons for being uneasy, hadn't he? Reasons for watching to see what happened. We've worked out exactly where he must have climbed to above the bridge, only about twenty-five yards away but high up. He obviously saw the tops of our cars and put two and two together. They were hidden from where he was meant to bring his car. And he was told to get out of it and away early. But he didn't. And he saw us.'

'So he shot young Vit.'

'So he shot young Vit. Realised Vit had shopped them. Let him have it. Good shooting, actually. I don't expect,' said Ponti, 'that we'll know what he used. I've a feeling young Vit's remains may not give Forensic much to go on, although I suppose a bullet might drop out of one of the parcels.'

'Do the Austrians think they'll get the other fellow?'

'They don't sound bursting with optimism,' Ponti answered with a grin. The Austrian police had been in position ready to grab Josef as he drove his car down from the point at which Miranda had alighted.

'Seems like he knows that bit of the mountains like a bloody goat. They may pick him up, but nobody's seen him. He'll probably just turn up for work somewhere and carry on as before.'

'There's the car. And the girl's description of how she was held ought to put them on to this Josef. There are a limited number of cable cars, after all. They'll go round them all, turn out all the huts, question the regular staff about extras they take on to help with maintenance, all that.'

'Yes,' said Ponti. 'Yes, all that. But I've a feeling Mr Josef is rather thorough about covering his tracks. They may get him. I hope not. After all, he really has solved at least one problem for us. Although I argued for it, I persuaded the boss, I feel sure we were in for trouble about not putting young Vittorio in the dock, using him again, letting him get away. It was authorised, mark you, but they didn't like it. Any more than they liked the idea of this Vanetti being given a safe-conduct by the Yanks. No, old Josef has solved that problem, anyway, although he's also deprived us of what might have been quite a useful asset. You can't have every-thing.'

They were driving south. It had been a hard three days. Ponti's companion said,

'It was a punishment killing, nothing else. Josef would have

268

known Vit had already given us most of what he could. Josef could have shot the girl, though – if he was as dedicated as he's always sounded. Branca's staying inside, orders are orders, the organisation's credibility is on the line, that sort of thing – so he could have shot the girl. But he let her go and shot the grass. That consistent, Ponti?'

'Maybe,' said Ponti. 'Maybe. We don't know Josef, so we can't say. We can't say what went on in that little mind of his. Anyway, let's be thankful it was as it was. Punishment killing, as you say. No other object. Revenge. Still, revenge is a sort of justice, didn't someone say? Funny thing justice, as you and I know well.'

# CHAPTER 14

I loathe the telephone, Franzi thought, but since it exists it becomes ill-mannered not to use it. He supposed that after her ordeal – recounted with vivid detail in both English and American newspapers, and described by Marcia Rudberg to Lise in an hour-long transatlantic conversation – Miranda would be recovering somewhere with friends. He rang her London number from New York with a quick-beating heart: no reply. No reply from Harry Wrench's number either. Marcia had had to remind him of both these numbers when he had displaced Lise at the telephone and had a briefer and rather stilted conversation with her.

'When are you coming to England?'

'Soon. Very soon.' Lise was returning to Germany in two days' time, imploring him without success to accompany her. Marcia's voice was movingly affectionate. Aunt by blood, albeit unrecognised, he had always loved her.

'Come and stay here. Come and relax.'

He was fond of Bargate, the Rudberg home, although it reminded him sadly of his first visit, that visit years ago which had culminated in a car accident and his true father's, Anthony Marvell's, death. Marcia's loved brother.

'Come whenever you can and for as long as you can, dear Franzi.'

Lise had said,

'You must now telephone this Miranda.'

'It's hard – there's so much that's unsayable. The telephone –'

'Of course it's hard, it will be an awful conversation. But you must do it. You cannot leave her in silence! She has saved your life!'

And he had, of course, rung. No reply.

'Now,' said Lise next day, implacable, when attempts to reach either Wrench had failed several times. 'Now you must telephone Marcia again and say you are trying to find Miranda. They have been in touch, I think, often through this whole business. I am sure they are in touch now.' It was the day before Lise's departure.

Another call to Bargate. A slightly hesitant Marcia. Yes, she thought she might be able to find Miranda. Yes, she was certainly back in England.

'I must talk to her myself. There is no reply from her flat.'

'Franzi, perhaps it will be better face to face – these things are so hard on the telephone, aren't they, so misleading –'

'Misleading!' said Franzi thoughtfully.

'That's perhaps a silly word –'

'No, it is not a silly word. Misleading. I agree.'

'Franzi, when are you coming to England?'

'Tomorrow!' Franzi had just and decisively made up his mind. Marcia asked whether he'd like to come at once to stay and he said he would. 'And if I can find her,' Marcia asked carefully, 'shall I ask Miranda down?' Franzi said that he devoutly hoped she could, indeed, find her. And next day, to their surprise, he and Lise found themselves at the airport together, her destination Hanover and Franzi's Heathrow.


Saturday, 23rd September. Bargate. The English weekend. Only a week ago Franzi had been operating in New York. An unsuccessful operation on Reno Vanetti. Reno's heart had, quite unexpectedly, failed after replacement in what had appeared a perfectly successful valve operation. Failed, and refused every inducement to resume its beat. It was Franzi's first such experience.

'Unsuccessful, hell!' his friend and colleague Dr Batley said. 'You did a good job. Nobody could have done it differently. Nobody could have done more.'

'He died.'

'People do die!' Batley sounded as rough as he knew how. It wasn't going to be easy to get Franzi over this one, he knew

271

that. Kidnapped and held a prisoner for six weeks; mutilated, never knowing what were his chances among the vicious and conscienceless zealots who were his captors, and who had killed and killed again, without pity or remorse; released on condition he operated, and quickly, on the extremely serious heart condition of one of his tormentors; finding that all this – and a successful operation – was to be insured by the giving of an English girlfriend – as a hostage, a willing hostage; learning, at the end, that because a terrorist-patient hadn't recovered from his operation and because the Italian Government refused to hand over yet another terrorist, the plan had been to kill that girl – and she'd escaped death only because the Italians had managed to catch and break one of the gang. It wasn't, Batley recognised, an easy sequence of events for someone as sensitive as Langenbach to live with, and he was profoundly relieved that his young friend had suddenly announced that he intended to go back to Europe, take a prolonged holiday. Then he'd see.

'You do that,' the Batleys had said warmly. 'And you'll want to see this little lady, this Miranda. Quite a heroine.'

Marcia welcomed him like a son.

'Miranda's being driven down by a friend, a girl who used to work at her gallery. Arriving about five, I think.'

'Have you gathered how she is?'

'I've seen her –'

'Of course. You told me.'

'I saw her as soon as she was ready to see anyone. She had a pretty shattering time, but no actual ill-treatment it appears. The greatest shock was the actual release, when she'd no idea what was going to happen. Then this member of the gang was shot through the neck a few yards from her. She thought she might have fainted and fallen off the ghastly little bridge she was on, over this gorge, of course you know the story –'

'More or less. This was the fellow who was meant to kill her, but who had been caught and turned by the police. I got the story pretty clear in New York.'

'I suppose he was one of those guarding you.'

'I expect so,' said Franzi. I expect, he thought, that he was

272

the one who hacked my finger off. Who looked at me, grinning, before doing it. And whom I never saw. He said, 'But you've not told me how you thought Miranda was.'

'She's a very beautiful girl, Franzi.'

'Yes, indeed.'

'She's also a formidable character. I've never met anyone with less self-pity. She laughs at herself over her fears, denies any real discomfort. But behind it, of course –'

'Of course. And she did it for me. It's incredible.'

Marcia privately thought it might be less incredible than he claimed. She said,

'Of course, as you know, she was named. They said they wanted, as a hostage, her or nobody. So it really did look as if the only hope of getting you was for her to surrender herself. And then, of course, be followed and picked up once you were safe. That was the idea.'

'Which didn't work.'

'Which didn't work. I must say we all felt absolutely ghastly when we learned that, when we gathered – confidentially, of course – from our people that the Austrian police had lost her.'

'What did her brother, Harry, say? They're very close. He must have been out of his mind.'

'He was.'

Miranda didn't say, would never say, that Harry Wrench, in one terrible, intolerable confidence, had told her that he might – just might – have been instrumental in financing Franzi's kidnap, Miranda's ordeal. By agreeing, secretly and humanely, to finance the paying of blackmail by a man who'd lost his daughter – paying it to something also called the European Liberation Movement. She'd told him it could never be certainly connected, he'd best forget it. She knew he never would.

'Well,' said Franzi, 'I have no words that are any use. What *can* one say?'


'What can one say?' asked Miranda Wrench. 'It's an embarrassing relationship. He has to regard me as some sort of

273

heroine who has sacrificed herself for him. He has to feel a sense of obligation. We can't meet in any natural way at all.'

Harry knew his sister very well. Everybody who loved her had hoped during recent years that she would find at last someone to whom she could give her heart, someone 'up to her' in every sense. She had married most unhappily. Then she had fallen in love with, had had a passionate love affair with an old friend of Harry's. It had ended in pain and disaster; it had ended in what had seemed, at the time, unforgivable betrayal. Since then Miranda, charming, intelligent, courted, had walked alone, Harry knew. She was just thirty, with beauty, strong character and a good deal of intolerance. But her heart, Harry surmised, a particularly constant heart, perhaps still beat only for that one man, damn him, who had first won it truly. There were women like that.

Yet now there was Franzi. Harry smiled at her.

'No doubt you'll swap reminiscences of kidnap and captivity. In our time, after all, it's the equivalent of the war stories of old soldiers. Terrorists I have known!'

Miranda smiled back sadly.

'I only knew one. Franzi's experiences are wider than mine. Bloodier, too. They –' Harry knew that the picture of a box with a severed finger would always recur to her mind's eye. He had, from the beginning, doubly admired her courage in placing herself at the mercy of people who could do things like that. Of course they had explained that it would only be for a few days, that she would be under covert surveillance, day and night – and a hell of a lot of use that had been! He looked at his sister with huge affection. If only –! But he knew he'd miss her if she married, all the same. Whatever the catchwords, matrimony was a sort of bereavement.

'Yes, it's going to be ghastly,' said Miranda, doing her best to sound neutral. 'Thank heaven for the Rudbergs, I am beginning to love them, really love them. And Bargate's a heavenly place, one will be able to take it gradually, no staged heart-to-hearts, no dramatic encounter before the curtain falls! I couldn't have borne dinner *à deux* in a restaurant – "I wish to express my profound gratitude, Miss Wrench," that sort of thing.'

'Franzi's not exactly formal, darling. After all, you know him quite well. Relax!' And Harry realised perfectly well that Miranda was disturbed not only by the fear of over-contrived drama on meeting Franzi but by uncertainty over what she really felt. 'You know him quite well,' he'd said, tongue in cheek. At one time, when they were flying to Italy, he could have sworn that they were lovers – or damn near it! But Miranda, trying to be brisk, said,

'Oh well, I'm sure it will all be perfectly easy. Anyway, what the hell does it matter! But what does one say?'


Marcia Rudberg had also given some thought to this matter. She, too, had suspected with pleasure that Miranda and Franzi were lovers or on the threshold of it. It must, however, be a shallow-rooted affair for they'd not been close, Marcia knew, until shortly before this extraordinary business started – only a few weeks ago, though it seemed an age. But though they might have been lovers, and might indeed be in love, it didn't necessarily mean this meeting would be easy. Perhaps Bargate's neutrality for both of them would help.

When Miranda first arrived she greeted her easily, said,

'How are you? Franzi and Toni have gone for a walk before it rains again,' settled Miranda comfortably into the atmosphere of Bargate, placed her, as it were, like an agreeable piece of furniture into the right place in the room and then continued with life and talk, showing no sign of strain. She talked about Franzi naturally, as if to a fellow nurse about a patient rather than to another patient suffering from the same disease.

'He's awfully tense, of course. It's really that operation going wrong that's upset him most, I think. He's like I know he was after my brother died, years ago. Do you know that story?'

'Not really.'

'Lise von Arzfeld, you know –'

'Yes, I know about her.'

'She told me Franzi was impossible to get near at that time. I suppose this business has been the next real upset in his life. Or in his adult life – there were plenty of upsets when he was a child, poor Franzi.'

They both heard a door opening. A silence, a tension, and then Franzi and Toni came in, and Marcia chattered, and gave them tea and chattered some more, and hardly gave Franzi or Miranda a chance to speak beyond a first tentative and oddly formal smile and embrace, so that Franzi felt – unusually in the case of Marcia – a certain irritation.

She's talking too much, he thought, putting on an act, to help. I wish she'd shut up. We need quiet.

But Marcia did not shut up and she had no intention of neglecting, as a forbidden topic, the question of kidnap. Unknowing that she was using words very close to those of Harry Wrench in London some hours before, she said,

'You'll be able to exchange prisoner gossip, both of you. I remember when my brother, Anthony, talked to people who'd been in prison camp with him they used to date everything from some incident about food. Whether it was before Red Cross parcels began to arrive or after, before their rations were halved or doubled or something. I know the feeling, that wartime feeling. Food, food! And prisoners must have had it worse than most. So no doubt you can swap memories about how they fed you before anything else!'

There was a silence. Franzi did not smile. Miranda played up to Marcia.

'With me it was tins. Not bad tins. And biscuits. Most of the time.'

She smiled at Franzi.

'And you?'

He seemed to be considering.

'I'm not sure I can remember. I never remember feeling hunger. Sometimes they cooked something, we had something hot.'

'"We",' said Marcia, '"We" all ate together, did we? And who cooked?'

'Sometimes, near the end, we ate together. Carla cooked.'

'Carla! The girl, the Belle of New York! Was she a good cook?'

And here, too, Marcia was stamping in with a deliberate tactlessness, a determination to show no delicacy. Some vulgarity, even, for she had understood very clearly from Lise what Lise's impressions of Carla had been, what her understanding about Franzi and Carla's relationship was. But Marcia had no intention of allowing the name of Carla to become something to avoid. As far as Franzi was concerned, she was sure, the less delicacy, the less avoidance, the better. She remembered her brother, Anthony, whose fault had been to erect walls too readily about his emotions and hang 'keep out' signs upon them. And Franzi was her brother's son.

Franzi just said, 'No, not a very good cook.'

Then, for whatever reason, he smiled, Marcia noted. She noted it with relief. A little later, and without visible contrivance she removed Toni for some domestic consultation. And Franzi and Miranda were alone.

Miranda said tritely, 'You know, I've not gathered exactly where my ski hut was. Perhaps near where you and I first met in that skiing party – 1957 was it?'

Franzi said, 'Yes, 1957 I think. Tell me, who brought the daily paper? Ah, your gaoler of course. Describe him, can you bear to?'

'Josef. He wore a mask all the time, of course. Small, very polite, very neat in all he did, very efficient. Very correct towards me. He went shopping for me, too.'

'Did he talk of his ideals? His motives?'

'A little. He wasn't a great talker. He was a soldier, a very young soldier in the war. Then he was a mechanic, did odd jobs for the ski lifts, worked in garages, that sort of thing.'

'He knew his way around.'

'He certainly knew his way around. I wonder if he got away.'

Franzi knew the story, knew that Josef, gaoler Josef, had undoubtedly shot Vittorio on the bridge. Since then, it appeared, nothing had been seen or heard of him.

Miranda said, 'The thing is, I don't believe the police necessarily know who it is they're looking for.'

'Perhaps not. You gave them, of course, a full description. Have you been shown photographs? By the Austrian police for instance?'

'Yes, and by the Italians. But I'm positive not one of Josef. I never saw him without his mask, of course. I think he may have faded back into ordinary life. I think he'll get away with it.'

Franzi said softly,

'And I think you hope so!'

Miranda smiled at him. It was getting easier now.

'Yes, I think I do. He was nice, you see. And, after all, he could have shot me instead of the other, couldn't he? They think Josef shot that other one because he spotted the police and realised he'd given their game away, the one he shot I mean. So he could have decided to shoot me instead. I was meant to die, after all. Because –' She checked herself: because Dr Langenbach's operation had not been successful? Because they'd refused to hand over someone called Branca? A bit of both, perhaps.

'But he didn't shoot me. Perhaps he meant to, and missed.'

'I doubt it, from what you say.'

'I doubt it, too. And you're right, I hope he gets away. Also I don't want to be badgered all the time, I want to get it behind me. If they catch him they'll obviously want me to give evidence and so forth. I don't want that.'

'No,' said Franzi, 'I can see you don't want that.'

He had a feeling, justified by subsequent events or lack of them, that she needn't worry. Nobody would catch Josef.

'And *your* gaoler? Do you want to talk about him?'

'Them.'


'It was a curious organisation,' Franzi said. He was finding unexpected relief in talking dispassionately about them like this, almost as if to a colleague about a point of technical interest to each.

'A curious organisation. The couple who held me were

278

important, had a lot of say in what was done, but there were others, quite powerful people I reckon, associates, not exactly superiors. It was cellular rather than hierarchical. And they – Reno, I mean, Carla wasn't an important individual in her own right – they had some helpers all over the place. The man, Josef, who held you, was one. There must have been others in Austria who managed the rest of that business, telephoned and so forth. And in Italy there were quite a number – several lived in the house where they kept me, on a lower floor. Sort of guards. It was quite a big set-up, but curious. It all went on in Reno's head, I think. Very secure.'

'What was he like?'

'Clever. Absolutely dedicated. He'd do anything for the cause. Perfectly convinced that our society must be shaken, terrorised, destroyed; so that better people can at last behave better in a better world.'

'That's like Josef.'

'I'm sure. Reno was ruthless. He was behind a big bomb outrage in Rome, so the police have told me. There was blood on his hands all right.'

'Did that show?'

'Not in the sense that he appeared a thug. Rather the reverse. You could feel his sincerity, his faithfulness (unless he had to tell a lie for the movement, that is), you could feel all that. But he was ready, of course, to do the most appalling things. Quite without pity, I'm sure. If something helped the Revolution it was right.'

'I suppose all fanatics are like that. One doesn't meet many. You and I have – although I still find it hard to think of Josef as a fanatic.'

The silence between them was companionable now. Miranda said quietly,

'What was the girl like?'


What was the girl like? It was a harder question. It was, by now, the only question. How to describe Carla? Whether to describe Carla?

Miranda said, 'Harry saw her on television when they showed you all at Milan airport. Which must have been awful.'

'Yes. Awful.'

'Harry said she was very pretty.'

Franzi still said nothing and he suddenly realised he was capable of saying nothing. Little terrorist Carla! Carla with her red-gold hair, her natural gracefulness, her enchanting, childlike air of being a cinquecento madonna, for all her generous sensuality and revolutionary ideals. Carla who had connived at murders, if not performed them. Who thought she had persuaded herself that any cruelty, any violence was justified if it led, by however small a step, to the radical changing of the world. Carla, who was prepared to suffer, to take risks – even, perhaps, to take enormous risks if it had come to it, for him, Franzi. Carla who had really very little thought of self, whatever her twisted ideology; who burned with fierce anger for the mother she had loved, the mother who had been kicked around by the world. Carla now living, once again, in the twilit world of conspiracy in Libya or wherever; almost friendless, it must be assumed, whatever her bravado. Carla who had, for those few, enchanted hours in squalid surroundings in Perugia, brought something golden, something that twisted the heart as well as teasing and pleasing the flesh. Carla, whose effect at such times was like those single, spaced, lingering notes in a sonata by Beethoven, drops of ice-cold water on the spine, echoes of wordless, indefinable longings, painful to listen to except infrequently. Carla to whom he had once said, 'I think I love you too,' as his arms were around her, his hands caressing her smooth, smooth skin. Carla whom he had ultimately known with self-dislike he could not possibly love in any lasting sense of the word.

Twice Franzi opened his mouth to say something acceptable about Carla to Miranda and twice he found it absolutely impossible to say anything at all. At last he murmured,

'She –'

and then found, to his embarrassment, that his eyes were smarting with unshed tears and his throat was dry. To the mature and distinguished surgeon, the experienced man of the world, the successful, admired and articulate Dr Langenbach, words would not come.

'She –'

Miranda had taken his hand and held it tightly. She sighed gently and they sat side by side on the sofa as it grew darker outside and it was time, when somebody thought about it, to switch on the lights in Bargate's inner hall. But Franzi and Miranda sat in darkness and, after a little, the darkness began to seem almost like peace.

'Well, Grasser,' said the Works Director of the large garage and service station on the eastern outskirts of Mainz, 'it so happens that we can certainly take you on. We've got a lot of work and I know you from when you were here before. I was sorry when you left. Hope you decide to have a proper contract with us, this time. You're too good a man to be on the move so often. You ought to settle down. Find a nice girl and settle down.'

'Thank you, Herr Direktor. I was happy here, I'm sure I will be again.'

'You know how things are here. You know our system.'

'Of course.'

'What have you been doing recently? When you left us you went down to Milan, as far as I remember. And you came to us from Vienna! You're a rolling stone, Grasser! But you're a good mechanic. You had two seasons down in Tirol, too, I remember, helping maintain the *skibahnen* and so forth.'

'That is so, Herr Direktor. I've travelled a good deal, I've no family. I generally manage to fit in wherever I am. I like change.'

'Start on Monday, OK?'

'OK, Herr Direktor.'

Josef moved away, having raised two fingers deferentially to the old peaked mountain cap he wore, in something like a military salute.

'Do you think –?'

Miranda held Franzi's hand easily, all tension gone now. Franzi said again,

'Do you think – perhaps –'

'Do I think that we might resume where we rather unsatisfactorily left off? Which was my fault! Do I think it might work?'

'Yes, my darling Miranda. That's what I mean.'

'No.'

Franzi sat in dead silence. Miranda sighed.

'The answer isn't "I don't think so", or "It's going to take a long time"! It's "No". No, in spite of the fact that you're immensely tempting to me, that I like and admire you, and feel intensely proud that I did something, I suppose, to help you. But no!'

Almost inaudibly Franzi murmured, 'Why, I wonder?'

'You know why, Franzi – and there are two reasons. The first is that you're not really hurt, are you?'

'Miranda –'

'Yes, you like me, I attract you, you'd enjoy making me love you, you can envisage life together being fun, we'd be in tune. But, my dear, you need to feel something overpowering, something to catch the throat, knock the breath out of the body. And you will. But not with me. You've thought about me – "She might do". You've reckoned "This, perhaps, is love". Franzi, it isn't. For a lot of people it would be excellent – sensual, companionable, satisfying, sensible. But that's not you. And it's not me. You were born wanting the moon, you see. So was I.'

They sat quiet for a little. Then Franzi said,

'The second reason?'

'The second reason you put to me yourself what seems like long ago and is actually a few weeks. My heart's not yet free.'

'Is that to wreck the whole of the rest of life?'

'Possibly.'

'Miranda,' said Franzi, and his voice was most unsteady, 'Miranda darling, I understand you. I don't even contradict you. But are you really sure that it's right to refuse something which may be – be less than romantic perfection, if it may, nevertheless, bring a good deal of happiness and content? Isn't that a bit –'

'A bit infantile? A bit neglectful of how seldom if ever human beings find their ideal? A bit ungrateful even?'

'All that.' He kissed her hand gently, moving his lips over it slowly. Miranda said, with a sigh,

'Yes, Franzi, I'm all you say. But so are you. You'll be transfigured one day, and then you'll be glad you didn't settle for second best.'

With a touch of bitterness Franzi answered,

'It may never come! This transfiguration for which I'm to reject ordinary human happiness!'

And Miranda inclined her head seriously and honestly and said, 'No. It may never come. To either of us.'

'Neither is ready for any sort of real relationship yet, anyway,' said Marcia. 'I know the feeling. I know it well. But in their cases when it comes, if it comes, it won't be for each other. Why should it be? It would be a nice romantic ending but a false situation. Each of them has hinted to me how things are, of course – it was obvious one might be looking for something to happen between them. It hasn't and it won't. The truth is, I'm sure of it, she's never got over that other business. I've never talked to her about it, how could one? But although it was three or four years ago I'm sure the flesh is still raw. Someone she never sees, or so one gathers.'

'I know that feeling too,' said Toni. He smiled at his wife. She had agreed, now, to believe that through thirteen years of prison her face, more than that of any other woman, had come before the eyes of his imagination. It happened to be true. Of Miranda, Toni murmured, 'What a waste!'

Marcia shrugged her shoulders.

'That's the way she's made. And as for him – well, I don't know about Franzi. He'll perhaps find someone permanent one day, someone special. I rather doubt it. Life is not as tidy as it should be. He may remain attractive, intelligent, highly successful – and inwardly always alone, with nobody, certainly no woman, reaching him except temporarily. And superficially. He'll be going back to America after Christmas. He was born to sadness really, however wide his smile. I've always felt that.'

Toni surveyed the events of these last months. He shivered slightly. September had turned surprisingly chilly and he thought it was time the fire was lit in the inner hall of Bargate Manor. His darling wife seemed to feel the cold much less than he did now. He grunted.

'All things considered, we ought to be grateful how it's all gone. Terrorism is the challenge of our time. When we were young, my love, there were wars to fight, nothing else was like it, war dominated everything. Now – well there are funny little wars here and there, maybe, or wars like the Americans have been fighting where nobody believes in winning. But on the whole it's not wars that threaten us now, it's this sort of thing, terrorism, kidnap, murder, the enemy within. And I reckon this has been quite a victory. For our side.'

Marcia smiled at him, her mind ranging over a long, long time.

'Perhaps,' she said, 'but is there really such a thing as victory? For anybody? In the end?'

As she said it, she knew the sentiment, tolerant and worldly-wise though it might sound, held a lie at its heart; and she was glad when her husband said quietly,

'Perhaps not. But there is certainly such a thing as defeat.'

It was a more defensible statement. Yet behind these outbreaks of fear and rage with their malign power to disturb and destroy, there were, Marcia reckoned, larger questions she felt too middle-aged and tired to explore, questions of justice and suffering and mercy or the lack of it, historic wrong, unfinished business. The younger ones can handle it, or fail, more likely, Marcia thought; whatever it is which is still upsetting this world of ours so cruelly. The evening was well advanced but nobody had drawn the curtains, although it was time; and the comfortable, lighted Bargate room felt vulnerable to whatever faces of incomprehension and resentment might one day peer through the glass from the darkness outside.